PRAISE FOR THE GABRIEL TRILOGY

"The Professor is sexy and sophisticated . . . I can't get enough of him!"
—*USA Today* bestselling author Kristen Proby

"[In *Gabriel's Inferno* and *Gabriel's Rapture*], I found myself enraptured by Sylvain Reynard's flawless writing. *Gabriel's Inferno* and *Gabriel's Rapture* are books I will always treasure and are among my top ten reads of last year."
—*The Autumn Review*

"An unforgettable and riveting love story that will sweep readers off their feet."
—*Nina's Literary Escape*

"Sylvain Reynard's writing is captivating and intense . . . It's hard not to be drawn to the darkly passionate and mysterious Gabriel, a character you'll be drooling and pining for!"
—*Waves of Fiction*

The Raven

SYLVAIN REYNARD

BERKLEY BOOKS, NEW YORK

THE BERKLEY PUBLISHING GROUP
Published by the Penguin Group
Penguin Group (USA) LLC
375 Hudson Street, New York, New York 10014

USA • Canada • UK • Ireland • Australia • New Zealand • India • South Africa • China

penguin.com

A Penguin Random House Company

This book is an original publication of The Berkley Publishing Group.

THE RAVEN

Berkley trade paperback ISBN: 978-0-425-26649-6

An application to register this book for cataloging has been submitted to the Library of Congress.

PUBLISHING HISTORY
Berkley trade paperback edition / February 2015

PRINTED IN THE UNITED STATES OF AMERICA

10 9 8 7 6 5 4 3 2 1

Cover design by Lesley Worrell.
Cover photos: Woman by Steffen Lachmann / Gallerystock; Archway by Giuseppe Paris / Shutterstock;
Figure by FZR / Shutterstock; Florence Duomo by RayTango / Thinkstock.
Interior text design by Tiffany Estreicher.
Page vii: Sandro Botticelli "La Primavera (Spring)." Reproduction from Encyclopedia "Treasure of Art,"
Partnership <<Prosvesheniye>>, Petersburg, Russia, 1906. Copyright © Oleg Golonev / Shutterstock.

*To the city of Florence
and my readers,
with gratitude.*

Primavera
Sandro Botticelli, c. 1482.
Galleria degli Uffizi, Florence.

Prologue

May 2013
Florence, Italy

Alone figure stood high atop Brunelleschi's dome, under the shade of the gold globe and cross. His black clothing faded into the encroaching darkness, rendering him invisible to the people below.

Not that they would have seen him.

From his vantage point, they looked like ants. And ants they were to him, an irritating, if necessary, presence in his city.

The city of Florence had been his for almost seven hundred years. When he was in residence, he spent the moments before sunset in the same place, surveying his kingdom with Lucifer-like pride. This was the work of his hands, the fruit of his labor, and he wielded his power without mercy.

His considerable strength was magnified by his intellect and his patience. Centuries had passed before his eyes, yet he remained constant. Time was a luxury he owned in abundance, and he was never hasty in his pursuit of revenge. Over a hundred years had come and gone since he'd been robbed of some of his most prized possessions. He'd waited for them to resurface and they had. On this night, he'd restored the illustrations to his personal collection, the sophisticated security of the Uffizi Gallery causing him only the most trifling of inconveniences.

So it was that he stood in triumph against the darkening sky, like a

Medici prince, looking out over Florence. He smelled rain on the warm air as he contemplated the fate of those responsible for acquiring his stolen illustrations. He'd intended to kill them two years previous, but had been thwarted by a tiresome assassination attempt. The war that ensued between the underworlds of Florence and Venice had kept him occupied since then. He'd won the war, successfully annexing Venice and all its territories. And his prey had finally returned to the city. Now was the time to have his revenge.

He had time enough to plan the killings and so he stood, enjoying his success, as a warm, persistent rain began to fall. The ants below scattered, scurrying for shelter. Soon the streets emptied of human beings.

He clutched the case under his arm more closely, realizing that his illustrations were in need of a dry space. In the blink of an eye, he traveled down the red tiles to a lower half dome before leaping to the ground and sprinting across the square. Soon he was climbing to the roof of the Arciconfraternita della Misericordia, an adjacent, aged building.

There was a time when he would have served the Arciconfraternita, joining in their mission of mercy, rather than treating them as a hurdle. But he hadn't been merciful since 1274. In his new form, the concept never entered his consciousness.

Some hours later, he flew across the tiled roofs at great speed, dodging raindrops and heading toward the Ponte Vecchio. The smell of blood filled his nostrils. There was more than one vintage, but the scent that attracted his attention was young and unaccountably sweet. It resurrected in him memories forgotten, images of love and loss.

Other monsters moved in the darkness, from all parts of the city, racing toward the place where innocent blood cried out from the ground.

He changed direction and increased his speed, moving toward the Ponte Santa Trinita. His black form blurred against the night sky as he leapt from rooftop to rooftop.

As he ran, the question uppermost in his mind was: *Who will reach her first?*

Chapter One

The streets of Florence were almost deserted at one thirty in the morning.

Almost.

There were a few tourists and locals, groups of young people looking for entertainment, homeless people begging, and Raven Wood, limping slowly down the uneven street that led from the Uffizi Gallery to the Ponte Santa Trinita.

Raven had been at a party with colleagues from the gallery and foolishly declined a ride home. Her friend Patrick had offered, since her Vespa was in the shop, but she knew he didn't want to leave Gina's flat. He'd been nursing a secret crush on Gina for months. On this evening, he seemed to have succeeded in attracting her attention.

Marginally.

Raven didn't have the heart to separate the prospective lovers. While she accepted that love was not for her, she took secret delight in the love lives of others, especially her friends. So she insisted on finding her own way home. That was how she found herself walking, with the assistance of her cane, toward her small flat in Santo Spirito, which was on the other side of the river.

Little did she realize that her decision to decline a ride home would have far-reaching consequences for herself and her friends.

Her colleagues wrongly assumed her limp was something she'd been born with, and so, out of politeness, they ignored it. She was grateful for their silence, since her limp held a dark secret she was unwilling to tell.

She didn't think of herself as handicapped. She thought of herself as mildly disabled. Her right leg was somewhat shorter than the other and her foot turned outward slightly, at an unnatural angle. She couldn't run and she knew it was painful to watch her walking. At least she tried to make her ever-present cane attractive, decorating it with whimsical designs drawn by her own artistic hand. She laughingly called it her boyfriend and dubbed him Henry.

Some women might have been worried about walking the streets of Florence late at night, but not Raven. She rarely attracted attention, apart from the rude stares at her leg. In fact, people often ran into or brushed past her as if she were invisible, making far too much body contact.

This was likely because of her appearance. The polite would have termed her figure Rubenesque, if they could have found it under her oversized clothes. To modern eyes she was overweight, her extra pounds compounded by baggy garments and well-worn sneakers that added little to her five-foot-seven height. Her hair was dark, almost as dark as a raven's wing, and carelessly pulled into a ponytail that swept her shoulders. In comparison to the many attractive and well-dressed women who inhabited Florence, she was considered plain.

But her eyes were beautiful, large and deep and almost an absinthe green. Alas, no one ever took the time to notice her eyes, hidden as they were behind oversized black frames. Not that Raven would have been comfortable with the attention. She wore the glasses in order to distance herself from people, switching them for reading glasses that actually aided her eyesight, when necessary.

As she approached the Ponte Santa Trinita from the Lungarno degli Acciaiuoli, she cursed the fact that she hadn't brought an umbrella. The rain was enough to clear the streets and bridge of pedestrians, but not enough to soak her. She elected not to seek shelter and simply continued, limping as she did everything else—with dogged determination.

She watched as a trio of rough-looking men approached the bridge ahead of her from Via de' Tornabuoni. They were not deterred by the rain, their speech loud and raucous, their steps unsteady. The sight of drunks in the city center was not unusual, but Raven's pace slowed. She knew too well the unpredictability of a drunk.

She clutched her old, worn knapsack more tightly as she continued toward the bridge. It was at that moment she saw Angelo.

Angelo was a homeless man who spent his days and nights begging for coins. Raven passed him on her way to and from the Uffizi. She always stopped to greet him and give him money or some food. She felt a kinship with him since they both walked with a cane. Angelo was developmentally disabled, which only increased her compassion.

As she walked, her gaze traveled from Angelo to the drunks and back again. A terrible feeling of dread passed over her.

"Good evening, friends!" Angelo's Italian pierced the rainy darkness. "A few coins, please."

The cheerful hope in his voice caused Raven's stomach to churn. She knew the cruel fate of hope when it was misdirected.

She began limping faster, her eyes fixed on her friend, willing herself not to trip and fall. She was almost to the bridge when she saw Angelo lifting his hands and crying out.

The largest man was urinating on him. Angelo tried to move away, but the man followed. The other men cheered.

Raven was not shocked.

Angelo was homeless, dirty, crippled, and slow. Each of these features would kindle any latent cruelty in the Florentine men.

She felt shouts of protest bubble up in her throat. But she didn't open her mouth.

She should intervene. She knew it. Evil flourished when good people walked by and said nothing.

Raven kept walking.

She was tired after a long day of work and an evening at Gina's. She was eager to return to her small, quiet flat on the Piazza Santo Spirito. All the same, she was conscious of Angelo's cries and the laughter and cursing of the men.

The largest man finished urinating with a flourish, returning himself to the confines of his jeans. Without warning, he lifted a booted foot and kicked Angelo in the ribs. He cried out in pain, slumping to the ground.

Raven stopped.

The other men joined in, kicking and cursing Angelo without regard to his screams. Blood poured from his mouth as he writhed on the sidewalk.

"Stop!" The loud cry, in Italian, filled her ears. In an instant, she felt joy at the fact that someone, anyone, had come to Angelo's rescue.

But her joy turned to horror when the men stopped and stared in her direction.

"Stop," she repeated, in a much quieter tone.

The men exchanged glances and the largest one said something derisive to his companions. He stalked in her direction.

As he approached, Raven could see he was broad shouldered and tall, his head shaven, his eyes dark. She resisted the urge to retreat.

"Go." The man waved at her dismissively.

Raven's green eyes darted behind him, to where Angelo was lying, curled into a ball.

"Let me help him. He's bleeding."

The bald man looked over his shoulder to his companions. As if in defiance, one of them kicked Angelo in the stomach. Her friend's cries filled her ears until finally and horribly, he fell silent.

With a predatory smile, the bald man turned back to her. He pointed in the direction from which she'd approached.

"*Run.*"

Raven contemplated an attempt to reach Angelo's side, but decided against it. There was no possibility of crossing the bridge to get home, either. The bald man blocked her path.

She began to back away, her gait unsteady.

The man followed. He flailed his arms and dragged his right leg in an exaggerated impersonation of her walk. One of his companions shouted something about Quasimodo.

Resisting the urge to tell the men that they were the true monsters, she turned around, struggling to move quickly. The sounds of hurried footsteps echoed in her ears. The man's companions had left Angelo and were pursuing her.

She heard one of them remark on how ugly she was—too ugly to fuck. The others laughed.

One of them observed that she could be fucked from behind. Then they wouldn't have to see her face.

Raven hobbled more quickly, searching in vain for a single pedestrian. The banks of the Arno appeared deserted.

"Not so fast!" One man's sarcasm was treated with laughter as they walked behind her.

"Come, play with us," another shouted.

"She acts like she wants it."

Raven increased her pace, but they soon caught up with her, circling like wolves around an injured deer.

"Now what?" the shortest of the three men asked, eyeing the others.

"Now we play." The bald man, who was evidently the ringleader, smiled at Raven. He pulled the cane out of her hand, throwing it into the street.

Someone else grabbed her knapsack, ripping it from her shoulder.

"Give it back!" she shouted, lunging toward him.

With glee, the man threw her knapsack to one of his companions, over her head.

She made a move to retrieve it, but it was quickly thrown over her once again. The men played keep-away for several minutes, taunting and teasing while she begged them to return her bag. They could not have known this, but her passport and other important documents were in the knapsack.

She couldn't run. Her disability prevented her. She knew if she went for her cane, they would only pick it up and possibly throw it into the Arno. She turned and began limping away from them, back toward the Ponte Vecchio.

One of the men tossed her knapsack aside. "Grab her," he said.

Raven tried to move faster, but she was already limping as quickly as she could. The man followed, closing in on her in three steps.

Frightened, she glanced over her shoulder. At that moment, her toe caught on a crack in the road and she stumbled. Pain lanced through her hands and arms as she tried to break her fall.

The bald man approached and grabbed her by the hair. She cried out as he ripped the elastic from her ponytail. Her long black hair fell around her shoulders.

He pulled her to her feet, grabbing her hair and wrapping it around his hand.

She scanned the area, trying to find a way of escape or someone to help her, but within seconds he was dragging her across the street and into an alley. The alley was so narrow she could almost span it with arms outstretched.

She went limp, pitching forward intentionally.

With a curse, he released her.

Raven whimpered as she fell to her knees a second time, her hands scraped and bleeding. A stench filled her nostrils. Someone had used the alley as a toilet.

She coughed, trying not to be sick.

The bald man grabbed her elbow and dragged her farther into the alley.

"Get up," he demanded.

She tried to pull away, but he had hold of her elbow. She twisted, rolling to her side and kicking wildly. He cursed and she scrambled away, trying to get to her unsteady feet.

Suddenly he loomed over her, grasping her arm and pulling her to face him. Without warning he punched her with a closed fist, breaking her glasses and her nose. Blood spurted, falling in great, fat droplets to the ground.

She howled in pain, tearing the broken glasses from her face. Tears sprang from her eyes as she covered her face with her hand, fighting to breathe through her mouth.

The man yanked her to her feet. He pulled her by the hair and swung her against the wall.

Raven saw stars, pain shooting from her forehead.

The world spun and began to slow as two of the men pushed her chest against the wall, pinning her arms out to her sides. The ringleader stood behind her, his hands lifting her shirt.

Roughly, his fingers climbed her naked skin until they closed over her bra. He squeezed her breasts, making a crude joke. His companions seemed to encourage him, but Raven was no longer able to understand the words they were saying.

She felt as if she were underwater. Her head pounded and she gasped for air, trying not to choke on the blood that dripped down her throat.

The man unzipped his fly and pressed himself against her backside. His hand trailed to her waistband. With a flick of his fingers, he unbuttoned her jeans.

She struggled as his hand slid into her pants.

"Stop! Please. *Please.*"

❀ ❀

A young woman's cries, slurred and desperate, reached the Prince's ears. In the distance, he could sense the approach of Lorenzo, his lieutenant, and Gregor, his assistant. Others of their kind were not far behind.

The Prince increased his pace, unwilling to share the source of the sweetest vintage he'd smelled in centuries. The scent seemed almost familiar, so much so that his already heightened desire was coupled with nostalgia. A nostalgia he had no wish to indulge.

His cunning and prudence had served him well, enabling him to survive while others had been dispatched to whatever afterlife abominations such as he deserved. He did not act without caution, which was why he stopped at the edge of a rooftop and peered into the alley below.

The narrow alley was lit by a single streetlamp. He could see a young woman who was being held by three men, one of whom was molesting her from behind, his fly open, his stiffened member rubbing against her. The other men cheered him on, pinning her against the wall like a crucifixion.

The imagery was not lost on him.

It would have been a simple thing for the Prince to steal the victim from her attackers and spirit her away, descending to another darkened alley in order to drain her of her prize.

He closed his eyes for a moment, inhaling deeply, and was seized by recollection: a half-naked woman lying at the foot of a stone wall, her body broken, her innocence taken, her blood crying out to him from the ground . . .

Revenge.

His appetite for food was swiftly replaced by a greater appetite, one that had been quietly fed over the centuries by anger and regret. The illustrations he'd taken great care to steal dropped from his hands unheeded as he leapt from the roof.

"What the—" The man was dead before he could finish his sentence, his head ripped from his body and casually tossed aside like a football.

The other men released the woman and attempted to run, but the Prince caught them handily, sending them to hell with a few swift movements.

When he turned to claim his prize, he found she'd fallen to the ground, the sweet scent of her blood heavy in the air. She seemed unconscious, her eyes tightly shut, her face battered.

"Cassita vulneratus," he whispered, crouching next to her.

She opened large green eyes and stared up at him through the raindrops.

"A girl. How disappointing." A woman's voice broke the silence. "From the scent of her I thought she was a child."

The Prince turned to find four of his citizens standing nearby— Aoibhe, a tall woman with long red hair, and three men, Maximilian, Lorenzo, and Gregor. All had pale faces and all stared hungrily in Raven's direction, but not before bowing to their prince.

"How did such a delicacy go unnoticed? If I'd smelled her in the street, I'd have taken her." Aoibhe moved closer, her posture regal and elegant. "Come, then. She's old enough and easily shared. I've not drunk a vintage that sweet since I fed on English children."

"No." The Prince's voice was low. He moved almost imperceptibly, standing between the girl and the others, obscuring her from sight.

"Surely, Prince, you would not deny us." Maximilian, the largest man, gestured in the direction of the various body parts of the three dead men. "The others are dead and reek of vice."

"There's an unspoiled corpse by the bridge. You can have it, with my compliments. But I have first rights to the girl." The Prince's voice was quiet, but it held an undercurrent of steel.

"Your prize is almost a corpse," Aoibhe spat out. "I can hear her heart stuttering."

In response to the woman's words, the Prince turned in the girl's direction. Her eyes were closed and her breathing was labored.

"What a mess!" one of the other men exclaimed, his Italian accented with Russian. He stepped forward, examining the bodies of her attackers, coming perilously near their victim.

A growl escaped the Prince's throat.

The Russian stopped abruptly.

"Pardon, my lord." He took a cautious step back. "I meant no disrespect."

"See to the perimeter, Gregor. If no one wants the other corpse, remove it."

The young assistant scurried off into the street.

"Not even a feral would want to drink from them." Everyone turned to look at Maximilian, his focus on the mutilated men.

His eyes moved to his ruler and narrowed. "I thought the Prince didn't kill for sport."

"*Cave*, Maximilian." The Prince's voice was threatening.

"Are you challenging the kill?" Lorenzo, the Prince's lieutenant, stepped forward.

A noticeable tension hung in the air at the sound of his words. Everyone stared at Maximilian, awaiting his response.

He glanced from the Prince to the bleeding girl and back again, his blue eyes calculating.

"If the Prince never kills for sport, why are these men dead? He could have stolen her easily."

"Enough!" Aoibhe sounded impatient. "She's dying and you're wasting time."

"The Prince is the one who enacted the laws against indiscriminate killing." Maximilian stepped forward. His eyes flickered almost imperceptibly to Lorenzo's, then fixed on the Prince.

Aoibhe stood in front of him, her tall form appearing slight in comparison to his great size. "You'd challenge the Prince of the city over this? Are you mad?"

Maximilian moved, as if to shove her aside.

In a flash, the redheaded woman caught hold of his left arm, wrenching it high behind his back and dislocating his shoulder with a sickening snap.

"Never lift your hand to me again. Or you'll lose it." She forced him to his knees, placing a velvet-clad foot to his lower back.

Maximilian gritted his teeth. "Would someone get this fork-tongued harpy off my back?"

"Aoibhe." The Prince's voice was low, but commanding.

"I just want to ensure this Prussian knight understands what I'm saying. His Italian is severely . . . lacking."

"Get off, you miserable wench!" he snarled, trying to shake her off.

"With pleasure." Aoibhe released her colleague with a string of Irish profanity and more than a few threats.

Max stood, popping his shoulder back into place with a groan and rotating his arm.

"Since I appear to be the only one interested in the laws of the city, I withdraw the challenge." He paused, as if expecting someone else to speak.

All were silent.

"Finally." Aoibhe turned her attention back to the Prince, who had moved closer to his prey, his back against the wall. "Your exceptional vintage is on her final breath. If she's to be had, it must be now. Will you share?"

On impulse, the Prince pulled the girl into his arms and in one quick motion leapt to the roof, leaving his fellow citizens behind.

Chapter Two

*C*assita *vulneratus.*

Raven awoke with a start.

She'd heard a strange voice whispering in her ear. Of course, there was no one else in her small bedroom. She couldn't remember what the voice said or if it spoke to her in English or Italian. Something told her the language was neither, but it was a dream, after all. She'd been known to dream in Latin on occasion.

She blinked against the streaming sunlight. It was unusual for the shutters on her bedroom window to be open, but open they were. (Not that Raven focused on the anomaly.)

She'd had the strangest dream, but all she could remember was a vortex of swirling emotions and colors. As an artist, it was not surprising for her to think and dream in color. But it was strange that her memory, which was usually as sharp as a knife, was amorphous.

Yawning, she swung her legs over the side of the bed, its narrowness a testament to her single status, and walked to her laptop. She opened her music application and began playing her favorite Mumford and Sons album.

When she entered the bathroom, she didn't bother looking in the mirror suspended over the vanity. The mirror was only large enough to show her best feature—her face. Even looking at that feature was something Raven avoided.

After her morning ablutions, she wandered into the tiny kitchen of her one-bedroom apartment and began making coffee.

It felt like a Saturday or Sunday, but she was pretty sure she needed to go to work. Seized by a sudden anxiety, she took a few steps to the left, peering into her bedroom. When she caught sight of her knapsack sitting next to the small table that she used as a desk, she breathed a sigh of relief.

She'd drink her coffee and check her e-mail, as was her custom, and figure out what day it was. According to the clock on the wall, it was seven in the morning.

She leaned against the counter. That was when she noticed something had changed.

The old-fashioned nightgown she was wearing should have attracted her attention, since it wasn't hers. But it didn't. Instead, she focused on what was visible beneath the hem of her gown. Her right foot, which was normally turned to the side, was symmetrical with the left, something it had not been for over a decade.

She froze. She shouldn't have been able to walk from her bedroom to the bathroom and to the kitchen without her cane. She shouldn't have been able to stand on both feet without pain. Yet that was exactly what she'd done.

Raven almost sank to the floor in shock, but she was too busy lifting her formerly injured foot, experimentally rotating the ankle. She repeated the movement with her left. Each foot moved with perfect ease and without discomfort.

She walked into the bedroom and back again. She held her breath and jumped.

Arms held wide, she ran in place, footfall after footfall a mad, enthusiastic triumph over what she knew to be impossible.

It was a miracle.

Raven didn't believe in miracles, or in any deity or deities who could possibly produce them. She closed her eyes, trying to remember anything from the night before—anything that might serve as a clue for this sudden, momentous transformation. Apart from the whispered voice whose words she could not make out, there was nothing she could hold on to.

Maybe I'm still asleep.

As if to test her hypothesis, she stretched her lower limbs and positioned herself into a wobbly, amateurish arabesque. She held the position as long as she could, revelling in muscle memories long since forgotten. When she finally lost her balance and placed both feet on the floor, she almost wept. Her right foot and leg had done what she'd asked them to, finally. All the damage that had been done to her that terrible, terrible night had been healed.

She heard the Moka espresso maker humming and spitting on the stovetop and rushed to switch off the gas. Opening the small fridge, she withdrew a container of milk.

She glanced at the label, reading it easily. Her eyes widened. She turned the container in her hands, reading the fine print. She blinked, feeling on her face to see if she was wearing her reading glasses.

She wasn't.

Without her reading glasses, she shouldn't have been able to make out the words printed beneath the label. But they were clearly visible.

This can't be happening. I'm delusional.

Raven put the milk on the counter and jogged to the bathroom.

In the mirror, she caught sight of a strange woman and shrieked.

The woman had long, shiny black hair. Her eyes were a sparkling green and she had a lovely oval face with high cheekbones. It was the kind of face, Raven thought, that deserved to be painted. In fact, the image reminded her of the actress Vivien Leigh.

She jumped back in fright.

So did the woman.

She moved to the right.

So did the woman.

It took a moment for her to realize the woman in the mirror was her reflection.

In amazement, she touched her face, her cheekbones, her mouth, with its full lower lip.

Raven knew how she was supposed to look—plain, overweight, and with a leg that didn't work right. Yet her appearance was that of a beautiful young woman with two completely functional legs.

Was she hallucinating?

But my senses seem to be working. I can hear, touch, see, and smell.

Was her previous appearance and injury a nightmare? She stepped into the hall and peered into her bedroom, which was decorated with framed prints of Botticelli's *Primavera* and the *Birth of Venus*, along with personal photographs. Pictures of herself and her sister, Carolyn, gazed at her from her bookcase, confirming her previous appearance.

She didn't believe in miracles, the supernatural, or anything that couldn't be investigated by science. She had to be hallucinating. There was no other scientific explanation.

She tried to remember what she'd done the day before. She recalled going to work, but she couldn't remember anything afterward. What if she'd been drugged?

Perhaps if she returned to work, her friends could help her. If she was ill, they could take her to a doctor. And if she'd been drugged . . .

Raven pulled the nightgown over her head, pausing to examine the material. It appeared to be made of cotton that had once been white but was now yellowed. The neckline was trimmed with ornate lace and a faded pink ribbon. A row of antique pearl buttons dotted the front from neckline to waist. In short, not only was the nightgown a stranger to her, it appeared to be from the previous century.

Now she was naked, next to the mirror.

She retrieved a small footstool from the kitchen and stood on top of it.

Raven never looked at herself naked. That was a sight she studiously avoided. But this morning she cursed the fact that her only mirror was so small.

Her skin was creamy and perfect, its surface unblemished by scars or stretch marks. Her breasts were firmer, sitting high on her chest. Her figure was an hourglass, her waist tiny, her hips gently flaring out.

She contorted herself atop the stool so that she could get a better view of her hips and backside. Cellulite was noticeably absent from her thighs.

I don't know what they gave me, but it must have been a very strong drug.

Worried she might have been assaulted, Raven examined her skin for any signs of trauma. She found nothing.

She cautiously parted her legs, slipping her hand between them in order to check for any tenderness. She breathed a sigh of relief when all seemed normal.

Of course, if I'm hallucinating my appearance, I could be hallucinating the absence of trauma.

Raven wondered if all victims of hallucination were so reasonable, and once again, she attributed both effects to the drug she'd no doubt been given.

She pulled on her bathrobe, though it dwarfed her now smaller size, and picked up her cell phone, quickly realizing that it was out of power. She moved to her desk with the intention of picking up the cord to charge her phone. A glance at her computer screen revealed that it was Monday morning. She didn't know how she'd forgotten her entire weekend, but she needed to skip checking her e-mail and get moving if she was going to make it to her job at the Uffizi by eight o'clock.

She gulped her coffee and dressed, pulling on an old pair of yoga pants and a T-shirt because they were the only items in her limited wardrobe that wouldn't be ridiculously oversized. Hurriedly, she brushed her hair and her teeth, switching off her music and tossing her cell phone and charger cord into her knapsack.

She tried to find her favorite sneakers, but gave up after a few moments, thrusting her feet into a pair of casual black shoes that had been carelessly tossed into her closet. She'd search for the sneakers under the bed later.

Consequently, she didn't see the unfamiliar box that was hidden below where she slept, just out of sight.

As she locked the door to her flat and stepped onto the landing, she saw Dolcezza, her neighbor's cat.

"*Buongiorno*, Dolcezza." Raven smiled at the animal and reached out a hand to pet her.

The cat withdrew, hissing and arching its back.

"Dolcezza, what's the matter?" Raven crouched, making another attempt to approach the cat, but it continued hissing, thrashing its tail wildly and lashing out with its paws.

At that moment, Signora Lidia DiFabio opened the door to her apartment and called for the cat, who raced past her legs as if a demon from hell were chasing it.

"Good morning." Raven waved to her neighbor, wondering how she would react to her change in appearance.

"Good morning, my dear." Lidia smiled.

"How are you this morning?"

Lidia rubbed at her temple. "Oh, a little tired. I just haven't been feeling well these past few days."

Raven came a few steps closer. "Can I help?"

"Oh, no. Bruno will be here later. I'm just going to go and lie down. Enjoy your day."

Raven waved good-bye to her neighbor and clambered down the stairs. She was surprised that Lidia hadn't seemed to notice her appearance or new, slimmer figure. Perhaps it was because Lidia wasn't wearing her glasses.

Raven was even more surprised by the cat's sudden change of temper. She'd always been on affectionate terms with Dolcezza and had frequently fed and cuddled the animal. Their relationship had never been anything but friendly.

Normally she descended the flight of stairs in her building like a turtle, moving slowly with the aid of her cane. On this morning, she ran.

It was liberating to be able to move without the burden of added weight or the pain she normally experienced. Without thinking much about it, she jogged all the way from her flat in Santo Spirito and across the Ponte Santa Trinita.

Then she stopped.

Angelo, the homeless man who was usually seated next to the bridge, was absent.

Raven took a moment to look for him, wondering if he'd merely changed location, but he was nowhere to be found. His belongings, which were normally placed next to the bridge in one favorite spot, were also gone.

She felt a prickly feeling on the back of her neck. In all the time she'd lived in Santo Spirito, Angelo was seated next to the bridge morning and evening.

She made a mental note to stop by the Franciscan mission, which he sometimes visited, in order to check on him.

Glancing at her watch and seeing she had mere moments before she was supposed to start work, Raven continued running to the Uffizi, a distance of one and a half kilometers. The sensation of her feet hitting the pavement, the jarring of her lower legs and knees—all these feelings were eagerly embraced.

A gentle breeze caressed her cheek and hair as it spilled over her shoulders and knapsack. She felt stronger, bolder, more confident. She felt as if she'd been given a new body and a new outlook.

With every step, she grew less and less concerned about what had caused such a dramatic reversal of her bad fortune.

Consequently, she was unaware of the mysterious figure who'd been shadowing her since she left her building.

It was the happiest morning of her life.

Chapter Three

The Prince climbed the stairs to his bedroom in the Palazzo Riccardi, an old Medici palace. He'd returned the wounded lark to her world. Now he returned to his.

And what a world it was—dark, violent, destructive.

As he entered the room, he caught sight of his reflection and pushed a few wayward strands of blond hair from his forehead. He never spent long looking at himself, despite the fact that his body was far more attractive now than it had been in life.

Favor is deceitful, and beauty is vain.

Funny how he could still quote Scripture. Funny how he, who had once been a servant of God, was now counted among the Church's enemies.

He frowned, thinking of a beautiful face with green eyes.

He pushed her image aside. He'd recklessly interfered in human affairs because of a centuries-old memory. Because of another beautiful face with haunting eyes . . .

He scrubbed his face with both hands. His body never tired but his mind needed rest. On this morning, he wanted nothing other than to spend hours in quiet meditation. But that would not be possible. He'd scented Aoibhe the moment he'd entered the palace, and she was behind him.

"You've been hiding." She spoke to her erstwhile lover in English, rolling to her side on the large bed and absolutely neglecting to cover her naked body.

(She had few virtues. Modesty was not among them.)

Dawn was just peeking over the horizon. In a few hours the lark, no longer wounded, would awake in her apartment. But at this moment, the Prince forced himself to forget her and gazed hungrily at Aoibhe's naked form, her firm, full breasts and long, tempting red hair.

He licked his lips. "Good morning to you, too. How did you know I'd be here?"

"I guessed. You've been in that impenetrable fortress of yours for days. I knew you'd have to feed eventually. Then you'd come here."

"I thought I changed the locks." He pulled the blackout shades over the windows. The action was for her comfort, not his.

Unbeknownst to the others, he could brave the sunlight.

Aoibhe rested her head on an upturned hand, looking remarkably like a Renaissance painting.

"You did. I wandered into the museum and persuaded one of the servants to allow me upstairs. I would have come to you at the fortress, but as you know, I can't pass through the gates."

The Prince ignored her pout, his gray eyes narrowing. "Is the servant dead?"

"Of course not. Merely—indisposed." She lifted a pillow and threw it at him. "I wouldn't kill one of your humans. At least, not without asking."

He cursed, batting the pillow aside. His memory was drawn to the green-eyed girl, cowering in an alley while Aoibhe begged him to share the "exceptional vintage." The memory, like the feelings that accompanied it, made him uneasy.

He turned his back. "Servants are easily replaced, but it's inconvenient to do so every time a guest gets hungry."

Aoibhe paused, for she'd seen the discomfort that flitted across his face a moment before. "You never used to care about them. I can recall when you executed your entire staff on a whim."

Her comment hung in the air as he crossed over to the aged wardrobe opposite the bed.

"I don't have whims, Aoibhe. I executed them for good reason, I assure you. Servants are like clothes. As long as they remain useful, I'll keep them. When they outlive their usefulness, I dispose of them. Perhaps it's more correct to say that I mourn the departure of a nice garment. A servant? Not so much."

The Prince removed his black jacket and hung it up before retreating to a chair and attending to his boots.

Aoibhe continued to watch him. "This is what I find so curious about you. You're the most human of any of us in some ways, but the least human in others."

"I'm sure there's a compliment in there somewhere," he said wryly.

"You're our prince, but no one knows how you keep your fortress secure or who your maker was." She lowered her voice. "Not even I know when you were brought across, although I surmise it was a few hundred years before me."

"Is there a question?" His tone was gruff as he placed his boots next to the wardrobe, avoiding her probing gaze.

She lowered her voice to a soft, seductive whisper. "We're lovers. Tell me your secrets."

He gave her a pointed look. "We aren't lovers, Aoibhe. We simply fornicate on occasion." As if to emphasize the point, he stood and removed his shirt.

She closed her eyes and inhaled as his scent swirled in the room. "You killed a human this evening, but fed on another. I smell someone's blood on you and a different one in you."

"A fool surprised me while I was feeding."

She opened her eyes. "Then why not enjoy dessert?"

"You're losing your sense of smell. I don't have a taste for rapists." He removed a man's silver Baume et Mercier watch from his pocket and tossed it to her.

She caught it and admired its elegant simplicity in the lamplight before dropping it on the nightstand. "A pity you were the one to end him, since you're so indifferent to human affairs. I would have made him suffer."

"He suffered well enough." The Prince's gray eyes twinkled. "You would have enjoyed it. He begged for his life, confessing his most secret sins. He even soiled himself." The Prince smiled, exposing white and perfect teeth. "He said his name was *Professor* Pacciani."

"The Paccianis produced a professor? I can hardly believe it."

(The name Pacciani was shared by a famous serial killer who had haunted Florence for decades. Of course, the humans didn't know that a number of the killer's alleged victims had been contributed by Aoibhe herself, and the others of her kind.)

"You killed a rapist. You ended three men last week in order to feed on that girl. This is strange behavior. Why the sudden interest in humans? You let the serial killer prey on the city for years."

He busied himself with his socks. "I interfere when it's in my interest."

Aoibhe rolled onto her stomach, exposing her beautiful back and backside. She tossed her hair over her shoulder.

"It wasn't in your interest to dismember the men in an alley and leave the pieces to rot."

The Prince's gaze flew to hers. "Gregor disposed of the corpses."

"You could have frightened them away or used mind control." She gazed at him curiously. "Max isn't the only one who found your actions peculiar. There's been talk among the Consilium members."

He leveled cold eyes on her, his expression menacing. "If Maximilian wishes to talk, he knows where to find me. He won't like how that conversation ends."

She shivered and looked away. "I spoke in your favor, of course. I would have done whatever it took to secure the girl, even if it meant dispatching the men. She was exquisite. And they were going to waste it."

The Prince said nothing but stood, removing his leather belt with a resounding snap.

Aoibhe toyed with the sheet, watching him. "How did it taste?"

He coiled the belt in his hand before placing it carefully on the wardrobe shelf. "My appetite is never quenched."

Once again, Aoibhe laughed. "You need to take a lover—a human pet to fulfill your needs, day and night. There are beautiful women and men at Teatro. You'd have your choice."

He hid his grimace by closing the wardrobe door.

The muscles of his naked chest and arms rippled with every movement, and Aoibhe admired them, wetting her lips with her tongue.

"In all the years I've known you, you've never had a woman for an extended period of time. Why?"

He turned his head minutely, spearing her with his gaze. "Humans aren't meant to be enjoyed for an extended period. They lack resilience. Besides, I had you."

"Our coupling has not been frequent."

The Prince pressed a fist to the wardrobe door and clenched his teeth. "You took a new human lover less than a month ago. Where is he this morning? Dusting your palace on his knees, naked?"

She rolled to her back, breasts exposed, staring up at the ornate canopy overhead. "Human lovers lack stamina. I nearly killed him within a week. And he has to sleep, on occasion."

"Ah, yes. Humans have to sleep." The Prince removed his black trousers and tossed them over the chair. "So you've enjoyed his body for the evening and now arrive to enjoy mine for the day. How flattering."

She turned her face toward him. "Nothing compares to our kind. And you've always been . . . attentive." Her dark eyes lingered on his muscled, lean frame before resting on the firmness of his backside. "I'm sure you were never in want of female company when you were human. There must have been a legion of sweet young virgins outside your home, begging to be seduced."

The Prince turned so quickly the movement was a blur, his eyes darkening and almost pinning her to the bed. "*Cave*, Aoibhe," he growled.

She lifted her hands in apology. "I beg pardon. I forgot you were a priest."

"I was no priest," he spat out. He crossed the room, planting his fists on the mattress and leaning over her. "I was a novice. Do you intend to talk all day or did you plant yourself in my bed for some other purpose?"

She reached out a hand and wrapped it around his wrist, her touch soft and sensuous. "You've been in Florence so much longer than the rest of us and you've guarded your past securely. Can you blame me for a lapse in memory? I know so little about you."

He gave her a heated look. "You know enough, it would seem, in order to bed me. You've entered my home, you've taken off your clothes, and you've deposited yourself between my sheets. Shall we get on with it?"

"Just a moment, my prince." She gave him a patient smile. "You served the Church. You lived in an age in which women were supposed to remain virgins until they married. Perhaps that's all you can countenance. Tell me, is that why you haven't chosen a consort?"

The Prince disentangled himself from her grasp.

"Precious few of our kind survive the change with virginity intact."

"I was a virgin once." Her tone was almost wistful. "Before my father insulted one of the English lords. My maker had a surprise when he took me. He favored virgins, too, but misread my scent."

"I'm sure you had other virtues that more than made up for it."

Aoibhe squinted, trying to read his expression. She shook her head.

"No human lover, no assignations at Teatro, and no consort. Of course you're angry and in need of release. Man cannot live by blood alone."

"If you're so concerned about my sexual needs, then you'd best do something about them." He spoke sharply. "I'm going to put something in your mouth to silence you if you don't stop talking."

"I'm trying to help. We are friends, are we not? After so many years?" She smiled prettily, sliding over so there was room beside her.

He stood naked and proud, his erection straining toward her. His hands clasped into fists at his sides and the tendons in his arms rippled.

"Friends? No. But you've certainly been a welcome ally." His gaze traveled the length of her body and up again, resting on her breasts.

She sighed and rolled her eyes heavenward. "I suppose that's the most I can hope for from an Englishman. It's a good thing I gave up killing your countrymen in the nineteenth century."

"Enough." He moved quickly, stretching his body over hers.

"Finally," she whispered, pressing her red lips to his neck.

His hands moved up and down her sides, digging into her perfect skin.

She purred like a cat at his touch and lifted her right breast to his open and eager mouth.

He licked it, encircling the nipple several times before drawing it between his teeth. She arched off the bed at the sensation, lifting her other breast for his attention.

He repeated the movement before closing his mouth and sucking.

Aoibhe moaned, thrashing her head from side to side. He raised her thigh, pulling her leg around his hip before entering her. She groaned heavily as he began to move.

Their coupling was active and frenetic, as was typical of their kind. The Prince's strength was such that he could hold himself over her with one arm, while he drove into her again and again.

Aoibhe lifted her hips to meet his thrusts before rolling him and climbing on top. With a triumphal cry, she rode him vigorously, head thrown back.

His hands explored her bouncing breasts before he sat up and replaced his hands with his mouth.

Aoibhe groaned her pleasure, trying to capture his mouth in a kiss, but he lifted her bodily and sprang out of bed, pressing her back against the wall.

She tried to kiss him again, but again he spurned her, whispering his lips up and down the column of her throat.

He felt her begin to orgasm and thrust into her more deeply. As was the case with their kind, her orgasm lasted several minutes.

When she had finished, she dragged him back to the bed and climbed atop him again, moving so quickly her body shimmered in the air.

With a cry, he thrust up his hips, emptying himself in her.

Aoibhe growled and bared her teeth, bending to sink them into his neck.

In an instant, he pushed her to her back, pinning her arms over her head. His body continued to shudder with his orgasm, his breathing almost labored.

"No," he snarled, his gray eyes flashing with anger.

She had no choice but to nod as he continued moving within her. They were almost matched in height and in size, but he was older and far more powerful. He could end her handily and take her body out of the city to burn it beyond recognition. No one would ever be the wiser.

She stared up with wide, panicked eyes, holding her breath.

When he was spent, he hung his head, a few locks of his hair skimming her breasts.

"Let me be your consort," she whispered, as her womb fluttered from the aftershocks, the pleasure continuing to flow through her. "We'll rule Florence together. Drink from me and I'll drink from you."

She exposed her neck and what lay below the surface of her skin.

The Prince opened his eyes slowly, like a gray-eyed dragon, and growled.

"Please," she begged.

He dislodged himself from her and walked naked toward the wardrobe.

She sat up, fanning a shaking hand over her throat.

"What are you afraid of, my love? The connection that comes from the exchange of blood?"

He glared. "Don't use appellations you don't mean. Your honesty is one of the few things I've always admired about you."

She pressed her lips together, but said nothing.

The Prince retrieved a clean set of black clothes from the wardrobe and approached the bed. "The palace is at your disposal until sundown. I'll instruct the servants. See to it you leave me with the full complement."

She studied him, her hair a riot of red curls around her lovely oval face.

"I thought we'd progressed a little over the past centuries. I was mistaken."

He clenched his jaw. "Don't lie to me. Everything you do is calculated."

"I don't deny it, but in this case I'm doing you a favor. We won the war with the Venetians, but how long will the peace last? And what about the attempt on your life? We still haven't discovered who helped the Venetians breach our borders. You must take a consort, if only to strengthen and protect your position. I'm one of your oldest friends. I'm the obvious choice."

He regarded her, studying her face and expression with restrained hostility.

She threw back the bedclothes and stood before him.

"You have to be thinking of the future. How old are you? Who knows how long you have before the—"

"Enough," he interrupted. "Our coupling has not been frequent, as you mentioned, but it has been fair. Until today."

He took a moment to admire her body, the creamy cast of her skin, her gentle curves and long legs. He shook his head.

"Your performance was unnecessary. I would have given you the same answer had you approached me in the street. We're allies, Aoibhe, not lovers. And from now on, that is all we shall be. Don't come here again."

And with that, he swept from the room.

Chapter Four

When Raven approached the Uffizi Gallery, she was stunned to find it cordoned off.

Several officers from the local police stood watch at the barricades, while carabinieri in their signature dark blue uniforms roamed the U-shaped courtyard.

A number of men in dark suits stood in a small group, talking to one another near the entrance to the gallery. Journalists from around the world gathered around the perimeter, shouting questions to the carabinieri in English and Italian. Their questions were ignored, but not by Raven.

Something terrible had happened.

The famed Botticelli illustrations—copies of Botticelli's drawings of Dante's *Divine Comedy*—were missing.

Raven covered her mouth, a sick feeling ascending from her stomach to her throat.

"*Permesso*." A masculine voice sounded in Raven's ear as someone tried to squeeze past her.

She turned and recognized Patrick Wong, one of her friends from the gallery.

"Patrick." She touched his arm.

His dark, almond-shaped eyes examined her face. "Do I know you?"

She switched to English. "It's me."

He looked at her in puzzlement and she remembered that her appearance was greatly altered.

"It's Raven."

Patrick shook his arm from her grasp and glared. "What do you know about Raven?"

"It's me, I swear." She retrieved her Uffizi identification card from her knapsack and held it out to him.

He snatched it from her hand, bringing his face next to hers.

"How did you get this?" he hissed. "Where is she?"

"Patrick, it's me. We work together, remember? I'm part of Professor Urbano's restoration team."

He curled his fingers around her identification card. "Everyone knows Professor Urbano's team. That doesn't mean anything."

She glanced around helplessly, trying to figure out how to prove her identity. Her gaze alighted on the edge of the Loggia dei Lanzi and its roof, which was barely visible.

"Remember we had lunch on the terrace? You told me about growing up with your grandmother in Richmond Hill and how she owned a restaurant. You told me you had a dog named Magnus, but he was hit by a car when you were ten."

Patrick's eyes widened. "Who told you those things?"

"You did. You're lactose intolerant, you were born in Toronto, and you have a crush on Gina. It's me, Patrick. I promise." She held out her arm. "Look at my watch."

He looked at her wrist, on which she wore an old, battered Swatch that he easily recognized.

His eyes met hers. "How do I know you didn't kidnap Raven and steal her watch?"

She rolled her eyes. "Listen to yourself. I'm not important. Who would want to kidnap me?"

"That isn't true." His expression grew fierce. "Raven is someone to me. She's important to me."

She paused, tamping down her emotions so she could focus on finding something that would prove her identity.

"Remember when you lost the copies of the radiographs of *Primavera*? And Dottor Vitali kept asking for them? I'm the one who put them in the bottom drawer of your desk."

Patrick shook his head. "I didn't lose the radiographs."

She smiled gently. "Yes, you did. You left them in the archives' reading room. I found them and put them in your desk so you wouldn't get in trouble."

Patrick stared, a look of incredulous fascination on his face.

"I didn't tell anyone about that."

"I know."

His expression slowly morphed from shock into concern.

"Raven?" he whispered, staring at her intently.

She nodded.

He lifted a hand to her face. "What did you do to yourself?"

She blinked and turned away, unable to meet his gaze.

Patrick dropped his hand quickly and looked around, noticing they had attracted the attention of one of the carabinieri, who was watching them from behind dark sunglasses.

"We need to get out of here." He grabbed Raven's arm. "Where's your cane?"

"I don't need it anymore."

"That's not funny." Patrick gave her a furious look.

Raven lifted her now uninjured leg and quickly demonstrated her range of movement.

"Fuck," he said under his breath, his eyebrows lifting. "What the hell is going on?"

Before Raven had time to venture an answer, the Carabinieri officer began walking toward them. Patrick pulled her around the corner and out of sight.

When they were several feet away, Raven planted her feet. "What about work? We're going to be late."

Patrick handed back her identification card. "I'm late every day because of the police. We have to go through a special security check before they let us in."

"Are the police here because of the illustrations?"

He looked at her suspiciously. "Of course."

"When were they stolen?"

Patrick stared.

When she didn't say anything further, he rubbed his eyes. "Holy shit."

"What?"

He exhaled loudly. "If you were in trouble, you'd tell me, right?"

"I'm not in any trouble."

"Are you kidding? I'm one of your best friends and I didn't recognize you." He cursed. "You don't need your cane. And you disappeared right after the biggest robbery in Uffizi history."

"What?" Raven practically shrieked, dropping her knapsack in surprise.

"Sssh!" Patrick gave her a furious look. "Do you want a half dozen carabinieri and God knows how many Interpol agents over here? Keep your voice down."

He quickly stepped away, looking in the direction of the Uffizi, before dragging her and her knapsack closer to the Ponte Vecchio.

"When did the robbery happen?" Raven asked, her mind almost numb with shock.

"The night of Gina's party."

Raven pressed her hand to her forehead. She remembered Gina's party. She remembered talking to Patrick about a ride home. After that, the evening was a blur.

She squinted in the sunlight. "How did the thieves get past the security systems?"

"No one knows. None of the alarms were tripped. They didn't find so much as a fingerprint. The special agents think it must have been an inside job, which is why they've been interrogating us. I've been interviewed three times."

"But who would do such a thing? Everyone we work with has a clean record."

Patrick's expression grew guarded.

"Raven, they've been looking for you. You've been gone over a week and no one knew where you were."

"A week?" she squeaked, eyes wide.

"Gina's party was the seventeenth. Today is the twenty-seventh. You didn't come to work last week at all. We thought you were sick. I texted you and sent e-mails, and Professor Urbano called your cell phone, but you didn't answer. I was pretty worried so Gina and I stopped by last Wednesday. One of your neighbors said he hadn't seen you in days. We reported you missing to the police and the American consulate."

Before Raven could respond, the Carabinieri officer suddenly appeared, flanked by two others.

"Do you work at the museum?" He addressed Patrick sternly.

Patrick's gaze flickered to Raven's. "Yes."

"Identification, please." The officer held out his hand expectantly.

Patrick gave him his Uffizi identification card. The man examined it carefully before returning it.

His attention shifted to Raven.

"And you?"

She nodded and handed him her identification.

The officer looked at the photograph and then he looked at Raven. He removed his sunglasses, folding them and placing them in one of the pockets of his uniform.

His eyes bored into hers. "You don't look like the photograph."

Raven shrugged. "That's me."

The officer peered at her thoughtfully before turning his gaze on Patrick. Patrick shifted his weight from foot to foot.

"You know this woman?" The officer gestured to Raven.

Patrick hesitated and Raven's heart began to pound.

He moved to stand closer to her. "Yes, we work together."

Raven tried not to melt with relief at Patrick's show of support.

The officer's attention snapped back to her. "Your identification says that you work for the Opificio delle Pietre Dure."

"I do. But I've been seconded to the Uffizi and that's stated on the card as well." She pointed to the identification he was still holding.

"Dottoressa Wood, come with me."

"She's an American." Patrick stepped forward. "You can't just take her."

The officer measured Patrick for a moment.

"We aren't *taking* her. We're accompanying her to the police station so we can interview her, just as we interviewed the other Uffizi employees."

Patrick grabbed Raven's arm, stopping her. "You interviewed the other employees at the gallery, not the police station. She isn't going anywhere with you."

"This isn't an interrogation or an arrest, it's simply an interview. I'm sure Dottoressa Wood wants to help the investigation." The officer gave Raven a pointed look.

She blinked, not knowing what to say.

Patrick held his ground, still holding Raven's arm.

The man cursed and removed something from underneath his jacket, flashing it under Patrick's nose.

"I am Sergio Batelli, the *ispettore* from the Carabinieri. She does not have a diplomatic passport and her name is on the list of Uffizi employees. Under Italian civil code, I can acquire information from her at the police station without notifying anyone, especially the Americans. *Capisce?*

"Perhaps you'd like to be interviewed with her, Signor Wong. Are you lovers? How long have you known one another?"

Patrick cursed and took a step forward, but Raven intervened, placing her hand over his.

"It will be all right. I'll just go and answer their questions. But please, tell Professor Urbano what's happening. He'll be expecting me in the restoration lab."

Patrick fixed the officer with a look of defiance. "I'll be notifying Dottor Vitali, the director of the Uffizi, and the American consulate. And I'll be naming names, Ispettor Batelli."

The officer shrugged.

"Dottoressa Wood." He gestured to the street, where a police car had just pulled up to the curb, lights flashing.

Patrick squeezed Raven's hand before sprinting in the direction of the Uffizi.

"This way." Batelli's voice was gruff as he and the other men led Raven to the car.

Chapter Five

"For your information, I should state that this is not an interrogation. You are not under arrest. We are interviewing you in connection with the theft of art from the Uffizi because you work at the gallery. This conversation is being video recorded.

"Dottoressa Wood, where were you on Friday, May seventeenth?"

Batelli sat across from her in a small interrogation room in the Florence police station, his dark eyes keen and peering.

He had files in front of him, but they were closed. He wasn't even taking notes. He was simply watching her.

Another man, wearing a dark suit, stood behind him and to his left. He'd been introduced as Alessandro Savola, an Interpol agent from Rome. He, too, was watching Raven, arms crossed, eyes alert.

She felt as if she were a sample being examined under a microscope.

She contemplated her options for a moment, staring back at the agents and wondering about her predicament.

She loved her work. She loved the Uffizi. She was willing to do anything to help the police find whoever had stolen the illustrations. That included answering the officer's very uncomfortable, potentially hazardous questions.

"I came to work in the restoration lab. At the end of the day, a group of us went to a friend's party."

"Which friend?"

"Gina Molinari. She works in the archives."

"Where did you go after the party?"

Raven focused on a spot on the wall, over his shoulder, willing herself to remember.

"I went home."

Ispettor Batelli leaned forward in his chair.

"What time was that?"

Her eyes met his.

"I don't remember, but the party was still going on. I said good-bye to Patrick and to Gina and walked home."

"Alone?"

"Yes, alone."

"Do you live with anyone? Did anyone see you when you arrived home?"

"I live alone and no, no one saw me."

"Do you have a lover? A boyfriend or girlfriend?"

"No." She crossed her arms over her chest.

"When did you first hear about the robbery?" The inspector's voice was casual. Too casual.

"This morning, when I came to work."

The agent's eyes narrowed. "What about newspapers? Radio? Television?"

"I don't take the newspaper and I don't have a television. Sometimes I listen to the BBC in the morning but I woke up late for work and didn't bother."

"Why are you carrying your passport and other important documents? Aren't you afraid of thieves?" Batelli gestured to the items, which were sitting on the desk next to her identification card.

"My old passport was going to expire. I picked this one up at the consulate the other day, but I had to present the paperwork that showed I was working in Italy legally. I must have forgotten to take everything out of my knapsack."

"The name on your documents doesn't match the name on your identification card."

She clenched her teeth. "My name is Raven."

"That's not the name in your passport."

That's because the name in my passport is dead, she thought.

She tried to appear relaxed, folding her hands in her lap. "In America, it's common for people to have nicknames."

"What part of America are you from?"

"New Hampshire."

"Your employee file states that you attended Barry University and New York University."

"That's right."

"How long have you been in Florence?"

"I spent a year here while I was finishing my master's degree from NYU. Then I returned three years ago while I was writing my dissertation. When I graduated last year, Professor Urbano hired me to work for him at the Opificio."

Batelli's eyes narrowed. "I thought Professor Urbano worked at the Uffizi."

"He does, but only on contract. He runs a lab at the Opificio, which is a world-renowned restoration institute. He was hired by the Uffizi, along with his team, to work on a single project. I'm part of that team."

"So you have a Ph.D. in art history and conservation?"

She squirmed. "And restoration. I was trained in both, but focused on restoration for my dissertation."

"Interesting," he said. "How is this restoration work done?"

"We begin by doing scientific research on the artwork. There's a lab in the Fortezza da Basso where we use microscopes, spectrophotometry, and X-ray machines. Sometimes we use ultraviolet rays or infrared photography. We also do archival work, comparing previous restoration and conservation attempts with current scientific findings."

The inspector stared. "You do all these things?"

"I help where needed, but on this project I spent most of my time removing layers of varnish from the painting so we could get at the paint beneath. Then, someone more accomplished than me fixed the cracks and flaking in the original paint. This week, we're supposed to start applying a transparent varnish to the artwork in order to protect it. Because of the size of the piece and its age, this process could take months."

Batelli nodded.

"Professor Urbano says you were absent from work all week and that you didn't call in. Where were you?"

"At home, I guess."

"You guess? You don't know?" The officer's tone was no longer casual. She didn't answer, for truthfully, she didn't know what to say.

"Is it common for you to disappear from work for a week and not remember where you were?"

"No." Unconsciously, her fingernails began digging into the palms of her hands.

"Where were you?"

"I don't remember."

Batelli exchanged a look with Agent Savola.

"Where were you yesterday?"

"I don't know."

"But you remember going home after the party?"

Raven closed her eyes, sifting through her memories. "I remember saying good-bye to Patrick and leaving Gina's party. I remember starting to walk home."

She opened her eyes. "That's it."

"Tell me, Dottoressa Wood, do you drink?"

She shrugged. "I'll have a glass of wine when out with friends. But no, I don't really drink."

"What about drugs?"

"Drugs?" she repeated, her body growing noticeably tense.

"Do you take drugs or medication?"

"Sometimes I take pain pills for my leg, but I have a prescription for them."

Batelli's gaze dropped to her leg. "Do you ever take too many pills?"

"No." She clasped her hands together, trying not to twist them in her lap.

"What about other drugs—cocaine, marijuana, ecstasy?"

"I don't do drugs."

"Tell the truth." Batelli gave her a hard look. "You go to a party. You miss work for a week. Somehow, during your absence, the Uffizi is robbed. Make this easier on yourself and tell us what really happened."

"I told you. I don't remember."

"This can become very unpleasant if you lie to me." His tone grew sharp.

"I'm telling you the truth!" She raised her voice, momentarily startling the two agents.

The inspector leaned closer.

"Where were you last week?"

"I don't know."

"Where were you yesterday?"

"I don't remember."

He slammed a fist down on the table. "Where were you last night?"

A hazy swirl of colors danced before her eyes, accompanied by a low whisper. All at once, she felt a sharp pain at the back of her head.

She closed her eyes.

"Dottoressa Wood?" he prompted.

She didn't respond.

"Signorina?" he said, slightly louder.

"Maybe I was drugged," she whispered, as the pain in her head subsided. She fanned a hand over her eyes.

"Drugged?" he repeated.

She dropped her hand. "Maybe someone drugged me."

"What makes you say that?" Savola spoke for the first time, his voice low and gravelly.

Raven's eyes met his. "I can't remember yesterday. I can't remember anything after Gina's party. I didn't drink much, but I had a couple of glasses of wine. Maybe someone slipped something into my drink."

Batelli waved Agent Savola over and whispered something in his ear. He nodded and left.

The inspector placed his hand on top of one of the files. "You can't remember anything from the past week? Anything at all?"

"No."

"Are you experiencing any pain? Dizziness?"

She rubbed at the back of her head.

"My head hurt a few minutes ago. But I don't feel dizzy."

He was quiet for a moment, studying her.

"What do you do for Professor Urbano?"

"I told you, I assist him with his restoration project."

"And what is he restoring?"

"The *Birth of Venus*."

The inspector nodded. "So you are a Botticelli expert?"

She shifted in her seat. "Not like Professor Urbano. He worked on the famous restoration of *Primavera* with Umberto Baldini."

Batelli looked at her blankly, not recognizing the name of the famous art historian and restorer.

"But it's fair to say you know a lot about Botticelli and his work?"

"Yes. I also know that the theft of great art is a crime against humanity." Her tone had the slightest edge to it.

The inspector appeared puzzled. "That's an unusual view."

"Not among those who devote their lives to preserving and protecting great works of art. That's why I came to Florence."

Batelli frowned. "The illustrations were copies."

Now Raven leaned forward in her chair. "Those *copies* were all we had. The full set of original illustrations have been lost. And the copies were beautiful."

"*We?*" he repeated, cocking his head to one side. "Who's *we?*"

She felt her cheeks flame. "Humanity. Whoever stole them, stole from all of us. Although I'm sure the Emersons are more upset than anyone, except maybe Dottor Vitali."

"And the Emersons are—?"

"The patrons who lent us the illustrations—Professor Gabriel Emerson and his wife."

"You know them?"

"Not really. They're patrons of the orphanage I volunteer at, but I've never met them."

The inspector opened his file and took out a series of printed sheets that had been stapled together. He pushed the pages toward her.

"This is a list of names. Tell me if you know any of them."

Raven picked up the pages and began reading.

She looked over at the inspector. "I recognize some of the names. They're patrons of the gallery. But I don't really know them."

"None of them?"

"I work in the restoration lab. The patrons don't interact with us." She placed the paper back on the desk.

"Would it be correct to say that you recognize all the names, or only some?"

"Only some."

Batelli uncapped a pen and placed it in front of her. "Please make a mark next to the names you recognize."

Raven frowned but did as she was told, marking about one-third of the names listed.

Batelli seemed to take restrained interest in what she was doing, but after she finished, he merely placed the papers aside. He withdrew a single sheet from the file and slid it across to her.

"Read that."

Raven picked up the paper.

The first thing she noticed was that the page was obviously a photocopy of some handwriting. The style of writing was old-fashioned. Very old-fashioned. It was precise, elegant, and very, very beautiful. A work of art in itself.

The second thing she noticed was that the language was Latin. Suddenly a phrase entered her consciousness.

Cassita vulneratus.

"What was that?" Batelli leaned forward suspiciously.

"I didn't say anything. I've read it. Now what?"

"Read it to me."

"It's in Latin." She gave him a questioning look.

"I know that. Read it in Latin, if you can, and translate to Italian."

Raven turned her attention to the page. "*Non furtum facies. Mihi vindictam ego retribuam.*" She looked over at the officer. "*Non rubare. La vendetta è mia; io ricompensèro.* You shall not steal. Vengeance is mine, I will repay."

Raven placed the paper on top of the desk.

"Why are you showing me part of a Latin manuscript of the Bible?"

"Why do you think it's from a manuscript of the Bible?"

"I'm not a paleographer, but I can recognize medieval handwriting." She gestured to the page. "The text sounds like the Bible, but I'm not an expert."

"Are the words significant to you?" Batelli gave her a questioning look.

"No."

"Interesting." He placed the page in his file and closed it. Then he put his hand, palm down, on top of the file.

"What can you tell me about the security systems in the gallery?"

"Almost nothing. I'm only an art restorer." She gestured to her identification card, which lay on the desk facing him. "I have access to certain rooms when the gallery is open. I don't have security codes to the building or to the individual exhibit rooms. I'm not sure what security systems the gallery has. It's all a big mystery."

"Would your card open the room that held the Botticelli illustrations?"

She shook her head. "I only have access to the rooms connected with my work—the archives, the restoration rooms, and the office I share with some of the other associates."

"What about keys?"

"Most of the rooms in the Uffizi are accessed by card. Some of the older rooms and the Vasari Corridor can be accessed by keys. But I wasn't issued keys. Even if I was, I couldn't access the building when it's closed."

"But you work after hours."

"Sometimes Professor Urbano asks the restoration team to work late, if we're doing something particularly delicate or time sensitive. But in those cases, the gallery is kept open, or at least the restoration lab is. Security lets us in if we arrive after hours and they escort us from the building when we're finished."

The inspector sat back in his chair. He watched her, unblinking, until she looked away.

"Were you working after hours on May seventeenth?"

"No. I'm working exclusively on the *Birth of Venus*. We're doing a complete restoration, which means the painting is no longer on display. We work normal hours except when Professor Urbano asks us to stay later. He hasn't done that for a couple of months."

"Your face doesn't match your card or your passport." He gestured to the identification on the desk. "I take it the photograph in your new passport is recent?"

"It is." She shifted in her chair.

"It doesn't look recent. Your employee file indicates that you are handicapped."

At this, his gaze dropped to her right leg, which was partially obscured by the desk. His eyes lifted to hers. "You don't look handicapped."

"The correct term is *disabled*." Raven straightened her shoulders. "And I'm not anymore."

"Explain."

She pressed her lips together tightly.

"I can't."

He lifted his eyebrows. "Excuse me?"

"I can't." She lifted her hands in an expression of frustration. "I have no idea what's happened. I already told you that."

A knock was heard at the door and Agent Savola entered. He whispered something to Batelli, who appeared disappointed. They exchanged a few quiet words, which Raven strained unsuccessfully to hear.

Agent Savola resumed his place on Batelli's left, arms crossed over his chest.

Batelli picked up the pen and began tapping it on top of the file.

"Have you seen a doctor?"

Raven shook her head.

"If you think you were drugged, why didn't you go to the hospital?"

"I felt fine. I was worried about being late for work."

Batelli scowled. "You have memory loss, a drastic change in appearance, a miraculous restoration of your ability to walk, and you're worried about being late for work?"

He cursed a few times, tossing the pen onto the desk.

Raven pressed her hand against her forehead.

"We can take you to the hospital." Agent Savola spoke in English, in a quiet tone.

She shook her head.

"I have to see Professor Urbano. I don't want to lose my job." She swallowed hard. "I have my own doctor. I'll make an appointment to see her."

Agent Savola nodded sympathetically. "Is your doctor a cosmetic surgeon?"

"No." Raven's tone was clipped.

"Only a cosmetic surgeon with great skill could transform you from that"—he pointed to her identification card—"to that." He gestured to her face.

"Are you trying to be insulting?" she fumed.

"Do you have a psychiatrist, signorina?"

"Of course not!" Raven snapped. "What about you, Agent Savola? Do you have a psychiatrist?"

The agent took a step toward her and swore.

Batelli held up his hands.

"This isn't helpful," he said, looking pointedly at Raven and his associate.

She pointed to the file.

"If you have my employee records, you know I've had a criminal background check. I've also had a psychiatric evaluation." She glanced in Savola's direction.

"More importantly, I've devoted my life to saving art, to preserving it for future generations. I don't destroy things and I don't steal. Art thieves are almost the lowest form of humanity, because they take something beautiful and hide it so the world can't see it."

Batelli looked at her with curiosity. "What's the lowest form of humanity, in your view?"

"Child abusers."

Both Batelli and Savola appeared taken aback by her remark, but they quickly regained their composure.

Batelli picked up her identification card, her passport, and her other documents. He looked at them closely before holding them out to her.

She reached for them, and for a moment he kept hold of the items, trapping her.

"You're free to go, after we fingerprint you. It's simply an effort to confirm your identity, since your appearance doesn't match your indentification. An officer will drive you back to the Uffizi.

"But I should warn you, Signorina Wood, we will want to interview you again. I would strongly urge you to stay in Florence. A note will be made with immigration, should you try to leave the country."

His eyes flickered to Savola's and back again. "For your own sake, I suggest you see a doctor."

Raven took her belongings from his hand and bolted from the room, leaving the door open behind her.

Chapter Six

When Raven finally arrived at the Uffizi, she had to submit to a scan of her fingerprints in order for security to admit her to the building. After that humiliating experience, she went to the office she shared with a number of different researchers. She greeted her colleagues with a tense wave before trudging to her desk, which was in a far corner.

She sank into her chair and looked around the windowless room. The office hummed with conversations and the occasional ringing of a telephone, while her colleagues stared. More than a few of her coworkers stopped by her desk, wondering who she was and demanding to see her identification. She had to summon security and ask them to vouch for her identity. Afterward, her colleagues continued to glance in her direction with expressions that ranged from surprised to censorious.

Her skin crawled under the scrutiny.

A number of messages sat on her desk, including a recent one from Patrick, asking her to text him when she arrived. She ignored them and placed her head in her hands.

She was in trouble.

Were it not for the fact that she felt pain when she pinched herself, she would have thought she was in a nightmare. There were too many incredible and inexplicable events. First, there was the sudden and spontaneous healing of her disability. Second, there was her loss of weight and radical change in physical appearance. Finally, there was her disappearance and lack of memory.

There was also the possibility that her personality had undergone a slight sharpening. Raven couldn't remember the last time she'd been so angry or rude. She'd always prided herself in being polite and controlled. But at the police station . . .

Raven's gaze alighted on a leaflet that she'd placed on her desk months before. The flyer included information about the Botticelli illustrations and had been distributed by the gallery to visitors.

She picked it up, glancing at the text.

Wordlessly, she stored her backpack in one of the desk drawers and locked it, looping her identification card, which was hung on a cord, over her head. She picked up her cell phone, which she'd barely been able to charge, clutching it in the same hand as the leaflet. Silently, she bemoaned the fact she was wearing yoga pants, which, although they made her derrière extremely attractive, lacked pockets.

She was supposed to report to the restoration lab for work, but instead she walked in the opposite direction, to where the illustrations had been on display. The exhibition hall was cordoned off, the corridor empty.

The hall boasted walls painted a bright blue in order to display the pen and ink illustrations to better effect. Inside the room was a series of cases, in which the artwork had been kept safe from exposure and human touch.

Raven scanned the now empty cases, noting that each of them, along with the walls and even the floors, had been dusted for fingerprints. Scaffolding stood in one corner, rising to the high ceiling. From the looks of it, someone had dusted the white ceiling as well. Sections of it were smudged with gray and black.

She began reading the description of the exhibit, which was printed on the leaflet. As Ispettor Batelli had mentioned, the illustrations were copies. Botticelli had prepared one hundred drawings of Dante's *Divine Comedy* for Lorenzo di Pierfrancesco de' Medici, who died in 1503. Unfortunately, eight of them had been lost. The Vatican owned a few of the originals and the rest were owned by the Staatliche Museen in Berlin.

The Emersons' collection was complete. Yes, they were only copies, but the Emersons owned the full one hundred of the original complement. This fact alone made the collection priceless.

Certainly the Uffizi was more than pleased to exhibit them. It charged extra for visitors to view the exhibition, using the funds to finance some of the restoration projects in the gallery, including the work that Raven and Professor Urbano's team were doing.

The illustrations had been on loan to the Uffizi for two years, since the summer of 2011. Raven remembered the announcement well, as she'd been researching her dissertation and doing work at the Opificio at the time.

Prior to the announcement, no one knew about the Emersons' collection. Raven had done some amateur investigation on the subject, but found nothing. For such important works of art, the lack of images or information was surprising.

Dottor Vitali had prepared an account of the illustrations' provenance, which was reproduced on the leaflet, but his information must have come from the Emersons themselves, for Raven hadn't found any independent confirmation of the facts presented.

She found this fact curious.

According to the leaflet, the illustrations had been prepared in the sixteenth century, probably by a student of Botticelli. Somehow they'd come to a Swiss family in the nineteenth century. They'd sold the illustrations to Professor Emerson in a private sale a number of years back.

The whereabouts of the illustrations from the sixteenth to the nineteenth centuries were a complete mystery. Certainly neither the Swiss family nor Professor Emerson had been in a hurry to disclose the existence of the illustrations to the public. It was said that Mrs. Emerson had finally convinced her husband to share the artwork with the world.

And now they're gone, thought Raven. She looked at the empty display cases and felt tears well up in her eyes.

She was about to report to the restoration lab, when her phone chimed with a text. It was from Patrick.

Where r u?

She quickly typed her reply.

Exhibition hall

She waited for Patrick's response, but none came.

She scrolled through the texts she'd been sent during the past week, noting that both Patrick and Gina had sent several messages, escalating in concern. She'd missed several e-mails and phone messages as well.

With a sigh she took one last, sad look at the empty cases and exited the room. Down the corridor, she saw Patrick striding toward her.

"How did it go with the police?" His face was creased with worry.

"Not good."

Patrick cursed.

"Come on."

He took her hand and led her to one of the back staircases. They climbed the stairs to the second floor and walked to a quiet corner.

He released her hand and crossed his arms over his chest, standing close to her.

"What did they say?"

"They asked me a bunch of questions. They're suspicious, obviously, and my inability to answer their questions makes me look guilty." She rubbed at her eyes. "I have no idea where I was last week. My memory is all screwed up."

"You don't remember last week at all?" He sounded concerned.

"Nothing since Gina's party. Maybe somebody slipped me something." She avoided his eyes, examining her feet.

"No way." Patrick's tone was firm. "I was pouring drinks, remember? I know everyone who was there. No one would have slipped you something."

"Then why can't I remember?"

"I don't know." His expression grew even more tense. "Dottor Vitali wants to see you."

"What?"

Patrick nodded in the direction of the director's office. "He's keeping tabs on everything having to do with the investigation, including your interview. And the Emersons just arrived. I saw the police escort them inside."

Raven groaned. Of course the Emersons would be upset about the theft. And Professor Gabriel Emerson had a reputation for being a trifle . . . *mercurial.*

Patrick continued. "I told Professor Urbano you were back, but I didn't mention the police. He wants to see you after Vitali is done with you."

"I liked it better when no one noticed me."

Patrick frowned. "Hey. That's the second time you've said something like that. Look around. I'm worried about you and so is Urbano. We've been stressed for a week wondering where you were."

She chewed at the inside of her mouth. "Maybe you should be suspicious of me. I'm suspicious of me."

Patrick took a step closer, leaning down so he was at eye level. "Don't start with that shit. Remember what happened to Amanda Knox?"

Raven shivered. "Yeah."

"She says she's innocent. Maybe she is. But she was caught up in an Italian police investigation. By the time they were finished, everyone thought she was guilty. The American consulate can't help you if you're charged with a crime. Don't give the police any ammunition." Patrick squeezed her arm sympathetically. "You'd better get going. Vitali wants to see you right away."

"He's going to suspend me, isn't he?"

Patrick squeezed her arm again. "I don't know. But there has to be a reasonable explanation for what happened. We'll find out, I promise."

She gave him a wan smile before walking the few steps to Dottor Vitali's office.

She knocked twice and waited.

The door was opened by a tall, handsome man with dark hair and piercing blue eyes. He was dressed in a white shirt and jeans, his feet clad in brown leather shoes.

His posture was anything but casual.

"Yes?" His expression, like his tone, was decidedly unfriendly.

"Good morning. Dottor Vitali asked to see me," Raven replied in polite Italian.

The man opened the door wider, and Raven saw beyond him that Vitali was seated behind his desk, talking to a young woman who was holding a baby on her lap.

"What do you mean there aren't any fucking fingerprints?" The man, who Raven surmised was Professor Emerson, brushed past her to stand in front of the desk.

"Gabriel." The woman, who Raven assumed was his wife, glanced from the professor to the child in her arms.

"I'm sorry, darling." Professor Emerson sounded contrite. He placed a hand on the baby's head. "I meant *fracking* fingerprints."

"That's not really an improvement." Mrs. Emerson gave him a half smile.

The child started fussing and tugging at her mother's dress. She balled up a chubby fist and began chewing on it, but not before making a noise that sounded to Raven like a squawk.

"I think she's hungry." Mrs. Emerson gave an apologetic look to their host.

"Vitali, can we have a quiet room somewhere so Julianne can feed Clare?" Professor Emerson placed a hand on his wife's shoulder.

"Of course." Vitali smiled, motioning to Raven to come forward. "And you are . . . ?"

Raven paused, embarrassed. "Raven Wood, *dottore.*"

Dottor Vitali took in her appearance with a look of incredulity.

Raven fidgeted.

Vitali glanced at his guests, appearing to recover from his shock.

"Miss Wood." He began speaking English. "Bring Mrs. Emerson to the conference room. Then return here. I'd like to speak to you."

"Of course." Raven forced a smile, for the director's tone and posture were noticeably cold.

"Thank you." Mrs. Emerson stood, holding the baby in one hand and attempting to lift a purse and a large Coach messenger bag with the other.

Raven gestured to the hallway. "This way, please."

The professor lifted the purse and bag, placing them over his wife's shoulder, before stroking the baby's head and kissing her.

Raven looked away as he embraced his wife, before stepping aside to let her pass.

"Come back when you're ready, darling." The professor smiled.

Mrs. Emerson nodded before addressing Raven in English. "Thank you. I tried to give Clare her breakfast at the hotel but she wouldn't eat. I'm afraid we're all jet-lagged."

"No problem. The conference room is private and it's just down the hall." Raven gestured to their right as they exited the office, responding in English.

Mrs. Emerson was dressed in a simple black shirtdress, with black espadrilles that tied in wide bands around her ankles and shapely lower legs. She had shoulder-length brown hair, highlighted with gold, and big brown eyes. She was petite and young looking, with a very gentle way about her.

Next to her, Raven felt enormous and dowdy, as she always felt when standing next to a thin and beautiful person. (She was forgetting that she'd recently undergone a tremendous physical transformation.)

"Can I carry your bags, Mrs. Emerson?"

She laughed. "Call me Julia. We have to be the same age."

"I'm almost thirty," Raven blurted out.

"I'll be thirty in a couple of years. So please call me Julia. If you'd carry the diaper bag, I'd be grateful."

She held Clare with one hand while Raven pulled the bag from her shoulder.

Raven was unprepared for the weight and nearly dropped it, but managed to keep it from hitting the floor at the last moment.

"I'm sorry. I should have warned you." Julia made a move to help her, but Raven waved her off and lifted the item with both hands.

"Gabriel wants to be prepared for any emergency and so he stuffs things into it when I'm not looking. I need a stroller for Clare and a stroller for the diaper bag." She laughed. "Actually, I need a stroller for myself. Traveling with a baby is more challenging than I thought."

"Are you staying nearby?"

"Yes, at the Gallery Hotel Art." Julia's expression brightened. "We're here for a week, then we're going to Umbria. Clare's godmother is with us."

"That's nice." Raven didn't really know what to say.

"But we're really upset about the robbery," Julia confided, holding Clare close to her body. "The illustrations are more than just artwork to us. They have sentimental value. When Dottor Vitali called to say they'd been stolen . . ."

Julia nuzzled her daughter, as if she were trying to hide her face.

"I'm so sorry," Raven whispered.

"Gabriel is hoping they'll be recovered, but I'm not sure how likely that is. I guess all we can do is pray.

"It's possible the illustrations were stolen once before and that's how they came to belong to the family who sold them to my husband." Julia sighed. "I guess we'll never know."

Raven was curious about her remark, since it was a possibility that had not been disclosed in Dottor Vitali's leaflet. She elected not to press the point.

"The police are doing all they can. I hope they find them."

"I hope so, too. You sound American." Julia looked at her with interest.

"I'm from New Hampshire. I lived in Florida so long I lost my accent."

"I'm from Pennsylvania, but we live in Cambridge." Julia grinned. "I don't think I'll ever sound as if I'm from Boston. What part of the gallery do you work in?"

"Restoration and conservation. I'm part of the team working on the *Birth of Venus*."

Julia's brown eyes lit up. "That's one of my favorite paintings. I don't suppose you let guests view the restoration? I promise not to get in the way."

"I'm sure Dottor Vitali can arrange something. I'd be happy to show you what we're doing but Professor Urbano is the one in charge. He worked on the restoration of *Primavera* under Umberto Baldini."

"That's another of my favorites. I've always loved Botticelli." Julia's tone was wistful. "That's why we wanted to lend the illustrations. We wanted other people to enjoy them."

Raven stopped, turning to face her. "Let me tell you how happy I was to be able to see them. I visited them almost every day. We were all so glad when you and your husband decided to extend the exhibit beyond a few months."

"Thank you." Julia's smile faded. "I can't help but think this is my fault. I persuaded Gabriel to let the gallery keep the illustrations while we were on leave with Clare. Now they're gone."

"I'm so sorry."

"So am I."

Raven regarded her curiously.

"You and Professor Emerson are both on leave? Are you a professor as well?"

"I'm a professor in training. I'm in the middle of a Ph.D. on Dante."

"Where are you studying?"

Julia smiled. "Harvard. I'm still finishing coursework."

"Professor Emerson is a Dante specialist, isn't that right?"

"Yes. Clare's godmother is a retired Dante specialist as well. Apparently, it takes three Dante specialists to look after one baby."

Raven laughed, opening the door to the conference room. She gestured for Julia to enter before her, and she changed the sign on the door to indicate that a meeting was in progress.

"No one will bother you here. Do you need anything?" She placed the diaper bag on the long table that dominated the space.

Julia quickly sat down and began rummaging in the bag. She removed a large bottle of sparkling water.

"If you have a glass, that would be great. I try to drink a lot of water while I'm breastfeeding." She removed her iPhone from her purse, placing it on the table in front of her. "If I need anything else, I'll just call Gabriel."

Raven retrieved a water glass from one of the cabinets on the far wall and handed it to Julia. She looked at the child, who had large blue eyes like her father and an abundance of fine, dark hair.

"How old is Clare?"

"She was born last September. She's almost nine months."

"She's beautiful." Raven touched the child's head gently.

"Thank you. I think she looks like her daddy. But everyone says she has my mouth. Do you have children?"

"No." Raven stiffened, looking from the child to her mother. "If you need anything, I'll be in Dottor Vitali's office."

Julia poured water into a glass. "We'll be fine."

"I hope they find the illustrations." Raven's voice was quiet.

Julia looked up at her.

"I hope so, too. Losing them is much more than losing art." Julia looked down at her daughter. "It's like losing family."

Raven nodded and exited the conference room, shutting the door firmly behind her.

Mrs. Emerson was not what she had expected. She was younger and much nicer than many of the important patrons and donors who visited the gallery on occasion.

Raven felt sorry for her, recalling the expression of sadness she'd worn when talking about the loss of the artwork. It sounded as if the Emersons truly loved those objects. Now they'd lost them.

As Raven approached Dottor Vitali's office, she noticed that the door was open.

Professor Emerson was speaking loudly in Italian, his voice trailing down the corridor.

"So the Carabinieri have interviewed all the local patrons and they've made attempts to speak to everyone who attended the gala when the exhibit opened. What did they think of William York?"

"Who?" Dottor Vitali sounded confused.

"The young man who accosted me at the exhibit opening. I pointed him out to you and you said he was a local recluse who'd given a substantial donation to the gallery in order to be invited."

"I don't know anyone by that name."

Raven approached the doorway, taking care to remain out of sight.

"Massimo, you recognized the man and had your assistant look up his name. Remember? He's shorter than me; about five foot eleven, with blond hair. He's English, from Oxford, I think. You said something about his patronage of the restoration of the Palazzo Medici Riccardi."

"Gabriel, my friend, I don't know anyone called William York."

Raven heard the sound of papers shuffling.

"Here is the guest list for the gala. His name isn't on the list. Certainly I know of no connection between an Englishman and the Medici palaces. Palazzo Riccardi is owned by the province. They financed the restoration, along with a select group of Italian patrons."

Professor Emerson swore in frustration and Raven heard the sound of a chair toppling over.

Without reflecting on her actions, she moved to stand in the doorway. "Dottor Vitali?"

She looked in anxiety from the administrator of the gallery to the professor, who was standing over the fallen chair with clenched fists.

"Signorina." Vitali gestured to her to enter before turning his attention to the professor. "My friend, please remain calm. Join your wife and your child and let me worry about this."

"I'm worrying about this, Massimo, because someone has stolen what is precious to me." The professor spoke between clenched teeth. "I will make it my life's mission to see that those illustrations are returned.

"I swear I met William York. He behaved very strangely at the exhibit, and you and I spoke about him afterward. He seemed resentful about the illustrations and, although he's young, he's a man with deep pockets. Someone needs to go through the donor records and find his donation. You told me he gave several thousand euros to the gallery."

Professor Emerson placed his fists on the top of Vitali's desk, leaning toward him.

"And if you or the Carabinieri won't see to this, I will personally hire agents who will complete this investigation."

A long look passed between the two friends.

Raven shifted uncomfortably, glancing back at the open door. She wished she could disappear.

"*Va bene*," said Vitali at last, waving at his friend. "Speak to Ispettor Batelli. He's in charge."

"Thank you." Professor Emerson straightened and, without another word, walked out.

Raven waited, watching as Dottor Vitali closed his eyes and bent forward, almost as if he were praying.

At last he opened his eyes and gestured to a chair. "Signorina Wood. Explain your sudden change in appearance. And tell me where you were last week."

Raven sat down, took a deep breath, and began her story.

On leaving Vitali's office, Raven walked, deep in thought, down the corridor.

He hadn't suspended her. He'd asked pointed questions about her appearance, her absence, and her interview with the police. His cool demeanor seemed to warm with her answers. By the time their conversation concluded, Raven believed she'd convinced him she had nothing to do with the robbery.

He'd sent her back to her job, informing her that the weeklong absence would be deducted from her vacation days. She was relieved she hadn't been suspended or fired.

She walked down the hall, reflecting on Botticelli's original illustrations of *The Divine Comedy*. They'd been prepared for Lorenzo di Pierfrancesco de' Medici, who also owned *Primavera*.

She wondered if the thieves knew that. She wondered if the thieves were particularly devoted to Botticelli or simply opportunist.

She imagined a group of hardened criminals, dumping the priceless illustrations into plastic bags and shoving them into backpacks. They wouldn't treat the artwork properly. They wouldn't protect it.

They've probably spread them on a kitchen table somewhere and are eating breakfast on top of them right now.

She shuddered, imagining drops of milk or coffee marring the beautiful ink and the rare, brilliant colors. She imagined the thieves smoking, perhaps flicking pieces of ash over the faces of Dante and Beatrice.

Assholes.

If the thieves were devotees of Botticelli, small wonder they stole the illustrations. The size and weight of *Primavera* was so great, the painting couldn't have been removed from the Uffizi without a team of men and the use of heavy equipment.

The thieves were probably unaware that the *Birth of Venus* was housed in the restoration lab on the lower floor. The lab was secure, but its security was not as elaborate or sophisticated as that of the exhibition halls. However, like *Primavera*, the painting was large and heavy and would require several people to carry it. It wasn't exactly a piece someone could pass through a window.

With such thoughts in mind, Raven found herself entering the Botticelli room. Immediately, she walked over to stand in front of *Primavera*.

The room felt off center. The large and imposing painting was usually balanced by the *Birth of Venus*, but it had been taken down almost a year before. It would be a few more months before it could be returned to its rightful place.

Raven stepped close to *Primavera*, her eyes alighting on the lone male figure on the left. She was drawn to his hands, the muscles and shape of his arms, and his perfect skin. She admired his chest and neck and, finally, his face. He possessed pale eyes and a straight nose, his lips full, his hair long.

Something about his hair displeased her, as if it were incongruous with the rest of him. But his face . . .

She heard a voice whispering in her ear, but she couldn't quite make out the words.

She whirled around. There was no one behind her.

She took a moment to close her eyes and focus on her breathing, trying with all her might to stave off the anxiety that plagued her.

With one last glance at the painted figure of Mercury, she walked to the door, bracing herself for her meeting with Professor Urbano.

Chapter Seven

After nightfall, Aoibhe sat in Teatro drinking from a glass specially designed to keep its contents warm and liquid.

Teatro was a secret club, located in the city center. It had been founded by the Prince in the seventeenth century as a kind of salon or meeting place. Over time, it had evolved into something far less intellectual. Now it was owned by the Consilium of Florence, although it hid its ownership behind the name of a Swiss corporation.

Florence and the other secret principalities in Europe predated the Romans. Shadow rulers and their advisers controlled the supernatural population within specific boundaries, usually cities. In the Middle Ages, the principalities in Italy had been organized under the ultimate rule of the King, in Rome.

Within the borders of Florence, the Prince had absolute power. In his wisdom, he'd put in place a Consilium, or ruling council, of which he was an honorary member. The Consilium functioned like a court and would punish or banish lawbreakers. It also oversaw the organization of the underworld society and its protection, particularly against incursions from other cities or territories.

When the Prince tired of dealing with Teatro, the Consilium took control, using it as a means of entertainment and nourishment.

The club contained a large central space with a dance floor and a bar; two sides of the area were dotted with tables and low couches. The walls and ceiling were painted a purplish black, the lighting was sensual and sparse, and the furniture was upholstered in velvet—black or red.

There was a stage on the other side of the dance floor that was hung with heavy red velvet curtains. The walls displayed large flat-screens, which cycled through projections of artwork and paintings in a variety of styles—all of the subjects profane, many of them sexual. From the central space, hallways led to private rooms, curving into the darkness like a spider's web.

The spiders of this web were the inhabitants of the underworld, with the exception of the Prince. It had been years since he'd crossed its threshold. Consequently, it was an excellent place for Aoibhe to recover her injured pride and contemplate how to change his mind.

Her dark eyes passed over the writhing bodies on the dance floor, her mind blocking out the loud, pounding music. Her kind were sensitive to sound and she always found industrial and gothic music dissonant. It was what attracted humans, so it was what the disc jockey played. (Aoibhe would have preferred Irish minstrel music but had no success in persuading the dj to play it. Next time, she was determined to bring earplugs.)

The bar served alcohol to the humans and drugs were freely available. Inebriated victims were easier to manipulate and confuse, but the substances affected the taste. Older, more powerful ones eschewed the usage, choosing rather to seduce or hypnotize their prey, rather than sedate.

Some couples and small groups were engaged in various sexual activities on the couches. Blood and sex went together for Aoibhe's kind, which meant there was a healthy amount of feeding going on as well. Her nose was filled with the various scents of individual bloods, the aroma heady and unbalancing.

She surveyed the activities with bored detachment. She'd seen it all before and for the moment, at least, nothing interested her. Actual intercourse and certain fetishes were reserved for the private rooms, in deference to the queasiness and social mores of some of the humans. The spiders needed the humans to come in droves every night, without fear and without disclosure.

Aoibhe didn't care what the others did with their human pets or what they did with one another. As one of the six members of the Consilium, she was obliged to follow the rules of Teatro and see that they were enforced.

No killing.

No transformations.

Feeding must be consensual but mind control and the use of alcohol and drugs are permitted.

The last rule was a puzzle to many, but it served to maintain the seductive atmosphere. Humans were unlikely to come and offer themselves night after night if they saw another human wrestled to the ground, raped, and drained of blood.

Mind control was ineffective on some humans. The strong-minded could not be swayed, nor could the particularly pious or those who wore certain talismans. But members of the latter two categories were not allowed entrance, even if they begged.

Aoibhe sighed. The rules must have been made by the Prince himself, despite his contempt for the club. They smacked of his temperance and control and the humanity that lurked just below the surface of his skin.

She smiled.

He'd let his body rule that morning. Those were the moments she enjoyed most; when the uptight, carefully controlled Prince gave and took pleasure. He was magnificent. He was powerful. He was dangerous.

She wanted him. He'd proved himself an excellent lover, despite his disdain for long-term affairs. Aoibhe felt not a small bit of longing for him and even some affection.

Even more, she wanted his city. As consort, they would share power, and when the eventual fate of their kind seized him, she would have control of the city.

Aoibhe drained her drink and signaled to one of the waitresses to bring her another.

She actively avoided André, the bartender and club manager, because he had a blood disease. His illness made him the ideal middleman between her kind and the humans. No one would touch him unless they were feral because his scent was sickening. She could only imagine how revolting his taste would be.

At that moment, a girl stumbled at Aoibhe's feet.

"Mercy," the girl begged, raising terrified blue eyes to Aoibhe's face.

She put down her drink.

She lifted the girl's chin, noting blood at the corner of her mouth and flowing from a wound on her neck. The girl was shaking in terror and began clutching Aoibhe's stilettos.

"Mercy," she repeated. "I don't want to die."

Aoibhe closed her eyes and inhaled.

Humans didn't realize their actions and emotions affected their scent. Just as a dog could sense anger or fear in a human being, or smell disease, so, too, could the members of Aoibhe's kind. They'd evolved to the point where they could scent a person's character. Certain vices, such as rape and murder, made their doers most repulsive, while those who were decent and good smelled—and, more important, tasted—delicious.

This girl smelled sweet enough. Not exceptional, like the one the Prince had found, but certainly tempting. She was clean and, by all signs, good. Aoibhe wondered what had possessed such goodness to come to Teatro.

A large hand reached out to grab the girl's curly blond hair, jerking her head back.

"For that, you'll pay."

"Mercy," the girl cried, wrapping her arms around Aoibhe's lower legs. "Please."

Aoibhe gave Maximilian an impatient look. "If you're going to flout the rules, do it elsewhere. Or I'll be forced to report you."

"Go fornicate yourself, Aoibhe. I'm a member of the Consilium, too. This is none of your concern."

He pulled the girl to her feet and she began screaming hysterically, thrashing about and trying to crawl into Aoibhe's lap.

Aoibhe scowled, noting that a group of humans and their nonhuman counterparts had begun to stare in their direction. "You're making a scene. Get her under control or let her go."

"No, no!" The girl screamed louder.

Maximilian appeared to be enjoying the spectacle. He wrapped his arms around her waist and pulled her against his body, grinding his groin against her backside. He placed his mouth to the wound on her neck and snaked out his tongue, lapping at the blood like a dog.

Aoibhe huffed before reaching out a single finger, forcing the girl to look into her eyes.

"Silence," she commanded.

The girl stopped moving, despite the man assaulting her neck. Her eyes widened as they fixed on Aoibhe, who spoke in soothing tones.

"You are not afraid. Not anymore. Look into my eyes and focus on the sound of my voice. I am your mistress now."

The girl nodded almost imperceptibly.

"Inhale deeply and feel your heart slow. That's a good girl."

"Aoibhe, stop it." Max lifted his head, tightening his grip on his prey.

Without breaking eye contact, Aoibhe spoke. "Too late. I told you to get her under control."

She lifted her hand, signaling to the bouncers, who stood by the door.

Max bellowed in anger and tried to wrench the girl backward. But he was stopped by the arrival of two large men. They functioned as a kind of security for the club and were of the same kind as he and Aoibhe.

She blinked, and the girl closed her eyes and sagged against Max.

"Tomas, Francesco. Be so kind as to escort Sir Maximilian to the exit. He has broken the rules." Aoibhe glanced at him in distaste.

"You can't do this! You can't evict me." Max leaned forward but Aoibhe held out her hand.

"One more step and I'll take you outside myself. I'm older than you by at least a century. Do you really want to challenge me?"

Max snorted derisively but didn't move. He knew, as did Aoibhe, that the older the supernatural being, the more powerful he or she was. Certainly her strength and agility were well-known. If she wanted Max dead, she could kill him. But not within the city—at least, not without cause.

The larger of the two bouncers glanced at the unconscious girl. "What about the human?"

Aoibhe waved a dismissive hand. "He can have her."

Max's head jerked in surprise.

She smiled slowly. "Think of her as a final gift. You are no longer welcome here. If you return, I'll report you to the Consilium and you'll lose your position."

Max spat in her direction but she turned her head swiftly, his spittle landing on the wall behind her.

She turned her head and gave him a long, slow smile. "Enjoy your takeaway."

He lifted the unconscious girl into his arms and the men escorted him from the club.

Those who had paused their activities to watch the clash between the supernatural beings quickly found themselves distracted by other pursuits.

Aoibhe straightened her dress. Dealing with Max and the other masculine egos of her kind was exhausting. Why the devil couldn't he follow the rules?

The Prince didn't make public spectacles, even when he happened upon an extraordinary vintage as he'd done recently. He'd simply taken the human and fed on her privately, discreetly disposing of the corpse or having Gregor dispose of it for him.

"You look in want of company." A smooth voice sounded in her ear.

"Ibarra." She smiled warmly at the tall Basque who leaned over her.

He kissed her cheeks and signaled to a waitress to bring him a drink.

"How is the fair Aoibhe this evening?" He sat next to her on the sofa, placing his arm around her shoulder.

"Annoyed, at the moment. I've just had to have Max thrown out." She sighed dramatically.

"I'm sure he deserved it."

"He did. Insolent fool."

When their drinks arrived, they clinked their glasses before drinking.

Ibarra placed his glass on one of the tables nearby. "We'll need more recruits if we're going to oust troublemakers like Max."

"Just kill him and get it over with."

"Not within the city." He winked at her and she laughed.

"Take him outside the city, then. I'll give you whatever you want if you rid me of him. I've had trouble with him twice in as many weeks."

"Anything I want?" He ran the back of his hand over her neck.

She leaned into his touch. "Within reason, Ibarra. Although I'm sorely tempted to offer you carte blanche at the moment."

He gave her a hungry look. "I'll remember that. Rumor says that Max's trouble was with the Prince."

"Trouble with the Prince is trouble with me." Aoibhe's tone was sharp.

Ibarra smiled sadly. "Alas, I'm too late."

"You aren't too late." She kissed him eagerly but pulled away before he was able to reciprocate. "How go the patrols?"

He groaned, wiping his mouth with the back of his hand.

"Give me a bit of warning before you do that. Now look at me." He gestured at his lap in frustration.

"I can arrange to have you serviced while we speak." Aoibhe turned in the direction of a group of young women seated nearby.

Ibarra placed his hand over her wrist. "I'd prefer you to service me."

"I'm too old to kneel in public." She gave him a frosty look and withdrew her hand.

"Who said anything about kneeling? Sit here and I'll pleasure you." He gestured to his groin.

She paused, her eyes darting to his lap. Certainly Ibarra was very attractive. And the Prince had always been indifferent to her romantic activities.

"Another time perhaps." She licked her lips. "Tell me about the patrols."

"I'll hold you to that promise."

"Please do."

He groaned again, muttering a Basque curse.

"The patrols are good enough. Our borders are secure."

She arched an eyebrow at him.

He frowned. "What? I speak the truth."

"A feral slipped past your patrols a few days ago. Pierre happened upon it but the creature got away."

"An isolated incident. We're already hunting it and will find it shortly."

"There are rumors that some of the ferals have banded together. I wouldn't be in a hurry to fight a war with them. They're animals."

Ibarra laughed. "With respect, Aoibhe, we're animals, too."

"Hardly." She sniffed. "And there's what happened two years ago. The Prince had to fight off a group of assassins by himself. They jumped him by a hotel."

Ibarra chuckled. "He's an old one. He can handle himself."

"A herd of ferals could take down an old one." She looked off into space for a moment. "How old do you think he is?"

"I'm newer to Florence than you are. You tell me."

She looked at his dark eyes curiously. "If you had to venture a guess?"

Ibarra ran his fingers through his thick black hair.

"Even if I knew nothing of his history, I'd guess he was an old one, given his strength and discipline. Old ones are at least seven hundred. Since he's been in possession of this principality since the fourteenth century, he's much older than that."

"His time is almost up," she murmured.

"I'm not so sure. I don't see any signs of madness. Do you?"

"No, but I'm told the madness creeps in slowly."

Ibarra waved his hand in the air. "If it truly is a curse, how could it affect all of us? Wouldn't *they* have to be aware of each of us and curse us individually?"

Aoibhe shivered, as she always did when their enemy was mentioned. "Don't speak of them."

"As you wish. But I don't think they are as powerful as everyone thinks."

"How is Venice?" She changed the subject.

"The Venetians seem remarkably placid, given their history. They tell me they prefer to be under our prince rather than Marcus. They think he was a tyrant."

"An extremely intelligent tyrant. I can't understand why he would have attempted such a sloppy coup when he knew the power of our prince."

Ibarra shrugged. "Our city is very desirable. Marcus wanted to expand his territory."

"The Roman would never permit that."

"Who knows if the Roman still exists? He'd be long past his thousand years, if he did. I think he was destroyed years ago but they kept his name alive, referring to whoever's in charge as 'the Roman' in order to keep everyone in line."

Aoibhe watched him for a moment to see if he was serious. Then she laughed.

"You spin fictions."

"I've never met anyone, or heard of anyone who is still alive, who has met the Roman. He's a figurehead for whoever assumed control of the kingdom of Italy."

She smiled. "I've lived in Italy a long time. I would have heard if the Roman had been deposed. We'll agree to disagree.

"Since Pierre's encounter with the feral, I've been meaning to call for a meeting. We need to increase the border patrols in order to protect against incursions. That means we'll need new recruits to fill the lower ranks so we can promote the young ones."

Ibarra stroked Aoibhe's cheek with a single finger. "I have no idea why you aren't the Prince's lieutenant."

She rolled her eyes. "Because Lorenzo *the magnificent* is a Medici. He was born here, while I merely arrived."

"The Prince is a fool."

"I won't argue with that."

Ibarra lifted his glass. "To your health, Aoibhe. May you live forever."

She lifted her glass as well.

"May I live longer than that."

Chapter Eight

Raven's kitchen table was littered with charcoal pencils, erasers, pencil shavings, cotton swabs, and paper. Two fingers on her right hand were black from blending and she'd taken to chewing the end of a pencil as she surveyed her most recent sketch.

It was a portrait of a man with haunted eyes and a square jaw. His short hair fell across his forehead carelessly, partially masking the creases above strong brows. His nose was straight, his mouth full and unsmiling.

There was something lacking in his expression. Raven didn't know what it was.

After a disastrous day at work, she'd gone to the orphanage where she volunteered. The children and workers were understandably confused by Raven's change in appearance, which she explained as the result of a crash diet and physiotherapy.

Raven confided in Elena, her friend and the orphanage director's assistant, about her troubles at the gallery. Elena had been alarmed and given her the name and address of one of her many cousins, who was a lawyer. Raven pocketed the information, promising to contact the cousin before she spoke to the police again.

Later, she walked to the Franciscan mission, looking for Angelo.

He wasn't there. No one had seen him in days.

She persuaded the director of the mission to file a missing persons report with the police, wisely deciding it was not in her interest to do so herself. Then she walked home.

Her apartment was a small one-bedroom unit that overlooked Piazza Santo Spirito. The green-shuttered windows of her room opened onto the square, affording an excellent view of the central fountain and the church that stood nearby.

Her kitchen was windowless and marked the entryway into the apartment. A simple table with four chairs was pushed close to one wall, while the counter and appliances ran the length of the other two.

She cooked well, if simply, her weight a constant concern. Her fondness for pasta, cheese, and desserts, and her disability's contraints on exercise, made weight loss seem almost impossible. She accepted the fact just as she accepted her solitude—with quiet resignation.

On this evening, she found little to work with in the cupboard or small fridge. She should have gone shopping after work, but she'd had more pressing concerns.

It was almost nine o'clock when she sat down to a modest dinner of pasta with pesto from a jar and a small salad made with wilted lettuce. She opened a bottle of Chianti, pouring herself a full glass before corking the bottle. The currant-colored liquid cheered her, but she only picked at her dinner, worried as she was about the theft of the illustrations, her sudden change in appearance, and Angelo.

Afterward, she cleared the table and spread her drawing materials across it, eager to draw Angelo's likeness. But something stopped her. Her hand froze, as if it were unwilling to commit him to posterity. As if it would be a sin against hope to relegate him to a drawing.

Instead, she put on some music and began to sketch a stranger's face.

When she was finished, Raven poured herself a second glass of wine, absolutely ignoring her discarded dishes. This was anomalous, since she normally washed the dishes after every meal. On this evening, she felt the need for fortitude rather than cleanliness and so she sipped her wine and stared at the sketch once again.

The face was handsome and symmetrical, with high cheekbones. Its almost feminine beauty was counterbalanced by the masculine jaw and brows. Apart from a slight resemblance to photographs of a young Sting, the man in the portrait was a stranger to her. She didn't know where his image came from or why she'd felt compelled to draw him.

Sometimes the Muses spoke in foreign tongues and she was ignorant of their meaning.

She was modestly pleased with the sketch, even though she knew there was something missing. On a whim, she signed and dated it and placed it on top of her dresser, at the foot of her bed.

Then, as if one of the Muses were whispering in her ear, she opened her laptop, taking note that it was now past eleven, and Googled the name *William York*.

She found several entries, one of which was to a story about a ten-year-old who'd murdered a little girl. Raven shuddered and moved past that link.

She skimmed through several pages of results, but nothing caught her attention. Certainly, if there were a William York living in Florence, he wasn't much of a public figure. There weren't any entries on him at all.

Raven hastily finished her second glass of wine, recalling what she'd overheard Professor Emerson say to Dottor Vitali. He'd described William York as a recluse who'd donated money to help restore the Palazzo Medici Riccardi.

When Raven clicked on the website for the palazzo, she found that the major restorations had been done long ago. There were restorations in 1874 when the building was taken over by the province. There were additional restorations from 1911 to 1929. The most recent modifications to the property began in 1992.

It was unlikely if not impossible that William York financed the restorations before 1929. That meant he had to be one of the patrons of the 1992 restoration. Dottor Vitali was already working at the Uffizi by then. Certainly he knew everyone of importance in the city. Since he didn't recognize the name, Professor Emerson must have been mistaken.

But he'd sounded so sure. And he'd been indignant when Vitali claimed not to know who he was talking about.

Stranger still, the professor had identified William York as a patron of the Uffizi. Raven was certain that his name hadn't appeared on the list Ispettor Batelli had shown her earlier that day.

The palazzo itself wasn't far. It was mere steps from the Duomo on Via Cavour. She could walk to the building, look around, and be back in bed in an hour and a half. Of course, it would be preferable to do so during the day or perhaps after work, but she'd draw attention to herself by visiting the palazzo during the day. And there was the matter of her work schedule.

It was possible, she thought, as she put on a hooded sweatshirt, that she could speak with a security guard about the building's patrons, since the guard would likely be unoccupied and perhaps bored at this late hour. The security guards at the Uffizi were a wealth of information and Raven had always found them to be extremely forthcoming, if one took the time to speak with them.

Perhaps the second glass of wine had made her bold. Perhaps it was simply her suspicion that she wouldn't be able to sleep without expending some energy. But whatever the true reason, she exited her apartment with her knapsack, hoping she would uncover something that would put her back into the good graces of Dottor Vitali.

Despite the late hour, the streets were alive with pedestrians and people visiting with one another. Raven passed a few young families on the piazza, wheeling sleeping children in strollers. She always found it surprising that Florentine parents were so lax with bedtimes.

When she approached the bridge, she took a deep breath and began to run. As she had that morning, she felt joy in every step, her body bursting with happiness.

She was so captivated by her experience she didn't notice the man who followed her at a distance on a black Vespa. He was dressed in black and helmeted.

She jogged to the Duomo, pausing to look up at the red-tiled dome. She could not have known this, but the Prince, who spent almost every sunset high atop the edifice, had not done so that evening. Instead, he'd spent hours on other, more important pursuits.

Not surprisingly, the palazzo was closed when she reached its double doors. Looking to the upper floors of the building, she saw light emanating from the windows. Someone was working, even at this late hour.

On a whim, she turned on Via de' Gori, following the exterior wall of the palazzo, and made a right on Via de' Ginori. Here she found the back entrance, its heavy wooden doors located inside an elaborate stone arch.

Enormous black iron rings flanked the doors and Raven guessed they'd been used to tether horses at one time.

At the right of the arch, set into the palazzo wall, was a small white box. Raven recognized it as part of a security system. Certainly whoever guarded the palazzo at night would be monitoring the door. It would only take a moment to ask him or her a few questions.

She pressed the call button and waited.

And waited.

She waited for what seemed like an age, watching pedestrians and the occasional car pass. She did not see the black Vespa at the corner, or the driver, who was pretending to check his cell phone. She did not see the mysterious figure that looked down on her from the rooftop of the building opposite.

With a sigh, she turned to leave, but static emerged from the speaker and she heard a voice.

"State your business."

She leaned forward, closer to the speaker. "Good evening."

"State your business," the man repeated, his tone bland and indifferent.

"I'm sorry to bother you," she stammered, wondering what she should say. "I should have visited during the day, but I was delayed. I'm looking for—um—Signor William York. Can you tell me how I can contact him?"

Raven waited for a response, regretting the impulse to use the recluse's name. But it was far too late for discretion.

Internally, she made an attempt to formulate an explanation for why she wanted to see William York. But the voice didn't ask her that question.

In fact, the voice asked her nothing at all. There was a long, pregnant silence.

"Just a moment."

Raven was shocked. She'd barely hoped to wheedle a little background information from one of the security guards. She hadn't expected them to recognize the name of William York, let alone to provide her with contact information. Could it be that Professor Emerson was correct and that William York was a patron of the palazzo?

And if Emerson had learned of William York from Vitali, why was Vitali denying it?

Raven grew very nervous. If there were such a person as William York and he'd taken care to protect his identity, how would he feel about her showing up and asking about him? What if he was connected with the robbery at the Uffizi?

She took a few careful steps backward, looking to see if anyone suspicious was nearby. For the moment, at least, she appeared to be alone.

She decided it would be safer if she left and left quickly. As she moved, she caught sight of a small black camera, located at the top of the stone arch and pointing in her direction.

Great. Now they know what I look like.

Static emerged from the speaker again and Raven started.

"There's no one here by that name. Leave now." Someone else was speaking. His voice was more melodic, it was true, but it was also hostile.

She moved in the direction of the speaker. "I'm so sorry, I didn't mean to bother you and—"

Raven was swiftly interrupted. "It's time for you to leave."

She didn't need to be asked twice. She began running in the direction of the Duomo, as fast as her legs could carry her. A black Vespa took off from where it had been idling around the corner, driving in the opposite direction.

Raven was too anxious to notice the man and his machine, or the fact that, by the time she passed the Duomo, he was following her.

Of course, she didn't realize she'd captured the attention of the decidedly nonhuman being standing on top of the building across the street as well.

Chapter Nine

By the time Raven returned to her building, her heart was beating furiously. Something momentous had occurred, she was sure of it, and she was fearful of the consequences.

She opened the door to her apartment and pressed the light switch on the wall.

Nothing happened.

Cursing, she closed the door behind her and blindly locked it, dropping her knapsack to the floor. She groped along the wall to the bathroom, reaching in to press the other light switch.

Nothing happened.

Muttering to herself about what she was going to say to the landlord the next time she saw him, she felt her way to the bedroom. She was just about to step through the doorway when she stumbled over something; something that felt suspiciously like a pair of feet. She flailed as she fell but before she hit the floor, a pair of strong arms came around her waist, catching her.

As soon as the intruder made contact with her body, she screamed and pulled away, falling on her backside. In the dim light that shone from outside the bedroom windows, she could almost see the outline of a figure lurking in the doorway. She scrambled backward like a crab, heading toward the only exit.

She felt the figure speed past her. Her hands collided with his feet as she approached the apartment door.

"If you scream again, I'll silence you." An angry voice, soft as silk, sliced through the darkness.

"What do you want?" Raven attempted to keep her voice steady. But she failed.

"I want you to answer some questions. Sit here."

Raven heard a chair scrape across the floor and felt one of its legs press against her hip.

She could try to crawl to her knapsack and retrieve her cell phone. The chance of success seemed remote. He'd probably grab her.

Her heart stuttered. "Did you shut off the electricity?"

"Don't give me a reason to hurt you." He thumped the chair on the floor, as if for emphasis.

She startled.

She could scream for help but her closest neighbor, Lidia, was hard of hearing and probably asleep. There was usually so much noise emanating from the Vespa traffic in and around the piazza, she wasn't sure her cries would be heard by anyone else.

"I am waiting," he growled.

Whoever the man was, he sounded young, but his fluid Italian was decidedly old-fashioned.

She moved slowly, placing a tentative hand on the chair and pulling herself up. She slid onto the seat.

"I don't have any money."

"A better question is whether you have any sense." He moved behind her.

She twisted, following the sound of his voice. "Who are you? What do you want?"

"I'm asking the questions. What were you doing at the Palazzo Riccardi?"

Raven's stomach dropped. Perhaps he'd followed her or perhaps he'd seen her at the palazzo. In either case he must be fleet of foot or he'd driven in order to arrive before her.

She wondered why he was hiding his appearance.

"You've been a stupid, stupid girl. Don't magnify your stupidity by trying my patience." His tone grew menacing.

She drew a deep breath, forcing the tension out of her voice. "It was a mistake. I shouldn't have gone there."

"What were you looking for?"

"Someone who works at the palazzo. I thought I'd stop by."

"At night? After hours?" the man said, pressing.

She forced a laugh, which sounded more like a strangled cough.

"Silly, right? It was a mistake."

"Who were you looking for?"

She hesitated and the man brought his face to within inches of hers. She could smell him—a scent of citrus and the woods. It was not unpleasant.

"William York."

If the intruder recognized the name or was surprised by it, he gave no indication.

"That's an odd name for an Italian." The man's tone grew conversational. "Is he a friend of yours?"

"No. I've never met him."

"Then why were you looking for him?"

"No reason."

A heavy hand rested on her shoulder. "That is not an acceptable answer."

The hand flexed minutely and Raven clamped her mouth shut to keep from screaming.

A myriad of old anxieties and fears swirled in her mind. She was terrified that the intruder was going to rape or kill her once he'd secured the information he sought.

She thought about her younger sister, Carolyn, and not being able to tell her one last time that she loved her.

The hand flexed again.

"Um, I work at the Uffizi and—"

"I know that," the intruder said, interrupting.

"You know that?" she repeated.

"I know a great many things. Continue."

She shifted in the darkness, wondering why, all of a sudden, his voice seemed familiar. He wasn't Agent Savola or Ispettor Batelli, she was sure.

But somewhere in the recesses of her memory, she knew she'd heard his voice before. She couldn't remember when.

"While I was at work I heard that this man, William York, was associated with the Palazzo Riccardi. That's all I heard."

The hand lifted from her shoulder.

Raven strained her ears, listening for any movement.

The man leaned over her, bringing his nose to her neck. She jumped at the contact, for his nose, like his hand, was cool.

The intruder inhaled slowly and deeply. Raven angled away from him, desperately trying to tamp down the nausea that was climbing the back of her throat.

He grunted and stepped back, as if he'd smelled something revolting. "I can tell when you're lying. What else did you hear?"

"Uh, that Mr. York donated money to the Uffizi in order to be invited to the opening of a special exhibit a couple of years ago."

"Who said this?"

When she didn't respond, a single finger made contact with her neck, sliding down her throat.

Raven cringed.

"Someone named Emerson. I didn't see who he was talking to."

He brought his lips to her ear. "Try again."

"Emerson was talking to Dottor Vitali."

At this, the man straightened. "Vitali? Are you sure?"

"Yes."

"Did you mention this conversation to anyone? A friend or the Carabinieri?"

"No."

The intruder was silent.

Raven waited for him to do something.

But he did nothing. He didn't move. He didn't sigh. She couldn't even hear him breathe.

She fidgeted, tapping her feet against the floor. She wondered if she could use the chair as a weapon, swinging it in the direction of his head and giving herself enough time to make it to the door. No doubt he'd be faster than her, and if she missed, he'd respond in kind.

She tapped her feet more quickly, wondering if she dared make a move.

Then the intruder's voice sounded near her ear. "You went to an orphanage and a mission today. Why?"

Raven froze.

"You followed me?"

"Answer my question. And tell the truth."

"I volunteer at the orphanage after work sometimes. A friend of mine, a homeless man, is missing. I went to the Franciscan mission to see if he was there. But he wasn't."

"A homeless man?"

"He's the one who sits by the Ponte Santa Trinita, on the other side of the river. He's disabled, like me."

She heard the man move, almost imperceptibly.

"Um, that is, I used to be disabled. I'm not anymore."

"Had Ordo Fratrum Minorum seen him?"

"Ordo Fratrum Minorum?" she repeated.

"The Franciscans," he clarified impatiently.

"No, they hadn't. I'm worried something happened to him."

"You care for this creature?" The intruder sounded incredulous.

"Don't call him that." Raven bristled. "Yes, I care for him. Most people ignore him. Some people, like you, ridicule him. But he's a beautiful person."

"I suppose you care for the orphans as well?" The man was contemptuous.

She frowned. "Of course."

"If someone attacked your precious homeless man and tried to kill him, would you intervene?"

Raven hesitated. "I'd be afraid to intervene, but I couldn't stand there and do nothing. I'd call for help."

The man hummed, as if her answer displeased him.

"I couldn't do nothing," she repeated, her voice breaking on the last word. An old memory tried to overtake her, but she stubbornly placed it aside.

She heard something then, as if he were rattling change in his pocket.

"If you had to choose between justice and mercy, what would you choose?"

"Mercy," she whispered.

"And if you were brought face-to-face with those who abused your homeless man, would you offer them mercy?"

She hesitated, and he laughed.

"I expected as much. Even the most magnanimous want mercy only for those who deserve it."

"No one deserves mercy. Not deserving it is what makes it mercy."

The man was quiet for so long, she wondered if he'd left. She looked behind her, scanning the darkness for any sign of him.

"What am I to do with you?" he wondered softly.

"Let me go. I answered your questions. I don't know anything."

"I made a grave mistake with you. Now it seems I'm destined to pay for it." The man's tone changed; it was low and ached with resignation.

"Please let me go," she repeated. "I won't be any trouble."

"I'm afraid that trouble is not what you do. Trouble is what you are."

The man sighed and Raven heard movement that sounded like he was rubbing his face.

"Leave Florence and never return."

"But this is my home," she protested. "My life is here. My friends—"

"Friends are of no consequence if you're in jail or dead," he snapped.

"Dead?" She shifted forward on the chair, preparing to run.

"You've attracted the attention of a group far more dangerous than the Carabinieri. For the moment, at least, you're safe. When they realize who you are, they will hunt you."

"But I didn't take the illustrations, I swear!"

The intruder laughed darkly.

"They care little enough about art, I assure you. No, their interest in you will be personal."

Raven's body tensed. "Why?"

"The less you know, the better."

Her spine stiffened. "I don't understand what they would want with me. I'm no one special."

"That's where you're wrong." The intruder grasped her wrist, plucking it out of the darkness as if it were low-hanging fruit. He placed two of his fingers across her pulse point and pressed.

Raven was seized with a sudden vision of being restrained in a hospital bed, an intravenous tube transferring blood to her body. Except the blood flowing through the tubes was black.

With a cry, she leapt to her feet. She lifted the kitchen chair, swinging in the direction of his voice, before turning toward what she thought was the door. She took only two steps before he caught her from behind.

She struggled, kicking and screaming, but his arms were like bands of steel. He pulled her flush against his front, lifting her so her feet dangled above the floor.

"Silence!" he hissed.

Raven's heartbeat was erratic. She tried to inhale but his arms squeezed too tightly.

"Can't—*breathe*," she managed to whisper hoarsely, twisting and squirming.

He loosened his hold but still held her aloft.

She gulped the air, her mind frantically assessing her predicament. She was not light, even in her new form. Still, he held her five-foot-seven-inch frame above the floor as if she were a doll. And he didn't seem to be exerting very much effort.

"I came here to help you," he whispered. "This is how you repay me?"

"You broke into my apartment. You're holding me against my will!" She scratched at his arms, but her fingernails met the fabric of what felt like a suit jacket.

"The others would have killed you, except they would have played with you first."

"How do you know so much about them?"

"Because I am one of them."

Raven stilled.

Her heart skipped a beat and began to thump loudly in her chest. She wondered if he was going to kill her.

With a curse, the intruder deposited her roughly on another chair, which he then slid across the floor to the wall.

He leaned over her, his voice dropping to a menacing whisper.

"Whether you believe me or not, I am your ally. Now sit still, be quiet, or I'll leave you to them. Do you understand?"

She nodded, trying to catch her breath once again.

"Good."

It occurred to her at that moment he must have seen her move, despite the lack of light.

"Do you have night-vision glasses?"

"I am the darkness made visible."

Raven shivered.

She heard the intruder begin to pace across her kitchen floor.

"Even if you avoid the others, you still aren't safe. The Carabinieri will be looking for a scapegoat in their investigation and you're the obvious choice."

She wrapped her arms around her middle. "I didn't take the illustrations. I don't know what happened to me last week. I think someone is trying to frame me."

The intruder stopped. "I can provide you with enough money to get home. Leave the city by train and travel south. Take a ship to Greece. Immigration at the Piraeus near Athens is very lax. From there you can get a flight back to America. You must leave Florence before two weeks have expired. In the interim, you're safe in this flat but I'd avoid venturing out at night."

She sat very still. "Why?"

"Partly because you're a terrible sleuth. Someone followed you to the palazzo and now he's sitting across the piazza, watching. Partly because the others will notice you. You don't want their attention."

Raven didn't respond, for leaving was the one thing she didn't want to do.

She heard him rattle something and take a few steps toward her. "I can see you're stubborn, if nothing else."

He placed something metallic and cool around her neck, from which was suspended something heavy. She reached up and felt a metal crucifix resting below her breasts.

"What's this?"

"It's a relic. From now on, you must always wear this. Never take it off."

"I thought I was safe so long as I left Florence."

"There are others in America, too."

Raven dropped the crucifix and it crashed against her chest. "How can some silly superstition protect me from the Mafia?"

A growl emerged from the intruder's chest and he grabbed the chain.

"Stupid humans don't deserve to live. I'll take back my gift and trouble you no more."

Panicked, her hand closed over his. "No, please. I want it."

He tightened his hold on the chain until it pulled against her neck.

"Perhaps when you have time to reflect on your situation, you'll assume a posture of gratitude."

"Thank you," she offered quickly.

"This relic offers protection from those who would kill you. Or worse."

"Will it protect me from you?"

She wished she could snatch back the words as soon as they left her mouth.

He dropped the chain.

"The relic has no effect on me. Best keep that in mind if you're tempted to speak to the Carabinieri about the palazzo or our conversation." His tone grew very sharp. "You don't want me as an enemy."

She clenched her teeth. "I won't tell them anything. I promise."

"You have two weeks. At the end of that time, if you're still here, you'll answer to me."

She nodded.

He grunted once again and much of his anger seemed to cool.

"I shall regret this. But it's far too late."

Out of the darkness, she felt his hand cup her face. His touch was light and surprisingly gentle.

"Beauty is vain. It appears and, like the wind, it's gone. Remember that." His thumb traced the curve of her cheek. "Good-bye, Jane."

Before Raven could react to the sound of her legal name coming from his lips, he'd withdrawn. His steps echoed in the apartment and she heard the sound of a window opening.

A few seconds later, the lights came on.

Chapter Ten

The Prince stood on a terrace at the Gallery Hotel Art, disturbed and angry. His evening had not gone as planned. Instead, he'd had to revisit one of his most recent, and serious, mistakes. She'd proved to be an even more attractive mistake than he'd remembered.

Cassita vulneratus.

Now the wounded lark had been healed and he was the vulnerable one. He'd heard truth in her voice when she promised to keep secrets, but he knew how easily human beings could be tricked. Her mind was too strong to control without making her drink from him. And he was unwilling to make her his slave.

If Maximilian or Aoibhe came upon her . . .

He shuddered.

Jane's scent was masked by what he'd fed her to save her life. Soon her true vintage would be detectable. He'd gifted her with one of his prized possessions, but he knew it would likely attract attention as well as repel it. He'd have to play guardian angel until she left the city, but from a distance.

Once again, a vision of a woman bloodied and abused burned before his eyes. And once again he resolved to stave off that outcome.

Whatever his commitment to Cassita, there remained the problem of the Emersons and Vitali. Emerson had received property stolen years before from the Prince's home and made the collection public, insulting him and drawing international attention to the illustrations. Vitali was complicit in the installation of the collection in the Prince's own city.

But Vitali's mind was susceptible to influence and so his memory of parts of the exhibit opening had been erased easily. The Prince saw no reason to take his life, despite his involvement with the Emersons. Having the director of the Uffizi in his control had clear advantages.

The problem of the Emersons, however, remained. The name *William York* needed to be erased from their memories and from any connection with the Uffizi Gallery and the theft of the illustrations. But Emerson's mind would not be controlled, nor would that of his wife.

Emerson would have to be killed and his wife would have to be traumatized into losing her memory.

The door that separated the terrace from their hotel room was ajar, in deference perhaps to their desire for fresh air. The Prince slipped into the darkened room.

The bed was only a few short steps from the door. Emerson was lying on his side, his back toward the Prince.

He closed his eyes and inhaled deeply.

Emerson's scent was distinctive and yet, somehow, it had changed since their last encounter. Certainly he was far more desirable now than before.

The Prince wondered idly what had precipitated the improvement.

At that moment, two other human scents assailed his nostrils, one new and pleasant and one familiar and unpleasant. Mrs. Emerson's scent had changed since he'd last been in her presence. Her aroma was noticeably sweeter, but there was still the undertone of disease. Whatever health problems she'd had before were still present. She gave the appearance of health, however. He could see her body visible in bed, curved into her husband's embrace.

The Prince reflected on the fact that he'd never enjoyed such a position, which seemed to embody the quiet trust that came from intimacy and love. He'd never wanted such closeness with Aoibhe. As for the others . . .

He felt his anger rise as jealousy overtook him. There was a time when he would have done anything to have a wife and a child. That possibility had been stolen from him.

He bared his teeth, a growl escaping his chest. Emerson had riches enough. Why did he have to steal?

The Prince approached the bed and was surprised to see a small structure standing next to it on the far side. In it, a baby was sleeping beneath a pink blanket. This was the source of the new, pleasant scent.

The Prince recoiled, the way some humans recoil from eating veal.

Standing at the foot of the bed, he regarded the parents. Emerson's wife had a light, floral scent that nearly masked the smell of her disease. Though he admired the virtues that gave rise to her fragrance, he found it cloying.

He craved the raven-haired beauty's blood. Or rather, what her blood was before he'd polluted it. She smelled of old arrogance and darkness now; her true scent, masked.

What he craved most, however, was a lively mind and a noble soul. Someone with whom he could talk about art and beauty. A companion and lover.

He bristled as he recalled Aoibhe's words. He'd been alone far too long. And he'd just persuaded the woman he wanted to flee the city, ensuring he would always be alone.

"Justice and mercy," he whispered.

Gabriel stirred and the Prince fled to the terrace.

He watched Emerson sit up and look around the room. He saw him reach for the lamp next to the bed.

The Prince moved so that he could not be seen.

For several moments, the Prince waited while Emerson walked about the room. With a muttered curse, he closed the terrace doors, locking them from the inside.

Strictly speaking, locked doors would not keep the Prince out. But the existence and presence of the child had changed his calculus.

As he stood in the shadows, he thought back to the first time he'd met the Emersons. He'd been impressed with the wife's virtues and decided not to kill her. Emerson, on the other hand, could be executed without misgivings. The fact that he'd procured stolen property meant a death sentence.

The Prince tried to persuade his feet to move in the direction of the door, but they wouldn't.

He was stunned to discover he couldn't kill Emerson in front of his child, even though the girl was an infant.

Something had happened to him. Something had changed.

Perhaps Jane had done it. She'd entered his life like a Trojan horse and brought mercy with her. He hated mercy, for it bespoke weakness.

What other explanation was there for his sudden change of heart? Just as he couldn't bear the thought of killing the baby or her ill mother, now he seemed unable to take the few steps necessary to kill the baby's father.

Emerson deserved it. He deserved death, if not for the sin of theft, then for the sin of pride, which still made his blood acrid and stark. And there was the small matter of William York . . .

The Prince would not tolerate weakness in himself. Neither would he pardon Gabriel Emerson.

As he dropped to the ground, he told himself he would spare the life of Emerson's wife and child, concealing his identity through some other means. He would wait and kill Emerson after Cassita left the city, when he no longer feared to see revulsion in her green eyes.

Mercy be damned.

Chapter Eleven

Just before sunrise, Raven sat on her bed, clutching a pillow to her midsection. The entirety of her apartment was bathed in electric light. The door and windows were locked, as were the shutters that covered her windows. An old plush moose she'd had since childhood sat next to her, as if it were a sentry.

She'd slept, but not for long. Fear and anxiety crowded her mind, haunting her dreams.

When she'd recovered from her shock the night before, she'd considered contacting the police. A glance across the piazza had changed her mind. She'd seen the man who lurked nearby, just as the intruder said.

She wasn't sure who the man who sat outside her apartment was. It was possible he was the intruder's accomplice. She wasn't going to court his attention by inviting a police visit.

The intruder, whoever he was, seemed to know her, or at least he'd spent the day following her. He knew she worked at the Uffizi. He knew she'd been interviewed by the Carabinieri. He knew she'd visited the orphanage and the Franciscan mission.

Somehow he knew about her visit to the palazzo. Whether he'd seen her or simply been told she'd been there, she didn't know. In either case, he must have raced to her apartment in a car or on a Vespa, gaining precious minutes in order to break into her apartment, cut off the electricity, and wait for her.

He'd exited her second-floor apartment through one of her bedroom windows. She assumed he'd entered the same way. Perhaps he was a rock climber—that would explain how he was able to scale the building and climb to the ground without injury.

She'd always kept the windows locked when she wasn't home. In her distracted state that morning, she must have forgotten. She wouldn't make that mistake again.

If she closed her eyes, she could hear the intruder's voice. Although it was familiar, she couldn't identify him. She could recall his scent, however.

A lot of good that will do. What would I say to the police? Arrest a suspect and let me sniff him?

She opened her eyes and looked over at the dresser. The sketch she'd completed the previous evening was missing, which meant he must have taken it. But why?

Her laptop and simple pieces of jewelry were left behind, as if he couldn't be bothered to steal them.

The reason could be pedestrian. Perhaps he'd stolen the sketch so he could dust it for fingerprints. He'd find her prints of little use. Patrick had told her that morning the investigators hadn't found any fingerprints in the exhibition hall.

Her cane was leaning against the wall, by her dresser. She didn't remember it being there earlier in the evening, but it was possible she hadn't noticed it. Why would the intruder move her cane?

In addition to these anomalies, he'd left gifts.

He'd placed a stack of money on her kitchen table. When she'd composed herself enough to count them, she discovered he'd left several thousand euros.

And he'd given her something else.

Raven lifted the crucifix from her chest. It appeared to be made of gold; the metal was thin and had been hammered from the underside in order to form the raised figure of Jesus. The design was primitive, the facial features of Christ barely distinguishable, which led her to believe the piece was pre-Renaissance and probably medieval.

Each point of the cross had two round loops on it, as if it had been made to affix to something. The gold chain on which it was suspended looked much newer than the crucifix, and it also appeared to be made of gold.

She knew a little about relics. She'd had a Catholic education at Barry

University, as an undergraduate. And there was Father Kavanaugh, the priest who'd intervened to help her and Carolyn when they were in trouble. Her love and respect for him didn't extend to his beliefs and she certainly didn't think there was anything efficacious about a piece of metal, no matter what shape had been hammered into it.

She couldn't imagine why the intruder would believe that a hunk of gold would protect her against "the others," whoever they were.

It won't hurt to wear the cross, just in case. Perhaps it works because the others fear it, not because it has magical powers.

But I'm not leaving Florence, not after I've worked so hard to build a life here. I don't care what he says.

She pulled her quilt around her shoulders.

The intruder was frightening and strangely strong. His command to leave the city was unambiguous, but she didn't know why the two-week mark was so important.

Maybe he has a source in the police force and knows what's happening with the investigation.

He'd recognized Dottor Vitali's name, although he seemed surprised to hear it. But it seemed to be the person of William York that he was most interested in. Raven found that puzzling.

And there was his speech. He'd called the Franciscans Ordo Fratrum Minorum, which, she'd discovered through the Internet, was their Latin title. And he'd warned her about going out after dark.

Raven couldn't imagine what the warning meant, or why, if he wanted her to leave, he'd given her the relic. His gift was strange enough. Then his disposition had changed and he'd touched her gently.

More puzzling, he'd called her Jane.

Raven's legal name was found only on her passport, work visa, and *permesso di soggiorno*, or "permission to stay" form, all of which were still in her backpack. However the intruder had discovered her legal name, it wasn't by searching her apartment.

Her legal name appeared in her employment file, so it was possible he'd learned it through the Uffizi. Raven dismissed that possibility, since everyone at the gallery called her by her chosen name, which was displayed on her security card. She hadn't been known as Jane since she was twelve.

So he's connected with either the gallery or the police.

Batelli and Savola knew her legal name. But they'd seen her Uffizi identification card and knew she was called Raven.

The intruder seemed to want to steer clear of the police, for whatever reason. He certainly hadn't learned her legal name through someone who knew her. At least, not someone who knew her in Italy. In Florida, it would be a different story.

Horror stabbed through her.

What if he talked to . . .

She couldn't finish the thought.

No, there was no point in entertaining the possibility. Florida was far away and so was any trace of her former life. Even her diplomas displayed her chosen name. If he'd opened the bottom drawer to her dresser, he would have found them, still encased in protective sleeves.

Putting the pillow and quilt aside, she stood in the center of the bedroom and took stock of her surroundings. The drawers to her dresser were closed, as was the door to her closet. Nothing seemed amiss, with the exception of the missing sketch and . . .

Her gaze alighted on the nightstand, on which were stacked several of her favorite books. She noticed the volume of the collected works of Edgar Allan Poe had been moved from the bottom of the stack to the top. *The Lion, the Witch and the Wardrobe* had been demoted to second place.

Once again, she wondered if, in a moment of distraction, she'd moved the C. S. Lewis book herself. It didn't occur to her to ask what, if anything, the intruder had against lions, witches, and/or wardrobes.

Raven rubbed her eyes in frustration. She had to report to work in a few hours, but she was too upset to go back to sleep.

With a sigh of resignation, she sat at her desk and opened her laptop. She'd catch up on her e-mail, which she'd been ignoring. When she logged in, she found a number of new messages, including one from her sister.

Hi Rave,

I tried calling you through FaceTime, but you never answer. Are you avoiding me?

Mom's wedding was beautiful. It's too bad you missed it.

Stephen is really nice. He was a plastic surgeon before he retired. He and Mom just moved into a big house on the ocean.

Raven paused her reading to roll her eyes.

Since you won't respond to Mom's e-mails, she asked me to ask you to come home for your birthday. She'll pay for your ticket and you can stay with me and Dan. Did I mention that we moved in together? I can't remember.

Mom wants to introduce you to Stephen and his kids. They're older than us—married with kids of their own. His son is a doctor and his daughter is a dentist.

Come home for a visit. We miss you. We can celebrate your birthday and I'll show you all the great hot spots in Miami.

You haven't seen Mom in years and I think it's time you two got over the past. I like Stephen a lot and he makes Mom happy. I think you'd like him, too, if you gave him a chance.

Dan is planning to take me to Europe to celebrate our two-year anniversary. I'm hoping we'll be coming over in the middle of June. We'll stay in a hotel, of course, but I'd like to visit you in Florence. Whether we visit Florence or not, I still want you to come to Miami.

Hey, what happened to that guy you had a crush on? I can't remember his name. Did you ever ask him out?

Let's talk soon.

Love,

Cara

XO

Raven sat back from her computer, resisting the urge to send a terse and angry reply.

She loved her sister more than anyone, but they had lived radically different lives. Carolyn was seven years younger, so she didn't remember their father or the happy life they'd had as a family living in New Hampshire. She certainly didn't remember the accident.

Raven took a moment to muse on the way her mind always attached a euphemism to the event that had disabled her. She flexed her feet be-

neath the desk, reminding herself that whatever she called it, its effects
had disappeared. That fact alone made her more positively disposed to
her mother, but barely.

When Carolyn was old enough, Raven had told her what had happened. Carolyn, to her credit, had listened carefully. But her memories
were so at odds with Raven's account, she had trouble believing it.

On one level, Raven viewed Carolyn's lack of memory as a good thing,
so she didn't revisit the subject. She remained silent, even in the face of
their mother's revisionist history.

But she refused to see her mother, speak with her, or be in the same
room as her until she acknowledged the truth. Which meant she hadn't
seen her mother since she'd left home for college over ten years earlier.

As for Carolyn's question about her old crush on Bruno, who was her
neighbor's grandson, well, of course it had come to nothing. She'd almost
forgotten about it, and him, given the previous day's events.

> Hi Cara,
> It's good to hear from you.
> I'll think about coming to Miami, but if I do, I'll pay my own way. I
> won't be seeing Mom. She knows why. There's no point in getting
> into it.
> As for your visit, it would be great to see you. But things are
> really busy at the moment. Let's talk later about this, okay? I'm
> swamped at work.
> I love you,
> Rave

Raven sent the e-mail and closed her laptop, not bothering to scroll
through the rest of her in-box.

She walked to the bathroom, putting thoughts of her troubled family
life aside.

She wondered why some unnamed group would take an interest in
her. She wasn't going to abandon everything she'd worked so hard for, just
because a mysterious criminal with connections to a secret association
told her to leave the city.

She bristled as she remembered what the intruder had said about her sleuthing skills. She was going to redouble her efforts at investigating William York and the Palazzo Riccardi and, hopefully, find something that would convince the police she was not an accomplice to the Uffizi robbery.

As she brushed her teeth, she began formulating a plan. She'd stuff the euros in a shoe box for now, then donate the money to the Franciscan mission.

She spat out her toothpaste and gazed at her appearance. It was still difficult to accept that the attractive woman staring back at her from the mirror was real.

Her gaze dropped to the relic around her neck. She was going to have to hide it under her clothes.

She muttered a few choice expletives and went to get dressed.

Chapter Twelve

"I'm telling you, the time is now!" Maximilian raised his voice, his imposing figure moving forward in the predawn darkness.

He and his companion stood high atop the Palazzo Vecchio, arguing. His interlocutor lifted a hand to stay him.

"Patience."

"We've been patient enough. I say we kill him tonight."

His companion sighed dramatically. "Have you learned nothing from the Venetians? It will take more than us to fell him, particularly if one of the others is with him."

Maximilian drew his sword. "We aren't exactly young. Who's to say the others will defend him? They're probably just as eager as we to seize control."

"Precisely why we must be confident in our alliances. Now is not the time for haste, particularly when you're in danger of losing your temper. It makes you reckless, Max, and that is something you cannot be when dealing with the Prince. He's more powerful than you can imagine."

Max cursed, swinging his broadsword through the air. "I disagree."

"Then you're a fool. Even I don't know the full extent of his power. I'm not about to find out only to lose my head."

"Must we wait until his thousand years have expired?"

"Don't be pessimistic. I made a mistake colluding with the Venetians. Now I'm cultivating other, stronger partners. And there's always the ferals and the hunters."

Max sheathed his sword. "Now you're talking nonsense. Ferals can't be controlled. And why would you want to work with the hunters?"

His companion smiled slowly.

"The Prince is old. The hunters would be only too glad to have his blood. They'd probably sign a treaty to leave the city alone if we were to deliver him up to them.

"Our borders have been somewhat porous recently. If a pack of ferals were to appear, they would wreak havoc. The Consilium will hold the Prince responsible. Not to mention that our noble prince has made a few *errors* recently—errors that threaten to expose him."

Max rested his large paw on the hilt of his sword. "The Consilium is riddled with his allies."

"And his rivals. They know his reign won't last forever. All they lack is a leader who is willing to depose him, and a little motivation.

"Be patient, Max. The city will be ours soon enough."

Chapter Thirteen

R aven sighed as she sat at a computer terminal in the archives of the Uffizi Gallery. She'd been demoted.

Professor Urbano had welcomed her back after her weeklong absence, but he hadn't allowed her to continue her work conserving the *Birth of Venus.* Perhaps this was his way of exercising his skepticism about her appearance, despite the fact that her fingerprints had been verified.

Yesterday, she'd been relegated to errand runner, while on this day, she'd been sent to the head archivist and told to follow her instructions. Someone else was sitting in her chair in the restoration lab, holding her brushes and carefully covering part of the surface of Botticelli's masterpiece with protective varnish.

Professor Urbano assured her she would be the one to apply the second and third coatings after Anja Pahlsmeier, a postdoc from Berlin, had completed the first. He was unwilling to interrupt the work she'd begun in Raven's absence. Or so he said.

Raven tried very hard not to be resentful, and failed.

The head archivist tasked her with organizing the printed and digital scientific reports the restoration team had done on the *Birth of Venus.* Then she was supposed to scan the printed reports and send all the digital files to Patrick, so he could input them into the archives' database.

The archivist had instructed Raven to familiarize herself with the files on the restoration of *Primavera* and to organize the new files in the same way. Raven was scrolling through the radiographs of *Primavera*, when she noticed something.

Radiographs are photographs taken by an X-ray machine, and they reveal details about a painting that aren't visible to the naked eye. In this case, Raven's attention was drawn to the radiographs that revealed the pentimenti, or outlines of the various figures Botticelli had drawn before he began to paint.

When she enlarged the radiograph of the figure of Mercury, she noticed something surprising. Originally, Botticelli had sketched him with shorter hair.

Raven had spent a lot of her own time studying *Primavera* and its restoration before she began working on the *Birth of Venus*. No one had ever commented on this particular change in Mercury's appearance or why Botticelli had lengthened his hair.

Puzzled, Raven clicked on another file, which featured an infrared reflectograph of the same image. In the reflectograph, the layers of paint were visible. It was clear that Botticelli had not only adjusted the length of Mercury's hair, he'd changed the color as well, darkening the strands.

Mercury was blond.

She sat back in her chair, staring at the computer screen.

On one level, her discovery was unremarkable. Artists in general, and Botticelli in particular, made changes to their paintings as they worked. Other changes to the original design of *Primavera* had been noted by the restoration team in their reports. But Raven couldn't recall anyone mentioning the changes made to Mercury's hair.

Curious, she scrolled through some of the written documents the restoration team had prepared. It took her some time to do so, but her investigation corroborated her suspicion. No one seemed to have noticed the change in Mercury's hair and this was very, very surprising given the fact that the change was obvious on a close inspection of the radiographs.

Lost in thought, Raven opened a digital copy of the finished painting and enlarged it, focusing on Mercury's head and shoulders. Then she switched to the radiograph.

She tried to imagine what Mercury would have looked like with shorter blond hair.

Discoveries such as this one could help an art historian make her career. But before she wrote a paper announcing her discovery to the world, she had to study the reports more carefully. And she had to be sure no one had written on this subject before.

Peering over her shoulder to be sure she wasn't being watched, Raven surreptitiously removed a flash drive from her backpack and quickly copied the relevant images. She could barely contain her excitement, her leg jiggling back and forth.

She'd just transferred the flash drive to the zippered pocket of her backpack when she felt a hand on her shoulder.

"Are you okay?" A voice addressed her in English.

She jumped in her chair and let out a loud expletive.

"Shhh!" the archivist hissed from her desk, which was across the room. She glared at Raven over the rims of her glasses.

Raven nodded meekly before looking up into the guilty eyes of her friend Patrick.

He mouthed a quick "Sorry."

"What are you doing?" she whispered, quickly closing the files that she'd opened on the computer.

"I came to ask you the same question." He nodded at the computer screen.

Raven glanced at the archivist, then at her friend.

"It may be nothing."

Patrick's gaze moved to the archivist as well before he spoke. "Gina wants you to come over to have dinner with us tonight."

Raven looked over at their mutual friend, Gina, who was working on the other side of the room. She waved.

"So it's official? You're an 'us'?"

Patrick grinned. "Yeah."

"I'm happy for you. I'd love to have dinner with you both, but I have to pick up a few things after work."

"That's all right. Do you have your Vespa?"

"It's waiting for me at the shop."

"I'll take you to pick it up after work and we can meet at Gina's later. Okay?"

"Thanks." Raven smiled.

Patrick picked up a piece of paper and scribbled a few words. He left the paper next to her computer before returning to his desk.

Raven glanced at his writing.

You forgot about the cameras.

"Shit!" she muttered.

She crumpled the paper and shoved it into her backpack.

She looked around the room, trying not to appear obvious as she located the security cameras in the four corners.

She'd been so excited about her potential discovery, she'd forgotten about them. Now the gallery had footage of her downloading files to a personal storage device without permission. It was a serious offense. And, given her recent circumstances, she doubted Dottor Vitali would be lenient.

She looked over at Patrick, who shook his head. He seemed just as worried as she.

He picked up his cell phone and began typing.

A few seconds later her phone chimed with a text.

What r u doing?

Raven quickly answered him.

Forgot about the cameras.

She could hear Patrick's huff of disapproval from across the room.

Raven turned to look at the archivist, but she seemed preoccupied by her own work.

Raven's phone chimed again.

You need to be more careful.

She couldn't disagree. She was about to type a suitably contrite response when the telephone on the archivist's desk rang.

As if in slow motion, she turned around.

The archivist was nodding and agreeing to something. When she finished her short conversation, she waved Raven over.

Raven walked to her desk, slowly.

"Dottor Vitali wishes to see you in his office. Now." The archivist's tone was brisk. "Make note of where you left off in your project and log out of your computer."

I am in so much trouble.

Raven ground her teeth as she returned to her desk. With a few short mouse clicks, she logged out of her computer. She took a clean piece of paper and listed what she'd accomplished that morning.

She picked up her knapsack and handed the paper to the archivist.

"Raven, wait," Patrick called to her.

He walked her to the door.

"Hand me the flash drive," he whispered, holding his hand out.

"What?"

"So they can see us." His eyes flickered to the side, where one of the cameras was positioned in full view of the door.

She shook her head. "You'll get in trouble."

"You're already in trouble." He lifted his hand higher.

Raven looked over at the archivist, who was watching them intently. "This is your job, Patrick."

"A job I have because you covered my ass when I forgot to file the radiographs. Now we're even." He moved his hand in front of her nose. "Give me the flash drive."

Raven muttered a curse and unzipped the pocket of her knapsack. She retrieved the flash drive and handed it to him.

"Thanks. I really appreciate it." His voice was loud, too loud, and the archivist hushed them once again.

He leaned forward to whisper in her ear. "Tell Vitali I asked you to copy the files. If they confiscate the drive, I'll help you get the files another way."

"I hope you know what you're doing." Raven gave him a worried look before exiting the archives.

"So do I." He grimaced.

As Raven climbed the stairs to the second floor, she contemplated an alternative explanation, one that would exonerate Patrick. Nothing came readily to mind. She couldn't even mention William York and his connection with Palazzo Riccardi.

Raven would never allow someone she cared about to be hurt. This was the core of her being. She'd made a mistake; she would take responsibility for it, even if it meant losing her position at the gallery.

She gave herself a short pep talk and approached Vitali's office just as a loud female voice, speaking English, echoed down the corridor.

"Codswallop! I've been wandering the streets of Florence since before you were born. Clare and I will be fine for a couple of hours."

Raven stood outside the open door, her palms sweating. She wiped them on her yoga pants.

"Katherine, the city isn't safe." Professor Emerson sounded exasperated.

"I don't believe that for one moment," the woman replied.

Taking a deep breath, Raven knocked on the door.

"Come in," Vitali called, in Italian.

She entered the room and found the Emersons talking with an older woman who had short white hair and snapping blue-gray eyes. She was pushing a stroller in which Clare was seated, playing with a toy bunny and oblivious to the tension around her.

"Julianne can take her tour, you can discuss your situation with Vitali, and I'll take the baby for a walk. It's a beautiful day. She needs fresh air." The woman wheeled the stroller around and headed for the door.

"No." Professor Emerson's voice boomed.

Everyone stared—at his sapphire eyes that blazed behind black-framed glasses, at his hands that were clenched into fists at his sides, and at his expression, which was frightening.

But Professor Emerson wasn't angry, although he'd adopted an angry posture.

Raven scanned his expression and was surprised to see fear behind his eyes.

"Katherine, it isn't safe. I can barely stand to have you, Clare, and Julianne out of my sight."

His eyes moved to his wife and he addressed her. "You can take your tour. But Katherine and Clare must stay inside the gallery."

His wife grasped his elbow and he unclenched his fists, his body relaxing.

Marginally.

"It's all right, Gabriel. We're safe now." She gave him a smile, which he did not return.

"And you will remain so."

Raven wiped her hands on her pants again and studied her feet.

She'd intruded on something she didn't understand, a private conversation between a protective husband and father and his family. She found herself strangely moved by his intensity. It had been a long time since someone had been protective of her. It had been a long time since she'd had a father.

"We can walk indoors." The woman referred to as Katherine turned toward Vitali. "Perhaps you'll assign us a guide. Would that be acceptable, Gabriel?"

It seemed clear from her tone that she was annoyed, but she seemed determined not to argue with him.

Raven lifted her eyes and saw Gabriel nodding in a restrained manner.

"Then it's settled. Now, if you'll be so kind as to find us a guide, I'll take Clare for a walk." Katherine gave Vitali an expectant look, almost as if he were a concierge rather than the director of the Uffizi Gallery.

Raven half expected Katherine to begin tapping her conservatively shod foot.

Vitali motioned Raven forward.

"Mrs. Emerson would like a tour of the restoration lab. Please escort her downstairs and introduce her to Professor Urbano. He's expecting her."

Raven blinked.

Vitali's eyes narrowed. "Miss Wood?"

Raven's anxieties at being summoned to the director's office because she'd copied files without permission began to lessen.

She cleared her throat. "A tour? Yes, of course. Of course. Thank you."

She paused, wondering if he was going to bring up the flash drive or mention anything about the robbery. She wondered if news of her midnight visit to Palazzo Riccardi had somehow come to his attention.

Vitali sat back in his chair and lifted the telephone, requesting that his assistant send one of the security guards to his office, that an important guest needed an escort.

Raven exhaled in relief.

Julia kissed her husband, patting him on the shoulder, before retrieving her purse and moving to Raven's side. Gabriel followed his wife's movements with a look of concern, his long fingers curving into fists once again.

With a nod, Vitali dismissed Raven, announcing that Katherine's guide would appear momentarily.

Raven was not about to delay and so led Julia to the hall. Julia trailed behind her, limping.

Raven stopped. "Are you hurt?"

"Not really. When I had Clare, I had an epidural. I've had nerve issues in my right leg and foot ever since. It's acting up today." She forced a smile, but appeared distressed.

Raven moved closer, noticing that Julia was wearing flat, comfortable shoes.

"Should I get a wheelchair?"

"It isn't that bad. Today my foot is numb so I'm having trouble walking."

"I'm sorry." Raven's expression was sympathetic. "I broke my leg once. There was nerve damage. Whenever the weather changes, I have pain."

"I'm sorry to hear that." Julia started walking again, slowly. "I'm lucky my leg only acts up periodically. I'm told the numbness will go away eventually."

"We'll take the elevator." Raven gestured to the far end of the hall.

"I know it's short notice, but I wanted to see the restoration work before we left." Julia spoke in low tones as they passed a few people in the hallway.

"No problem." Raven watched her from the corner of her eye. "I thought you were staying in Florence for a week."

"Our plans have changed." Julia's expression grew grave. "We're checking out of the hotel this afternoon and going to Umbria."

"Umbria is beautiful."

Raven was distracted, thinking about what had occurred in the archives. It was possible the security guards hadn't noticed what she'd done. Maybe she'd implicated Patrick for no reason. She'd have to warn him.

"Have you heard any rumors about the Gallery Hotel Art being haunted?" Julia's voice intruded on Raven's thoughts.

She turned her head to meet Julia's eyes. "Haunted? No. I always thought it was peculiar their restaurant served Japanese food, but I haven't heard anything about the hotel being haunted. Why do you ask?"

Julia fidgeted with her purse strap. "This is going to sound strange, but my husband thinks there's a ghost in the hotel. That's why we're leaving."

Raven's eyebrows shot up. "A ghost? Why does he think that?"

"He woke up last night convinced someone was in our room. He couldn't see anything but he felt a . . . dark presence."

Raven's heart began to speed.

"Did someone break in?"

"I don't think so. Nothing was missing and he didn't see anyone. But he felt like someone was there and the doors to the terrace were open." Julia smoothed her long hair behind her ears. "If it were anyone other than Gabriel, I'd dismiss it. But he's seen—and felt—strange things before."

Raven bit her tongue. She desperately wanted to ask Julia what strange things she was referring to, but she was an important donor and barely an acquaintance. Raven didn't want to seem nosy.

"I don't believe in ghosts. But it's possible someone broke into your hotel room. Petty thefts are common in the city and, as you know, that hotel attracts wealthy guests."

"I suppose that's possible."

"I hate to say it, but I'm wondering if the Uffizi robbery is connected to what happened in your room."

Julia eyed Raven as they entered the elevator. "Why would you say that?"

"Your names are connected with the gallery. If someone found out you were staying in the city, they might think you're carrying expensive jewelry or artifacts."

"That makes sense. I'm not in a hurry to stay in the same hotel room, even if it was a burglar. This makes me sad because we stayed in that room before." Julia appeared wistful.

"Did your husband mention the break-in to Vitali?"

"Yes. He didn't mention the ghost to anyone. He simply said he had security concerns about the hotel, and he cited some recent reports in the newspaper about missing people and bodies being found downriver." Julia shivered. "I wish he hadn't told me."

Raven toyed with the security card around her neck, resisting the urge to touch the relic she was wearing under her shirt.

"I hadn't heard about the bodies."

"There was an article in *La Nazione* yesterday. Several bodies were found on the banks of the Arno. The police aren't releasing any details."

"Men or women?" Raven's mind went immediately to Angelo.

"Men." Julia took a step closer. "Are you all right? You've gone pale."

"I'm fine. I hate to mention it, but since you're leaving anyway, I'll say that Florence had a serial killer for decades. I hope he hasn't returned." She exited the elevator, holding the door open for Julia.

"I thought they caught him." Julia followed her into the hall.

"I thought so, too."

Julia sighed. "Our trip to Umbria has poor timing. We're thinking about adopting a little girl from the Franciscan orphanage and we were supposed to be spending time with her."

Raven stopped. "I volunteer there. Which girl?"

Julia smiled widely. "Maria. She's five."

Raven's heart leapt. "I know Maria. You're going to adopt her?"

"We're thinking about it. We can't apply to adopt her until we've been married for three years and that isn't until January. But we want to get to know her and have her know us. When we first met her two years ago, she didn't speak. But she's been seeing a therapist and is talking now."

"I help the younger children learn their letters and their numbers. I work with her."

Julia placed a hand on Raven's arm. "Then thank you. She's very different from the girl we met two years ago."

Raven found herself unable to respond. She swallowed, trying to rid herself of the lump she felt in her throat.

"You're welcome," she managed to say.

Julianne gave her a wide smile and followed her down the long corridor that led to the large restoration lab.

Before they entered, Raven paused.

She felt like she should mention the intruder who broke into her apartment, but she was worried about the repercussions. Nevertheless,

Julia had a baby. What if the intruder broke in where they were staying in Umbria, and they were hurt?

She cleared her throat. "I hope there isn't a connection between what happened at the hotel and the robbery here. But you should be cautious, even in Umbria. Whoever stole the illustrations did so without leaving evidence. As far as I know, the police don't have any suspects. Please be careful."

"I will." Julia offered her an appreciative look before they opened the door to the lab.

❀ ❀

The morning came and went. Raven continued her work in the archives and no one mentioned the flash drive. In fact, the archivist seemed all too eager to let Raven leave at lunchtime, in order to visit the doctor.

Raven's doctor was stunned at her sudden transformation. A series of X-rays was scheduled after the appointment, so the doctor could learn what had happened to Raven's leg.

Blood and urine were sampled in order to test for any drugs. But the doctor warned her that even if she had been drugged, the drugs might not be in her system. It depended on when she was drugged and what she'd been given. Rohypnol, for example, showed up in urine tests no more than sixty hours after ingestion.

Having been x-rayed and tested, Raven grabbed a quick lunch at a café before returning to the gallery.

She was dismayed to see Ispettor Batelli at the entrance. He eyed his watch, then turned to her with more than a modicum of distaste.

"A long lunch, signorina?" He sounded contemptuous.

"I'm working in the archives and the archivist gave me permission to see my doctor."

"Interesting," the inspector said. "Is there anything you'd like to share with me about your visit?"

"No."

Raven brushed past him, but she could feel his eyes on her as she retreated.

❀ ❀

Working in the archives was not that interesting. Patrick returned the flash drive while they were standing in the hall, away from the security cameras. She hid it in her knapsack.

"Nice hardware." He gestured to the crucifix around her neck.

Raven glanced down at the relic. She'd forgotten she was wearing it.

"Oh, this." She lifted it and looked at it for a moment.

He gave her a questioning look. "May I?"

"Sure."

He examined the cross more closely, looking at the raised figure in the sunlight that streamed in from one of the windows. "This is really old. Where did you get it?"

"A friend."

He released the cross into her hand.

"Must be some friend. It looks like a museum piece."

Raven moved the necklace so that it was hidden under her shirt.

Patrick dropped his voice. "I wouldn't let the carabinieri see you wearing that."

"Why not?"

"They'd probably confiscate it and run the image through the Interpol database, trying to figure out if it's stolen."

"It isn't stolen." She sounded indignant.

"Speaking of which . . ."

At that moment, Ispettor Batelli walked by with Agent Savola. Both men stared at Raven and Patrick before continuing down the hall.

Patrick shook his head. "Try to keep a low profile, okay? We'll talk more at Gina's tonight."

Raven gave him a small smile. "Thank you."

He ruffled her hair. "When do I get to meet the boyfriend who's giving you museum pieces?"

She rolled her eyes. "After I meet him."

Patrick laughed and accompanied her back into the archives.

After work, they went to the mechanic's shop to pick up her Vespa.

Patrick went home to Gina, and Raven went to one of the shopping areas near the Duomo. One could buy Prada and Salvatore Ferragamo over by the Ponte Santa Trinita, but Raven's fellowship didn't afford her that kind of budget.

She'd worn old yoga pants two days in a row because none of her other clothing fit. She had to buy new clothes for work, as well as underwear and pajamas.

It was more exciting than she could have imagined.

Raven detested shopping. Her weight and the European sizing system conspired against her. It was difficult to find clothes that fit, and when she did, they were always expensive. Not so now.

Owing to her smaller size, she was able to buy clothes off the rack and quickly spent several hundred euros on the essentials. She even bought a few pieces of lingerie.

By the end of her shopping spree, she was dressed in a black linen sundress, a pale yellow cardigan, black wedge-heeled sandals, and extremely attractive pink underwear. She even bought a pair of large black sunglasses.

She threw her old clothes in the garbage.

The relic was not so easily hidden by the sundress and cardigan as it had been by her large button-down shirt.

She toyed with the idea of placing the necklace in her knapsack, but the intruder had been adamant she wear it. Given the strange events that had befallen the Emersons, and the reports of bodies found near the Arno, she decided that trading on someone else's superstitions wouldn't really harm anyone.

She bought a floral silk scarf and wound it around her neck in such a way as to cover the chain and cross, hoping no one would notice it.

Looking very chic and feeling more confident than she had ever felt, she bought a few groceries and a bottle of wine to take to dinner. Having deposited her purchases safely in her apartment, she drove the Vespa to Gina's, very much looking forward to a relaxing evening with friends.

❊ ❊

By the time Raven left her friends, it was after eleven. Their dinner had extended to drinks and dessert and an evening of conversation and music.

The skies had opened, pouring rain. As usual, there were still a few pedestrians and drivers on the slick streets. Everyone else had retreated indoors.

Or so it seemed.

Raven was glad she kept a long raincoat under the seat of her Vespa. She wore it as she drove, wincing at every drop of water that fell on her new sandals.

When she arrived at Santo Spirito, she discovered the piazza was empty.

Usually patrons sat outside the bar across from her apartment or at one of the cafés. The square itself was often filled with students. Several American universities had study-abroad programs that were housed nearby. But since the rain was falling heavily, the emptiness of the piazza was unsurprising.

She parked her Vespa and had just returned her helmet to the storage space beneath the seat when she heard something. The sound itself was strange, a cross between a growl and a roar.

She whirled around and saw something move at the far end of the piazza.

The falling rain partially obscured her vision and the dimness made it difficult to see. She could discern something large and black moving toward her.

As the figure approached, she realized it was too large to be a dog. It was moving quickly, its outline a blur against the rain.

She turned and tried to run, but her sandals slid on the slick cobblestones and she fell. Hard.

When she came to her senses, she saw that the animal, which was now running on two legs, was bearing down on her. Snarls and growls echoed across the piazza as it drew nearer.

She tried to stand, her new shoes slipping beneath her. She could hear the animal approaching, its footfalls heavy in her ears.

She scrambled to her feet and was about to sprint toward her building, when she dropped her keys.

"Shit!" She bent to retrieve them just as the creature roared.

Chapter Fourteen

Raven expected the worst. She expected the thing—whatever it was—to crash into her.

She glared at the relic that swung from her neck. She didn't have time to indulge herself in an "I told you so," directed at the absent intruder. Silly superstitions had never done her or anyone else any good. They certainly weren't helping her now.

She braced herself for impact, knowing it was too slippery to run.

There's nothing I can do.

It's going to kill me.

She heard sliding and scuffing, as if something had tried to come to a sudden and abrupt halt.

She turned her head just as the dark creature came to a stop several feet away. It roared and lunged toward her with its arms, but its feet did not move.

"Take that fucking thing off! Take it off!" it bellowed, in Italian.

Raven peered through the falling rain at what she realized was a man. He was dressed in dark and dirty clothing, his hair long and matted. A stench filled her nostrils as he moved, as if he hadn't been washed in a very, very long time.

What she noticed most were his eyes. They were very dark, as if the pupils had expanded to obliterate the whites of his eyes, giving him a strange, insectlike appearance. When he opened his mouth, he exposed a pair of fangs among broken, yellowed teeth.

She moved to run, and once again her ridiculous shoes slipped out from beneath her, landing her hard on her bottom.

The creature roared expletives, waving his arms and pacing back and forth. But he maintained his distance.

"You whore. Take that fucking thing off," he shouted. "I'll rip your head off and drain your blood. I'll fuck you until you die. Take it off!"

Raven moved back, placing more distance between them as he continued to rant almost incoherently.

He started shrieking Latin profanities, which she barely understood. He described someone, a man, as a pedophile and a deviant. He said she was the deviant's whore and that he was going to kill her.

But, strangely and inexplicably, he came no closer. He simply paced back and forth, like a lion in a cage, roaring and gnashing his teeth.

Raven righted herself and was prepared to flee into the house, when she heard footsteps. Someone was approaching from the direction of the church, which stood to their right.

"Police!" a man called. "Put your hands on your head."

Raven saw someone dressed in black run toward them, pointing a gun at the madman. It was dark and still raining, so she couldn't make out the policeman's features.

In an instant, the madman leapt, knocking the gun out of the other man's hand. He pulled the policeman's head back by his hair, baring his neck, and bent over him.

Raven heard a ripping sound and saw blood spurt.

She looked away in horror as the madman bent his mouth to the wound in the policeman's neck.

Without a backward glance, she skidded to the door of her building, her hands shaking as she fumbled with her keys. She slammed the door behind her, climbing the stairs as fast as she could.

It was only when she was in her apartment, with the door locked and every light on, that she sank to the floor, clutching the gold she wore around her neck.

❊ ❊

Aoibhe closed her eyes and inhaled.

"Blood." She drew her lips back, exposing her fangs. "Let's go, Ibarra. It smells delicious."

Together, they leapt from roof to roof, racing from where they'd been conversing, under the loggia near the Uffizi, to Santo Spirito. As they dropped to street level and crossed the bridge, Aoibhe stopped.

"Do you smell that?" She grabbed Ibarra's hand, rain pouring down on them.

He inhaled and his expression shifted. "A feral."

"Hurry," she cried.

The two beings climbed a nearby building, continuing their course across the roofs. When they arrived at the piazza, they stopped, their eyes scanning the space below.

They located the feral easily. It was feeding from a human in full view of the buildings. Based on the strength of the scent, they inferred the human had almost been drained.

"How did it get past the patrols?" Aoibhe cast a furious gaze on her companion.

"This must be the one Pierre spoke of."

She surveyed the apartment windows that lined the piazza on both sides. Many of them were illuminated.

"No doubt it's been seen."

"It's too late to worry about that. There are too many witnesses." Ibarra glanced in her direction. "Can you tell how old it is?"

Aoibhe wrinkled her nose. "It isn't old enough to be a challenge. We can take it, if there's only one. How much faith do you have in your patrols?"

"I have absolute faith in them." He met her gaze.

"Good. I'll approach from the front and you, from behind. We'll attack and drag it into one of the alleys."

They nodded to one another and Ibarra raced across the roofs to get behind the feral, while Aoibhe landed on the wet cobblestones.

She approached him slowly.

Ferals were unpredictable, as well as strong. They were outcasts, eschewing covens and living and hunting in the countryside. Many were mad and behaved like animals, although some of them maintained vestiges of rationality.

Aoibhe begun running toward the feral as soon as her feet hit the ground. Whether it saw her or merely scented her, it dropped its prey immediately.

Its blood-smeared mouth snarled and it bared its teeth, lowering into a crouch.

Aoibhe changed direction, but it was too fast. The feral came at her with speed, its fingers stretched like claws toward her head.

She vaulted over its shoulder, surprising it. She placed a knee to its back and grasped its head with both hands. With a twist and a crunching sound, she wrenched the head from the body and dropped back to the ground.

The feral continued moving, its arms and legs shaking, black blood oozing from its neck.

Aoibhe held the head out to her side, taking care not to be bitten by its snapping mouth. She scowled in disgust as the stench filled the air.

"I was going to do that." Ibarra appeared at her side.

She laughed. "Next time. But you'll have to be faster."

She shook the head by its hair, the way a cat shakes a mouse, until the eyes closed and it stopped moving.

"What a nasty piece of filth." She tossed the head aside and picked up her skirts, wiping her hands carefully on the white slip she wore underneath. "And the smell. Good hell."

Ibarra coughed, as if in agreement.

"What now?"

"You take the human; I'll take the feral and its head. We'll meet in the alley." She nodded across the piazza.

Ibarra did as he was told, grabbing the human, and his gun, and lifting him over his shoulder. He ran between the raindrops to the alley, then dumped his burden on the ground. Something fell from one of the human's pockets.

It was a black leather wallet.

Ibarra almost threw it away. Money in small amounts was uninteresting to him. But when he picked it up, he caught sight of something that gave him pause.

"What's that?" Aoibhe looked over his shoulder curiously.

He pointed at the identification in the wallet. "Interpol."

"Damnation!" Aoibhe kicked at the feral's beheaded corpse. "Not only does it trespass on our city, but it feeds in public on a damn policeman!"

Ibarra tossed the wallet to the ground. "What now?"

Aoibhe turned furious brown eyes in his direction. "What now? I'll tell you what now. You and your border patrols are appearing before the Consilium. If you don't have an explanation as to why our borders were breached, I'll kill the lot of you."

Ibarra took a step backward, lifting his hands. "Aoibhe, stay calm. Let's find out what happened before we involve the Consilium."

"It's too late! The humans are probably reporting what they've seen, including our little maneuver, to the police. The feral spilled blood on the ground. The piazza will be crawling with policemen in minutes. Don't you understand what this means?"

He dropped his hands and his black eyes narrowed. "Don't patronize me, Aoibhe. I know exactly what it means."

She gave him a furious look.

"Then help me clean up this mess before they arrive."

Ibarra cursed and did as he was ordered.

Chapter Fifteen

The Prince was restless.

His network of spies informed him that the Emersons had left the city for Umbria. On the whole, their departure mattered little. There was nowhere in the world that was beyond his reach, only places that were more inconvenient than others.

Umbria was not inconvenient.

He would have to apply to the Princess of that region for permission to hunt on her territory, but they'd been on good terms for years. He doubted she'd withhold her assent. It was possible she'd request a sexual favor, as she had in the past.

She was beautiful and very desirable, but the Prince found himself indifferent to the possibility as his thoughts shifted to a raven-haired woman with large green eyes.

His quest for revenge against the professor would have to wait. He had more pressing concerns.

He'd watched the woman from afar, hoping she'd obey him and flee. She didn't.

She went to work. She went to the doctor's office. She went shopping. The Prince cursed.

Yes, he'd given her two weeks, but that had been a concession. She needed proper motivation. She needed to be shown what true danger was.

He'd fed himself in his villa, indulging in human blood followed by one of the rare, bottled vintages he'd procured in centuries past. This was one of his secrets.

Over time, he ingested the blood of old ones; blood he'd carefully extracted and saved or acquired through various means. His economy in not ingesting the blood of an old one all at once was rewarded every time he took a drink. He felt himself renewed in strength, his intellect sharper, his senses heightened.

Ingesting blood sated one desire but aroused another. On this evening, he wanted a human woman—young and soft. He wanted to kiss her mouth and thrust inside her. He wanted to look into her eyes and see trust, not fear, and to have her sleep in his arms the way Emerson's wife slept in his.

He wanted Cassita.

For various reasons, he couldn't have her. This meant he needed to go in search of a convenient substitute.

On a rainy evening, when the streets were almost empty, it would be difficult to find a woman who met his standards.

That was how he found himself outside Teatro, a place he had not visited in over a century.

When he entered the club, those who recognized him fell silent. He was greeted enthusiastically, if carefully, by the bartender and his citizens, who bowed deferentially, offering their seats.

The music played on and he found himself grimacing. Surely, *music* was used equivocally when applied to the pulsing dissonance that resonated from the sound system. He didn't find it entertaining. He didn't find it enjoyable.

In fact, it made his already impatient and aroused mood that much more dangerous.

Luckily, the humans ignored him. To them, he was one among many. Handsome, it was true, but not obviously powerful or as large as some of the others.

He took a proffered seat and goblet of warmed blood and sat in silence, scanning the crowd. If he couldn't have Cassita, at least he could have someone who looked like her. He doubted anyone would smell as sweet.

Within minutes he found an olive-skinned, dark-haired woman who boasted an hourglass figure and bright blue eyes.

Close enough.

"Good evening, my lord."

The Prince's musings were interrupted by a female who bowed before him. She was dressed in red satin, her sandy-colored hair pinned up, exposing pale shoulders and an elegant neck.

He tamped down his annoyance at being interrupted and nodded at her curtly, putting his drink aside.

"May I service you, my lord?" Her hazel eyes lifted to his.

He stared at her.

"Service me, how?"

"In any way you wish." She knelt before him and placed her hands on his knees.

He undid her hair, wrapping it around his wrist.

"Your name?"

"Svetlana, my lord." She searched his eyes for permission.

His expression did not change.

"Your age?"

"I was changed fifty years ago, my lord. I was visiting from Russia." She parted her red lips in anticipation.

"A youngling," he muttered. He released her hair and pushed her hands aside. "Stand up."

Her face registered her surprise as she stood.

He tugged impatiently on the cuffs of his black shirt.

"Since you're a youngling, I'll forgive this impertinence. But in future, know that I am the hunter, not the hunted." His gray eyes narrowed.

She bowed her head. "Forgive me. Your presence is a great honor. I merely meant to show my respect."

The Prince lifted a skeptical eyebrow.

"I'm sure some of the members of the Consilium would welcome your . . . generosity," he said. "Not all of us are the same. If you wish to reach old age, you'll remember that."

With a nod, he dismissed her.

She bowed again and retreated, disappearing into the crowd.

The Prince scowled.

He hadn't always behaved thusly. When he was newly turned, he'd indulged in the pleasures of the body. But the chains he'd worn in life were difficult to break. Even now, he wore them. He was, perhaps, the only one of his kind who still had sexual compunctions.

He took great care to hide them, which was why, among other reasons, he avoided Teatro as one might avoid plague.

Aoibhe spoke the truth. He could have his choice, as Prince. But what he desired was a human female, not a succubus.

He rubbed his face. Perhaps he should go home.

But home held memories of Cassita, of her broken body sliding perilously close to death. It was not a place to go in order to forget her.

Anger began to build in his chest. He finished his drink in one swallow, determined to have the satisfaction he craved.

He searched the crowd and eventually located the dark-haired woman he'd been admiring. Surely she was reason enough for him to court a little guilt.

He stood, adjusting the sleeves of his jacket. Eyes on the woman, he walked toward her.

Humans and supernatural beings alike parted in front of him. Soon he was at the center of the dance floor. Her back was toward him.

He leaned forward, his lips brushing her ear. "Good evening."

She shuddered. "Hi."

She turned her head and he was disappointed momentarily at how different her facial features were from Jane's. This woman was more beautiful, but the fact that she was not who he really wanted diminished her appeal. Greatly.

He closed his eyes and inhaled. Her scent was enticing.

And she was willing. Her heartbeat quickened, as did her breathing, as soon as he made eye contact.

The Prince placed a hand on her hip, drawing her to his body. Ignoring the pounding music, he began to sway, moving with her to his own sensual rhythm.

She lifted her hands and slipped them between the lapels of his jacket, tracing the planes of his pectorals with pink-tipped fingers.

"You're very strong. Are you an athlete?" She raised her voice so she could be heard, but she needn't have bothered. His hearing was excellent.

"Of a sort. What brings you here?" He smiled, watching her reaction.

She returned his smile and moved nearer. "I came in search of pleasure."

His grip on her hip tightened. "And have you found it?"

She shook her head.

He spanned her waist with his hands, bringing their lower bodies together. Her breasts brushed across his chest and he felt the stirrings of desire.

"You're attractive."

Her smile widened. "Thank you. So are you."

He laughed and she joined him.

He moved her hair behind her shoulder and stroked her cheek with his thumb. Then he brought his lips to her neck.

Instantly, he could hear her heartbeat speed, the blood pumping through her veins. She slid her hands up his chest and brought them to his hair, gently scratching at his scalp.

He brushed his nose against her throat and kissed her intently, careful not to let his teeth puncture her skin. There would be time enough for that. Satisfaction was always sweeter when delayed. And he had always prided himself in being a master of satisfaction.

She sighed in his arms, pulling him closer.

He continued to kiss her, enjoying her enthusiastic moans. When the scent of her arousal became too much, he pulled back.

She opened her eyes. "Why did you stop?"

He stroked his thumb across her lower lip. "I want to be the only one to hear your cries when I taste you."

She nipped at his thumb, her eyes sparkling. "Yes, please."

He took her hand in his. "Come."

He led her from the dance floor and toward one of the halls. A youngling, who acted as a guard, bowed to the Prince and stood aside so they could pass.

At that moment, someone moved to stand in front of them.

"Lorenzo." The Prince nodded at his second in command, gripping the woman's hand more tightly.

Lorenzo was Italian by birth and a distant cousin of the Medici family. Born in the sixteenth century, he had transformed when he was twenty years old. His dark hair was curly and hung to his shoulders, while his eyes were a light brown. In size, he matched the Prince, but he was younger and far less powerful.

"Forgive the intrusion, my prince." Lorenzo's eyes flickered to the woman's and back again. "But there's a situation that requires your attention."

The Prince swore. "Can't it wait?"

Lorenzo lifted his hand, revealing a cell phone. "I'm afraid not."

The Prince scowled at the device. He despised them. They weren't permitted in Teatro for security reasons.

If Lorenzo was using one, something must have happened.

He turned to the guard.

"Escort the woman to one of the rooms and see she is not disturbed."

He lifted her hand and pressed his lips to the back of it. "I'll be with you momentarily. There are drinks in the room. Please enjoy yourself while you wait."

She smiled up at him and nodded, following the guard down the hall.

The Prince watched the curve of her backside as it swayed in her tight blue dress.

"What is so important as to interrupt my entertainment?" The Prince turned angry eyes on his lieutenant.

"An incident at Santo Spirito."

At the very mention of the name, the Prince stilled.

Cassita.

"What kind of incident?"

"Perhaps we should move this conversation somewhere private."

Angrily, the Prince stormed toward the exit of the club, pushing beings and humans aside as he crossed the dance floor. He threw the door open and stepped into the alley. It was raining.

Lorenzo followed, closing the door carefully behind him.

"We need privacy," he said to the security guard.

The guard nodded and moved to the far end of the alley.

"What happened?" The Prince placed his hands on his hips, his voice low.

"A feral appeared in Santo Spirito. It killed an Interpol agent."

The Prince pressed his lips together. "Witnesses?"

"I'm told there are a few. Fortunately for us, the agent was not in uniform."

"Other casualties?"

"Just the feral. Ibarra and Aoibhe killed it and gathered a few young-lings to help them remove the corpses and attend to the scene."

"What about the border patrols?"

Lorenzo shook his head. "No one reported a breach."

The Prince scowled. "Double the border patrols immediately and call a meeting of the Consilium after sunrise."

"The local police received reports by telephone. Officers are at the scene, but our contact has delayed the face-to-face questioning."

"Exactly what was reported?"

"Witnesses saw a man dressed in black threatening a woman. She escaped into one of the apartment buildings. Then the man attacked an-other man, killing him. There were reports about Ibarra and Aoibhe, but those reports have mysteriously disappeared."

Lorenzo smiled.

The Prince took a moment to process the report. "The woman was threatened by the feral?"

"So I've inferred."

The Prince's eyebrows knitted together. "Why isn't she dead?"

"Witnesses claimed it didn't approach her. She must have been wear-ing a talisman."

The Prince rubbed at his chin thoughtfully. "Do we have names for these witnesses?"

"Yes."

"We cannot erase the event without arousing more suspicion. Have our contact see to the interviews personally. Remind him to check for cameras or telephones that might have taken photographs. He can amend the reports, if need be."

Lorenzo bowed. "Yes, my lord. And the woman?"

The Prince forced himself not to react. "If she's wearing a talisman, no one will be able to approach her. I'll investigate the matter personally."

The lieutenant gazed at him curiously.

"What about the dead agent?"

"Aoibhe has probably burned the corpse by now. Tell our contact to focus everyone's attention on the missing person investigation that will no doubt ensue and to plant evidence that links the scene to organized crime. That's plausible enough. The witness reports and physical evidence should support a knife attack, rather than a feeding. If an unruly witness were to disappear . . ." He gave Lorenzo a meaningful look.

"And the other woman?"

"What other woman?"

"The woman you left in the club." Lorenzo gestured toward the door. The Prince startled, for he'd forgotten her.

"Find out her name and address and ask one of the guards to escort her home. She is not to be touched by anyone."

"As you wish."

The Prince dismissed his lieutenant and instructed the security guard to return to his post. Then he ran in the direction of Santo Spirito, as if the very forces of hell were chasing him.

Chapter Sixteen

In the Prince's experience, coincidences were rare. That was why he flew with great speed to Jane's building.

It was possible another woman had evaded the feral because of a talisman. It was possible a policeman other than the one he'd seen following her had been killed.

He wanted to ensure she was safe, although he took great care to conceal his movements. He didn't want to draw more attention to her and he certainly didn't want it known that some relics had no effect on him.

Maximilian and his allies would have declared the Prince's tactics paranoid and unnecessary. But there was a reason why his coven had lasted so long. There was a reason why his principality was safe, while others around the world were threatened or even destroyed. He kept his secrets secret.

What humans did not know about, they couldn't fight. Certainly they couldn't recruit the coven's enemies without knowledge of the coven itself.

There'd been a time when he and his kind were well-known in Europe and had not lived in secret. Then came the Black Death, poisoning their food supply. His brethren had shrunk in numbers, some being destroyed in their hungry, weakened state while others quit Europe for unblighted parts of the world.

Then the Curia had emerged. It was a mysterious group, formed by human beings, but wielding limited supernatural powers. It had tried to eradicate his kind and had waged a war against them. When the war ended, neither side won, although both claimed victory. The uneasy truce that emerged between the European covens and the Curia required the covens to live underground, in shadowy, secret societies. Any public exposure was perilous.

With the rise of the Enlightenment and the triumph of science over the supernatural, first-person accounts of encounters with his kind became stories, and the stories eventually became myths. The Curia intervened to protect the public from what lay hidden in their midst only when provoked. The covens did their best not to provoke it by attracting attention.

Thus, the Prince jealously guarded his city, even to the point of killing to secure it. The feral and its witnesses threatened his world, as did whoever escaped the feral.

And if it were Cassita . . .

He surveyed the piazza from the building next to hers.

He could have chosen a better vantage point, that of the church nearby. But despite his ability to walk on holy ground, he couldn't do so unscathed. He tended to avoid the pain, unless it accompanied his daily triumphal climb to the top of Brunelleschi's dome. And he only visited the dome before the sun set and his brethren awoke.

From his vantage point, he could see the police. They'd cordoned off an area in front of Jane's building, erecting tents to stave off the rain. He saw one of the officers wheel a black Vespa toward the tent. The Vespa looked familiar.

Keeping to the shadows, he leapt to the ground at the back and walked to Raven's building. He unlocked the back door and swept inside, out of the rain. The stairwell was illuminated but empty.

Brushing the rain from his blond hair and face, he held his breath. The woman in the apartment next to Jane's had cancer. He'd smelled the stench before and it was most unpleasant. He didn't relish inhaling it again.

As he gazed at the staircase, he contemplated cutting off the electricity to Jane's apartment.

Truthfully, he both wanted and did not want to speak with her.

He wanted to shake some sense into her and force her to leave the city. But he also wanted to ascertain that she was safe and that she hadn't volunteered any information to the police. These goals would be difficult to achieve without speaking with her and, he admitted ruefully, frightening her.

When he'd saved her life that night, over a week before, he had no idea his very existence would change—that he would be forced to come to her aid again and again.

She needed to leave the city. For her own safety and for the security of his principality, she needed to flee Florence and never return.

Within minutes, he'd cut off the electricity to her apartment and unlocked her door, slipping inside.

He moved through the kitchen, purposefully making a few muted sounds. He wanted to announce his arrival, but softly, so as not to frighten her. By what he could hear of her heartbeat and breathing, he knew she was awake.

As he walked toward the bedroom, she began moving.

"Are you injured?" he whispered in Italian.

He knew she wasn't. He could smell her blood, of course, but the scent was muted. She didn't have any wounds and there was no indication of tears, either.

His Cassita had not cried. He took pride in the fact.

He paused for a moment, listening to her struggle to breathe as quietly as possible. But to no avail.

He entered her room.

Just as his foot crossed the threshold, she leapt from behind the door, swinging something in the direction of his kneecaps.

He jumped, evading the object.

She swore as she swung in vain, pitching forward on unsteady feet.

When he landed, he pulled what turned out to be her cane away from her, breaking it in half with a loud, angry crack. He threw the two pieces across the room, ignoring the sound of them striking the wall. Then he pulled her against his body, so they were chest to chest.

For a moment he stared. Having her in his arms provided a tangible distraction, as did her large, unseeing green eyes.

"Let me go!" She struggled, pushing against his shoulders.

"I came to see if you were hurt. Clearly you aren't."

"I said, let go!" she shrieked, pushing and kicking at him with all her strength.

With a loud curse, he held her more tightly, lifting her off her feet.

Now they were close, very close. He could feel her breath on his face and if he moved a few inches, her lips would be his.

Instinctively, he moved toward her mouth.

"You came back," she managed to say, breathing roughly.

"Yes, Jane."

"You're hurting me."

The Prince paused, eyeing her attractive mouth.

He placed her on her feet and loosened his grip, but did not let go. His arms encircled her, pressing their bodies together from shoulder to thigh.

He brushed the hair from her face.

She turned her head. "Don't touch me."

Now he released her.

She tried to get as far away from him as possible. Disoriented in the darkness, she tripped and fell.

The Prince watched in horror as her forehead caught on the metal frame of the bed. The tang of her blood sliced through the air.

She cried out in pain.

He was at her side in an instant, crouching beside her. "Let me see."

Raven didn't answer, holding her hand to her wound.

He pried her fingers away and swore.

"Don't move."

He withdrew a handkerchief from his pocket and walked to the bathroom, where he soaked it in cold water. When he returned, she was still sitting on the floor, stunned.

"This should help." He placed the cloth to her forehead.

She winced from the cold.

"I hit my head."

"Yes, I see."

"Not all of us can see in the dark, you know." She glared in his direction.

"I'm beginning to realize that."

He found himself inhaling her scent. It wasn't particularly enticing. Her own sweet vintage was muddled with the blood of the old ones he'd transfused. He'd never found their scent attractive.

"You'll heal more quickly than usual, but you'll have a wound tomorrow."

"Why will I heal more quickly?"

He pressed his lips together. "You have larger problems to worry about."

"My health is a pretty large problem. Tell me why I'll heal quickly."

"Leave the city and I'll tell you."

He lifted the handkerchief in order to inspect the gash and shook his head.

Her heart rate had slowed somewhat and her breathing evened out, but she still wore the scent of fear.

There were dark circles below her eyes. She looked exhausted.

"I didn't mean for this to happen," he said softly.

"I'll be fine." She tried to push his hand away, but he resisted, pressing the cloth to her wound.

"It may scar."

"There goes my chance at Miss America."

"What?"

She sighed. "Never mind."

"You confound me," he whispered, more to himself than to her.

Lightly, he brought his other hand to her face and traced the ridge of her cheekbone.

Raven was surprised at how comforting his touch was. She rationalized she was feeling shaky after hitting her head and that there wasn't anything special about how he was touching her. He could have been anyone—any Good Samaritan who came to her aid.

Abruptly, he helped her to her feet and directed her toward the bed. When she was seated, he positioned her so she was holding the handkerchief to her wound.

"Something happened in the piazza this evening. Did you see it?" He tried to sound casual.

She shuddered. "Yes."

"Were you afraid?"

Her heart skipped a beat, providing him with an affirmative answer.

"Are you going to kill me?" she whispered.

The edges of his lips turned up.

"If I wanted to kill you, you'd be dead by now. I wouldn't have bothered to lend you the relic. Or my handkerchief, which you can keep."

Raven removed the cloth from her head and turned it over in her hands. She couldn't see it but she could feel it. It felt like linen.

She placed it back on her wound.

"The man who killed the other man, is he who you warned me about?"

"It wasn't a man." The Prince's response was swift. "And no, I hadn't expected one of those creatures to enter my city."

"Your city?"

"The city," he amended quickly.

"If it wasn't a man, what was it?"

"We call them ferals. As you saw, they're dangerous."

"Are there more?"

"Yes, but we keep them outside the city. Somehow that one breached the border."

"But he wasn't what you were warning me about."

The Prince clenched his teeth. "No."

Adrenaline spiked in her system. He could smell it and hear the way her heart rate increased.

"He was a cannibal," she managed to say.

"In a manner of speaking."

"He saw me first. Why didn't he attack?"

The Prince frowned. "I should have thought it would be obvious. It's because of what you're wearing around your neck."

Raven removed the handkerchief from her forehead. "Bullshit."

"Ignorance," he rejoined, sounding cross. "You modern people live in your own version of the Dark Ages, dismissing anything you can't understand. If the relic didn't stop him, what the hell did?"

Raven shut her mouth abruptly, not knowing what to say.

The Prince relaxed his posture and lowered his voice. "Are you in pain?"

"I'm fine."

"Hardly. You're in danger and the danger is real. Tonight you watched a feral feed but you didn't dissolve into hysterics." His tone bore the merest hint of admiration. "I thought you lacked an appreciation for the true danger you are facing. Now I know that isn't true. I'm beginning to think you may have courage."

She shifted, picking up a pillow and hugging it to her chest.

"Why are you here?"

His smile faded.

"As I said, I came to see if you were all right."

"Why?"

"Does it matter?" His tone cooled.

"Why do you keep cutting off my electricity?"

"Why don't you do as you're told and leave the city?" he snapped.

"You gave me two weeks. I was hoping you'd keep your word."

"That was before a policeman was killed by a feral in front of your building. How dangerous do things have to be before you decide to leave?"

Now he'd lost his temper.

He turned his back on her and walked toward the door.

"It's likely he was the same man who has been following you since yesterday, but I can't say for sure."

Raven hugged the pillow more tightly. "He saw the man yelling at me. He came to help."

"Policemen tend to do that." The Prince sniffed.

She pointed a contemptuous look in his general direction. "You don't care, do you? You don't care that he died trying to protect me."

"No, I don't. His protection was unnecessary. I was protecting you, through the relic."

"Why?"

"Why, indeed?" he muttered to himself.

"There has to be a reason." She turned toward the window, which was shuttered. "I don't have any money. I don't have anything of value. What do you want?"

Several answers sprang to the Prince's mind. But he was not about to entertain them. Or confess them.

He moved toward the bed and adopted a lighter tone.

"Perhaps I'm captivated by those green eyes of yours."

Raven blinked in the darkness. "Now I know you're lying. Why don't you tell me who you are and what you really want?"

The Prince's gaze focused on her so sharply, she almost felt it.

"I want you to leave the city."

"You seem to know a lot about what goes on in Florence. Something happened to me last week. I lost my memory and—things changed."

"I know that." His voice was low.

"Tell me what happened." She put the pillow aside and moved to the edge of the bed. "Please."

He ground his teeth together. "No."

"I have a right to know. You have to tell me." Her expression twisted his insides.

"Promise me you'll leave the city and I'll tell you everything you wish to know."

She sat back on her knees. "If I have the relic and it seems to work, why would I need to leave?"

"Are you mad?" he growled.

"Is the man who attacked the policeman the one who killed the others?"

The Prince froze. "What others?"

"*La Nazione* reported that several bodies were found downriver."

His eyes narrowed. "When?"

"It was reported yesterday, but I haven't had a chance to read the article."

He swept away from her to the far side of the room, his mind spinning. He was unaware of the bodies and his anger at being surprised was almost boundless.

She heard him move and shifted to the side of the bed.

"Why won't you go to the police? Interpol is here, investigating the Uffizi robbery. Why not turn these others over to the police?"

"Because I can't."

"Why not?"

"Don't presume to give advice about things you don't understand!"

Undeterred by his temper, Raven continued.

"You won't turn them in, but you'd go against the others to protect me? Why should I believe you?"

"You don't have to believe me." His voice lowered into a growl. "Just leave the city."

"You gave me the relic to help me. You warned me about the others. Tonight, you heard about the feral and came to see if I was all right. Obviously you don't want me to get hurt. If you're powerful enough to know what's going on in the city, you must be powerful enough to help me.

"Please don't make me leave," she whispered. "This is the only place I've ever been happy."

For a moment he was silent. He closed his eyes and began rubbing his forehead.

At length, he spoke.

"A long time ago, I came here in search of happiness."

"Did you find it?"

"No."

"I did." Raven's tone bespoke her truthfulness. "I left the U.S. to start a new life. If you send me back, I'll have nothing."

The Prince watched her in the darkness—her uplifted face with the creamy skin and perfect features, her long black hair. She was beautiful, she was intelligent, and she was brave. Something akin to admiration began to grow and warm in his chest.

He shook his head. He hadn't come to her home in order to admire her. Any connection to her could only lead to darkness.

He changed the subject abruptly. "Do you know the story of Cupid and Psyche?"

"What does that have to do with anything?" There was an edge to her voice.

"Learn from Psyche's mistake and do what I tell you."

"So you're Cupid?"

He stepped closer and dropped his voice to just above a whisper. "I am the monster, hiding in the darkness."

"I doubt that a monster would hand out religious artifacts to damsels in distress."

"In case you haven't noticed, I'm not exactly 'handing them out.' I gave you money. Use it to go back to America."

"It's in a shoe box in my closet. I don't want it."

"You'll need it."

She lifted her hands. "All of this must have a perfectly reasonable explanation. The man who killed the other man was disturbed. It isn't kind to refer to him as *feral*. And you and the others are part of a crime ring. Obviously." There was more than a note of hope in her voice.

"Your denial is amusing, but it won't change reality." He crossed his arms in front of his chest.

"I'm grateful for your help. I don't know why the man was upset by the cross I was wearing, but I'm glad he was. He could have killed me. But you're mistaken about the danger. I promise, I'm no one special. I work at the gallery, I go out with my friends, I draw and I paint. I don't know state secrets and I don't have access to the security of the gallery. I'm just a boring, average postdoctoral research associate. That's all."

"I disagree. But I've been here too long already. If tonight's events won't convince you to leave, there's little else I can do. I've warned you twice. What happens next is your responsibility." His voice was cold.

"I won't leave the city."

His expression grew fierce.

"Even if it costs you your life?"

Raven faced him stubbornly. "It won't come to that."

"Very well."

The Prince cursed, before lifting both hands, holding them out in front of him, palms up.

"*Innocens ego sum a sanguine.*"

He dropped his hands and walked to the door. "When you come to beg for my help, I will remind you of this moment. I'll demand something of you. And you'll give it to me."

"I won't come to you and I certainly won't beg." She sounded contemptuous.

He returned to stand next to the bed.

"Yes, you will."

He stroked the curve of her cheek with the back of his hand. "You have no idea what you've done."

The Prince indulged himself in the feel of her skin and the beauty of her eyes.

When the lights came back on, Raven was alone.

Chapter Seventeen

Beneath the city of Florence lay a labyrinth of tunnels, secret passages, and catacombs. The tunnels were used by the citizens of the underworld, especially in daylight when they could not travel aboveground.

The focal point of the tunnels was the great hall below the Palazzo Riccardi, which was used for Consilium meetings and other formal events of state. Its stone walls were hung with tapestries and panels illustrating the history of the city. Several suits of armor along with various swords and weapons were also displayed.

The room was dark. The underworld wasn't wired with electricity and so torches burned in wall sconces, while elaborate iron candelabras illuminated the cavernous space. Shadows flickered across the faces of the beings who'd assembled.

Interestingly enough, the tunnels were noticeably absent of rats.

"This meeting of the Consilium will come to order." Lorenzo thumped a tall staff, which boasted a carved gold lily on its top.

At his announcement, the other five Consilium members came forward and sat in tall wooden chairs that were upholstered with red velvet. The seats were arranged in sets of three, facing the front on either side of a central aisle that featured a long, red velvet runner.

Moments later, the Prince entered the hall through its large double doors, his black velvet robe billowing behind him. He strode up the aisle to a large gold throne that stood on a raised platform.

He did not look pleased.

While the Consilium members wore formal clothes in the style of the Renaissance, capped with red velvet cloaks, the Prince was dressed in modern clothing, with the exception of his robe. As always, he wore black.

The council members stood as soon as he entered and, when he'd taken his place, they bowed. He acknowledged them impatiently, waving at them to be seated before turning to his lieutenant.

"Clear the gallery. Offer my apologies to the citizens and see that they are fed."

Lorenzo bowed again, trying to hide his displeasure. He quickly directed the sentries to escort the citizens from the hall. Then he whispered instructions to Gregor, the Prince's assistant, with respect to the feeding.

It was customary to have humans held in reserve during council meetings, in case someone grew hungry.

(It appeared the Consilium members would have to forgo their catering on this occasion.)

The Prince regarded the council members with a look of cold detachment, his piercing gray eyes moving from face to face.

The members were seated in order of rank. Lorenzo sat in the place of honor at his right. Niccolò, a famous Florentine who'd been a chancellor of the city when he was human, sat next to Lorenzo. Aoibhe was seated to Niccolò's right.

Across the aisle and to the Prince's left, sat Maximilian, Pierre, and Ibarra.

"There are a number of important matters that must be addressed." The Prince's tone was brisk. "Regular business will be tabled until our next meeting.

"Aoibhe." The Prince's eyes met hers and she stood.

"Yes, my lord."

"Tell me about the feral."

Aoibhe's brown eyes slid to Ibarra's and a look passed between them.

"Last night Ibarra and I happened upon a feral in Santo Spirito."

Her colleagues remained quiet, despite her troubling announcement, for the news had already reached their ears.

"For the benefit of the council members, please tell us what you saw." The Prince focused his gaze on Ibarra, his expression harsh.

"The feral killed a human in the piazza. When we approached, it attacked. I beheaded it and we took the body and that of the human outside the city to be burned."

"Pierre." The Prince turned his gaze to the Consilium member in charge of human intelligence.

The Frenchman stood and bowed. "Yes, my prince."

"What of the police?"

"The dead human was an Interpol agent who was doing surveillance on a woman in Santo Spirito. I'm told the woman is being watched in connection with a theft at the Uffizi."

At this the Consilium members murmured among themselves.

"And?" the Prince prompted.

"The investigation is now focusing on organized crime, following our suggestion that the policeman was knifed in the piazza and his body taken. The police are planning to interview the woman to see if she has any information in connection with the agent's disappearance."

The Prince carefully controlled his reaction. "Remove the woman from the police records and implicate the Russians. They've grown arrogant and fat in recent years. It will be amusing to see them scrambling. A war between the Mafia and the Russians will distract the police from these concerns."

"What of the human witnesses?"

"All have been attended to, my lord. The record consistently reflects reports of a knife attack. Those who resisted mind control have been dealt with."

"Are you sure?"

Pierre looked confused. "Of course, my lord."

"There's no room for error," he warned.

"Certainly not, my lord."

"It's clear this trouble could have been prevented had the feral not entered the city." The Prince glared at Ibarra before returning his attention to Pierre.

"Am I to understand that the feral Aoibhe disposed of is the same one you saw the other night?"

"I cannot say, my lord. Certainly there haven't been any other reports of ferals in the area and no other unexplained killings."

The Prince lifted his eyebrows. "None? The newspaper is reporting that several bodies were found by the river. What of that?"

Pierre's blue eyes went wide.

"Several bodies?" he repeated.

The Prince nodded curtly.

"I'm sorry, my lord. I know of no such finding. I will speak with our contacts as soon as possible and discover what is known."

"A sad state of affairs when you don't know what's going on with the police, Pierre."

"The matter will be rectified immediately and our police informant will be dealt with." Pierre bowed low and withdrew to his seat.

"What of my lieutenant? Lorenzo, did you know about the bodies?"

Lorenzo stood, adopting a chastened posture. "No, my prince."

The Prince huffed in frustration.

"Am I to dissolve the council in view of these failures?"

The council members shifted uneasily in their chairs.

He turned his attention to the head of security. "Ibarra, what has been done to locate the feral Pierre saw?"

The Basque stood, his expression tight.

"We increased the number of patrols. We've also organized searches of the city and the catacombs. The feral has not been found, which leads me to believe that the one we disposed of is the one Pierre saw."

"A convenient conclusion. What of our borders?"

"I've spoken with all those on duty last night and there were no sightings of ferals nor was there evidence of any breach. The feral must have been hiding within the city. Perhaps the bodies of which you spoke belonged to him."

"Perhaps." The Prince's expression shifted and he glared. "As a Consilium, you've all grown lax."

He turned his attention back to Ibarra.

"Our borders were breached by the Venetians, under your predecessor. His ashes are now fertilizing an obliging field. Now the border has been breached by at least one feral, and your patrols knew nothing of it."

Ibarra curled his hands into fists. "With respect, that's a hasty conclusion, my lord. We don't know the feral came through the border. With a full investigation, I can—"

"You can do nothing," the Prince snapped. "You're relieved of your duty and of your position on the Consilium."

The other council members began murmuring and looking at one another.

"Silence," he hissed. "Our survival requires security. Because of Ibarra's failure, our city is threatened. Niccolò will assume control of the borders and the patrols, along with his other duties as head of intelligence, effective immediately."

At this, the Florentine stood and the Prince addressed him.

"I want the patrols increased, I want their schedule varied, and I want daily reports. See to it I am not disappointed."

Niccolò bowed. "Yes, Prince."

The ruler continued barking out instructions.

"Maximilian, redouble your efforts at training the younglings. Aoibhe, see that more human beings are transformed so as to expand our numbers.

"And I expect a full investigation of those bodies, Pierre." The Prince jerked his chin in his direction.

"You would replace me because of one feral?" Ibarra took a step closer to the Prince. "It's possible it's been in the city for decades. It's possible it's one of our own gone mad."

"So you recognized it?" the Prince mocked.

Ibarra didn't answer, his face a mask of fury.

"It wasn't one of ours," Aoibhe answered quickly. "It was an older feral. I can't imagine it was in the city long. We'd have had more than several bodies piling up."

Ibarra cursed Aoibhe in Basque, using extremely derogatory terms.

"Enough!" the Prince growled. "Ibarra of the Euskaldunak, you are hereby banished from the city of Florence.

"Aoibhe and Niccolò, escort Ibarra from the council chambers and remain with him until sunset. Take a detachment of guards with you and escort him to the border. If he resists, kill him."

The Prince dismissed them with a wave of his hand and turned toward Lorenzo.

"See that the banishment is publicized among the citizens and that it is strictly adhered to."

Niccolò and Aoibhe exchanged a look and moved to flank Ibarra.

"There was no breach." Ibarra spoke through his teeth. "I would have heard of it. It would have been reported."

The Prince didn't bother looking in his direction. "If you return, you will be executed."

Ibarra cursed. "Our borders are sound. Our patrols our vigilant; I trained them myself. If the feral came from outside, someone must have helped it enter the city."

"That's preposterous," said Aoibhe. "Who would do such a thing?"

Ibarra gave her a hard look. "The Venetian informer. We were never able to discover who sold the schematics of our old security systems. He must still be in the city, trying to wreak havoc. How else was the feral able to slip past our patrols?"

"An expedient excuse," Lorenzo commented. "Can you produce evidence of this?"

"No, but I will."

The Prince lifted his hand and all grew silent.

"Ibarra, you've had two years to find the traitor. You investigated everyone who knew of the weakness in our security systems and yet you were unable to discover which of them betrayed us. I have no confidence in your ability to discover the traitor now. You have failed in your duties and are lucky to be leaving the principality with your head. Get out of my sight."

The Prince nodded at Niccolò and Aoibhe, who began escorting Ibarra to the door.

Ibarra cursed as he was led away, shouting his displeasure at the Prince and the Consilium.

When he was halfway down the aisle, he flew to the nearest wall and tore a sword from its hooks. Brandishing it with both hands, he sprinted toward the throne.

In an instant, the Prince was on his feet.

"Take one more step and it will be your last."

Ibarra ignored the old one's warning and ran toward him, lifting the sword.

Lorenzo retrieved a matching sword from a nearby suit of armor and tossed it toward the Prince.

He caught it and tore the robe from his shoulders, lifting the sword high just as Ibarra lashed at his head.

The clash of metal against metal echoed in the hall as the two supernatural beings did battle.

The Prince had the advantage as he stood above Ibarra on the platform. But he advanced down the stairs, striking blow after blow.

Ibarra was strong, but clearly no match for the Prince. Again and again he lunged, looking for an opening, while the Prince easily deflected every thrust.

At once Ibarra swung at the Prince's legs and the Prince jumped, somersaulting over his back. Before Ibarra knew what was happening, the Prince slashed at his head, the sword whistling as it sliced through the air.

Ibarra's head took flight from his shoulders and rolled across the floor. It came to rest at Aoibhe's feet.

She sighed as she looked down into her recent lover's eyes.

The Prince lifted his bloody sword, so that all could see it, and drove it deep into the stone at his feet.

"Let this be a sign to traitors."

He returned to the platform and retrieved his robe, wiping his hands with it before tossing it away in contempt.

"Lorenzo, take the traitor's head and display it on a spike next to the sword. Parade the citizens in to look at it. Maximilian, you and Pierre take the body outside the city and burn it."

The Prince made eye contact with each of the remaining council members.

"The next one who betrays me will not receive so swift a death."

Chapter Eighteen

Raven believed in science, the testimony of the senses, the power of human reason, and the veracity of her own perceptions. She did not believe in religion, sacred texts, the supernatural, or the afterlife.

And that was why she believed the intruder was a member of an organized crime faction and that the so-called feral was someone who was in mental distress and in need of help.

Three days after she gashed her forehead, the wound had healed, leaving only a pale, shiny scar. She was still struggling to formulate an adequate, scientific explanation for that fact, and for the piece of metal that was stuck in her bedroom wall like a dart in a dartboard.

She knew enough Newtonian physics to conclude that the intruder must have incredible strength if he could hurl the cane at so great a force it would pierce the plaster and stone. But to have the cane embedded several inches into the stone . . .

(Perhaps he took steroids.)

And what of his words to her, in Latin?

I am innocent of the blood.

She had no idea what he meant, but it certainly frightened her. As did her reaction to the gentle way he'd touched her face.

As she swung her legs over the side of her bed, she shivered, realizing she needed to develop a social life. If she was lonely enough to enjoy the touch of a stranger, then she must be in desperate need of human contact.

Yet, there was something about him. There was something sincere in his distress over her injury. If he was worried she'd be upset about what she'd seen in the piazza, so much so that he would come to see if she was all right, and if he was upset when she injured herself, surely he couldn't be a completely coldhearted criminal.

He praised my eyes.

Raven had been paid few compliments about her physical appearance in her life. She knew she ran the risk of attaching more importance than was prudent to the one the intruder had paid her.

Thankfully, she had a date that evening.

Bruno was Lidia DiFabio's grandson. He was about Raven's height, with dark, wavy hair and large brown eyes. He was athletic and intelligent, and Raven had nursed a secret crush on him almost from the moment they met, which was why her sister teased her.

He visited his grandmother regularly, usually for a short breakfast before work. Until the day before, he'd always been polite but detached with Raven, despite his grandmother's repeated matchmaking efforts.

When he saw Raven exit her apartment Thursday morning, he hadn't recognized her. She'd introduced herself (again) and he'd stared, openmouthed, his dark eyes raking up and down her new yellow sundress.

He'd liked what he'd seen and said so.

Moments later, she was promising to go out with him for sushi Friday night and he was kissing her cheeks, murmuring how glad he was to have finally seen her.

Raven e-mailed her sister about the surprising turn of events and had been pleased by her sister's enthusiastic response. Of course, she didn't tell Cara that Bruno's change in demeanor had been precipitated by a marked change in her own physical appearance. She didn't want to portray Bruno as shallow.

Even if he only wants to go out with me because I'm pretty now, I don't care. I deserve a little happiness.

She placed her legs on the floor and found herself cringing. Pain shot through her right foot and up her leg.

She sat back on the bed and the pain lessened to a dull ache. She was able to move her leg, even though it felt a bit stiff. Leaning over, she started massaging the tense muscles, moving down to gently manipulate her ankle.

As she took a closer look at the exposed skin of her right leg, she noticed something.

The scar that she'd had for years, ever since the accident, had returned. Oh, it was less visible than it had been before, the mark pale and shiny. But she was pretty sure it hadn't been visible the day before, or any day since she'd woken up Monday morning without it.

The realization made her stomach flip, especially when she compared the appearance with the scar on her forehead.

She wasn't delusional. She pinched her arm to prove that point.

She reached for her cell phone and quickly scrolled through the photos she'd taken of herself that week. Comparing the photos with her leg, the changes were noticeable. The scar had reappeared and her foot had begun to turn out slightly. Still, it was a far cry from what her injured leg and foot had been before.

Putting her phone aside, she placed both feet on the floor and stood. She found that she could walk without limping, but the pain flared during her first few steps.

When she looked in the mirror in the bathroom, she was surprised at what she saw. Her face was a little fuller, her hair not quite as shiny, and dark circles lay beneath her eyes.

She looked, she thought, as if she hadn't been taking care of herself. Once again, the changes from her appearance the day before were dramatic, but not so much as to return her to her previous appearance.

It was as if the physical transformation had been undone, but not completely.

She readied herself for work, showering with her favorite rose-scented soap and washing and drying her hair. She struggled into her new green sundress, finding that the linen fabric pulled across her now slightly protruding abdomen and softly padded hips.

She wondered how the dress had shrunk in her closet. She wondered how, in the space of a few hours, she'd gained enough weight to have a rounded belly.

If someone is trying to make me think I'm crazy, they're doing a hell of a good job.

At least the photographs didn't lie. She had pictures of what she looked like before she'd lost her memory, a few self-photos of what she looked like afterward, and now she took pictures of the most recent changes.

There was no doubt about it. She'd changed.

The pain in her leg could be explained by overexertion. Perhaps the exercise was catching up with her. But overexertion didn't explain the reappearance of the scar.

Raven had no scientific explanation for any of her early morning discoveries and so she ignored them, taking two pain pills with her breakfast.

As an act of contempt for superstitions in general and the intruder's superstitions in particular, she removed the relic from around her neck and placed it in her knapsack. She closed her eyes for a moment, trying to discern any noticeable change in her body or her emotions.

She opened her eyes. She felt the same as she had a moment before. However, she was unwilling to leave the relic behind, especially since every time she closed her eyes she could see the so-called feral standing a distance away from her, cursing. With dead bodies showing up near the Arno and in her piazza, she needed whatever help it could offer and so she brought the relic to work with her, hidden in her knapsack.

Raven spent the day in the archives, completing menial tasks and trying not to draw attention to herself.

Her doctor called, informing her that her blood test was inconclusive because the sample had been contaminated with at least two foreign substances of indeterminable origin. Unfortunately, the window to see if she'd been drugged was now closed. The doctor apologized on behalf of the lab, which had obviously made an egregious error in contaminating her sample, but said there was no point in repeating the test.

The X-rays, however, were another matter. The films the doctor had received obviously belonged to another patient, because they showed no evidence of the break in her leg and ankle that had occurred when she was twelve. So the doctor suggested Raven be x-rayed again.

Raven declined, citing a busy schedule. She said that she would follow up with the doctor when things at the gallery calmed down.

She didn't bother trying to explain that it was possible her injury had been spontaneously reversed. Certainly she didn't want to have her doctor examine her leg only to see that the scar, which was absent on Tuesday, was once again visible.

Given all the strange and unexplained events swirling in her head, she was grateful for the distraction work provided. She spent the afternoon compiling files on the digital database and staring from time to time at an image of *Primavera*.

She wanted to ask Professor Urbano, who'd worked on the restoration of the painting, if he'd realized that Mercury's appearance had been altered. But since, for the moment at least, she was not welcome in the restoration lab, she didn't.

She spent some time examining the images of Cupid and Venus, recalling the intruder's reference to the myth of Cupid and Psyche. According to myth, Zephyr, who hovered in the orange grove at the right-hand side of *Primavera*, had helped Psyche when she was in distress.

I am the monster, hiding in the darkness, the intruder had whispered.

She wondered idly if he was like Zephyr.

Raven was glad she'd studied Greek and Roman mythology as an undergraduate, for it helped her understand Botticelli's work. She knew, for example, that Maia and Jove were the parents of Mercury and that Atlas was his grandfather.

She knew that Chloris had been raped by Zephyr but that he'd repented of his violence and married her, renaming her Flora. Ovid, who told the story in his *Fasti*, quoted Flora as claiming she had no complaint in bed, which signified that her husband was kind to her after his former brutality.

She wondered if the intruder was like that—a man who'd engaged in acts of violence, only to regret them later and repent.

She gazed at Zephyr's face and quivered, recalling how gentle the intruder's touch had been.

Raven closed the window on her computer and quickly logged in to her e-mail account. Scrolling through a few unopened messages, she found an e-mail from Father Jack Kavanaugh.

Dear Raven,

I hope this e-mail finds you well.

I've been transferred to Rome, effective July 1st.

It's a long, Jesuitical story. The short of it is that I've had to resign my position at Covenant House in Orlando. Don't worry, I'm leaving the house in good hands and I intend to continue helping them in any way I can.

I'm hoping to visit Florence and hear about your good work at the Uffizi Gallery.

How is your sister?

How is your mother?

I remember you and your family in my prayers, praying that you all will find peace, forgiveness, and hope in the extravagance of God's love,

Fr. Jack

Raven sat back in her chair.

This was an e-mail she had not expected to receive.

She'd known Father Kavanaugh for years. He'd helped her and her sister when they were in crisis. Later, he'd helped her attend Barry University, finding scholarship money to pay for her tuition and residence. Even now, long after graduation, he was still trying to help her by praying to a god she didn't believe in.

Father Kavanaugh was a holy man. He was pious and he was good. He'd worked with Mother Teresa in Calcutta, and he'd founded orphanages and schools in Uganda.

But more than that, he was the one person in Raven's life who had never disappointed her. She knew without doubt that if she were in trouble and went to him, he would do everything in his power to help her and he would expect nothing in return.

She wondered what he'd say when he saw her altered appearance. She wondered what miraculous account he would give of her experience wearing the relic.

Although she respected him, loved him even, she was not looking forward to those conversations.

It would be some time before he was settled in Rome and able to travel. She would have to work up the courage to listen to him and not blurt out cynical, offensive words.

She sighed at the thought.

"You don't look so good."

Raven was jolted from her musings by Patrick's voice. He was standing next to her desk in the archives, wearing a concerned expression.

"Thanks a lot." She grimaced.

"I didn't mean it that way." He touched her shoulder. "Are you sick?"

She shook her head.

"Dark." He pointed to the purple smudges below her eyes. "Aren't you sleeping?"

"Not really." Her eyes moved in the direction of the archivist and back to her friend. "I can't talk about it here."

"Fair enough. I need to make some photocopies and use the scanner. I probably need help. Join me?"

"What about the archivist?"

"I'll speak to her. Hang on."

Patrick walked to the archivist's desk. Raven closed her computer windows in anticipation and logged out of her computer.

The archivist looked over at her and she offered a restrained smile.

"So what's up?" Patrick asked as they walked down the hall toward the photocopying room.

"I'm still freaked out about the mugging in Santo Spirito."

Patrick grimaced. "I don't blame you. Has there been any other trouble?"

"No. But every time I close my eyes I see it."

Patrick shook his head. "I'm beginning to think the city isn't as safe as it used to be."

"You can say that again."

They continued walking and Patrick looked down at her feet.

"Are you limping?"

"A little. My leg is stiff today."

"Do you need your cane?"

"I don't think so."

Patrick seemed suspicious. "I thought your leg was better."

"It is." Raven straightened her leg and set her teeth against the pain. "Did you ever look at the radiographs of the figure of Mercury from *Primavera*?"

"Not very closely. Why?"

"It looks like Botticelli changed Mercury's hair."

Patrick gave her a puzzled look. "Changed? How?"

"He had short blond hair in the beginning. There's a ghost underneath the figure."

"I don't remember hearing about that."

"Me, neither. That's why I saved the files to my flash drive. I wanted to look at them at home."

"Did you?"

"I expanded them on my laptop, but the quality isn't that good. Still, you can see the ghost."

Patrick whistled. "That's a pretty incredible find. How did everyone miss it?"

"I don't know. Maybe I'm looking at it wrong. I need to ask Professor Urbano."

They entered the photocopying room and closed the door behind them.

Patrick quickly set up his photocopying jobs so they could continue talking.

"How's life in the archives?"

Raven's shoulders slumped. "Not that great. Hopefully, Urbano will let me come back on Monday. He said it depended on my replacement."

"What about Vitali?"

Raven shook her head. "I was his resident gopher this week."

"I didn't think Italy had gophers."

Raven rolled her eyes.

"It does now."

❋ ❋

On the way back to the archives, Patrick and Raven climbed the steps to the second floor and entered the Botticelli room. Patrick wanted a closer look at *Primavera*.

"I can't imagine why Botticelli would change the hair. Mercury is supposed to be modeled on Lorenzo, one of the Medici. He had long brown hair." Patrick stepped closer to the painting.

"Perhaps another patron commissioned the painting, then failed to pay. That kind of thing used to happen all the time." Raven found herself gravitating to the figure of Zephyr, on the other side of the painting.

"Maybe. I doubt Botticelli would start the painting without a large deposit and a contract. I suppose he could have had a falling-out with whoever commissioned it first."

Raven nodded.

Neither of them noticed the figure of Ispettor Batelli, who stood at the entrance to the room, watching them.

Chapter Nineteen

When Raven exited the Uffizi after work, she found Bruno waiting for her, handsomely dressed in a gray suit and blue tie.

She was tired and her leg was troubling her. But she pushed everything aside and walked to him, her knapsack on her shoulder and her head held high.

Bruno greeted her with a smile.

His smile faltered as she approached.

Raven traced the scar on her forehead self-consciously before balling her hand into a fist and lowering it. Clearly he'd noticed the change in her appearance. From the looks of it, he was surprised, if not disappointed.

"Hello." He kissed each of her cheeks and motioned to her scar. "Are you all right?"

"I fell, but I'm okay. How are you?"

"Good. And your cane? Don't you need it?" His gaze traveled to her legs, fixing momentarily on her scar.

"No." She shifted her weight awkwardly.

His eyes moved to hers again. "You smell fantastic. Like roses."

"It's Jo Malone soap. My sister sends it to me."

Bruno closed his eyes and inhaled. "It's tremendous."

"How's your grandmother? I haven't seen her for a while."

He opened his eyes. "She hasn't been feeling well. She's been spending her days in bed and not eating. My mother is with her."

"I'm sorry to hear that. She's always been so kind to me. When I first moved into the apartment, she took pity on me and taught me how to cook. If there's anything I can do, let me know."

"Thank you." Bruno gave her a warm look. "What would you say to a drink over at the Gucci Museum before dinner?"

"I'd like that."

He took her hand in his and they walked across the Piazza Signoria to the Gucci Museum, which boasted an open-air bar under umbrellas. They sat on comfortable banquettes and enjoyed their Prosecco, while Raven told Bruno about her work in the restoration lab.

If Bruno continued to feel disappointed by her appearance, he kept the fact well hidden.

Yet, Raven was uneasy. His lack of regard for her previously, and the way the smile had slipped from his face when she approached, distressed her.

Of course, his reactions held far more weight since she'd admired him from afar, knowing she could never have him. To have caught his attention only to lose it would be painful. Raven subtly began to steel herself against that possibility.

Conversation between the two flowed easily and so it was hours later that they strolled the short distance to Gallery Hotel Art. Its restaurant, Fusion, served the best sushi in the city.

Although Raven had walked by the hotel on many occasions, she'd never been inside. Anticipation made her eager.

That was why she forgot that the building they were entering was the one in which Professor Emerson had sensed what he thought was a ghost.

✾ ✾

Over dinner, Bruno was charming and attentive. He didn't bore her with stories about his work—he was a banker—with Monte dei Paschi di Siena. Nor did he focus on the familiar topic of his grandmother, although he admitted she'd been trying to match them up ever since Raven moved into the building.

No, the conversation focused primarily on Raven.

Bruno asked questions and listened to the answers. He laughed when she said something funny and was gently sympathetic when she said something sad. They ordered several plates of food and shared them, while he chose a very expensive bottle of Brunello di Montalcino as an accompaniment.

In short, it was the best date Raven had ever had. But it was also the worst.

Bruno didn't ask if she wanted to see his apartment or if she wanted him to take her home and spend the night. Instead, he offered to walk with her downtown before he escorted her home.

It was a first date. Raven probably would not have spent the night with him. Even so, she took his lack of initiative as an indictment of her physical appearance.

He held her hand loosely as they wandered the city streets after dinner.

Raven meditated on how handsome and gentlemanly he was. She did not think about the slight twinges in her leg and ankle. She did not think about her temporary demotion at the Uffizi, or of the strange discovery she'd made about *Primavera*, or about ferals, mysterious intruders, or the relic that had sunk to the bottom of her knapsack.

They admired the way the Duomo was illuminated against the night sky and sat with the tourists on the front steps. They talked about the approaching summer and the special events the city planned.

When it was almost midnight, Bruno suggested he walk her home. As they entered a deserted alley, he took her knapsack from her shoulder and placed it on the ground at their feet. Then he spun her in a circle, over and over, as if they were dancing. At the other end of the alley, he pulled her into his arms.

He whispered a few words about how he'd enjoyed her company.

She responded in kind.

Bruno smiled, his eyes darting to her lips.

He leaned forward.

Raven closed her eyes.

She felt his nose brush hers. He murmured something about how her mouth was tempting.

A low chuckle sounded nearby.

Bruno retreated, looking at the opening of the alley. When he saw a large, oddly dressed man standing nearby, he placed Raven behind him.

"It isn't her mouth that tempts me." The man, who was bearlike, with long hair and a full beard, closed his eyes and sniffed.

His eyes fixed on Raven's. "Who are your masters?"

"Come on." Bruno took her hand and quickly led her away from the man and toward her knapsack, being sure to shield her from view with his body.

No sooner had he done so than the man seemed to fly over their heads and land in front of Raven, blocking their path.

Raven glanced at the knapsack, realizing he'd cut her off from it.

Her eyes met his.

"Oh, did you want what's in that bag?" He jerked his thumb over his shoulder. "Then come and get it."

When Bruno tried to pull her away, the man came a step closer.

"I asked a question." He glared at Raven, his voice a low rumble. "You have three bloods in you. Name your masters."

"I don't have a master."

He smiled, exposing yellowed, jagged teeth. "That's what I thought. No one would be mad enough to master you and allow you to have a talisman."

As soon as the words left his lips, he leapt forward.

Bruno saw him move and pushed Raven out of the way.

She toppled over and fell on her bottom.

The man grabbed Bruno by his suit jacket and hurled him through the air. A sickening sound filled the alley as he made contact with the stone wall and slid down. Blood began to pour from a wound on the side of his head.

Forgetting the relic entirely, Raven ran to him. "Bruno, get up."

She snaked her arm around his waist and managed to pull him to his feet.

He was unsteady and slumped against her. Blood smeared the thin strap of her sundress and the skin of her shoulder.

The man took two long steps toward them and grabbed Bruno again, shoving him against the wall. This time Bruno fell and lay unmoving.

"I'm going to get help." Raven wasn't sure Bruno could hear her.

She tried to run in the direction of her knapsack, but once again the man blocked her. She turned quickly and fled in the opposite direction.

She'd taken only three steps when he got hold of her arm and wrenched her backward. She felt as if her arm was being pulled out of its socket and howled in pain.

"Now you're mine." The man spun her around. "I'm hungry."

Raven reached out her uninjured arm and began pushing against his chest, trying to get free.

"You seem incapable of following the rules these days, Max. Are you really hunting someone else's pet?"

Raven turned and saw a beautiful red-haired woman standing nearby, maintaining her distance from the knapsack.

Her appearance must have surprised the man because he released Raven's arm.

She stumbled, trying to put distance between them. When she regained her balance, she began running as fast as she could, away from the man and woman.

"Don't interfere!" Max snarled at the redhead.

She stood in front of him.

"As a Consilium member, I'm bound to enforce the laws. As are you. I kept your secret about what happened at Teatro. I'll be damned if I keep this one."

Max grabbed at the woman, but she was too fast. She caught hold of the side of one of the buildings and began climbing until she was out of sight.

With a curse, Max ran after his prey.

It wasn't much but the short delay gave Raven a few precious seconds to disappear into another alley, eluding her pursuer. She ran toward the Duomo, ignoring the shooting pain in her leg and ankle.

The sounds of growls and heavy footfalls filled her ears, as the large man approached with great speed.

She slipped into a dark corner by the side entrance to the Duomo. Hiding in the darkness, she glanced around.

The man had stopped a few feet away. He was glaring in her direction. Somehow, the shadows did not shield her from view.

She saw movement in the distance. The red-haired woman descended from one of the buildings behind him, dropping almost elegantly to the ground.

Raven stared, mesmerized by the couple's strength and appearance. She felt as if she'd seen them before, perhaps in a dream.

"Come away from there, you bitch!" the man bellowed.

Raven pressed herself into a corner, trying to fade out of sight. But still, the couple continued to stare in her direction.

"Oh, this is delightful. You've lost her now, Max." The red-haired woman clapped. She lifted her hand as if saluting Raven and addressed her. "Your masters, whoever they are, taught you well. Although I'm wondering why they let you near a talisman. What say you, Max? Has she been a naughty little pet?"

Raven's courage was bolstered by what she believed was their repeated reference to the relic, but she was confused by the mention of masters. A cold finger of fear traced the length of her spine. She wondered if the couple were connected with a human trafficking ring. She wondered if she resembled someone they kept as a slave.

Raven scanned the area for pedestrians, hoping she could find someone to help her.

No one came. She wasn't visible to those congregated at the front of the Duomo. She didn't even have her cell phone, which was still in her knapsack.

"Tell your masters this rogue is called Maximilian. They'll know how to deal with him." The woman laughed again.

Without turning around, Max lifted his bearlike paw and swung in the direction of the woman's head.

She ducked.

While bent double, she struck him with her fist, plowing it into his kidneys.

"You're lucky her masters aren't about, Max. She's owned by two old ones; I can smell their age from here."

Max bellowed in anger and moved toward the woman, as if he were going to tackle her.

At that moment, sirens sounded in the distance.

The man cursed Raven and spat before fleeing to a nearby building. He scaled it quickly, moving to the roof and out of sight.

The woman lifted her skirts and ran around to the back of the Duomo, disappearing from view.

Raven leaned back against the exterior wall of the Duomo, breathing a sigh of relief. The sirens offered hope that help was on its way.

She hoped Bruno was still alive. She exited the shadows and made her way toward the alley.

Suddenly a large Triumph motorcycle approached from the front of the Duomo, skidding to a stop in a wide arc and cutting her off.

"Get on!" the driver shouted to her, in Italian.

Chapter Twenty

The motorcyclist was wearing a black leather jacket, black jeans, and black boots. His helmet, which had an opaque shield, was also black.

Raven wondered if he were a policeman, assigned to follow her.

She didn't bother to find out. Breaking into a run, she skirted him in order to return to Bruno.

"We have to go. Now!" the driver shouted.

Raven increased her speed, fighting the pain in her leg, as she heard sirens approach.

When she came to the alley, she saw Bruno lying on the ground. She could see blood on his face and a dark pool on the cobblestones beneath his head. He wasn't moving.

A police car turned into the alley several feet away, followed closely by an ambulance.

She was going to run to him, when an arm curled around her waist and pulled her back. The motorcyclist clutched her to his side, kicking and screaming, as he pulled away.

The driver was strong, but even so, it was nearly impossible to drive with one hand and hold a squirming woman with the other. He came to a halt near the Duomo.

"If you're caught by the police, they'll arrest you," he hissed behind his helmet. "Is that what you want?"

"I didn't do anything! A man attacked us."

"They won't believe you. And the boy's blood is on your clothes." The motorcyclist pointed to her dress.

"I have to help him." She struggled. "I have to get my knapsack."

He gripped her arms, his gloved fingers biting into her flesh.

"Jane, *get on the bike.*"

At the sound of her former name, she stilled. She couldn't see his face from behind his helmet. Since his voice was muffled, she couldn't swear that he was the intruder.

But a policeman wouldn't want her to evade his fellow officers and, certainly, no one she knew ever called her Jane.

Before she could respond, the driver pressed a helmet over her head and tugged her to sit behind him. He pulled at her arms, but she resisted, favoring her right shoulder.

"Are you injured?" He turned in his seat to examine her.

"The man who attacked us wrenched my arm." Raven massaged her shoulder, eyes screwed shut in pain.

"I'll fix it after you're safe."

"Are you the intruder from my apartment?"

"Of course," he snapped. "Who else would help you?"

"Let me go. I have to help my friend."

"You can't help him from a jail cell."

Instantly, Raven thought of Amanda Knox.

She knew she would come to regret her decision, but, with a deep breath, she wrapped her arms around the intruder's waist.

"Hold on," he commanded.

The bike shot forward, almost toppling as it approached the Duomo and made a hard left to go around it.

The sound of a siren pierced the air as another police car, which was parked on a street nearby, began to pursue them.

Raven shut her eyes as the motorcycle wove in and around traffic, shooting through red lights and barely avoiding pedestrians.

Still the police car followed, now joined by a second one.

With a burst of speed, the motorcycle crossed one of the large vehicular bridges that spanned the Arno before darting up the winding road that led to the Piazzale Michelangelo. Trees and houses flew past them as they raced around the curves.

Raven felt sick, but the driver would not slow.

They raced past the *piazzale* and around a tight curve, losing the police cars for a moment. The motorcyclist shot into a hidden driveway and climbed another hill, putting them out of sight.

The sounds of sirens grew close and then far away, as the police cars sped past the driveway and continued along the main road.

Raven tried very hard not to throw up, swallowing down urge after urge to heave.

The driver slowed the motorcycle to a moderately quick speed, making several turns before stopping in front of a tall metal gate. He pushed a few buttons and the gate opened.

He entered the gate, which closed behind them, and drove along a paved driveway that led past trees and what appeared to be an orchard.

They came to a stop in front of a freestanding triple-bay garage.

Raven was clutching the driver so tightly, she couldn't let go. He had to pry her fingers from his jacket.

"Inside. Now." He jerked his head toward the large and palatial villa visible via the floodlights that illuminated the garden and driveway. "Ambrogio will attend to you."

The driver helped Raven from the motorcycle and removed her helmet.

"Her right arm and shoulder are injured. See to it." He addressed a man who hovered nearby.

The motorcyclist turned his back on her and rolled his machine into the garage.

"Signorina, please." The man, who Raven inferred was Ambrogio, gestured toward a stone path that led through the garden and to the back door.

Raven took one tentative step and threw up the entire contents of her dinner on Ambrogio's impeccably shined shoes and suit-clad legs.

Chapter Twenty-one

Ambrogio said not a word as Raven's vomit splashed on his legs and feet. He merely placed an arm around her waist, supporting her.

She heaved until she could do so no more.

"I'm sorry," she rasped, wiping her mouth shakily with the back of her hand.

"Signorina, come inside." His tone was calm, too calm, as if the sight of blood on her skin and the vomit was not only unsurprising, but expected.

Raven gazed at him curiously.

He was about her height, with gray hair and dark eyes. He looked as if he were in his sixties and was carefully dressed in a well-cut dark suit. Raven found something troubling about his demeanor, but she could not articulate what.

She tore her eyes from his impassive expression and looked toward the garage. "My friend Bruno is hurt. He may be dead. I have to go to him."

"Everything will be attended to." Ambrogio deftly turned her to face the villa.

"I don't have my cell phone. Or my wallet. My knapsack is in the alley, where Bruno is."

"This way, please."

Raven turned toward the garage, hoping to catch sight of the intruder. "But—"

"It would be best if you came into the house." Ambrogio interrupted her with a tone that held a warning.

With one last, vain glance, Raven allowed herself to be led on shaky legs to the back door.

She was escorted through a modern, eat-in kitchen and a large, opulent dining room to an immense central foyer. A wide wooden staircase led to the second floor, while a huge antique chandelier sparkled overhead.

But it was the artwork that captured her attention.

The walls were painted a deep red and hung with oil paintings that varied in size and composition, all encased in glass.

Raven gaped at the sight and muttered a few stunned oaths.

She'd spent years studying Renaissance art and art restoration. The collection on display was of works from that period she had never seen. Paintings by Raphael, Botticelli, Caravaggio—and something that looked surprisingly like a Michelangelo—stared at her from their ornate frames.

She lifted a trembling finger and pointed to a medium-sized painting on the far wall.

"Is that—? It can't be. Is it?" she stuttered.

"Michelangelo, yes. *Adam and Eve before the Fall.*" A gray-haired woman, wearing a smart navy sheath dress and jacket, strode across the floor.

"But Michelangelo is thought to have completed only one painting and it's in the Uffizi. An uncompleted work that may be his is in the National Gallery in London."

The woman ignored Raven's protest. "I'm Lucia."

"Raven," she murmured, crossing the floor so she could get a better look at the alleged Michelangelo.

"I thought your name was Jane. Jane Wood." Lucia followed her with a frown.

Raven kept her eyes fixed on the painting. She looked at it from the side, trying to discern the brushstrokes.

"The intruder calls me Jane, but my name is Raven."

The couple seemed taken aback by her remarks but commented no further.

Ambrogio apprised Lucia of Raven's injury. He bowed, declaring he would find out about Bruno's condition and attempt to locate her knapsack, before disappearing into the dining room.

Lucia gestured to the staircase. "Your room is upstairs."

"This painting," Raven managed to say, fixated as she was, "where did it come from?"

"It's part of Lord William's extensive collection. But the best pieces are in there."

The woman nodded toward a closed set of double doors to the left of the staircase.

Raven reluctantly tore her gaze away from the painting and stared at the closed doors.

She shook her head, as if to clear her mind.

"You said Lord William?" she whispered. "William York?"

"Of course." Once again, Lucia seemed puzzled.

"The intruder is William York?"

"I don't know anything about an intruder. The gentleman who owns this estate is Lord William York. He brought you here." Lucia took a step closer, examining Raven intently. "I will send for a doctor."

"No, I'm fine. I was just a little—motion sick." She wiped her mouth self-consciously. "Can you tell me if Lord William recently acquired something in the style of Botticelli? Such as a set of illustrations?"

"You were bleeding." Lucia ignored Raven's question, pointing at the dried blood on her shoulder and dress.

"No, it's Bruno's. My friend." Raven fought back tears. "I'm worried he's dead. I need to see him."

"Ambrogio will attend to it."

Raven stared at Lucia suspiciously, wondering why she was repeating the intruder's rote remark.

"I really need to go. If you could just call a taxi for me, I'll leave."

"It's past one o'clock. His lordship would like you to clean up and rest." Lucia's expression brooked no argument.

Raven began moving toward the front door, which was a few feet away. "I don't want to impose. You've been very kind."

"Stop." Lucia's polished demeanor dropped for a moment and an icy coldness filled her eyes. "His lordship's orders are always obeyed."

"I just want to go home," Raven whispered.

As if on cue, Ambrogio returned. He stood in front of the door, effectively blocking Raven's escape.

Her eyes moved from him to Lucia.

"You must obey his lordship." Lucia gestured in the direction of the staircase. "He has been expecting your return."

"My return? I've never been here before."

"This way, please." Once again Lucia ignored her comment. She walked toward the staircase.

Raven lifted her right foot surreptitiously, trying to figure out if she could outrun Lucia and Ambrogio and make it to the back door. Of course, it was more than likely that the intruder was outside and would come after her.

She didn't want to think about what he'd do to her if he caught her.

She forced an artificial smile and joined Lucia on the stairs. "A shower and a rest sound like a good idea. Thank you."

Lucia's frosty attitude thawed marginally as she ushered Raven upstairs. She brought Raven down a long central hall, pausing in front of a tall wooden door. "In here, please."

She opened the door.

In keeping with the rest of the house, the large bedroom boasted dark hardwood floors that were covered by elaborately woven antique carpets. A massive four-poster bed hung with wine-colored velvet curtains stood at the center of the wall to the left.

The walls were painted to match the curtains and all the other furniture in the room was dark, polished wood, with the exception of a large divan near what looked like the entrance to the bathroom en suite. The divan was covered in wine velvet and held a single gold damask cushion.

When Raven crossed the threshold, she felt a prickling at the back of her neck. Something about the room seemed familiar.

Ignoring Lucia, she walked to the bed, noting that a white Turkish cotton bathrobe had been placed at its foot, along with a pair of slippers. A blue silk slip-style nightgown rested on top of the duvet, which was covered in gold damask.

"If you sit down, I'll examine your shoulder." Lucia gestured to the divan and Raven lowered herself to its edge.

That was when she saw the painting.

On the wall opposite the door, and therefore hidden from initial view by the bed curtains, hung a large oil painting behind glass.

Raven turned to her right, craning her neck so she could see it.

Her eyes widened in shock.

Without a word, she pushed past Lucia to get a better look at the painting.

The composition was similar, almost identical, to Botticelli's *Primavera* but on a smaller scale. There were three notable differences: the figure of Flora was absent in this version, and Mercury and Zephyr featured radically different appearances than their Uffizi counterparts.

This Mercury had gray eyes and a wreath of short blond hair.

In gazing at his face, Raven immediately thought of the drawing she'd done a few days earlier. The drawing that had mysteriously disappeared after the intruder's first visit.

Then there was the figure of Zephyr, on the right-hand side of the painting.

Zephyr was clothed in blue garments, but his face and body were decidedly flesh colored, if not a bit paler than the other figures. He, too, had blond hair.

Raven glanced from Zephyr to Mercury and back again. The two figures were almost identical, except that Zephyr had paler skin and a more muscular body. There was also a refinement in his facial features that made him more beautiful than Mercury.

Whoever painted this picture had used the same model for Mercury and Zephyr. And his face was not unknown to her.

Adding to her confusion was the fact that this Mercury, with his short blond hair, largely resembled the ghost she'd found in the radiograph of *Primavera*. It was almost as if Botticelli had seen this painting, copied Mercury's appearance, then painted over it, changing his hair from blond to brown.

Raven felt light-headed.

"You should sit down." Lucia pulled her back to the divan and proceeded to prod her right arm and shoulder.

"I don't understand," Raven murmured, her eyes glued to the painting.

"The shoulder isn't dislocated. Would you like an ice pack?"

Raven peered up at Lucia, who was staring at her with a distrustful look.

Raven shook her head. She tried to remain calm, but her mind was racing.

How could William York have a reproduction of Primavera *that I've never heard of? And how could it be a reproduction if Botticelli's original Mercury matches this one?*

"I could run a hot bath or you could shower. Perhaps you should wait until you have something in your stomach. I'll bring some tea and toast."

Raven's attention was drawn back to Lucia.

"I should get out of these clothes. The smell . . ." Her voice trailed off.

"I'll be back shortly." Lucia pointed to a long, thin piece of tapestry that hung from the ceiling at the right side of the bed. "If you need me, pull the cord."

Raven nodded, her eyes moving to the painting again.

As Lucia approached the door, Raven spoke.

"You prepared this room for me?"

"His lordship wanted you to stay here, in his room." Lucia disappeared through the door.

Chapter Twenty-two

Although Raven would have liked the opportunity to examine the faux *Primavera* and the alleged Michelangelo in a leisurely fashion, she was not about to put her passion for art above her safety.

Neither was she going to spend the night in his lordship's room.

She was clever enough to realize she needed to wait until the appropriate time to make her escape. The intruder's staff was disturbingly loyal.

After her short confrontation with Lucia and Ambrogio downstairs, Raven decided her best strategy was temporary compliance. Her knapsack had been returned without her cell phone and without the relic. She elected not to press the issue, intending as she was to slip out of the house after everyone was asleep.

She was relieved to learn that Bruno was still alive. She was told he was in an induced coma at the hospital while the doctors waited for the swelling in his brain to go down. It was too early to tell if he would survive.

At this news, Raven cried. She shed her tears in the shower, where no one could hear.

Lucia had stationed herself in the bedroom while Raven used the bathroom, as if she were standing guard.

Raven scrubbed her hair and body with a finely milled Florentine soap that smelled of lemon. She'd found the soap in a decorative box on top of the vanity and recognized the scent as being that of the intruder.

Since it was the only soap on offer, she couldn't be bothered to care that it was his.

After drying her hair and changing into the silk nightgown and plush bathrobe, she dutifully drank mint leaves steeped in hot water and choked down dry toast and a couple of aspirin.

She feigned exhaustion and declared to Lucia she was going to bed. Thankfully, the housekeeper departed, bidding her good night.

Raven was sure to lock the bedroom door from the inside.

At four o'clock in the morning, she padded over to the closet. Divesting herself of the nightgown, she pulled on a green wrap dress that was exactly her size. She bent to reach for a pair of black ballet flats and stopped cold.

Sitting on the closet floor, next to several pairs of shoes and boots that looked to be of her size, were her own sneakers. She picked one up, inspecting it. They were the black Adidas sneakers she wore almost every day and had been unable to find since Gina's party.

Why would the intruder steal my sneakers?

Raven lifted the other shoe, turning it over in her hand. A couple of rust-colored spots decorated the toe.

A sick feeling came over her as she wondered whose blood was on her shoes.

She shoved the sneakers in her knapsack and slid on the ballet flats. She'd worry about the blood spatter later.

She pulled her knapsack onto her uninjured shoulder and crept down the dark hallway to the stairs.

Her plan was to escape the estate as quickly and quietly as possible. She'd walk down the hill to the Arno, even if it took hours. Then she'd go to one of the hotels, borrow a phone, and call the police.

There wasn't a telephone in her room. In fact, she hadn't seen one in the house.

No doubt Ispettor Batelli would be glad she'd located William York and that she'd seen his vast and secret art collection.

No, she hadn't seen the illustrations, but, given his other treasures, it was possible he had them. It was also possible other works in his collection were stolen. Surely this was enough information to place the police's suspicion where it belonged—on the shoulders of Lord William York.

She descended the stairs slowly, trying not to make a sound. The foyer, like the hallway above, was bathed in darkness, although lights at the front of the villa shone in through the glass of the front door.

As she reached the first floor, she noticed that the doors that led to the more extensive part of William's collection were open.

Curiosity tempted her. If she could see the stolen Botticelli illustrations with her own eyes, it would make her testimony much more valuable.

She padded lightly to the entrance.

The room was pitch-black.

She placed a hand on the door frame and leaned inside, willing her eyes to grow accustomed to the darkness.

"Psyche awakes." A low voice spoke to her from inside the room.

She startled, jumping back.

"I'm surprised it took you this long to try to make your escape." The intruder continued speaking Italian.

Raven turned, intending to run.

"I wouldn't do that if I were you."

She paused. For the moment, at least, her arm and leg were only aching. But she knew she couldn't evade him on foot.

The realization discouraged her.

"I'm already furious with you," the voice announced. "Don't anger me further. Come inside. Now."

"Why should you be furious? I'm the one who's been kidnapped." Raven clutched her knapsack more tightly.

"You're the one who's been rescued. You'd have been charged with attempted murder and be rotting in a jail cell by now if I hadn't dragged you from the scene of the crime. I should add that the police station is only a short ride away, if you'd prefer their company."

Raven huffed. She didn't want to deal with the police. It seemed an audience with the intruder was her only option at the moment.

She lifted her chin and walked through the doorway.

The room gave the impression of being large, but she couldn't see for sure. Like the foyer, it was bathed in darkness.

The intruder had the advantage of being able to see in the dark.

She took another hesitant step forward and stopped. "So you're William York?"

"In a manner of speaking."

"What manner is that?"

"It's a name I use, in certain circles. But York is where I'm from, not my surname."

"Then what's your name?"

"Do you really wish to waste time on such inconsequential questions?" He sounded impatient.

"The questions aren't inconsequential to me." She lifted her knapsack higher on her shoulder. "I want to go home, please. Will you call a taxi?"

He laughed and it was not a happy sound.

"Do you think I went to all this trouble only to send you home in a taxi? Hardly."

Raven felt her heartbeat quicken. "The policemen investigating the Uffizi robbery are already looking for you. If you let me go, kidnapping won't be added to the charges."

"Kidnapping is the least of my worries. And the least of yours."

Raven tensed. "You brought me here. You must have been planning to reveal yourself. Why won't you show me your face?"

"Oh, Psyche.

> *"'Fortune doth menace unto thee imminent danger,*
> *wherof I wish thee greatly to beware. . . . thou shalt*
> *purchase to mee great sorrow, and to thyself utter*
> *destruction. . . . Beware that ye covet not . . . to see the*
> *shape of my person, lest by your curiosity you deprive*
> *your selfe of so great and worthy estate.'"*

"You're quoting Apuleius?" She sounded incredulous.

"It seemed appropriate. Psyche wasn't satisfied with what she had and she wouldn't do what she was told."

Raven straightened her spine. "I'm not a dog to be told to sit or stay."

"Obviously," he said dryly.

"Besides, Psyche loved Cupid. She wanted to know the person she loved."

The intruder seemed to move closer. "She was a human who fell in love with a god."

"Are you saying you're a god?"

"Are you saying you're in love with me?" His tone was mocking. "I suppose you love that boy who's lying in the hospital."

Raven flinched.

"I know better than to fall in love with a man who's attracted only to beautiful women."

"If he's attracted to beautiful women, ergo he must be attracted to you."

She scowled. "That isn't funny."

"You'll discover in short order I am never humorous. Did he say you weren't beautiful?"

She squirmed. "Not in so many words. I've known him awhile and he only paid attention to me when my appearance changed."

"If he's foolish enough to think beauty is in the skin and not the heart, then I hope he dies quickly and rids the world of his stupidity."

"How dare you! He's my friend!" Raven took a blind step forward.

"Clearly you should rethink your choices in friends."

The sound of a match striking caught Raven's attention.

She turned to see a single candlestick illuminated. It was standing on a table in the center of the room, next to a large, burgundy chair.

Behind the table stood a man.

Raven stared.

When she regained her composure, she blinked a few times, her eyes struggling to become accustomed to the dim light.

The man was younger than she'd expected. She was nearing thirty and he looked to be a few years her junior. He had blond hair and gray eyes. His face was attractive, even beautiful, with full lips and a straight nose.

It was difficult to tell more about his appearance, since he was clad all in black and the room was still dark, but in size he appeared to be of medium height and build.

Raven already knew his clothes hid muscles that were deceptively stronger than their size led one to believe.

Her eyes fixed on his face.

A strange dryness filled her mouth and she struggled to swallow.

He was the mysterious man she'd sketched earlier that week. She surmised he'd stolen her sketch for that very reason.

She fanned a hand to her throat as she tried once again to swallow. The intruder's face was familiar not only because she'd drawn him. He bore more than a passing resemblance to the figures of Mercury and Zephyr in the painting upstairs.

She puzzled how that could be.

"Sit down." He spoke English with a British accent, pointing to the now vacant chair.

Something about his voice speaking English nudged her memories. She sat in the proffered chair, clutching her knapsack in her lap.

William gestured to a bottle of wine and a single glass that stood on the table. "Would you care for something to drink?"

She shook her head, lifting her eyes to examine his appearance.

He was wearing a black dress shirt with the top two buttons undone and black jeans. He'd removed his motorcycle boots and was now wearing black shoes. For some reason, he'd rolled up his shirtsleeves, exposing muscled forearms and pale skin that was lightly dusted with fine, blond hair.

In short, he was probably the most attractive man she'd ever seen.

"Shall we begin our discussion, or would you rather examine my collection?"

He gestured to the room proudly.

It was difficult to make out all the works by the light of a single candle, but Raven took her time scanning the space. There were Renaissance paintings on the walls and marble sculptures positioned at different points in the room.

On the far wall, directly in front of her, was an elaborate display of illustrations, under glass.

Raven pushed her knapsack aside and marched over.

Her suspicions were correct. He had the missing Botticelli illustrations, unashamedly arranged.

"You stole them," she whispered.

"I most certainly did not." He sniffed.

She turned to face him. "Semantics. You hired someone to do it."

He gestured to the display. "They were stolen from me years ago. I simply took them back."

"Dottor Vitali said they belonged to a Swiss family for generations before the Emersons bought them."

William's eyes narrowed. "The story is a long one and I'm not interested in telling it. Sit down."

Raven stubbornly remained where she was.

"How did your people get past the security systems?"

He made a sweeping gesture, as if to brush aside her question. "Stop wasting my time with trifles. Tell me why you aren't wearing the relic I gave you."

"I told you I don't believe in that shit."

"That 'shit,' as you so ignorantly put it, would have saved your precious boy from being injured. He's in the hospital now because of you. In addition, the police found your knapsack next to his body, making you a person of interest."

"You put a lot of faith in inanimate objects." Raven glanced over at her bag. "If I'm a person of interest, how did you get it back?"

"Bribery and threats. I should note that I'm tired of expending energy and manpower on your account."

William's tone was credible and Raven believed him, momentarily stunned into silence.

He regarded her with narrowed eyes.

"I warned you about going out after dark. You caught Maximilian's attention tonight and it was only through the miracle of Sanctuary that you escaped."

"What do you mean by Sanctuary? I didn't go inside the church."

"Where do you think the efficacy of Sanctuary comes from? From the holiness of ground. You stood on holy ground and they couldn't follow you."

"How do you know there was more than one?"

He scowled. "I make it my business to know what's going on in the city, especially concerning you."

Raven exhaled loudly. "I never asked for your help. I don't even know you."

William approached her. "We met before. You simply don't remember."

"I would have remembered," she mumbled, her cheeks beginning to warm.

William noticed her reaction and tilted his head to the side, as if he found it curious.

"Do you find me handsome?"

"I'm physically disabled, not visually impaired," she snapped.

Anger moved across William's face.

"No one ever speaks to me as you just did. No one who retains his head."

Raven's cheeks flamed again and she avoided his eyes. "I didn't mean to be rude. I was in trouble and you helped me. Thank you."

She pushed her long black hair behind her ears. "I'm sensitive about my disability."

William's gaze dropped to her right leg. "Are you in pain?"

"Just a dull ache." She flexed her foot and rotated her ankle, as if hoping the movement would soothe the discomfort.

It didn't.

"Wait a minute." She paused, examining him closely. "How did you know which of my legs was injured?"

"That is a very good question." He gave her a knowing look.

"Are you going to answer it?"

"Perhaps."

Raven was about to say something insulting but she caught herself. She tried to adopt a conciliatory expression.

"The man you mentioned, Maximilian, he asked me who my master was. He said something about blood."

"I can explain that," William said quietly. "And if you were to ask me politely why you lost your memory, I'd tell you."

He gave her an expectant look.

She took a step closer. "I'm asking politely—please tell me what happened. I've been going crazy trying to figure it out."

"As you wish." He thrust his hands in his pockets.

He paused, as if he were trying to figure out where to begin.

"A week ago, I was downtown after dark. I came upon a young woman who was being attacked by three men. They'd beaten her and dragged her into an alley in order to rape her.

"I'd come across similar scenes in the past. I always ignore them."

Raven gave him a censorious look.

He returned her gaze. "It isn't my job to rid the world of such animals.

"This was different. I knew she was good. I knew she hadn't led an easy life, but she'd led a brave one. Later, I would discover that the reason she'd been attacked was because she'd seen a homeless man being beaten and she'd intervened."

Raven felt a piercing pain at the back of her head. The pain was so great and its onset so sudden, she failed to notice the strangeness of William's claim to have moral perception.

But she would notice it later.

Raven heard the sound of quick, sure footsteps, which stopped about two feet in front of her.

"Are you all right?"

She rubbed the back of her neck. "My head aches."

"Here." He took her by the elbow and led her to the chair. "Do you want a drink?"

"No." She sat down heavily. "What happened to the girl?"

"She was dying. They'd smashed her head against a wall and caused a brain injury."

Raven fought back bile.

"Did they rape her?" she whispered.

"I killed them before that happened."

An expression of horror flashed across her face. "You killed them?"

"Yes."

"Why didn't you call the police?"

"I have no use for police."

"You didn't have to kill them." Her voice was unsteady.

William's eyes glinted a cold, steel gray. "Would you have preferred I leave them to their next victim? Another woman? Another homeless man? Or a child?"

"No, but death is final."

"In some cases." He cast her a meaningful look.

Raven could see there was more, much more, that he wasn't telling her. She felt her grasp on what she thought she knew begin to slip, like a lifeline being pulled out of her hands.

She gazed up at him, wide eyed. "How can death not be final?"

"Now is not the time for theological questions."

William paced to her left and back again. "Faced as I was with a dying woman, I had to make a decision. I could let her die, I could hasten her death, or I could save her.

"I thought about ending her suffering." He paused his pacing. "I couldn't do it. She hadn't done anything to deserve the attack. Her death would have been a tragedy.

"I brought her here, to my home. She nearly died in my arms. There wasn't time to fetch a doctor, and in any case I doubted one could help her. So I did what I could."

Raven shuddered. "And what was that?"

William turned to face the illustrations and she was treated to the sight of his back, his wide shoulders and narrow waist. He was quiet, as if he were reading the answer to her question in the drawings of Dante and Beatrice.

"I used—alchemy."

Raven stared at his back. "Like turning metal into gold?"

"Not quite. It took time and care, but she recovered. She was now my guest. I'd taken care of her. I'd washed her, clothed her, fed her." William turned toward Raven. "Do you understand guest friendship? The rules of hospitality?"

She looked down at her lap.

"Um, I think Homer describes it. Guest friendship is supposed to govern how a host treats the people in his house." She clutched the sides of the chair, her knuckles whitening. "Since you're my host, you're supposed to protect me and keep me safe."

William's eyes seemed to glow in the darkness as they fixed on hers. "Precisely."

He ran his fingers through his blond hair, pushing the strands back from his forehead.

"What happened to your other guest?" Raven fidgeted in her chair.

William put his hands back in his pockets. "I returned her to her life. Because of her head injury, her memory was affected. I was confident she wouldn't remember me or the attack and I thought that was for the best. Her body healed and her amnesia would allow her soul to heal."

"There's no such thing as souls."

"Call it a mind, then," he growled. "In any case, I hoped that, having been restored by my good deed, she'd live her life and that would be the end."

"But it wasn't," Raven prompted, still gripping the armrests of the chair.

"No. The woman began to draw attention to herself—attention that would lead to me. I tried to put a stop to it, but she persisted."

Raven blinked. "What kind of attention?"

"Going to the Palazzo Riccardi and asking for me by name."

"But that was a coincidence! I learned your name from Professor Emerson. If I hadn't been missing for a week, the police wouldn't have questioned me. And I wouldn't have gone looking for you, thinking you had something to do with the robbery."

William's eyes glinted angrily, but Raven ignored his look. "You robbed the Uffizi Gallery and stole priceless pieces of art. That's what caused this mess. Not me."

William lifted his gaze to the ceiling and proceeded to address it. "A perfect example of the young woman's absolute intractability. She will not listen; she will not heed advice."

He lifted his arms in frustration. "What shall I do? Tell me. Shall I kill her and violate the principle of guest friendship? Or shall I try to reason with her? Again."

Raven's breath caught in her chest.

He strode toward her, his face a mask of fury.

"I told you to leave the city. You refused."

"You broke into my apartment. You wouldn't tell me who you were. It would have been irrational for me to listen to you."

He leaned over her, his gray eyes piercing hers.

"I gave you something to protect you, but you called it 'shit.' Tonight you came to the attention of two people who saw me with you after you were attacked. It's only a matter of time before they realize I didn't let you die. My good deed will be exposed, along with my weakness."

"What weakness?" Raven whispered, unable to look away.

"You." He lifted his hand and brought it to her cheek.

Raven ignored the feel of his touch and glanced in the direction of the door. She felt panicked, as if she stood on the edge of a precipice. At any moment, her host could push her over.

And she was unable to run.

Her mind raced, wondering what would happen if she reached over to grab the candle. Could she risk maiming him in order to make her escape? Would she have the nerve to throw the candlestick at one of the paintings, and destroy a priceless work of art?

William's eyes took in her reaction and he dropped his hand.

"What shall I do with you, Jane?"

Her eyes met his again.

He was staring at her with a conflicted expression. "Shall I prove myself devoid of honor by killing a guest in my home?"

"You said I was your weakness." Her voice broke on the last word, her body shaking.

"You are."

She cleared her throat. "If you kill me, all your striving was for nothing."

William's eyes narrowed almost imperceptibly.

Raven lifted a finger and touched the scar on her forehead.

"You said you didn't mean for this to happen." She gave him a searching look. "You wiped away the blood with your handkerchief."

His eyes moved to her scar.

"Please," she begged, knowing that her life hung in the balance. "If your story is true, you saved me from being raped and killed. Would you kill me now, after all that?"

He closed his eyes for a moment.

"Cassita vulneratus," he whispered.

At the sound of those words, images crowded Raven's mind. She saw William's face, and the faces of the man and woman who'd chased her to the Duomo.

She saw herself in a dark alley, her hands covered in blood.

She saw herself in William's room, lying on his bed while he stood over her, a tortured expression on his face.

She heard his voice, murmuring in English and in Latin.

"'Wounded lark,'" she translated, lifting her eyes to him in wonder.

William's lips curved into a half smile. "The wounded lark with the great green eyes and the maddening, courageous soul."

Raven broke eye contact as she tried to come to terms with the images she'd just seen. Unless he was a hypnotist and a master of the power of suggestion, she was beginning to remember what had happened to her. Shockingly, the memories were consistent with the story he'd told.

She wrapped her arms around her middle, trying to manage the fear and wonder that coursed through her.

"I went to a party that night," she mused aloud. "I couldn't remember what happened after."

"You had a brain injury."

She looked up at him. "Is that why I found my sneakers in the closet upstairs?"

He nodded. "The rest of your clothes were ruined—stained with blood."

Her stomach twisted.

"The homeless man you mentioned, was that Angelo? The man who stayed by the Ponte Santa Trinita?"

"I don't know his name, but that's where we found his body."

Raven's eyes filled with tears. "He never hurt anyone. All he did was draw pictures of angels and ask people for charity."

William watched Raven's reaction, an unfamiliar emotion rising in his chest.

"From what I've inferred, you saw the homeless man being attacked and intervened. That's why they turned on you. You're noble, but lack prudence."

"What should I have done? Stood by and watched?" Her green eyes flashed.

He gestured to her knapsack. "You own a cell phone. Why didn't you use it?"

"I don't remember. Probably I thought there wasn't time to wait for the police."

"Precisely." He gave her a look that was heavy with meaning.

She swiped at her eyes. "Will my memory return?"

"I don't know." His tone was sincere. "Perhaps it's a mercy you don't remember."

She nodded absently.

After a moment, something occurred to her.

"You said earlier you could tell I was good and that's why you intervened. How can you tell someone is good just by looking at her?"

"It's a skill acquired over time, of which I have had a great deal."

"I can't be much older than you. Is it part of your alchemy?" She watched him carefully.

His posture was casual, too casual. "A kind of alchemy, perhaps. Mostly, the judgment is made based on perceptions. Your character was evident to me even as you lay dying."

Raven turned away, her stomach churning.

"What did you give me to save my life?"

William opened his mouth to answer but stopped. He noted her tense posture, her still wet eyes, and the ferocity with which she held on to his chair.

"I think you've had enough for one evening." His voice was quiet. "Go to bed. We'll continue this conversation tomorrow."

"I want to know about the alchemy. I want to know why my wound healed quickly." She gestured to her forehead.

He reached out to trace the scar, his touch featherlight.

"This is a tragedy." William's tone was heavy with meaning.

Raven heard much more than a description of her scar in his voice. From his eyes, his face, the way he caressed her, she started to believe he didn't want to hurt her.

He withdrew his hand. "I gave you something to heal your injuries, but the change in your leg is temporary. It's already beginning to wear off."

A look of horror flashed across Raven's features. "Temporary?"

"Unless the treatment is repeated," he qualified, searching her eyes.

"Will my head injury return? Will I die?" Raven's heart thumped in her chest.

His hand slid underneath her hair to the back of her neck.

"Look at me," he ordered, his gruff tone at odds with the lightness of his touch.

He brought his face close to hers.

"The mortal wounds were healed. But your appearance and the old injury of your leg will return to what they were before, perhaps with some small variations."

Her gaze dropped to his mouth. "How is that possible?"

"How is it that a relic deters a feral, and holy ground repels Maximilian and Aoibhe?"

"You're a murderer." She changed the subject.

He did not blink. "Yes."

"And a thief."

William released her neck and straightened.

"With respect to the illustrations, I merely repossessed them."

"But you came to see if I was frightened after I saw the policeman being killed."

He nodded once.

"And you came to me tonight, when you thought I was in danger. Now I discover you fought three men to save my life, even though you didn't know me." She gazed up at him in wonder.

He moved to cup her face.

"I know you.

"I know you live alone and have few friends. I know you walk with a cane because of your leg and ankle.

"I know you weep over a homeless man and risked your life to save him.

"I know that, despite the quiet and simplicity of your life, you've been happier in Florence than anywhere else."

He drew a circle on her cheek with his thumb before dropping it to her jaw.

"You are my greatest virtue and my deepest vice."

He leaned forward and pressed their lips together.

Anguish and desire flared in his chest as his mouth touched hers, his kiss becoming firm and insistent. His thumb traced a tempting trail down her beautiful neck and he groaned, the sound throaty and carnal.

Raven had been taken by surprise. At first she was motionless, trying to get her bearings. At the sound of his groan, which she took to be an indication of genuine desire, she relaxed against him.

His mouth was sensuous, his lips softer than she expected. And he kissed with the intensity of a condemned man.

Suddenly he pulled away.

"Good night, Cassita." His words were a command and not a suggestion.

He turned his back on her, walking to the far end of the room where the Botticelli illustrations were displayed.

Raven wanted to ask him questions. She wanted to ask why he'd kissed her. Why he'd changed his mind and stopped.

She wanted to ask about the medicine he'd used to save her.

His mood had shifted. He seemed irritated, if not angry, and she was wary of him.

Her wariness was enough to propel her to obey his command and delay her escape. She had too many unanswered questions to leave now.

Without a word, she lifted her knapsack and exited the room, touching her lips in wonder.

Chapter Twenty-three

William strode to his library and shut the doors, locking them from the inside. Bookshelves ascended from the floor to the domed ceiling. A sliding metal staircase ran on a track that curved around the room, enabling one to climb to the tallest shelf.

Not that he needed the staircase.

Through the immense glass panes that formed the ceiling, he could see the moon, and the stars winking above him. Year after year, century after century, he'd gazed at that same sky. Its response was always the same—beautiful, cold indifference.

Just like God.

He growled at the thought.

He hadn't chosen this life; it had been forced on him.

So much for the justice that governs the universe. Dante was a fool to believe such myths. Some of us are damned by the actions of others and exiled to hell through no fault of our own.

It was rare that he indulged himself with such thoughts. They stoked his anger and tested his discipline. On this evening, they could not be put aside.

He'd served God, even after God had taken what he treasured most. And in such a sick and twisted way.

Then God had taken from him again.

Twice he had seen goodness disappear from the world, watching the very life ebb away. Twice he'd been powerless to stop it. On the third occasion, when he came upon Cassita, he had the power to do something.

So *do* something he did.

Interestingly enough, Cassita's goodness wasn't cold and indifferent, as her tardy response to his kiss indicated.

The thought seared him.

He sat behind his wooden desk and opened the center drawer, withdrawing a small, black velvet box.

He opened it.

A pretty face looked up at him from behind glass.

The face was of a woman, young and fair, with large blue eyes and an abundance of long, reddish blond curls.

William remembered his anger, long since buried, as he stroked the girl's cheek. He remembered the centuries of despair and hopelessness he'd weathered until the night he'd found the girl with the green eyes, slumped in an alley.

With her face firmly fixed in his mind, he closed the box and put it back in its place, sliding the drawer shut.

The next morning, Raven awoke late. She'd tossed and turned most of the night, her mind active and worried.

She found a card on her nightstand that indicated she should ring Lucia for breakfast. The card itself was unremarkable. What was remarkable was the fact that Raven found herself squinting in order to read Lucia's elegant script.

Her heart sank as she realized that her eyesight, like all the other changes to her body, was reverting back to what it had been before William rescued her.

If, in fact, he had rescued her.

In the bright light of day, she wondered about his story. He claimed she'd had a head injury, but apart from a headache or two and her memory loss, there wasn't any physical evidence.

Of course, there was the strange matter of her changed appearance. She wondered how William had been able to bring that about.

William.

The name, like the man, was deceptive. His attractive exterior and elegant name belied the criminal who was prone to violence.

The man who'd kissed her the evening before.

She had limited experience when it came to kisses, but she recognized his expertise. The recognition was accompanied by the cooling tide of guilt.

William was handsome and he could be charming. Certainly he'd helped her more than once. But he was an art thief, a member of almost the lowest form of humanity.

And I let him kiss me.

Raven told herself she hadn't pushed him away because she'd been emotional. She'd been frightened. She couldn't be attracted to a criminal.

More precisely, she wouldn't allow herself to be attracted to a criminal. No matter what.

She pulled on a robe to greet Lucia and was delighted when the woman set her brunch out on the balcony that opened from the bedroom.

Raven was grateful that two aspirin had been left on the tray, since her leg and ankle were aching. If the pain worsened, she'd have to start taking her prescription pain medication again.

She sighed at the thought.

As she enjoyed the noon sunshine her mind naturally drifted to the evening before.

William York was behind the theft of the illustrations from the Uffizi Gallery. Whether they'd belonged to him in the past or not, Raven didn't know. Certainly his story was at odds with the account the Emersons had given.

In addition, William seemed almost too young to be a serious art collector. The collection he'd amassed downstairs rivaled that of many museums in quality, if not quantity, leading Raven to believe it had been acquired over decades, if not centuries, by his family.

Since Professor Emerson had already mentioned William as a potential suspect, it was more than likely he'd been investigated. Knowing he was guilty, she wondered why he hadn't fled the city and returned to England.

Raven looked down at her half-eaten sweet roll. She'd suddenly lost her appetite.

William claimed to have saved her life, and killed in order to do it. While it was possible he'd lied about that, too, she couldn't explain the strange images that continued to flood her consciousness—images of a dark alley and blood and the faces of the man and woman she'd seen the night before.

And there was the fact that she'd sketched William's face before seeing it. She must have met him before.

If he'd killed to protect her, she certainly didn't condone it. But she knew her story would be too fantastic for the police to believe. She'd had enough trouble with them already.

She could try to persuade William to give the illustrations back, so they could be enjoyed by everyone and not relegated to a private room in his villa. Given his attitude and the way he'd spoken about the illustrations, this task would not be easy.

A shadow fell across the table.

"Good morning," William greeted her. "Did you rest well?"

"I found it difficult to sleep." She pulled the edges of her bathrobe closed. "Would you like to join me?"

"I've eaten already." He stepped out of the sun and back into the master bedroom, hovering in the doorway.

She found the movement strange.

"Don't you want to sit in the sun?"

"Not particularly." He sounded prim.

She gestured to his fair skin. "Do you burn easily?"

"I find the sun uncomfortable and tend to avoid it. Is breakfast to your liking?"

"Yes, thank you."

Raven felt conspicuous eating in front of him, especially since her waist had noticeably thickened overnight. She pushed the tray aside and sipped her coffee, looking out over the extensive gardens and trees at the back of his villa.

"You have a beautiful home."

"Thank you."

Raven shifted in her chair in order to appraise him. His clothes were impeccable and clean, although he appeared to be wearing the same black shirt and jeans he'd worn the night before.

Raven inferred he was wearing new clothes that resembled the others.

"Do you always wear black?"

He seemed taken aback by her question. "Ah, yes."

"It's a warm, sunny day. Aren't you hot?"

"Not really." His body tensed.

His nearness reminded her of the kiss they'd shared the evening before. It also reminded her that he'd had to convince himself not to kill her. It was time to disentangle herself from this situation.

"Thank you for your hospitality and coming to my rescue last night. I really should be going. I'd like to visit Bruno in the hospital." She placed her coffee cup on the tray and gave him a smile calculated to disarm him.

"I'm afraid I can't let you go."

A feeling of alarm coursed through her. "Why not?"

"A longer conversation is in order. I'll leave you to dress and meet you downstairs. You have one hour."

Raven watched as he strode through the bedroom toward the door, his spine ramrod straight.

"I don't want to wait," she called. "Let's talk now."

William paused before turning around. He did not look pleased.

"We can't talk here."

"Because?"

William walked back to her so quickly he was almost a blur.

"Because your proximity to my bed reminds me of all the things I'd rather be doing with you."

Raven's mouth dropped open.

William took a moment to regain his control, willing his body to obey his mind.

"Get dressed and come downstairs."

He returned to the door, closing it loudly behind him.

Raven sat in her chair, dumbfounded.

She was not accustomed to receiving attention from men. Mostly she'd been treated a little like wallpaper or a piece of furniture.

At college, she'd had two boyfriends. The first one was affectionate, but not especially passionate. The second was duplicitous. Neither of them ever looked at her as William had just done, even in their most intimate, secret moments.

William had seen her and wanted her. He knew she wasn't a size zero, with a dainty figure. Still he wanted her in his bed.

She tried to reconcile his expression of wanton desire with the tenderness with which he'd kissed her the night before. And the way he called her Cassita.

He doesn't even know my true name.

Raven's realization was enough to stop her speculation about William's desire and his probable talent in bed. She was not lonely and desperate enough to trade her respect for herself (and her name) for an afternoon of pleasure.

Plus, he's a criminal.

She needed to remind herself of the fact.

There was also the small matter of William's anger. He seemed cross with himself for wanting her.

She wondered if his anger was because she was troubling his well-ordered criminal life or for other reasons. Probably he resented his attraction, knowing there were exceptional Florentine women ripe for the taking.

Raven decided not to dwell on the subject. She'd long since discarded the belief that all puzzles in the universe could be solved. Some puzzles didn't have solutions, and she suspected William was exactly that sort of puzzle.

The internal struggles of a criminal were not her concern.

With a labored gait, she walked to the closet. As she sorted through the hangers and shelves of clothing, she realized it held an assortment of sizes, ranging from the size she'd been a few days past to the size she was before she lost her memory.

Either he'd provided clothes for her while he was saving her life or he'd anticipated her return to a larger size. She didn't know what to think about either possibility.

She chose a raspberry-colored sundress, calculated to contrast with the green of her eyes; a white cardigan; and a pair of simple, low-heeled sandals. Then she locked herself in the large bathroom to get ready.

When Raven reached the first floor, Lucia was waiting. She escorted her to a room down the hall, which she said was the library; she opened the door, then left Raven to William's company.

Raven found the term *library* a gross understatement. The room was larger than the central archives at the Uffizi Gallery. She stared at the books openmouthed, turning in circles as she tried to take in the enormous and varied collection.

She was amazed someone so young could have amassed such an extensive library. What she would not give to be able to spend hours perusing the shelves.

William stood at the far end of the room, in front of a massive window that ran from the floor almost to the domed ceiling, facing the gardens. He did not turn around.

The air was filled with one of Rachmaninoff's piano concertos. Raven recognized the music, which seemed to emanate from nowhere and everywhere all at once. She looked around the room for the source but couldn't find it.

She resisted the urge to limp and walked to a chair in front of his desk, sitting down with a barely repressed whimper.

"Are you in pain?" he asked, still facing the window.

"A little. The aspirin is helping."

He turned. "I can make the pain stop."

"How?"

"Alchemy."

She wrinkled her nose. "What does alchemy entail?"

"Prepare to have your universe expanded, Jane."

She stiffened at the sound of her former name.

William rested his hip against the front of the large desk, crossing his arms in front of him. "You said last night there was no such thing as souls. Your disbelief doesn't negate reality."

"Your beliefs, however fantastic, don't create reality."

William's expression hardened.

"Your ignorance will get you killed."

"Then enlighten me." She mirrored his posture. "You've been speaking in riddles and esoteric circles. It's time for the truth. Who are you and what are you involved in? Why does it put me in danger?"

William's eyes flared gray fire.

"You saw the feral for yourself. Last night you encountered Maximilian. Either of them could have drained the life out of you in minutes."

"I thought Florence was relatively safe at night. I'll be more careful."

"You need to stop being so damned dogmatic and open your eyes," William snapped. "You wore a relic, and a feral kept his distance. You ran to holy ground, and Maximilian didn't follow you. Isn't that enough empirical evidence for the supernatural?"

Raven opened her mouth to argue, but found herself unable to formulate an intelligent response.

William shook his head.

"Use your reasoning, Use your powers of observation. They weren't choosing to stay away from you; they were forced to stay away. What more proof do you need?"

"I agree, they avoided me. The question is why. Maybe there's something to your belief in relics and the power of Sanctuary. But maybe it's just the placebo effect."

William lifted his hip from the desk and growled.

Raven leaned back in her chair.

The sound coming from his chest was unmistakable—he was growling like an animal. She didn't know what to do with that realization.

William moved closer.

"Your leg was healed, temporarily, and you changed in physical appearance. What are your scientific explanations for that?"

"I don't have one. Listen, Mr. York. I think I deserve the truth. Something strange happened to me. My memory is confused. Just tell me what you gave me so I can go and see a doctor."

"A doctor wouldn't know what to do with you. He'd draw your blood, test it, and discover that it contains substances absolutely foreign to human biology."

Raven started, visibly shaken by what he'd said. She remembered her doctor's remarks about her blood work and the incompetence of the lab. She'd said the lab contaminated the blood sample.

"What did you give me?" she whispered.

"You're asking the wrong question. You should be asking *who I am*."

Raven pressed her lips together.

"I know who you are. You're the thief who stole the illustrations from the Uffizi."

"As I said, I didn't steal them. They were stolen from me, originally."

"Dottor Vitali said they belonged to a Swiss family since the nineteenth century."

William tilted his head to one side.

"From whom did they acquire them?"

She lifted her shoulders. "I don't know."

"Precisely. They appeared in Switzerland after they were stolen from me."

"Before the turn of the nineteenth century?" Raven laughed. "But that would make you—"

"Yes."

She rolled her eyes in disbelief. "What's your connection with Palazzo Riccardi?"

"None of your business."

"The painting in your room upstairs, who's the artist?"

William stopped, pinning her to the chair with a look so sharp, she felt it. "You know who the artist is."

"I've never seen that painting before."

"You have, actually, when I brought you here to save your life. The artist, of course, is Botticelli."

"Impossible."

"Why?"

"Because of Mercury and Zephyr. Their faces . . ." She stopped, confused.

"It isn't impossible. Use your powers of inference."

"I am. I'm familiar with all of Botticelli's works. I've never seen that painting before."

He smiled. "Because I've owned it for years and I've never let anyone see it."

"How long have you owned it?"

William clenched his jaw. "Since it was painted."

Raven erupted in a scoffing laugh. "Nice try, ancient one. Botticelli died in 1510."

"He nearly died earlier. When I discovered he'd painted my likeness in a work, I decided to kill him. He offered me a few things and I changed my mind."

Raven stood and began walking toward the door. "I don't find your delusions funny. I find them pitiable. You need to get help and I need to go home."

William blurred past her and stood at the door, barring her way.

Raven's eyes widened in shock. "How did you do that?"

"I'm quick." He moved away from the door and stalked toward her.

She retreated, holding her hand up as if to keep him away.

"You're disturbed. Let me go."

He approached her determinedly.

"If I let you go, all my striving will be for naught. Someone like Max will come upon you and kill you. Or worse."

She froze. "Like what?"

William stopped when their feet were almost touching.

"Like keeping you as a pet until he tires of you."

William stood so close she could feel his breath on her face.

She focused on the door, willing herself not to be distracted by his nearness.

Realization suddenly dawned on her.

"You traffic in humans." Her gaze moved to his face. "You sell them as sex slaves."

William's expression quickly morphed from anger to surprise to amusement.

"Not quite."

"Who else keeps human beings as pets?" she demanded.

"Those who feed on them."

"Feed?" Raven began backing away, keeping her gaze fixed on William. "You're a cannibal."

William drew himself up to his full height.

"Hardly.

"I am a vampyre."

Chapter Twenty-four

If time could be measured by grains of sand flowing through an hourglass, there would have been enough sand to form a small sand castle in the bottom of the glass. That was how long it took for Raven to process William's declaration and react to it.

"You're sick."

(She had difficulty coming up with a more descriptive response, given the fantastic nature of his claim.)

"No, I am not." William was visibly irritated. "I am perfectly well."

"I think cannibalism counts as a mental illness. I don't mean to make light of it, because clearly you need help. And a dietician."

Raven was not trying to be funny, but found herself giggling out of nervousness.

William was not amused.

He walked past her and circled his desk, opening one of the side drawers.

Raven should have taken that opportunity to flee the library, but she was curious about what he was doing. Until she realized he was withdrawing a dagger.

It was old-fashioned and far from small, boasting a gold handle.

"What's that for?" She started backing away from him.

"I'm going to challenge your view of the supernatural. I'd advise you to stay. You'll want to see this."

Raven continued moving toward the door, but she kept her eyes on him.

He went to one of the bookshelves and withdrew a large, heavy volume. Raven noticed that it was a copy of Dante's *Divine Comedy*.

William placed it on the center of his desk. He glanced in her direction as the music swelled.

Raven's hand found the doorknob and she twisted, eager to leave.

Unfortunately, the doorknob wouldn't move.

She tried it again. The door was locked.

"Jane," he called to her.

She was about to pound on the door and scream for Lucia, when she saw William put his left hand on top of the book.

Staring at her, he lifted the dagger and plunged it into the back of his hand.

Raven screamed.

"Oh, my God! Oh, my God. Oh, my God. What are you doing?"

Without thought for her safety, she raced forward, ignoring the pain in her leg.

She saw a blackish fluid pouring from the wound in his hand. She wondered if it could be blood.

"You're okay, William. You're going to be okay. It's just a cut," she lied as she pulled her white cardigan from her shoulders. "We'll take you to the hospital." She tried to press the sweater around the dagger, which was still sticking out of his hand, pinning him to the heavy book.

William's face was impassive.

He hadn't cried out. He hadn't even flinched.

Calmly, he pushed her cardigan aside and, with a great wrench, pulled the dagger out.

The sound was sickening.

"Why did you do that? You're going to bleed to death!" Raven pushed the sweater toward his hand.

Once again he waved her aside. With a handkerchief, he swiped the blackish substance from the center of his hand and held it in front of her face, palm toward her.

The hole in his hand was so large, Raven could see through it.

He must have shattered bone with the dagger, or perhaps he'd missed the bones entirely. She couldn't be certain.

She dropped her cardigan to the floor. "Holy shit."

William came around the side of the desk to stand in front of her.

"Watch carefully." His tone was ominous.

A moment later, the wound in his hand began to close. Raven watched as a milky film formed over the hole. Sinew and skin seemed to grow over the film before her eyes.

He moved his hand, displaying the back as well as the front. The wound had disappeared.

Thinking it was an illusion, Raven grabbed his hand, peering at it closely.

She traced the palm with her finger. It felt like flesh and not a prosthetic. She couldn't even see a scar.

On his desk was the book with a large, deep incision still visible.

She lifted her face. "How did you do that?"

"I could repeat the experiment, if you like. I could do it a thousand times, but the outcome will always be the same. I'm not human; I am a vampyre."

Raven dropped his hand and tried to race for the exit.

He cut her off.

He lifted his hands, palms toward her.

"Jane."

She retreated to the metal staircase and scrambled to the top, shouting as she climbed. "Help! Help!"

"No one will come to your aid. Lucia, Ambrogio, and the others do exactly as I tell them, without exception." William stood at the bottom of the staircase. He did not look pleased. "Climb down from there before you fall."

"Don't come near me!" She reached over and pulled a very heavy atlas from one of the shelves.

"*Sard*," he swore, throwing the bloodstained handkerchief on the floor next to her cardigan. "I'm sure the revelation comes as a shock, given your preconceived notions. But you should remember that I've done nothing but help you."

"Let me go."

He straightened his shoulders. "I can't do that."

"Yes, you can. I've done nothing to you. Just let me go."

William regarded her, his face taking on a contemplative expression.

"You thought I was a cannibal and yet you came to my aid. You sacrificed your white sweater for my wound."

"You were bleeding, for God's sake! Of course I tried to help."

"Not *of course*. Few have ever lifted a finger to help me in the past few centuries. When they did, it was always with an agenda. You've not only surprised me, you've impressed me. And I am not easily impressed."

He stepped to a table nearby and poured a deep purplish liquid into a goblet.

"You need a drink." He lifted the glass.

"No, I don't." She shifted the atlas to her other hand. "I need to get out of here and away from you."

"Finally you're making sense."

William approached the staircase. He was unhurried in his movements, almost relaxed. He placed a hand on the railing.

"If you'd come down from your perch, little bird, I'll tell you more."

"You're a bunch of sick people."

"Strictly speaking, we aren't people. We're vampyres."

"Whatever."

William smiled, revealing an array of straight white teeth.

"You've already met several vampyres, including me."

Raven felt unsteady. "Who?"

"The feral. And Maximilian and Aoibhe."

"Who's Aoibhe?"

"The female who chased you to the Duomo."

"So there are three of you?"

William pressed his lips together. "'Our name is Legion, for we are many.'"

"How many?" Raven's eyes widened.

"We exist worldwide, usually congregating in cities. Some of our kind live as ferals, alone and in rural locations."

Raven gripped the railing. "I saw the feral kill the policeman. Is that what you do?"

"No. Ferals abandon reason and live like animals. The civilized ones among us feed on humans, but try not to kill them. Humans are a renewable resource."

"Like trees," she said weakly.

"What's that?"

She closed her eyes. "The feral said I was a pedophile's whore. He told me he'd fuck me until I died. Are you a pedophile?"

She opened her eyes and saw William's expression change. A wave of fury passed over his features.

With a roar, he lifted the wine bottle and threw it against the heavy wooden doors. The bottle broke on impact, the top quarter of it embedding in the wood.

Raven clutched the atlas to her chest, clinging to the staircase rail with all her strength.

William rubbed his face with his hands. After a moment's silence, he turned to her.

"I didn't know that it spoke to you. I hope you never encounter one again, but if you do, you mustn't listen to what it says. They're devoid of reason and entirely dark."

"Dark?"

He shifted his feet. "Something dark animates us. In a feral, the darkness overtakes it completely and the result is what you saw with the policeman.

"They aren't without perception, however. It realized you had a relic and it must have divined where it came from, which is why it insulted the former owner and you."

"You gave me a relic from a pedophile?"

"He was not a pedophile," William snarled, baring his teeth. "He was a saint. Only a feral would suggest otherwise."

Raven shrank from his anger. But after a minute her curiosity got the better of her.

"Which saint?"

William gestured to the chair she'd sat in previously. "You need to sit down before you fall down."

When Raven made no movement, he told her, "I shall keep my distance and stand by the door."

"Not until you tell me what you gave me."

William did as he'd offered, stepping carefully between the shards of broken glass and pools of Chianti to the door. "In order to save your life, I fed you vampyre blood."

"You *what*?" she shrieked.

He lifted his hands as if to calm her. "It has certain properties that can keep a human being alive."

"This is impossible." She swayed on the staircase, switching the atlas back to her other hand. "This must be a nightmare."

Before she was aware of what was happening, William was at her side. He'd flown across the room and ascended the staircase.

He lifted the atlas from her shaking hand and reshelved it.

"Cassita." He spoke firmly, looping an arm around her waist. "Stay with me."

Her eyes focused on his. "I didn't see you move. How did you do that?"

"Speed and agility are two of our talents. Now come down."

She tried to push him away.

He was immovable.

"Look at me." When their eyes met, he spoke in a low voice. "I won't harm you. I—I swear by the relic."

His voice and expression seemed sincere. Certainly he was superstitious about the relic, whatever its power or lack thereof. Would he swear by it and lie intentionally?

She wasn't sure.

Raven considered her options and realized she couldn't remain on the staircase forever. The only exit from the room was the door. At least if she descended the staircase, she'd be closer to the exit.

William took her hand and patiently led her to the chair.

"Drink this. It will settle your nerves." He handed her the glass that held the remaining Chianti.

She eyed the contents.

"It isn't blood, is it?"

He seemed offended. "Of course not. It's wine."

She sniffed the liquid before draining it. The wine was good but she barely tasted it. She closed her eyes as she willed the alcohol to give her strength.

"I thought vampyres were supposed to be cold." She handed him the glass and he placed it on the desk. "Your skin is cooler than mine, but I wouldn't call it cold."

"Some of our mythology was propagated by our enemies. Some we circulated, hoping to confuse them."

"I can't imagine Bram Stoker as someone's enemy."

"Probably because he was a paid propagandist."

Raven peered at his mouth.

"You don't have fangs."

William frowned. "Our teeth are sharp enough, I assure you."

"So you have enemies?"

"Every predator is prey to something."

"What would prey on you?"

"Not what—whom. And that is a story for a different day." He appeared impatient.

"You look human."

"I was human once. My body has been perfected. I'm faster, stronger, and I don't age. I still feed and breathe but can go a long time without air. As you saw, I heal quickly."

She lifted her hands before dropping them to her lap. "How can this be?"

"Your mistake is in assuming that the supernatural springs into existence uncaused. It doesn't. It obeys certain rules; it follows certain patterns. In summary, a vampyre's supernatural properties come from the darkness."

She rubbed at her eyes. "Metaphorical explanations are useless. If you aren't human, why do you look human? Why don't you have a different kind of body?"

"Why do the elements of the Eucharist retain their physical properties after transubstantiation in the Mass?" Once again William sounded impatient.

Raven made a face.

"They didn't quite cover the transubstantiation from human to vampyre in my catechism class, but perhaps my parish was conservative."

William's features softened into a smile.

He chuckled.

"It's been a long time since I've laughed." He gave her an admiring look.

Raven tried very hard not to roll her eyes. Then something perilous, something terrible, occurred to her.

She regarded him with a worried expression. "If you gave me vampyre blood, does that mean I'll become a vampyre, too?"

"Not from that, no. The blood I gave you was harvested from two vampyres who are no longer alive. You have to be changed by a living vampyre in order to become one."

"I thought vampyres were supposed to be immortal."

"Not quite."

"How can they be killed?"

William's smile disappeared. "We don't discuss those things."

"The man who approached me last night—he mentioned the term *masters*. What was he talking about?"

William muttered something under his breath.

"You still have vampyre blood in your system. Max must have assumed you'd been kept by two vampyres as a pet and they'd let you feed from them as a reward."

"That doesn't sound rewarding." Her lip curled in disgust.

"It is when you're dying." He spoke sharply. "Vampyre blood reverses the aging process and modifies nature, which is why it changed your appearance and healed your head injury.

"Your leg injury is obviously old, which is why it's coming back. The older the injury, the greater the amount of blood it takes to heal it, but the less permanent the change. How did you break your leg?"

"That's a story for a different day." Raven directed her own sharp tone toward him before focusing on her hands, which were clenched in her lap. "So my leg will be like it was before?"

"Yes. In order to heal your leg permanently, you'd have to become a vampyre. But you could heal it temporarily by continuing to ingest vampyre blood."

His expression changed. He seemed thoughtful, searching.

Raven felt more than a tinge of regret. She'd enjoyed the changes to her appearance. She enjoyed being pretty and thin. Most important, she enjoyed having a functional leg that worked properly and without pain.

She enjoyed it so much she was almost ready to ask William to give her whatever it would take to heal her.

The realization made her cold.

"What happened to the man who attacked Bruno?"

"Maximilian is not a man. And nothing happened to him. No doubt he's resting privately. Vampyres can't survive in the sun."

"But you can. You stood in the sun when you came to my room."

William leaned forward at the waist and dropped his voice.

"That is an exception you'd best forget."

She turned her head to the side, avoiding his eyes.

"And Bruno? How is he?" she persisted.

"There's no change in his condition. The doctors don't know if he'll recover."

"I want to see him."

"I'm afraid I can't let you leave. It's for your protection."

Raven stood, panicking.

"But I have to go home. I have to see Bruno."

William glared at her.

"I asked you repeatedly to leave the city. You refused. I warned you that you would come to me for help. And here you are."

"You brought me here!"

"To save your life." He crossed to her in two long strides. "Again and again, I offered help and you spurned it. You could have left the city, but you didn't."

"It would have been irrational for me to leave on the advice of a stranger who broke into my apartment."

"My warnings were given in good faith. You ignored them. Now you've come to the attention of two of my associates. Ergo, you have entered my world whether you realize it or not."

"What does that mean?"

He straightened proudly. "It means, Jane, that I shall offer you my protection. In return, you'll give me what I want."

"What's that?"

William gave her a sensual look.

"You."

Chapter Twenty-five

"Excuse me?" Raven wasn't sure she'd heard what she thought she'd heard.

William's expression left no ambiguity, as his eyes traveled the length of her body.

"I warned you that I would exact a price. The price is you. You'll be safe living here. If you wish, I can continue administering blood so your leg will remain sound.

"I have the largest private collection of Renaissance art in the world. Much of it has never been restored. I'll give you free rein to assess my collection and restore it. I'll even build a lab for you, out there." He pointed to the gardens that lay beyond the library windows.

"I'd live here as your personal art restorer?"

His lips twitched. "I'd have other, personal expectations of you."

"Sex?" Her voice sounded higher than normal.

"Of course."

"Why?"

He seemed surprised by her question.

He reached out to cup her face and his eyes grew soft. "Because you interest me. It has been many, many years since someone caught my attention."

Raven couldn't pretend she didn't like his gentle voice or the way he touched her, as if he truly found her pleasing.

She didn't know him well enough to know if he was lying or not. It was possible this was some tortured game and that she was merely a pawn in a greater contest.

His kiss the previous evening had felt sincere. But Raven had been deceived before, and so she didn't trust her feelings.

She wished she were more used to a man's attention. Perhaps then she wouldn't be so affected. So vulnerable.

"Is sex the same for vampyres?" She pulled away from him.

His hand dropped to his side and he frowned. "The same as what?"

"The same as when you were human."

"I couldn't tell you," he said coolly.

His demeanor didn't invite interrogation and so she elected not to pursue the ambiguity in his statement.

But she made a mental note to ask about it later.

He ran his thumb across his lower lip. "When a vampyre feeds from a human, the urge to engage in intercourse is overwhelming. Sex and feeding go together, almost universally."

Raven wrinkled her nose in revulsion.

"Do vampyres ever have sex with one another?"

"In some cases."

"Do they feed from one another, too?"

"Sometimes, but vampyres need human blood in order to maintain their health."

Raven decided to keep William's attention fixed on answering questions, in order to give herself time to plan an escape. She tried to look curious.

"Why would a vampyre feed from another vampyre?"

"It bonds the two. There may be political or expedient reasons to forge that bond. The blood of an older vampyre can strengthen a younger one."

"Are you bonded with anyone?"

"No." He moved away from her abruptly. "I need to disclose that when a vampyre takes a human lover, the human becomes overwhelmed by the experience and develops an addiction to it. In some cases, the human begs to become a vampyre. In other cases, the vampyre gets carried away and kills the human."

He paused, noting her reaction.

Her jaw had dropped open and she was gazing at him in horror.

He hastened to explain himself.

"You should know that I am what they call an old one—I've been a vampyre for centuries. I have more power than the others and I have much more control. I won't be carried away when I drink from you. You're safe with me."

Raven laughed without amusement. "Safe? Nothing you have said so far makes me feel safe. And thanks for the invitation, but I'm not interested in having sex with you."

William smiled a slow, sensuous smile. "You say one thing but your body says something else. Your heart rate escalates when I touch you and you hold your breath. Your pupils dilate and your skin warms. One might almost think you are aroused."

Raven felt her cheeks flush.

"I can't help biology."

"Neither can I," he retorted, coming nearer.

"Are all vampyres misogynists? I had no idea."

His eyebrows lifted. "I am not a misogynist. In fact, I'm a great admirer of women. I'm simply stating what your body already recognizes—you are attracted to me."

"Find another art restorer to snack on."

He moved closer, his eyes fixed on hers. "You don't know the pleasure I'm capable of giving you. There are those who would beg to become my lover, just for one night."

Raven's gaze dropped to his mouth.

He licked his lips.

She shook her head, as if trying to snap out of it.

"Then you should have no trouble finding a *willing* partner. Now, if you'll excuse me—"

He stepped in front of her. "In a few days, the two bloods I administered to you will disappear from your system and I'll be able to enjoy your true vintage. I've been looking forward to sampling it for a while."

"You'd drink my blood?"

He gave her a half smile.

"Vampyres tend to do that."

"I'd rather die."

"What?" His tone was harsh, if not incredulous.

"You stole the illustrations from the Uffizi and now you've kidnapped me. I don't care what you are. I have no intention of staying with you as a sex slave or a fountain drink or anything else."

He scowled. "You wouldn't be a slave. You'd be royalty."

"You said I'd be under your control."

"I said that's usual. You should know by now that you are far from usual. In fact, I think you're strong-minded enough to maintain a degree of autonomy despite an intense sexual relationship with me."

"A degree of autonomy isn't freedom."

"Being my lover is." He reached out and traced her collarbones from shoulder to shoulder. "Freedom to enjoy the pleasure I'll give you. Freedom to leave your cares behind and focus only on living a life of erotic delight."

"That isn't an inducement." She set her teeth. "I'd rather kill myself than be touched against my will."

William glared. "I am not a rapist."

"So you say."

"I saved you from being raped and I killed three men in order to do it," he hissed.

"Maybe because you wanted to finish the job."

"*Cave,*" he warned.

He was perilously close to losing his temper, but, through a visible effort, he restrained himself.

He clenched his jaw.

"You'd end your life, simply to avoid this?"

Raven lifted her chin. "Yes."

"Do you know what happens to suicides after they die?"

She shrugged. "They go to sleep and never wake up."

"No, they don't. Suicide is the worst thing a human being can do. You shouldn't even consider it." William looked deeply into her eyes. "You say you don't want this, but I saw you blush. You want me to touch you. You want to be in my bed."

"No." She spoke defiantly.

"Convince me."

His gray eyes dropped to her lips.

He brought his body to within a hairsbreadth of hers, but didn't touch her. His mouth hovered close.

Raven waited, expecting him to kiss her.

He didn't.

She inhaled deeply.

Still, he didn't move.

"Cassita," he murmured. The movement of his mouth brought their lips in contact, but only for a second.

Then his lips were on hers and he was kissing her.

His hand sifted through her long hair, cupping the back of her head. He brought their bodies together, erasing the space between them.

Then he slowed the tempo of his lips to an agonizing crawl. He pressed against her, brushing his lips across hers as if the distance were interminable and he had all the time in the world.

She didn't push him away, but she didn't kiss him back. She was as still as a statue, motionless in his arms.

Then his lips were gone.

She opened her eyes and saw him staring at the door.

"We're about to be interrupted."

"Interrupted?"

No sooner had the word left her mouth than there came a knock at the door.

"Enter," William called.

There was a click and a scrape of the lock. The door opened.

Ambrogio appeared. "Forgive me, my lord. An urgent message has arrived."

"Place it on the table."

If Ambrogio was surprised by the shards of glass and wine droplets he had to step over in order to walk to the side table, he hid it well. He put a white envelope next to Raven's empty wineglass.

"Will there be anything else, my lord?" He ignored Raven and looked only at William.

"No. That is all."

Ambrogio bowed and withdrew, closing the door behind him.

William released Raven, walking over to the table. He ripped open the envelope and scanned the written contents.

"*Sard*," he cursed, stuffing the letter back into the envelope.

"What does that mean?"

"It means *fuck*."

"In what language?"

"English." He tossed the envelope on the table. "I had hoped to spend the day with you. Unfortunately for us both, business intrudes. We'll continue this conversation later. In the interim, the villa is at your disposal. Lucia will prepare your meals and see that you have what you need. I'll seek you out when I return, which may not be until tomorrow."

He nodded at her and made for the door.

She followed him. "Wait. What's going to happen to Bruno?"

William frowned. "Why must you keep mentioning him?"

"Because his grandmother is my neighbor. And he may die because of me."

William's demeanor cooled. "You won't have to worry about her much longer. She has cancer and will die soon."

"What?" Raven croaked.

"When I visited your apartment, I could smell the cancer from the hall. It's very advanced."

"How can you smell cancer?"

He pressed his lips together. "It's one of our talents. We can smell disease. And death."

Raven placed a hand on the back of the chair for support. "Why didn't Bruno tell me?"

"It's possible he doesn't know. I didn't scent any drugs in her system. Perhaps she declined treatment."

"Can you help her?"

"I could, but I won't." His tone was matter-of-fact.

"Why not?"

"Using vampyre blood to help you has already exposed me. I'm not about to do it again."

"But if I asked you to help her?"

A muscle jumped in his jaw.

"I'd still say no. The blood will heal her cancer but I'd have to give it to her in such a large amount, she'd end up much, much younger. It would attract too much attention."

"Could you give her a little, just to ease her suffering?"

"Death is the only thing that will help her."

Raven let out an anguished sound. "Please."

"We don't interfere in the lives of human beings. You were an exception." His eyes glinted cold steel.

He turned his back on her and reached for the doorknob.

She swallowed hard as tears pricked her eyes. "William, wait."

She cleared her throat.

"What if I begged?"

William kept his back toward her.

"My answer won't change."

"I tried to protect Cara," Raven whispered. "I failed."

Now William turned around. "Who's Cara?"

"I am not going to watch this happen and do nothing."

William exhaled loudly.

"It isn't your responsibility to save the world. Let people save themselves."

Raven let out an anguished sound. "If what you said about the relic is true, it's my fault Bruno was hurt. If I'd been wearing it, no one would have bothered us."

"It's too late for regrets." He reached for the doorknob once again.

"No, it isn't."

She approached him, standing a few feet away.

"You said I'd come to you and beg for help." She lifted her chin. "I thought I was too proud to beg. But I'm not. I beg you for Bruno's life and the life of his grandmother."

William remained stubbornly fixed on the door.

"No."

"Please, William. Please."

He exhaled loudly. "As difficult as it may seem to you, we try not to draw attention to ourselves. You're asking me to expose myself."

"I'll stay with you."

William's eyes flew to hers. "What?"

"If you heal Bruno and help his grandmother, I'll stay with you. I'll work on your art collection. I may even do . . . other things, eventually. I just ask that you don't force me."

William simply stared.

"Please," she repeated. "Help them."

William stood still so long, Raven worried he'd gone into a trance.

She wrung her hands, anxiety making her fidget.

His gaze moved to her hands and then to her face. "You'd live with me until I let you go? That could be decades from now."

She nodded.

"I can't help your neighbor. The risk is too great. But I could help the boy."

"It has to be both."

William gave her a hard look. "I'm not wasting my precious vintage collection on an old woman. I will, however, give something to him to save his life. But I won't risk healing him completely."

Raven contemplated her options, which were limited.

William's expression began to shift. She worried he'd change his mind.

"All right." Her shoulders slumped.

He walked toward her, his shoes crunching over the broken glass.

"You'd give up your life, your position at the gallery, in exchange for helping that ridiculous boy? He barely knows you."

A single tear trailed down her cheek.

"I don't want to see him die, knowing I could have done something to stop it."

William huffed in exasperation. "He isn't worthy of you. You said yourself he never noticed you until your appearance changed."

She wiped her face with the back of her hand. "You were never going to let me go. At least now, something good will come of it."

He took her face in his hands.

"Do you understand what you are offering me?"

She closed her eyes. "Yes."

For what seemed like a long time, he didn't move.

"You shame me," he murmured.

Her eyelids opened.

He brushed his lips across hers. "It's been a long time since I felt shame."

Uncertainty flashed across his features and Raven began to worry he'd retract his offer.

Impulsively, she reached up to kiss him.

He was surprised by her action, but welcomed it, his closed mouth moving over hers, unwilling to break their connection.

When he took over the kiss, she felt off balance, her hands gripping his biceps for support.

He propelled her backward, almost waltzing her across the room, until her back was against a bookshelf. And still he kept his lips on hers.

His hand slipped between her head and the shelf, cradling her. Protecting her.

She felt the movement for what it was and opened her mouth.

Instantly, his tongue began to play with her lips. He tasted and licked at an unhurried pace, but did not venture inside.

He trailed her jaw with his thumb, as he kissed and teased, tempting her to reciprocate.

She slipped her tongue into his mouth and he gently stroked it with his own, a deep sigh emanating from his chest.

He tasted different. His mouth was cool against her tongue, his movements leisurely but purposeful.

When she retreated, he kissed her lightly once again and pressed his forehead to hers.

He waited for her to open her eyes before he spoke. "Do you know how rare self-sacrifice is? How magnificent you are?"

Raven bowed her head. She was selling herself into slavery, not saving the world.

He toyed with her hair. "Spend the day enjoying my art collection. I'll try to rejoin you tonight."

She kept her eyes on the floor.

He kissed her once more before exiting the room.

Raven heard the door open and close.

She collapsed on the lowest rung of the staircase and placed her face in her hands. Her black hair fell forward, partially covering her arms and flowing over the shoulders of her raspberry-colored sundress.

She did not cry. But her heart ached.

She pushed aside thoughts of herself and her fate to think about her neighbor, Lidia.

She loved her. And she was very, very sick.

Raven exhaled in anguish.

Chapter Twenty-six

William took three steps outside the library and realized he'd forgot-ten the letter Ambrogio had delivered earlier. He returned to the library to retrieve it.

As soon as he entered the room, he saw Cassita huddled on the stair-case, her face in her hands, her shoulders shaking. She was crying.

Something twisted in his chest.

No doubt she was overwrought. She'd said herself that she'd left Amer-ica and come to Florence in order to find happiness. She'd told him she'd found happiness here.

Now she was giving up that happiness and the work that delighted her so he would save the lives of her friends. And he wouldn't agree even to that. He'd promised only to help the boy.

The sensation in his chest increased, feeling a great deal like pain.

It was a foreign feeling.

He picked up the letter and put it in his jacket pocket, with the inten-tion of leaving her to her tears. His gaze dropped to the floor, alighting on two items resting a short distance away: her simple white cardigan and his handkerchief.

The cardigan was no longer pristine. Like his handkerchief, droplets of vampyre blood blackened its appearance.

His eyes traveled from the cardigan to its owner, who was huddled into a defensive ball.

He found that the sight of her in that posture displeased him. Greatly.

It had been a long time since he'd concerned himself with the feelings of a human being. Because of the nature of vampyric transformation, many of his human feelings and memories were gone.

But he remembered loss. He remembered the pain that accompanied anxiety for someone you loved, even though he'd not loved anyone for centuries. Truthfully, he believed himself and his kind incapable of love.

Although he wasn't practiced in empathy, he felt it at that moment, watching the beautiful, brave Cassita weep for her friends. And perhaps, for herself.

More than that, he was able to discern the central aspect of her character.

Cassita was a protector.

She was the kind of person who cared so deeply for others—even homeless men and neighbors—that she would do anything to help them, including sacrificing herself.

He hadn't recognized this quality in her before but as soon as the thought occurred to him, he knew it to be true. He also knew that this trait of her character went very deep, to the core of her being.

In this respect, as in several others, she resembled the young woman whose image he kept carefully concealed in his desk. He'd failed her, many, many years ago, and she'd paid the ultimate price.

His regret and anger over what had happened to her were what propelled him to make an exception and save Cassita's life. Now he'd taken the wounded lark and manipulated what made her noble and good, and for what? For his own selfish purposes? For sexual intercourse?

He looked down at the white cardigan she'd used to try to stem his bleeding and despised the blood that fouled it. She'd come to his aid, knowing he was a vampyre. Now she sat in his library, crying, because he'd forced her to trade herself for her friends' lives.

William despised himself.

"Cassita," he whispered.

When she lifted her head, he expected to see cheeks streaked with tears, but they were merely blotchy and red. Her green eyes were watery and she looked miserable. Miserable and contrite.

The pain in his chest increased.

"I changed my mind."

"No," she cried, panic overtaking her. She scrambled from the steps to stand in front of him. "Please don't go back on your word. Please."

He shook his head, lifting his hand to quiet her.

"I've decided to let you go."

"You can't! We had an agreement. You said you'd help him."

"I did." He fixed his eyes on her and gave her what he thought was his most sincere expression. "I will honor that promise and help the boy. I will instruct Ambrogio to find medical help for your neighbor as well. That's the best I can do for her."

Raven's eyes narrowed suspiciously. "What's the catch?"

He shook his head. "No catch. I offer these things to you as a gift."

"You brought me here as your prisoner. Now you're going to let me go and give me what I asked for? I don't believe you." She wrapped her arms around herself.

His face grew pensive.

"You shamed me by offering yourself for the lives of others. I am regaining my honor."

She eyed him skeptically, but said nothing.

He lifted his hand, touching her face. "A bird in a cage is never as beautiful as a bird that is free, Cassita. You've been wounded enough. I won't add to your wounds."

He bowed stiffly and turned to go.

She grasped his arm. "Can I go home?"

His gaze traveled from where she was touching him to her eyes, which looked hopeful.

He felt her hope like a brand on his skin.

"You'd be safest here, with me. But I won't keep you."

She released his arm and placed a hand to her mouth, relief washing over her.

He lifted his hand in caution. "But you must promise me something."

"What?"

"That you will accept my protection. It's for your safety, I assure you."

"As long as I can go home."

He dropped his hand. "When I return, I want to introduce you to my brethren."

Raven opened her mouth to protest, but William interrupted.

"Maximilian and Aoibhe have seen you. If they see you a second time, they'll take you. Once I've asserted my protection and put a few measures in place, no one will dare touch you. Then I will take you home."

"I'd rather go home now."

His expression grew momentarily severe. "My condition is inflexible. You either agree or not."

"I agree," she said quickly.

"Good." He pushed a lock of hair back from her face, an ancient sadness visible in his eyes. "Enjoy your day, Jane."

He turned toward the door.

She watched him walk a few steps before she called to him.

"My name is Raven."

Chapter Twenty-seven

Raven's view of the world had been transformed. It was, she thought, much like the switch from a geocentric view of the universe to a heliocentric one. Except her heliocentric universe included supernatural creatures that healed from knife wounds in minutes and fed on human beings.

She'd experienced a myriad of emotions—fear, wonder, relief, anger, and even, at some moments, desire. Raven was exhausted by the time William left her and so she ventured upstairs to the master bedroom and curled up on the bed. Within a few minutes she was asleep.

When she awoke, she felt much better. William had promised he would let her go and he'd also promised protection from the other vampyres.

He'd protected her in the past, but she worried what his future protection might include. He'd already revealed his plan to take her to meet Maximilian and Aoibhe. She did not relish a formal introduction.

If she were to be honest, she'd have to admit she was attracted to him. His eyes, his appearance, his mouth . . . he was handsome and magnetic in many ways. He kissed with such focus she almost believed he felt more than just attraction to her.

Almost.

She'd changed his mind, at least. That was no small victory.

She was relieved to be able to focus on William's art collection, rather than the events that had transpired between them and the looming danger of her forthcoming meeting with William's associates.

After a late lunch she engaged Lucia and Ambrogio in the task of helping her to examine two pieces—the Michelangelo in the front hall and the version of *Primavera* in the master bedroom.

They removed the works from the walls and placed them carefully on the dining room table, which had been shrouded in a white sheet.

Raven was careful to touch the paintings only while wearing white cotton gloves, obligingly provided by Ambrogio. She examined every inch of the works with a magnifying glass, dictating any damage or wear to Lucia, who made copious notes.

Without testing the age of the paint and using much more sophisticated equipment than was available in the villa, Raven had to guess at the dates of the paintings. By her estimation, both pieces seemed genuine.

She wished she could ask Professor Urbano's opinion, especially of the purported Michelangelo. If authentic, that work would change art history.

Michelangelo was thought to have completed only one painting in his lifetime. He'd sketched in chalk and ink and painted on wood, but had focused much attention on sculpture and, of course, the ceiling of the Sistine Chapel.

Throughout the afternoon, Raven tried from time to time to engage Lucia or Ambrogio in conversation. They were polite but distant and entirely mirthless.

She asked questions about William, but most of her inquiries were met with either silence or a change in subject. His staff gave a respectable account of his membership in British aristocracy and his love for the city of Florence. They avoided any hint of impropriety.

She wondered if they knew anything about his supernatural activities. She wondered if they'd enrolled in a Stepford-style training program for domestic servants.

In any case, Raven was certain that William's staff would never disclose any of his secrets, nor would they ever, ever disobey his orders.

Chapter Twenty-eight

At ten o'clock that evening, Raven and William were seated in a black Mercedes, driven by a large man called Luka. The windows were tinted, keeping them safe from prying eyes.

When William had returned to the villa, two hours previous, he'd instructed Raven to dress in black and to cover as much skin as possible. When asked for his rationale, he'd patiently explained he was taking her to meet some of the others of his kind.

(His explanation was not extremely informative since she already knew that.)

Raven was terrified but bolstered her resolve by reminding herself that after the meeting he would take her home.

While she was grateful for her freedom, she was saddened to be leaving his art collection. She hoped she'd be able to return in order to examine and perhaps restore some of the works. More than a little of her curiosity had been piqued by their owner, as well. In a more relaxed setting, she wondered if he'd tell her about living through the Renaissance.

The possibility intrigued her.

As they drove down the winding road toward the city, she adjusted the hem of her black silk dress to cover her knees. Her legs were encased in black stockings, her feet placed in extravagantly expensive black designer heels.

William had been insistent she cover her neck, so Lucia had supplied a black vintage Hermès square in a conservative pattern and Raven had knotted it carefully.

(Raven was beginning to get the impression that his lordship had a thing for the color black.)

She was completely covered, with the exception of her face and hands. She fidgeted with her fingernails, unable to keep still.

William reached over to take her hand, clasping it in his.

"Sorry." She gave him an embarrassed smile. "I'm anxious."

"That is an appropriate reaction. Do you like the dress?"

"Very much, thank you."

He smiled. "You look beautiful."

Raven squeezed his hand in thanks, but she didn't believe him. The fabric of the dress was handsome, but silk clung. Even though Lucia had provided her with underthings that smoothed out her body, she knew her stomach, hips, and backside were far too prominent and that the fabric of the dress only emphasized their size.

William's appetite for blood must be impairing his vision.

"Lucia said you picked the dress."

"She bought it on my instructions, yes." His focus moved from her face down her body to her legs. He gave them an admiring look. "I like to surround myself with beauty."

Raven resisted the urge to scoff.

"I'm surprised vampyres travel in cars. Or on motorcycles." She glanced at him out of the corner of her eye.

"This car provides a measure of security. As for the motorcycle, I like speed." He flashed her a winning smile. "So, beautiful Jane, why did you say your name is Raven? Ravens are scavengers. They feed on carrion."

She turned to look out the window. "It doesn't matter. That's my name."

He tugged at her hand. "Tell me why you want to be called Raven."

"Because they're intelligent. They're independent." She paused. "They're survivors."

William stroked his thumb across the back of her hand. "And what have you had to survive, little Raven?"

The tone of his voice, low and inquisitive, caused her to meet his gaze once again. He wasn't hiding his concern, as if her answer mattered.

"I don't want to talk about it. Especially tonight." She disentangled herself from his grasp.

Involuntarily she glanced down at her right leg.

William's eyes followed the path of hers. He frowned.

"Something made you strong. It's common for vampyre blood to have that kind of effect in humans, but I think your resilience is your own." He paused, then asked, "Who is Cara?"

"My sister," she whispered.

"I had a sister."

Raven turned to him with interest. "Older or younger?"

"Younger. I was the oldest. There were six of us, four boys and two girls."

"I always wanted a brother."

"It was just you and Cara?"

Raven nodded.

William regarded her, his face unreadable.

Under his gaze, she grew progressively more anxious. She swept her hair behind her ears.

"Stop staring at me."

"Why? I like to look at pretty things."

"So you say," she huffed.

"And I haven't seen anyone as captivating as you for a long time. But you're a lark, not a raven."

"I have a large number of euros that belong to you." She changed the subject pointedly.

"Keep them, in case of emergency."

She wanted to argue with him, but concluded the exercise would be fruitless. "Does it bother you to be near me?"

He looked puzzled. "Bother me, how?"

"Does it make you—hungry?"

She almost winced when she said the last word. She didn't like to think about his feeding habits.

"I've already eaten. Your true vintage is masked currently by the blood I gave you a week ago. In a few days, however . . ." His voice trailed off suggestively.

She looked at him in revulsion.

"It doesn't hurt, when done with care." William brought his face close to hers. "I'd take you to my bed and we'd engage in all the sensual delights lovers enjoy. I'd touch you, taste you, bring you pleasure. Vampyres can engage in intercourse for hours. I can promise you the best delectation of your life. Only when you were in the throes of climaxing would I feed from you. It would be very pleasurable, very erotic."

Raven began to feel a little warm at the sound of his words and the movement of his perfect, sensual lips.

She closed her eyes to dispel the magnetic pull of his mouth and the way his voice pronounced the words *climaxing* and *erotic*.

The car approached the bottom of the hill and turned.

She looked outside.

"Where are we going?"

William's expression grew grim. "We're going to the hospital. Your boy has taken a turn for the worse. I need to see him immediately."

"Can you help him?"

"Yes, but I'll only give him enough to keep him alive. That will buy me enough time so I can schedule a more convenient visit. Being in the hospital exposes me."

"Thank you." She made eye contact so that he would see her sincerity.

"You're welcome. While I'm in the hospital, you'll wait with Luka. Under no circumstances are you to get out of the car. Do you understand?"

"What happens if Luka decides to take a nap with some fish?" She tried to suppress a grin.

And failed.

William's eyebrows drew together. "What are you talking about?"

Raven took a moment to assess him. He was not amused.

"Haven't you seen *The Godfather*?"

William's face was devoid of recognition.

"You know, the movie?"

He cleared this throat. "I find film—banal."

Raven laughed. "Of course you do. One of these days, you need to see *The Godfather*. It's the best film ever made, next to *Casablanca*."

"Would you watch these films with me?"

She blinked in surprise. "Would you want me to?"

He stroked her wrist with his fingers, back and forth across the skin.

"I can think of few things more pleasant than an evening in your company, even if it includes a film."

Her attention was drawn to his fingers and what he was doing to her. It felt incredible.

"Okay, but I have a condition."

He paused his movement. "What?"

"That you let me examine your art collection."

He frowned. "That's it?"

"I'd like to see what you have and assess the condition of each work. Then I can let you know what should be done to restore them."

"In exchange for this work, which will be extensive, given the size of my collection, you'll watch films with me?"

She mirrored his frown. "I'd need your word that you won't try to detain me. I want my freedom."

"I already gave you my word." He sounded offended.

William adjusted the cuffs on his black dress shirt. Raven noticed that the cuff links were in the shape of a lily and appeared to be made out of gold.

"I'll make arrangements for you to have access to the villa." He gave her a heated look. "Perhaps in time you'll come to desire my company for other reasons."

"You made me an offer I couldn't refuse," she muttered, turning back to the window.

"What's that?"

"Nothing."

His eyes narrowed, but if he was going to scold her, he appeared to think better of it.

"After the hospital, I will take you to meet my brethren. They will not be expecting you. No matter what happens, you will act as if you are perfectly at ease with everything that is said and done."

Now Raven was afraid. His words caused her stomach to flip.

He reached out a finger to lift her chin, angling her head so he could see her eyes.

"I am about to bring you into the underworld, Persephone. Can you be brave?"

She swallowed. "I think so."

"I know so." He hazarded a smile and swiped his thumb across her lower lip.

"There's just one last thing."

She gave him a questioning look.

His gray eyes glinted as he brought his thumb to his mouth and tasted it.

"You need to pretend you've spent the last twenty-four hours in bed with me, mindless with pleasure."

❋ ❋

Raven was terrified of William's associates. She hoped she wouldn't witness a human feeding frenzy or some other horrific event. She doubted very much if she could be brave under those circumstances.

He didn't spend a long time in the hospital. He reported that he'd been able to slip into Bruno's room and administer a small amount of vampyre blood, enough to stabilize his condition. A contact at the hospital would provide updates, which would be shared with Raven.

As the Mercedes approached the city center, William withdrew a length of black silk from his pocket and gestured for Raven to turn her back.

She eyed the silk with alarm. "Why?"

"The blindfold will enable me to ease you into the experience."

"I don't think there's anything easy about being blindfolded." Her green eyes were wary.

William ran the black silk through his fingers.

"I'm taking you to a place you are not supposed to see. This will protect you and make it easier for you to stay calm."

Raven stared at the fabric, unmoving.

He cocked his head to one side, listening to the escalating rhythm of her heart and her shallow breathing. He could smell the anxiety on her skin.

He placed the silk across his knee and eased his arm around her shoulders, pulling her against his body.

"Raven."

The sound of her true name from his lips caught her attention. She stared into his eyes.

"I need you to be brave and I need you to be calm. The blindfold will help. If you won't wear it, I'll have to use mind control."

"Mind control?" she repeated.

"Vampyres have the ability to manipulate human beings, but it doesn't work on the strong-minded. I doubt it will work on you. I'll have to try it if you won't cooperate."

"Is it like a Jedi mind trick?" She waved her hand in the air. "Pay no attention to these familiar looking droids."

He scowled. "Can you stop indulging in non sequiturs? What we are about to do is dangerous. I'm not the one who will end up dead if something goes wrong."

"I was trying to be funny."

"Vampyres don't indulge in comedy. Now, will you wear the blindfold or not?" He was moving swiftly from impatience to anger.

"I'll wear it." She turned her back.

He placed the silk over her eyes and knotted it behind her head. Then he rested his hand on her shoulder.

"Be brave, Raven."

She didn't feel brave, but she had no choice but to act the part. She focused on her breathing, trying to inhale and exhale deeply. She felt the car continue for a while, until it turned and seemed to enter a building of some sort. Shortly thereafter, the car came to a halt.

William helped her from the vehicle and held her elbow as he escorted her through a door. The ground beneath her feet felt like stone, which indicated to her that they were probably in one of the older buildings in Florence.

She wondered if they were in the Palazzo Riccardi.

William led her through a series of hallways and doors and down a winding staircase that seemed to last forever. She was almost convinced they were journeying to the very center of the earth.

Once they descended the staircase, they walked through a door and down a long, echoing corridor. She heard voices—men and women, but no children. She heard scraps of conversation in various languages, some of which she couldn't identify.

She heard laughter and the very obvious moans and rhythms of sexual encounters.

She felt the color rise in her cheeks, wondering if the underworld was actually a sex club for vampyres. She wondered if the erotic groans and sounds were those of human men and women, giving up their blood as they climaxed.

"Steady now," William whispered.

His hand slid down her arm and squeezed before returning to her elbow.

Raven took a deep breath, trying not to shake.

The air surrounding them was damp and carried with it a hint of mold. She coughed.

"Be brave and be silent, no matter what you hear." William's grip tightened on her arm.

Her stomach pitched.

A door opened and they entered what must have been a huge hall or theater. Raven could hear the echoes of metal clanking against metal, and the sounds of grunts and yells.

She lifted her chin slowly.

Despite William's best efforts, the blindfold had shifted. It was failing to cover a tiny field of vision to the right of her nose. If she moved her head, she could see.

And what she saw overwhelmed her.

She was on a balcony that overlooked an immense space, like a gymnasium. Men and women were engaged in various kinds of combat on the floor below. Some used weapons; some used just their bodies.

As Raven tried very hard not to move, she saw people leaping from the ground and seeming to fly through the air. She also saw them inflicting what she thought would be mortal wounds, although the victims remained unscathed.

She cursed impulsively.

"No sounds." William squeezed her once again.

What she had just seen was impossible. It defied gravity. It defied everything she had come to believe about human beings and their abilities.

It confirmed what she already believed—that William and his kind, whatever they were, weren't human.

He led her through another door and into a hallway. It was dark and appeared to be lit dimly by torches that were placed on the walls.

As they moved forward, Raven noticed that the underworld was hewn out of stone.

She heard voices in the distance, but no one passed them.

They stopped and Raven heard another door open. William led her inside a small, dark room.

She heard the striking of a match and inhaled the scent of smoke. A small light grew visible from a short distance away.

He must have lit a candle.

"Take a few moments to calm yourself."

Raven breathed deeply.

She heard the opening of a bottle and the splash of liquid. He placed a cold, smooth object in her hand and closed her fingers around it.

"This is Vin Santo. Sip it slowly, but drink all of it. It will relax you."

She brought the glass to her nose and sniffed.

She pressed the glass to her lips and drank.

"Humans are not allowed here unless they're under mind control and reserved as food. You must pretend your very will is slave to mine. You cannot reveal what you've seen. Or I'll be forced to silence the lark I've come to admire."

Chapter Twenty-nine

"What is the meaning of this? Why have we been convened?" Aoibhe strode into the council chambers below the Palazzo Riccardi. She was in a foul mood.

Pierre shrugged. "No one knows. The order came from the Prince himself, and he would not accept delays."

"But for what purpose?" She turned her attention to Lorenzo, who shook his head.

"Something came in from the human intelligence network but the report went straight to the Prince. I haven't seen it."

Aoibhe frowned. "That's irregular. You're second in command."

Lorenzo opened his mouth to comment, but closed it almost immediately.

"Where's Max?" She scanned the large room.

"He's been summoned." Lorenzo took his place at the front of the hall, holding the staff of the city out to his side.

Aoibhe approached Niccolò, who was already seated. "Are there problems with the patrols?"

"Not at all. Everything is proceeding according to plan." Niccolò's tone was not friendly.

Aoibhe clapped slowly. "Eager to keep your head, Nick?"

"It's attached to my body."

"For now," she muttered.

"*Perché la fortuna è donna, et è necessario, volendola tenere sotto, batterla et urtarla,*" Niccolò stated, his dark eyes taunting her.

She scowled and took a threatening step forward. "Five hundred years later and you're still spouting that ridiculous drivel? I'll show you what it is to be beaten, you ridiculous cretin."

"Aoibhe." Lorenzo spoke sharply. "Stop antagonizing Sir Machiavelli."

She opened her mouth to protest, but at that moment Max entered the room, followed by Gregor.

Aoibhe reluctantly took her seat, but not before hurling a few insults in Niccolò's direction.

"This meeting of the Consilium will come to order." Lorenzo tapped his staff on the floor.

The Consilium members stood as the Prince entered the room.

As soon as they saw the young woman beside him, a series of growls left their throats. All six vampyres inhaled her heady scent, turning with hunger in her direction.

Chapter Thirty

It was all Raven could do to keep moving. Her leg was troubling her but she refused to limp. She walked slowly, navigating the stone floor in her high heels like a cat mincing across a hot surface.

William had hold of her arm, but his proximity did nothing to stave off her fear. She heard animalistic snarls and growls. They seemed to surround her, echoing in a large space.

For one desperate moment, she wondered if William had escorted her to her death.

As he led her forward, she glimpsed a chair to her right and two pairs of feet encased in men's shoes. William positioned her in front of them, next to a series of steps.

When his hand fell away, she had to fight the urge to reach after it.

Her heart beat furiously as she worried he'd abandoned her.

She could feel eyes burning into her back. She sensed the closeness of the two men behind her.

She closed her eyes beneath her blindfold, willing herself not to show any reaction.

"A situation has arisen that requires our attention." William's commanding Italian broke into Raven's musings, and her head moved in the direction of his voice. "First, I have an announcement.

"I have taken a pet." He paused, as if gesturing in her direction. "No one is to speak to her, approach her, or touch her. This announcement is to be made to the plebs, as well, and it admits no exception."

Raven heard movement to her left.

"Forgive me, my prince. It pains me to remind you that human beings are not permitted in the underworld, with the exception of Teatro, unless they are part of the catering." The man's voice was respectful but firm.

"Yes, Niccolò, I am well aware of the rules since I am the one who established them." William's tone was cool.

It took Raven off guard, for Lucia and Ambrogio had referred to him as a lord. Now he was addressed as a prince.

She had to stifle a verbal reaction, her mind racing.

William continued. "As you can see, precautions have been taken. I'd like it noted that this visit would not have been necessary if it weren't for Maximilian."

A chorus of murmurs filled Raven's ears.

"Maximilian approached my pet, spoke to her, and tried to take her. I am also told that Aoibhe spoke to her as well." William's voice was glacial.

"With apologies, my lord. I had no idea she was yours." A woman's voice, young and attractive, sounded to Raven's ear like music. She recognized the voice from the night before.

"Am I to assume the pet will always be in your company, Prince?" a younger man asked.

"It pleases me to give her a measure of liberty, Lorenzo. I am busy with the affairs of state and cannot fornicate all the time."

A few chuckles sounded.

Raven felt her face grow hot.

"But she will wear your mark?" Lorenzo asked.

"Of course. To avoid misunderstanding, I am also presenting her with this."

Raven heard footsteps approach.

"Kneel," William commanded, his voice about a foot from her face.

She made a show of reaching out blindly in front of her, before dropping to her knees. The stone beneath her was hard and damp.

He lifted her right hand and slipped something cool over her wrist.

From under her blindfold Raven could see that it was a bracelet, fashioned from three intertwined strands of gold. A carved gold lily was affixed to the center of the bracelet.

Raven noticed that the lily matched the carving on William's cuff links.

"As long as she wears the symbol of the principality, she's mine. Anyone who interferes with what is mine shall be destroyed." William paused, as if for effect. "Remember Ibarra's fate."

His hand slipped over hers, the smallest, most unobtrusive touch, before disappearing. In it, Raven found comfort.

He must be worried about me.

"You may stand," his voice commanded.

Raven stood carefully. She heard William walk away.

"You cannot claim another master's pet."

Raven recognized the low, gravelly voice as that of the man who'd attacked Bruno. She felt a shiver travel up and down her spine at the realization that he was standing just behind her.

She fought the urge to cringe away from him.

"Explain yourself," Lorenzo barked.

"I came across this little one last night. She has two bloods in her, in addition to her own. Someone else has been keeping her."

"Silence," William growled.

The room grew quiet. Raven strained her ears for any sound.

"There were two others, yes. I destroyed them." William sounded impatient.

"She had a talisman. How were you able to take a pet who had a charm?" Murmurs sounded in the great hall.

"I was fortunate, Maximilian, that you separated my pet from her talisman, allowing me to claim her. Since I destroyed her previous masters, she belongs to me. Unless you'd rather challenge me for her." William waited, but only for an instant, before lifting his voice to address the group. "Does anyone else have an objection? There are enough swords on the wall to dispatch all of you."

Silence filled the chamber.

"Come now, don't waste time. I'd like to put this matter to rest so I can enjoy my new pet."

When no one responded, William continued. "I find your attitude troubling, Maximilian. This will be the last time you trouble me."

Raven heard movement behind her but she didn't know what it was.

"Since there are no further questions, we shall proceed. Gregor, escort my pet to the side chamber. Bar the door and stand guard outside. Anyone who approaches the chamber is to be destroyed. Do you understand?"

"Yes, my lord."

Raven felt someone move to her side and lightly grasp her elbow. He turned her around and accompanied her for several steps before they exited through a door.

She heard the scraping of something and the opening of another door. Gregor escorted her forward a few steps, placing her hand on the back of a chair.

He withdrew, leaving her in total darkness.

She heard the door close and something heavy fall into place. It was only then that she allowed fear to overtake her.

Chapter Thirty-one

"I received a message this afternoon from the human intelligence network. A group of hunters were sighted outside the city this morning."

Inside the council chamber, the Consilium murmured their reaction to the Prince's announcement.

"The network intercepted them as they tried to enter the city. They were interrogated and destroyed. Unfortunately, it appears they were part of a larger party, some of whom entered the city on the other side."

"Were they members of the Curia, my lord?" Niccolò asked.

"No."

The Council members breathed a collective sigh of relief.

The Prince lifted his hands.

"Those who were part of the human patrols today have been destroyed for their failure. I have also dispatched their leadership. They have been replaced and I am assured by the head of the network that this lapse will not happen again.

"With hunters in the city, everyone is at risk. Lorenzo, make sure word goes out to the plebs.

"Niccolò, take Max, Aoibhe, and your best patrols and search the city, going building to building. I want the hunters destroyed, but reserve two. I will interrogate them personally."

Lorenzo and Niccolò bowed their acquiescence.

"Prince, a missive has arrived by courier from the Princess of Umbria."

Lorenzo produced an old-fashioned envelope, sealed with wax, from under his robe.

The Prince cracked the seal and opened the letter. After he'd perused its contents, he nodded at the council.

"The Princess sends her greetings. She reports all is well and that our alliance is intact." He stuffed the letter back into the envelope and placed it in the inner pocket of his jacket, ignoring the quizzical gazes he received.

"Niccolò and Lorenzo, I want the city to be impenetrable. I want our army at the ready. It's possible this hunting party is a sortie for a larger incursion."

The Prince stood, as did the council members, who bowed as he swept from the throne and down the aisle.

Before he reached the door, Aoibhe was at his elbow.

"May I have a word, my prince?"

He turned, examining her face.

She appeared calm, if not curious. Seemingly satisfied, he gestured to a corner and followed her.

"I see you took my advice." Aoibhe smiled, but it did not reach her eyes.

William's expression tightened. "The girl is a diversion; not a consort."

"Then there's room in your bed for me."

William simply returned her stare. Aoibhe tilted her head as she scanned his features.

"No doubt it will take some time for you to tire of your new pet. I can be patient. Is she under mind control? I couldn't tell."

"Is there a point to this conversation?"

Aoibhe tossed her long red hair.

"Your pet's scent is masked. Was she a virgin?"

William gritted his teeth. "Be alert this evening, Aoibhe. The hunters will find you irresistible."

"I suppose that means she wasn't." Aoibhe tapped a finger to her lips, as if she were deep in thought. "If she wasn't a virgin, I'm surprised you bothered with her. Tell me, was she sweet?"

The Prince glared. He was about to leave, when something over her shoulder caught his eye. The other council members were turned in their direction, observing them with more than a little interest.

His eyes returned to hers.

With practiced ease, he lifted his right hand and brought it to her face, swiping his thumb across her lips.

Her dark eyes widened in surprise and she drew his thumb into her mouth, sucking deeply.

"She's a pet. Nothing more." He kissed her aggressively and she reciprocated, nipping at his lower lip.

William pulled back with a scowl, lifting a hand to his mouth. Mercifully, she hadn't drawn blood.

Aoibhe winked at him.

"I'm glad we have an understanding. You know where to find me when you grow tired of your pet."

She turned to rejoin the other council members, but spoke over her shoulder.

"I'll be waiting."

Chapter Thirty-two

Somehow the journey up the spiral staircase seemed much longer than the downward climb. Raven clung to William's side, eager to flee the strange world he inhabited.

Inhabited.

Her thoughts caught on the word. William didn't simply inhabit the underworld; he ruled it. Judging from the deference she'd heard in the voices of his associates, they feared him.

She had thought of him as a member of a group of vampyres, not as the leader. If she'd been afraid of him before, her fear had tripled.

Now I'm his pet.

She cringed. The term, as well as the experience, was demeaning. If she hadn't been afraid for her life, she would have objected. Loudly.

Her commitment to the laws of nature and what was physically possible had been weakened and almost destroyed. She'd seen and heard too much, both above and below the mysterious staircase. And the way the men and women in the gymnasium moved . . .

She wondered why vampyres hadn't taken over the world.

Raven stumbled and she felt William's iron grasp on her right elbow. "Keep going," he whispered.

She didn't know if they were visible to the others. Certainly she didn't hear any other footsteps on the staircase.

Her heart was beating very fast. She was sure the adrenaline was what was staving off the discomfort of wearing high heels.

William didn't speak, but he moved so that his arm was wrapped around her waist.

Raven found his touch comforting.

A few more minutes and they were moving through doors and down hallways. William helped her into a car and sat beside her, removing her blindfold and shoving it into his jacket pocket as they drove through the city streets.

She exhaled a sigh of relief.

His face was watchful, careful. "It's possible my brethren might follow us, but they'll be stopped at the gate to the villa. They can't cross onto the property."

"Why not?" she croaked, her mouth dry.

William retrieved a bottle of water from Luka, who was driving.

Raven accepted it gratefully.

"Let's just say there are certain things in my possession that prevent the others from troubling me."

"You didn't tell me you were a prince."

"The title refers to my position." William watched as she drank half the bottle. "The ruling vampyre of a principality is known as the Prince. Thus, I am the Prince of Florence."

"How long have you been prince?"

"Since the fourteenth century."

Raven began to choke, water spilling into her lungs. She coughed and spluttered while William looked on helplessly.

"Are you all right? What should I do?"

She waved aside his hand and continued to cough, clearing the water from her throat.

"Luka, stop the car," William instructed.

"No," she managed to say, though she continued coughing. "I'm okay."

"You don't sound okay." He placed his arm around her shoulder.

She coughed a few more times.

"I'm fine."

Carefully, she sipped her water. Then she took a deep breath and exhaled.

"Are you all right now?" His pale eyebrows had drawn together.

"Much better, thanks."

"You have to be more careful."

"I didn't realize that drinking water while you were talking was hazardous." She glared at him. "If you became prince in the fourteenth century, you must have been born earlier than that."

He nodded once.

"How much earlier?"

"I've kept my age a secret, for various reasons."

She frowned. "What kind of reasons?"

He gave her a look calculated to end her line of inquiry.

"How does one become a prince?"

"Usually, by destroying the previous one." His tone was casual, too casual.

Raven's blood grew cold.

"I never destroyed anyone who didn't deserve it. Remember that before you condemn me."

He withdrew his arm from her shoulder and turned his attention to the darkened cityscape.

Raven took another drink of water, not knowing how to respond.

William was unaccustomed to justifying his actions. Since he'd become prince, he hadn't had the need.

But even as he explained himself to the young woman who sat beside him, he felt a new emotion. He pushed it aside, not wanting to deal with it.

"You were very brave this evening. I would have liked to reward you by showing you the wonders of my city, but there are hunters about. Our tour will have to wait."

Raven put her empty water bottle aside. "Who would be crazy enough to hunt you?"

"Two groups. This is the weaker one. Some of the weaker ones hunt for sport, but most do so in order to harvest blood."

"Vampyre blood?"

"Wealthy humans use it for healing purposes but also to combat aging. We're difficult to kill, which makes our blood rare and very valuable. So valuable the hunters sometimes target ferals."

"Is their blood similar?"

"Feral blood induces madness."

Raven swallowed hard. "If someone thought she was taking vampyre blood but got feral blood instead, she'd go mad?"

"Whatever animates a feral is transmitted by the blood. The darkness migrates to whoever ingests it." He looked over her shoulder briefly, as if he were considering something. "It's similar to possession."

Raven rubbed her temple as the ghost of a headache emerged. Clearly her body was having trouble processing these successive revelations.

"If that feral had bitten me the other night, would I go mad?"

"If there'd been a transfer of blood in a suitable amount, yes."

Raven closed her eyes, trying with all her might to keep a close rein on her emotions. Her heart thumped in her chest and she felt a cold clamminess pass over her skin.

William took her hand in his.

"Are you going to be sick?"

"I don't know."

"Luka, stop the car."

Obediently, Luka slowed the car and pulled into an alley.

William turned, giving Raven his full attention.

"If you took a catechism class in your parish, then you know all about angels and demons and supernatural events."

"I stopped believing that shit when I was twelve."

"Why?"

Raven answered by leaning back against the headrest and breathing deeply, eyes still closed.

"If you believed in it once, you can believe in it again. Just add vampyres and ferals to the angels and demons."

"Are you saying there are angels and demons?"

"Undoubtedly."

Raven cursed.

William moved closer to her. "Ferals kill; they don't maim. If one attacked you, you'd be dead in seconds. After that, it would feed from you. Vampyres prefer their food alive."

"Strangely, I don't find that comforting."

He pulled her into his side and lowered his voice.

"Take comfort in the knowledge that you are under the protection of the most powerful vampyre in the kingdom of Italy, with the exception of the Roman."

Raven opened her eyes. "Who's the Roman?"

"The Roman is the ruler of the principality of Rome. Since ancient times, the Roman was also considered to be the king of the principalities that now make up Italy."

"He's more powerful than you?"

"Much."

Raven blew out a loud breath. "Where does your power come from?"

He tugged at a lock of her hair.

"Not so fast, Delilah. I'm not about to reveal all my secrets."

"I didn't know vampyres went to Sunday school."

William's smile faded.

"The less said on that subject the better. Not that my training protected me."

Raven felt his anger. It seemed to seep out of his skin, filling the car. But it wasn't directed at her.

"Lucia packed up your belongings at the villa and Ambrogio has transferred them to your flat. If anything was missed, tell him and he will deliver it to you."

"The things at the villa aren't mine. I arrived only with this." She pointed to the knapsack that sat on the floor.

"The clothes were bought for you."

"You didn't need to do that." Her cheeks pinked in embarrassment. "Some of them won't fit."

"Weight loss is an unfortunate side effect of ingesting vampyre blood. You'll be back to your healthy weight soon enough."

Raven's mouth dropped open.

She was going to protest, or at least ask him to clarify what he'd said, but he'd already continued speaking.

"Ambrogio had to remove the relic from your flat before you returned."

Raven's attention shifted immediately.

"You took it back, remember? It was in my knapsack when Bruno was attacked."

"I placed another in your flat the night I returned you."

"I didn't see it."

"It was hidden under your bed. I had no intention of seeing you again. I left a relic to protect you."

Raven gave him a searching look.

"That was very . . . good of you. Why are you taking it back?"

"The others will be curious about you. They'll find your apartment. The relic must be gone by then. And I won't be returning the one I gave you before."

"But why?"

"You're supposed to be my pet. Relics deter my kind." He spoke abruptly.

"They don't deter you."

William gave her a look that was dangerous, if not cold, and she found herself inching away from him.

"You don't need to worry about me telling tales."

He glared his warning. "I hope for your sake that's true."

"A vampyre's pet wouldn't have relics because they would deter her vampyre."

"Exactly."

"What about Maximilian? He knew I had a relic in my knapsack. I'm sure of it."

"Don't worry about Max." William's voice was clipped.

"So your brethren don't know that relics have no effect on you." She looked at William with new eyes. "Why do you keep it secret? Don't you want them to know how powerful you are?"

"Power is at its most powerful when it is concealed." His face, like his tone, grew dark.

"Okay," she whispered.

"Are you going to be sick?"

"No."

William turned his attention to the driver. "Luka, we can proceed."

Silence filled the car as they crossed the Arno. William placed his palms on his knees, tapping his fingers against the wool.

Raven was seized with the impression he was anxious or impatient about something.

As they approached Piazza Santo Spirito and Raven's apartment, he spoke.

"I promised to help the boy and I will do so until he recovers. I will also endeavor to ease the suffering of your neighbor."

"Thank you."

"The depth of your concern for your fellow human beings took me by surprise." He paused, his gaze suddenly fixed on one of the buildings. "I am not usually surprised."

His remark didn't seem to require a response, so Raven didn't answer. She leaned forward to pick up her knapsack and settled it on her lap.

Luka parked the car near Raven's building and immediately got out. He closed the door and stood behind the car, his posture alert.

"I realize that your willingness to stay with me was based on your wish to help your friends. But it is my hope that you—" William stopped, his voice filled with longing.

"What do you hope?" She tried to make eye contact.

"Nothing." He kept his gaze fixed on the street. "I hope for nothing because hope is vain."

Raven toyed with her knapsack. "Despair is the absence of hope."

"Don't presume to lecture me on despair," he snapped.

Raven twisted her fingers.

"I'm sorry," she said meekly.

He turned, placing his hand under her chin. "You are the only ray of hope I've seen since 1274. You're the only one who has caused my heart to beat again."

For a moment, Raven saw something much deeper than physical desire in his eyes. She didn't know what it was, but she saw it and felt it, shimmering in the air between them.

All at once, he covered her mouth with his own, his tongue tracing the seam of her lips.

She opened to him.

William swept the knapsack aside, tugging her into his arms.

His tongue pushed past her lips, sliding against her own. His hand moved to her neck.

In a few swift movements, he undid the knotted silk at her throat. Then his lips were on her neck.

Raven's eyes shot open.

He nipped at her skin before laving it with his tongue. Over and over he repeated the sequence as Raven's heart sped in her chest.

She shifted her legs as heat flared in her middle and lower down. Tentatively, she touched his hair, pushing back the strands with her fingers. Still his lips moved against her throat.

He drew some flesh into his mouth and sucked.

Raven gasped.

William's mouth gentled. He kissed the tender spot on her neck, his tongue fluttering lightly over the skin.

He pressed a few small kisses to the indentation at the base of her throat before brushing his lips across hers.

"Was that a bite?" she whispered.

William moved back. "No."

She touched her neck. The skin wasn't broken.

She examined her hand. There wasn't any blood.

He bent to retrieve her scarf, which had fallen to her feet. He placed it in her lap.

"I would never feed from you unless you offered yourself."

"Isn't that what vampyres do?"

"Don't tempt me." His voice grew cold.

"I don't understand you." She shook her head.

"What's not to understand?"

"How you can be so harsh and kiss like that."

William's face broke into a smile and he placed his arm around her.

"I predate the advent of psychology, Cassita. I can't offer that kind of self-analysis."

Raven tentatively rested her head on his shoulder and was rewarded when his other arm wrapped around her waist.

"I know you're dangerous," she confessed. "But I know without doubt that I'm alive because of you and for that I'm grateful."

"Gratitude is a start," he mused.

"Bruno's grandmother was kind to me when I first came to Florence. Thank you for helping her and for saving Bruno."

William nodded against her hair.

She placed her hand on his chest, near his heart.

"Can I ask you something?"

"Of course. I don't promise to answer, but you can ask."

"When we were with your people, I heard someone mention something about a mark. What was that about?"

"If you were my pet, I'd have fed from you by now." He gestured to her neck. "They'd see more than just a bruise. From now on, you'll need to cover your neck whenever you're in public."

"I can do that. I like scarves."

"You can keep this one. Lucia can buy another."

Raven lifted her head. "Won't she want it back?"

"Not if I tell her not to."

Raven decided not to argue with him. She'd see that Lucia's scarf was returned later on.

William glanced in the direction of Raven's apartment, wearing a look of displeasure. "You'd be safer at the villa. As I said, vampyres can't cross the property line and my security team keeps out the humans. But I promised to bring you home and here you are.

"Tonight we're hunting hunters. Once they're disposed of, you'll have more freedom. Until then, I'm assigning Luka to keep an eye on you. He'll follow you to work Monday morning and stay close during the day."

"Is that really necessary?"

"The hunters are human. If they learn I have a pet they may decide to use you."

"Wait—what?" Raven pushed back from his embrace. "How can a human being hunt you?"

"They use weapons and various tools. They also use subterfuge, which is why I want you to be careful."

"Do you think they'll come after me?"

"It's possible. But most vampyres wouldn't be lured out of hiding to save a pet. Pets are disposable."

Raven cringed.

"You are not disposable, Cassita, I assure you." He kissed her lightly. "But it's safer for you if I keep that secret.

"I doubt the hunters would target me, in any case. Wise hunters realize it's easier to capture newer vampyres—younglings, we call them. But young blood is never as powerful as old, which means older vampyres are a greater prize."

"You inhabit a strange world."

"No stranger than yours. Except, in my world, everyone is a villain."

Centuries of betrayal and mistrust flashed before William's eyes. Even though he respected his Consilium and relied on them in certain circumstances, he didn't trust them.

No. The young woman in his arms was the only person he'd come close to trusting for years. And he couldn't bring himself to tell her even some of his lesser secrets.

Raven flexed her right foot, trying to alleviate the ache in her ankle. It occurred to her that the adrenaline in her system must have receded.

"If I were to ask you to heal my leg, would it be your blood you'd give me?"

William stiffened. "No."

He kept his arms around her, but moved to look straight ahead.

Raven wanted to press the matter, to pepper him with questions, but she didn't. He'd already grown cross with her once that evening.

She was grateful he was going to help her neighbor and he was going to let her go. She didn't want to do anything that might cause him to change his mind.

William released her.

"It's time. Luka will accompany you and make sure you're safely inside. He will be replaced by a guard who will watch your apartment from across the piazza.

"Monday morning, Luka will take you to the Uffizi."

"Thank you."

She gave him a small smile before picking up her knapsack.

"What, no argument? No protestation?" William gazed at her curiously.

"You brought me into a world where, even blindfolded, I could feel the power and hunger of the beings who surrounded me. Then you told me that there's a class of humans who hunt you, who may decide to use me as bait. I need all the protection I can get."

He took her hand and kissed the back of it, holding it gently.

"Noah released the raven and the raven returned. If I were able to hope, I'd hope you would return to me. Good night, Cassita."

"Good night." Raven tried to hide her surprise at his remark and the delicate way he'd kissed her hand.

As she exited the car, she was surprised to feel a sudden sense of loss.

Chapter Thirty-three

Just before sunrise, William sat behind his desk rereading the letter Lorenzo had delivered to him earlier that evening.

To His Lordship, the Prince of Florence,
    Greetings.
    It was with joy we received your missive. As ever, the Principality of Umbria welcomes the friendship of the powerful Principality of Florence. We pledge our continued fidelity to our great and important ally.
    The human beings you inquired about are indeed resident in our territory. There are four of them: one adult male, two adult females, and one female infant. As of the date of this letter, they inhabit a house near Todi.
    It would be an honor to deliver these humans to you as a gift. Or, should you prefer, we will dispose of them in the manner you request and provide you with the remains.
    If these possibilities are not to your liking, you have our permission to enter Umbria in order to hunt them. Please do us the kindness of notifying us in advance of your visit, as we would like to welcome you in a manner that befits a person of your rank.
    I would like nothing more than to entertain you, should you be able to spare a few days. I remember your previous visit with much pleasure.

I remain,
Your loyal ally,

Simonetta,
Princess of Umbria

William tossed the inked parchment on his desk.

His situation had grown a good deal more complicated since he'd written to Simonetta, requesting permission to hunt Gabriel Emerson in her territory.

He hadn't forgotten him. But he knew the laws concerning illegal incursions and was not about to risk a war with one of his most important allies over a common thief.

Now that he had Simonetta's permission, he could go quickly, kill Emerson, and return to his own principality in a single evening. But he would not leave his city while it was infested with hunters.

Nor would he leave Raven now that he'd known the pleasure of her mouth.

Her mouth.

His plan to take her as a lover had gone awry. While it was true he hadn't loved anyone in centuries, he felt something for her, and the feeling was beginning to deepen. He'd hoped they'd be able to explore their mutual attraction and that something between them would blossom and grow.

He'd been sorely mistaken.

Her horror at his proposal and her subsequent offering of herself in exchange for a favor had more than surprised him. He knew himself to be far from noble, but he prided himself in doing the noble thing, just this once.

He'd released her.

But he had no intention of abandoning his plan to seduce her. In fact, his desire for her had increased exponentially.

When he finally had her in his bed . . .

William restrained himself from fantasizing. He needed to clear his mind through meditation and rest while the sun shone. Or at least until it was almost sunset; then he could climb the Duomo and enjoy the view of his city.

It was true that he could walk in direct sunlight, but he found it uncomfortable. Like all vampyres, he needed to rest during the day and clear his mind.

There was a suspicion among his kind that madness descended on those who did not adequately and regularly clear their minds—something about the weight of immortality causing rationality to fail. If there was one thing William needed as prince, it was rationality.

Hunters plagued his city. They'd evaded the search party and murdered two younglings over by Santa Maria Novella Station, draining their blood and dumping their decapitated bodies on the train tracks.

As was their custom, the hunters had taken the heads. If a vampyre head was left in proximity to its body, the two pieces tended to go back together, reanimating the vampyre. Hunters knew that they could fetch a higher price for vampyre blood if it was sold with the head, proving authenticity.

William shuddered to think what the hunters would do to Raven, should they become aware of her. Which was why on a hunting party a few hours before, with Aoibhe and the others, he'd made sure to mention that Raven was safely ensconced in his villa, awaiting him in his bed.

He hoped he'd been believed.

Chapter Thirty-four

Raven stood in her bedroom early Monday morning, staring at her new cane.

It had made an innocuous appearance when she'd arrived home after Ambrogio's visit. On this morning, she stared at it with utter hatred.

Most of the changes in her appearance had been reversed. Her disability had returned almost completely. Her weight had increased so she was, perhaps, a size smaller than she'd been. No one who saw her now would think she'd undergone a miraculous change.

She was angry with herself for enjoying her brief experience of beauty and for mourning its departure. She'd never thought of herself as shallow; she thought of herself as stoic. Clearly she didn't know herself as well as she thought.

She was also angry with herself for hating her disability. No sooner had she limped out of bed that morning than she'd begun thinking of asking William to give her vampyre blood to heal her leg.

Her willingness to entertain the idea upset her greatly.

Her disability divided her from those who did not have visible disabilities. She knew this.

But in her view, all human beings were disabled in some sense—physically, socially, mentally, morally, etc. She thought that accepting the truth about oneself, and perhaps even coming to embrace it, was the correct way to deal with a disability, not denying it, hiding it, or, God forbid, trying to eradicate it from society.

So it was with scorn that she regarded herself in the bathroom mirror—her sad eyes and downcast expression. She was manifesting the same bigoted sadness she'd seen in others when they pitied her. She despised pity and its attendant low expectations.

Raven paused to note the fact that William had not pressed her to take blood.

He'd mentioned it, but seemed to leave it as her choice. He didn't seem bothered by her disability. It was almost as if it escaped his attention most of the time. Maybe that was why she was strangely drawn to him, even more so after he'd released her and promised to help Bruno and Lidia.

She limped to the cane and gripped it as if it were a sword, swearing she would accept herself as she was and that she would no longer entertain any thought of healing. The cane itself, new and black, was far more functional than her old ones, especially the one that was still (artfully) sticking out of the wall.

She decided she liked it there and would not remove it.

While she wasn't sure how she felt about William buying her a new wardrobe, she was grateful for the nice clothes. Lucia must have sorted the items and sent only the larger sizes, because most of them fit, including two pairs of designer jeans.

On this day, she wore a navy dress with matching cardigan and simple flat navy shoes. Obediently, she was wearing a scarf and the bracelet William had given her. She wondered if it had some historical connection to the city of Florence or if it was something he'd acquired during his long and mysterious life.

He'd become prince in the fourteenth century, but had mentioned something about losing hope in 1274. Raven didn't have time to Google the date to see what was significant about it, but she intended to do so later.

She retrieved her new reading glasses from atop her bedside table. Her old ones had been in her knapsack the night of Gina's party. She hadn't been able to find them. Ambrogio must have known her prescription because he'd replaced them—and with smart Prada frames.

She tucked her glasses into their case and made her way to the kitchen table, where she retrieved her new iPhone. Ambrogio had left it for her in its box, with a note that indicated the information stored on her old phone had been transferred to it, along with contact information for himself, Lucia, and Luka.

William's name and contact information were noticeably absent. From this, she surmised that vampyres didn't carry cell phones.

(They probably used carrier pigeons.)

Unfortunately for Raven, all the photographs she'd taken of her changed appearance hadn't been transferred to her new phone. She no longer had visual proof of the healing of her leg, since her old phone was missing.

The absence of photographs seemed intentional. Certainly she hadn't done it. She wondered what William's reasons were.

Perhaps he was protecting her. Perhaps he was protecting himself. He certainly wasn't demanding she maintain her changed appearance. Maybe he truly was attracted to her ordinary self.

As promised, Luka was waiting for her downstairs. He was a large man, standing well over six feet, six inches and probably weighing about three hundred pounds. He was also spare with his words.

When he saw her, he walked in front of her to the door and escorted her to the Mercedes, which was parked around the corner.

During the short drive to the gallery, Raven fingered the scarf around her neck. It was covering William's mark now. He'd left behind a love bite.

She tried not to think about how pleasurable it had been to be in William's arms and how sensual it had felt to have him kiss her neck.

She sighed.

He hadn't mentioned anything about seeing her again when he dropped her off. In return, she hadn't named a day for their film night.

Her apartment had certainly seemed spartan and lonely next to his opulent villa.

Truly her life had taken a surprising turn when it was clear that her next most likely date would be with a vampyre prince.

"Are you all right?"

Patrick greeted Raven with concern as soon as she entered the office space she shared with several other people. Other colleagues filtered in, chatting at one another's desks before starting the workday.

She hobbled to her workspace, leaning on her cane. "I'm perfectly fine."

"You're using your cane again."

Raven shrugged. "I guess the new treatment I was trying failed."

"You didn't mention anything about a treatment. I thought your leg improved on its own when you disappeared."

Raven lowered herself to her chair and placed her knapsack on the floor. "I don't like talking about it."

"Right." Patrick didn't sound convinced.

He approached her, his hand reaching for her wrist. "What's this?"

Raven tried to pull her hand away, but he'd already seen the bracelet. "It's a gift."

"From whom?"

"Just a friend," she said airily. She began withdrawing items from her knapsack and placing them in a neat row on top of her desk.

"The same friend who gave you the other museum-quality piece you had on last week?" He let go of her wrist. "That's gold, Raven. How much do you think it's worth?"

"Listen, Patrick, I met someone who's a bit of a collector. He's just lending me things for fun. No big deal."

"Okay, okay." Patrick lifted his hands in surrender. "I'll stop being nosy. But you have to realize how this looks. You disappear for a week and come back looking like a totally different person. A week later, you're back to normal, but you're wearing expensive gifts. And I'm not talking about things any asshole could buy from Tiffany. I'm talking about medieval and Renaissance pieces that are probably traceable to a collector."

Raven wracked her brain for a plausible lie.

She offered him a conspiratorial smile. "Okay. The deal is that I met someone. It's early yet so I don't want to say too much. He has some money and likes to spend it."

"So is this the friend who gave you the gold cross?"

She peered around the room, making sure no one could hear their conversation.

"Yes. We're just getting to know one another."

"I thought you were going out with Bruno."

"He had to cancel." She twisted her hands in her lap.

Patrick's expression shifted. "I'm sorry."

"Thanks," she said weakly.

"But you've met someone else and that's good. What does he do?"

"Uh, he deals in—rare vintages."

Patrick smiled. "Well, if he ever has any extra, send a bottle over to me. Gina loves that stuff and it isn't exactly cheap."

Raven nodded, trying very hard not to squirm.

Patrick moved to sit on the edge of her desk. "Unfortunately I have some bad news for you."

"What?"

"The head of security stopped me on my way into work this morning."

Raven clenched the top of her cane tightly. "Why?"

"He saw the tape of you handing me the flash drive in the archives."

"Oh, no. Are you okay?"

"I'm fine. Luckily I had a similar flash drive in my pocket that was filled with files I'd been transferring for the project I'm working on. I showed it to him and said you'd been helping me.

"He checked with the archivist, who confirmed I had clearance to copy the files, and that was the end of it. The archivist was puzzled when your name came up, but I covered for you."

"Thank you." Raven leaned back in her chair. "I'm really sorry about that. I owe you one. Again."

"It's fine. Did you ever find out anything else from those files?"

"I haven't had a chance to work on it. I know that Botticelli changed Mercury's hair, along with some other changes that are well documented. But this weekend I was a little busy."

Patrick smiled. "Busy with your vintage collector?"

She looked away. "Maybe."

"Good. I'm glad you can get out and have some fun. I saved the good news for last. Professor Urbano was in here a few minutes ago. He wants you to report to the restoration lab. I'm supposed to notify the archivist that you're no longer working for her."

"Really?" Raven almost clapped her hands. "Can I go now?"

"He said to report in as soon as you arrived."

"Thank you." She flashed him a wide smile and he grinned, hopping off the desk.

She zipped her knapsack closed and carefully stood, leaning on her cane. She crossed over to the wardrobe that sat at the end of the room and withdrew her lab coat, folding it carefully over her arm.

Patrick followed.

"I ran into Ispettor Batelli after I left the security office," he announced, shoving his hands into his pockets.

"What did he say?"

"He said that the Interpol agent assigned to work with him disappeared last week."

Raven stopped. "When?"

"The night you had dinner with Gina and me."

"Agent Savola," she whispered.

"That's right. That was his name."

Shakily, she leaned against the wardrobe door.

She had no idea that it was Agent Savola who'd popped out of the shadows the night the feral appeared. That he was the man who'd given his life trying to save her.

Her stomach heaved.

"Are you okay?" Patrick peered at her face.

"I think so. Why did the inspector tell you that?"

"I have no idea. I saw him talking to Dottor Vitali a few minutes ago. Neither of them looked happy."

Patrick jerked his chin at her wrist. "For the love of God, hide that. You don't want to be conspicuous with the inspector walking around."

Raven pulled her cardigan over the bracelet, hiding it.

"Thanks, Patrick. I'll be careful."

Slowly but surely, she made her way across the room and down the hall to the restoration lab, wondering what Batelli and Vitali had been talking about.

Just as she was about to put her hand on the door, she stopped.

Probably there were witnesses who'd seen her, along with Agent Savola and the feral.

Raven didn't know what to do with the realization. It was bad enough having captured Batelli's interest in connection with the theft of the illustrations; she didn't want his attention in connection with Savola's murder.

And there was also the matter of Bruno's attack, which William said he had handled. But had he?

She contemplated telephoning Ambrogio with a message for William, but decided against it. She was going to be late for work and didn't want to upset Professor Urbano.

William was probably resting somewhere, anyway, out of the sunlight.

❊ ❊

Raven spent the morning in Botticelli's world, painstakingly applying a coat of varnish to the *Birth of Venus*.

Professor Urbano had decided that Anja, her replacement, had not progressed at an acceptable pace. There was also some question about the quality of her work. Urbano simply replaced her, assigning her to another project.

Raven was sympathetic with Anja's plight and moderated her joy at being able to return to the lab. But it was with undisguised delight that she sat on a high stool, slowly and carefully restoring one of the greatest works of art in the world.

"Dottoressa Wood."

Raven heard the voice but dimly. She was working on the figure of Zephyr, marveling at the way his face differed from the Zephyr who appeared in William's version of *Primavera*.

She heard footsteps and the slight clearing of a throat.

She turned to her left and saw Professor Urbano standing there. He was smiling.

"Can I look?" He gestured to the patch she'd been working on.

"Of course." Raven put her supplies in order and obligingly climbed down. She pointed out what she'd accomplished and where she'd left off.

She removed her glasses and waited nervously for him to pass judgment.

He took her place and used a series of magnifying glasses and other instruments to check her progress. When he descended from the stool, he was smiling.

"Very fine work. Thank you."

"My pleasure."

"I think now is a good time for lunch."

She looked around, noticing that their colleagues had already left.

"Before I go, Professor Urbano, could I ask you a few questions?"

"*Certo.*" He gestured to a nearby set of chairs and they sat down.

"When you worked on the restoration of *Primavera*, did you ever notice anything about Mercury's hair?"

Urbano looked puzzled. "Such as?"

"Such as evidence of changes in color or length."

Urbano looked off into space for a moment, as if he were regarding the painting in his mind's eye.

"There was some slight change around the edges of the hair, as I recall, but nothing about the color or the overall length. Why do you ask?"

"I thought I saw something in one of the radiographs that suggested Botticelli changed the hair color."

Urbano smiled. "Impossible. We went over the radiographs very, very carefully. Everything we found was documented and published."

"Oh." Raven nodded. "I have a couple of other questions, if you don't mind."

He gestured to her to continue.

"Did you know of any other version of *Primavera* that was painted by Botticelli, perhaps prior to the one upstairs?"

Urbano stroked his chin. "There were studies for the figures and drawings."

"But not a painting?"

"No. Why?"

"Uh, when I thought I saw something about Mercury's hair, I wondered if Botticelli had painted a previous version." She lifted her new glasses. "It was just a thought."

"Of course." Professor Urbano gave her a patient smile and excused himself for lunch.

Raven watched him leave, mulling over their conversation.

She considered William's account of how he'd acquired his *Primavera*, wondering if that was why no one had ever heard of it.

What she couldn't understand was why no one seemed to have noticed the change in Mercury's hair in the Uffizi's version. She knew evidence of the change was visible. She knew she hadn't made a mistake.

Your memory hasn't been that great lately. You can't even remember what happened the night of the accident.

It occurred to her that William might be the one behind Urbano's lack of awareness, as he was behind so many odd events. Since Urbano had worked on the restoration of *Primavera*, he should have seen the change. Perhaps William had adjusted his memory during the restoration.

But why didn't he delete the records?

Raven didn't have an answer to that question, but she was determined to ask him. Her need to speak to him reminded her of what Patrick had said earlier about Agent Savola and Ispettor Batelli.

Raven walked with her cane to her knapsack and picked up her new phone. She called Ambrogio.

"Good afternoon, Signorina Wood." He greeted her in English. "How may I help you?"

Raven grew flustered. "Um, hello, Ambrogio. Can I speak with William?"

"I'm afraid his lordship cannot be disturbed. How may I assist you?"

"Can you give him a message for me? It's urgent."

"Of course."

She paused, feeling awkward. "Can you tell him that, um, the man I saw being attacked in Santo Spirito was an Interpol agent named Savola, who was working with the Carabinieri to investigate the robbery at the Uffizi?"

Raven's tone grew urgent. "William needs to know this right away. The police haven't approached me, but one of the officers is here and he spoke to one of my colleagues. Because the agent was attacked in front of my apartment, I'm worried they'll put it together and come looking for me."

"Please don't worry, signorina. I will see that your message reaches his lordship. Is Luka with you?"

"I think he's outside the gallery, waiting."

"If there are any problems, go to Luka. He will bring you here."

"Yes. Yes, thank you."

"May I help you in any other way?"

Raven sighed. "No. Thank you, Ambrogio. That's everything."

"Then good-bye, signorina."

"Good-bye."

She ended the call, staring at her cell phone.

She'd passed along the information, but felt far from comforted. At that moment, however, there was nothing she could do.

She lifted her knapsack and began walking toward the door, leaning heavily on her cane.

That was when she saw Ispettor Batelli striding toward her.

"You saw Agent Savola being attacked?" he asked, in Italian.

"What?" She stalled.

"You just said that you saw him. What did you see?"

Raven frowned. "You misunderstood my English. I didn't say that."

Batelli swore. "I heard what you said. And my English is perfect. Savola's Vespa was found outside your apartment."

"Really? That's strange." She forced a smile. "I'm afraid I'm late for my lunch. If you'll excuse me . . ."

"Who is William?" he asked, intercepting her.

"I have no idea."

"Your telephone call. You wanted to speak with William. William who?"

"A family friend." She smiled again. "Now I really have to go."

She tried to move past him but he stood in front of her.

"William York?"

Raven attempted to hide her recognition, but she suspected she failed based on Batelli's triumphant expression.

"Where is he?"

"I don't know what you're talking about." She skirted him and limped toward the door.

"Why didn't you call the police? Why didn't you report it?"

"Because I didn't see anything." She spoke over her shoulder.

"The investigating officers were told that Agent Savola was following you after hours. When they found his Vespa, they should have interviewed you as a matter of procedure. Why didn't they?"

Raven didn't turn around. "You're harassing me. If you don't leave me alone, I'm going to Dottor Vitali."

"And tell him what? I overheard you confess to having witnessed a crime."

"I didn't witness anything."

Batelli brought his body in front of hers. "I saw the police reports. Your name doesn't appear. Why is that?"

"I have no idea what you're talking about."

She continued her way to the door, desperate to get away from him.

"Someone is protecting you," he called. "I'm going to find out who. You're going to be questioned."

Raven increased her pace.

"This time it will be with the public prosecutor!"

She exited the lab, ducking into the women's bathroom. Leaning against the wall, she screwed her eyes shut and tried to calm herself.

She was in trouble.

Raven didn't see Batelli when she exited the bathroom. In fact, he seemed to have disappeared.

She sent a text to Ambrogio, not wishing to court disaster by speaking to him on the telephone again.

He texted back five words:

His lordship will address it.

Raven took only a small measure of comfort from that text.

She was too agitated to eat lunch and so she wandered the second floor of the gallery, moving past the Botticelli room to look at Michelangelo's *Doni Tondo*.

She hung back, allowing the visitors to admire the work.

She forced herself to stop worrying and simply focus on the great artist's depiction of the holy family. Her eyes traced the figures, the folds in the fabric, and the men in the background.

By the time she was finished, her lunch break was almost over. She felt much, much better. Great art had the ability to soothe as well as nurture the heart.

Having taken what amounted to a mental vacation, Raven returned to the lab. She was pleased to be able to lose herself in the restoration work, finding a comforting rhythm in every brushstroke.

Soon it was time to go home. She deposited her lab coat in the office wardrobe and slowly made her way outside to where Luka was waiting.

He drove her to Santo Spirito and accompanied her up the stairs to her apartment. He searched her rooms before he allowed her to enter, then nodded at her and descended the stairs.

Clearly he was still a man of few words.

Raven checked her phone for messages, e-mails, or texts, but there weren't any. It seemed as if everyone she knew was busy with other things.

Her apartment seemed small and maybe even a little sad. She'd spent a glorious day working on a beautiful piece of art, but now she felt unaccountably lonely. It was as if her world had transformed from a brightly colored Renaissance painting to the dark, somber work of a Dutch master.

She switched on her laptop and began playing Mumford and Sons, finding the music a pleasant distraction. She changed into a black T-shirt and jeans, placed her gold bracelet on her nightstand, and ate a modest supper.

After a solitary glass of wine, she retired to her bed, putting on her glasses and picking up *The Lion, the Witch and the Wardrobe*.

In chapter eight, one of the characters warned the others about beings who used to be human or should be human but weren't, suggesting when they met such a creature they should reach for their hatchets.

She'd read the passage before. She'd read the entire book before. Now the passage took on a new meaning.

The hunters made it their mission to kill vampyres and harvest their blood. If they'd been hunting humans, the world would have cried out to stop them.

Genocide.

Ethnic cleansing.

Raven wondered if such moral prohibitions applied only to human beings or whether they could be applied to other species.

And what of William? If he needed human blood to survive but did not kill those he fed from, should he be destroyed? Or denied his only source of food?

She was attracted to him. He'd rescued her on more than one occasion. Raven was not used to being protected, at least, not since her father died. Her mother hadn't protected her or her sister.

The fact that a mysterious vampyre would protect her, at great risk to himself, and that her mother would not, pierced her.

Even now, as she looked around her empty apartment, she wished he were there. She wished she could communicate how important his care had been. She'd been alone and self-sufficient for so long. It was nice to have someone to approach with her problems.

He was gentle when he touched her. And he kissed with tremendous passion. Raven pondered the vagaries of sex with a vampyre and, more improbably, love.

The song "Awake My Soul" began playing. Raven put her glasses and book on the nightstand and focused on the lyrics, staring at the ceiling.

William believed in souls. She wondered if there really were such things.

She wondered if vampyres had souls.

"Why the long face?"

"Ah!" Raven screamed, scrambling toward the window.

William was leaning against the doorpost, wearing a black dress shirt and black jeans, his arms crossed over his chest.

He was chuckling.

"I didn't mean to frighten you."

Raven clutched at her heart, willing it to slow. "You scared the hell out of me. What are you doing?"

He frowned. "I came to see you, of course."

She leaned back against the pillow and closed her eyes. "Can't you use the doorbell? You gave me a heart attack."

William stood by the bed and leaned over her, bringing his ear close to her chest. "Your heart sounds fine—strong and healthy."

"Very funny. How did you get in?"

"Magic."

She turned on her side, facing him, her head resting on an upturned hand. "Just knock next time. Okay?"

His grin faded.

"That reminds me. Don't let anyone into your apartment, especially if they ask to be invited."

"Why?"

"Vampyres have to be invited into a home; otherwise, they can't cross the threshold."

"You must have entered uninvited when you brought me back the first time."

"You invited me; you just don't remember." He gave her a knowing smile. "And the rules are somewhat flexible when it comes to me."

"Why is that?"

"I don't know."

She lifted her eyebrows.

He shrugged. "It's true. I don't know the reason. It's possible there are others, but so far I'm the only one I'm aware of who's able to skirt the rules."

"There must be an explanation."

"Naturally." He spread his arms wide and turned around. "Perhaps you'd like to examine me? Come up with a scientific explanation?"

She rolled her eyes, trying not to examine his very attractive backside. "Why are you here?"

He lowered his arms. "Am I not welcome?"

"You're welcome; just unexpected."

He approached the bed. "I came to give you something."

"What?"

"This." William placed a fist on either side of her hips and brought his mouth to hers.

Like his presence, his kiss came without warning.

He kissed her lightly at first, becoming more insistent as she responded.

She brought her hand to his chest and up to his shoulders, reveling in the strength beneath her touch. She could feel his muscles, his lean power, and the attraction that flared between them.

When she opened to him, his tongue slid against hers. He growled appreciatively, angling his head.

He toyed with her for a moment before withdrawing, making her follow him into his mouth.

She enjoyed his taste and the way he moved in an unhurried fashion, focusing only on the interplay of mouth, tongue, and lips.

She rolled to her back and he followed, bringing his body to cover hers.

It had been a long time since Raven had been in such a compromis-ing position. Her hands slid up and down his back, pressing their chests together.

She could feel his arousal hard against her thigh.

Suddenly he lifted himself on his forearms.

He kissed the corner of her mouth. His eyes glittered and he seemed very pleased with himself.

But Raven also saw regret.

"I can't stay," he rasped, sliding his nose along hers.

"Why not?"

He kissed her again, a searing, toe-curling kiss. "Do you want me to stay?"

She turned her head from the burning intensity of his eyes.

"When you ask me to stay, I'll stay." He shifted to his side and placed his hand on her abdomen.

"We're still searching for the hunters. The patrols need my help."

She looked at him askance. "You left the search so you could kiss me?"

William lifted the hem of her T-shirt and slid his hand over her bare skin, back and forth, back and forth. "Is that an objection?"

She shook her head.

William continued his movements, lightly tracing the curves of her waist. "Tell me what happened at the Uffizi today."

She placed her hand over his, stilling his movements. She found it dif-ficult to think while he was touching her.

She recounted her conversations with Patrick and with Batelli, explain-ing how the inspector had threatened her with a formal questioning.

"Don't worry about that." William slid his hand to her hip and squeezed.

"He heard me talking on the phone to Ambrogio about Agent Savola. If he goes to the public prosecutor and has me brought in for questioning, I'm sunk."

"There's a security guard at the Uffizi who's part of our network. He made a videotape of Batelli's encounter with you and presented it to the director of the Uffizi this afternoon.

"He also sent me a copy. There wasn't any sound from the security cameras, but what I saw was extremely damaging to the inspector. He accosted you, shouted at you, and tried to prevent you from leaving. The director reported him to his superiors and he was escorted from the gallery."

Raven was surprised. "No one at work said anything."

"Since the investigation at the Uffizi is ongoing, I'm sure things are sensitive." He brought his face closer to hers. "When I promised to protect you, I meant it. No one, human or vampyre, is going to intimidate or harm you."

She kissed him, bringing her hand up to brush through his hair. "Thank you."

"The inspector is still in charge of the investigation but he's been ordered to stay away from you and he's been formally reprimanded. Now the police can't bring you in for questioning in connection with the Interpol agent's disappearance, even if they wanted to." William tugged a lock of her hair. "The outcome is better than expected."

Impulsively, Raven wrapped her arms around him, shoving her face into his neck.

William seemed taken aback by her reaction, but he recovered, hugging her back. "What's that for?"

"For helping me. I'm used to having to rely on myself."

"I'm more than willing to help you, in almost anything. Just say the word."

"He scared me," she whispered. She'd become emboldened, perhaps by their closeness.

William held her more tightly. "I could see that. But you stood your ground."

"I didn't realize it was Agent Savola who was killed by the feral. I didn't get a good look at him."

William brought his lips to her neck.

"Um, I spoke to Professor Urbano about the restoration of *Primavera*."

William ignored her remark and continued to kiss her throat.

"When I was in the archives I noticed that Botticelli changed Mercury's hair color and length."

"I told him to," William murmured against her skin.

It took a moment for Raven to process his remark.

"Because?"

"Because he was trying to paint me into the painting. I instructed him to adjust the features and the hair."

"Mercury still looks like you."

"Perhaps. But Zephyr doesn't." He kissed her once again, moving to the indentation at the base of her throat.

"Why doesn't Urbano know what's in the radiographs? He worked on the restoration with Baldini."

"Probably because I used mind control to adjust his memory."

"You did that?" She pushed back to look at him.

"Of course." He frowned. "Their interest in Mercury would have raised questions. I've been known to visit the Uffizi on occasion. I didn't want to be recognized."

"How did you get into the gallery the night you took the illustrations?"

"Don't ask those kinds of questions." He nibbled on her skin.

"I can't help it. It bothers me."

He pulled away, his eyes hard.

"They were stolen from me. I've owned them since Botticelli completed them. I had no idea where they were until they materialized at the Uffizi over a century after they were taken from my home."

"Wait a minute. You said Botticelli completed them?"

"Of course." He sounded cross.

"But they're copies, made by one of his students. The originals are in the Vatican and the Staatliche Museen in Berlin."

A ghost of a smile appeared on William's lips.

"No, the illustrations in Rome and Berlin are copies. I own the originals."

"Holy shit." Raven clapped a hand to her mouth.

Now William was grinning.

"During the Renaissance, I took an interest in human affairs. There were tremendous innovations in architecture, science, painting, and sculpture. I moved in human circles from time to time.

"Botticelli heard rumors about my true nature and decided to illustrate it in the original version of *Primavera*. I appear as Mercury and as Zephyr. A human woman who fell in love with me was the model for Chloris as well as the second of the three Graces.

"I was angry when I found out what he'd done and intended to kill him. He begged for his life, offering me the painting in question and a set of illustrations of Dante's *Divine Comedy*. I agreed. He completed the copies later on."

Raven dropped her hand.

"A human woman fell in love with you?"

"Yes," he replied tersely.

"What happened to her?"

William ground his teeth. "She climbed Giotto's bell tower at the Duomo and jumped to her death."

"Good God! Why?"

"Because she fell in love with a monster." William lowered his voice, his eyes steel gray.

"Did you love her?"

"No."

Raven felt pain lance through her. Few things were more tragic than unrequited love. It was easy to imagine a young Renaissance woman falling in love with William, only to discover that he was a vampyre.

"I'm sorry."

"So was I." He shifted to lie on his back, folding his hands on his chest.

"Was she your pet?"

"No."

Raven was uncertain what to do with that information. Whatever William's relationship with the woman, centuries later he was still upset about her death.

She looked over at him as a terrible feeling passed over her. He'd mentioned many disturbing things, but all of a sudden several of them came to mind, forming a picture she did not like.

She decided to change their topic of conversation. "Are you hungry?"

Now it was his turn to lift his eyebrows. He stared unashamedly at her neck.

"I meant for food," she clarified. "Human food. Or wine?"

"I could take a glass of wine, but our bodies don't digest human food."

She moved as if to climb off the bed, but he stopped her, placing an arm on either side of her body.

"Are you in pain?"

"No." She looked away.

"Then why are you upset?"

"I'm not."

William's eyes narrowed.

"You are. I can see it, hear it, and, more importantly, I can smell it. What's the matter?"

She made a face.

"And don't lie." His tone grew serious.

Her eyes moved to his. "Did you eat before you arrived?"

"Of course."

"How many times a day do you eat?"

"It depends. Old ones can feed once per day. Younglings need to eat frequently. I feed when the mood suits, either once or twice per day. It depends on what's on offer and what my appetite is." He smiled at her slowly. "I've been known to have a healthy appetite."

"Whenever you feed, you have sex?"

His smile disappeared. "Why are you using that tone?"

"I'm not using a tone." She tried to shift away from him but he hovered over her, caging her with his body.

His eyes narrowed. "You sound upset."

"Well, I'm not," she huffed.

"It's usual for a vampyre to have sex when he or she feeds. But I tend to be a bit more discerning."

She looked up at him with interest. "So you don't have sex every time you feed?"

"Why are you so concerned about this?"

"No reason. Can I get up now?" She glanced at his arms pointedly.

"Cassita." He ran his nose down the side of hers. "Are you jealous?"

"Of course not."

He fought a smile. "Then why are you asking about my sexual assignations?"

"You said you wanted me. I was curious if you were building a harem."

"Such things don't interest me."

She hummed in response. "I'm sure you could find someone who didn't need a cane."

He brought his lower body to hers. "Are you considering engaging in intercourse with me?"

She reddened. "I'm just trying to figure out what your game is."

"It isn't a game. As I told you before, you're the first to capture my interest in a very long time."

He bent down and kissed her firmly. He swept her hair to the side and stroked her neck, lightly, up and down.

When he pulled back, her eyes were still closed.

"Your beauty is a feast for the eyes as well as the senses."

At that her eyes opened. "I hate it when men lie."

"Look at me," he ordered, his tone momentarily harsh.

Their eyes met.

"I have no reason to lie. While it's true that flattery is a means of seduction, I have no reason to use it with you. I think you're beautiful. If you want me to heal your leg, I'll do so. But stop playing the jealous mistress. I don't owe you explanations or fidelity, unless you agree to be mine."

He rolled to the side and left the bed, moving to stand next to her desk.

She sat up, watching him. He looked very unhappy.

"Are vampyres faithful to their pets?"

"No."

"And you?"

"I've never had a pet," he confessed.

"Never?"

"That's correct." He looked at her thoughtfully. "I can only surmise that part of your reaction has to do with my story about Allegra, the young woman who killed herself. The story is not a pleasant one. Perhaps I'll tell you someday.

"In the interim, I'll reiterate what I have already said. You are not my pet and if anything were to develop between us it would be pleasurable and enjoyable."

She toyed with her fingernails, avoiding his eyes.

He lifted his arms in frustration. "Why don't you tell me what is really going on?"

"I think I missed you," she blurted out. "When I came home after staying with you, the apartment seemed so quiet."

William smiled, and the smile lit his entire face. "You missed me?"

Raven looked down at the bedcovers. "What kind of person am I? You kidnapped me, you threatened to keep me as your sex slave, and I miss you? I must have serious issues."

William's expression darkened. "Is it really so terrible to desire my company? Am I so repulsive that you'd despise yourself for wanting to see me again?"

"It isn't exactly natural. You're a vampyre."

"I may as well be human. I'm not feeding on you." He gave her exposed throat a hungry look. "If fidelity matters, I'll volunteer the information that, for the present, I'm not having intercourse with anyone—vampyre or human."

Raven tried to ignore the strength of feeling that bubbled up inside of her. But she failed.

He sat next to her on the bed once again. "There is mutual attraction between us. Clearly we enjoy one another. Spend the night with me, just once, and you'll see how magnificent we will be together."

He traced her cheekbone with his finger. "It will be the greatest evening of your life, I swear it."

Raven closed her eyes and leaned into his touch.

The music shifted and her laptop began playing Madeleine Peyroux's "Dance Me to the End of Love."

"I like this," he whispered, kissing her neck. "I never listen to modern music."

He traced the V-neck of her T-shirt, his finger descending to just above the curve of her breasts.

She grabbed his wrist.

"Are you positive the illustrations you have are original?"

"Yes." His eyebrows knitted together in irritation. "Forget about them. You're the only work of art I'm interested in."

He brought his lips to her throat.

Raven knew she was fighting a losing battle. His touch was light but sensuous, leaving a scorched trail across her skin.

No one had ever made her feel this way before. She felt as if he were drawing away her resolve, little by little, and soon there would be nothing left.

"You have to give them back."

William lifted his head.

"Absolutely not."

"You own a lot of beautiful things," she said quietly. "Don't you want to share them?"

"No. And I'd rather not discuss them, especially when I'm trying to seduce you."

"Is that what's happening?"

"This is the dance of love. Men and women have been doing it for centuries. What did you think was happening between us?"

"No one ever looked at me with . . . desire." She fumbled her words, embarrassed.

"Because human beings are shallow, ignorant creatures." He lifted his eyebrows, as if daring her to contradict him.

Her eyes dropped to her hands, which were gripping the quilt. "You don't mean love, you mean sex."

He frowned. "I am not capable of love, Cassita. No vampyre is."

He lifted his hand and ran it through her hair.

"But I am capable of tenderness, I think, at least with you. Can't that be enough?"

Raven fought the urge to wince.

Perhaps these had been the words William spoke centuries earlier to the woman who jumped from the bell tower. For her, it had not been enough.

Raven had always discounted love, thinking it wasn't possible for her. She wondered bleakly if William was offering her the best she could do.

She moved toward the head of the bed, putting space between them.

"Let's not talk about love, okay? It's ridiculous to have that conversation when we barely know one another."

William's expression tightened, but he did not disagree.

"Would sex bond us?" she asked.

"Bond us?"

"You mentioned something once about vampyres bonding."

He shook his head. "That bond is through the intake of blood."

"Oh."

"The sexual act unifies the two, unless the parties will that it doesn't."

"So is that what you'd do? You'd have sex with me, but will that it didn't bring us closer together?"

"I never said that." His eyes took on a strange light.

Raven didn't want to consider what that meant.

"Getting back to the illustrations, since they're original, why don't you share them with the world? The way the Emersons did?"

William stood, placing his hands on his hips. "Don't mention the name of those thieves. They stole from me and they're going to pay for it."

At that moment, Raven was almost grateful for William's anger. It was a great deal easier for her to deal with than his hands on her body. But she found his response distressing.

"You're talking about a man and his wife and child. You wouldn't harm them, would you?"

His expression remained unchanged.

"The Emersons weren't alive a hundred years ago," she persisted. "They didn't break into your house."

"That is no excuse."

"They're a young family with a baby. I don't know the professor, but I met his wife. She told me they're going to adopt a child from the Franciscan orphanage."

Something shifted in William's eyes, but he didn't speak.

"It's true. They're going to adopt a little girl who has special needs. I volunteer at that orphanage. I know Maria. No one wants her. If you kill the Emersons, that little girl will never have a family."

William clenched his jaw.

"That is not my concern. I cannot tolerate thievery. If the others realize I let this go, it will weaken my authority."

"Can't you strengthen your authority in other ways? Find out who stole from you originally?"

"I have my suspicions."

"Then leave the Emersons alone."

"Never," he said haughtily, moving toward her bedroom door.

"William," she called. "I need to tell you something."

"Proceed." His tone was cold but his eyes radiated concern.

"I think it's obvious I'm attracted to you. And I—" She struggled for the words. "I feel something for you."

She held up her hand. "Not love. I'm not sure love is for me, anyway. But if you harm the Emersons, whatever is between us will end. I can't condone punishing the innocent for someone else's crime, especially a mother and child."

"I've already decided not to harm the family," William responded primly. "But Emerson received stolen property. That hardly makes him innocent."

Raven's eyebrows knitted together. "Do you think whoever sold him the illustrations revealed they'd been stolen? The Swiss family probably wasn't even alive when they were taken from you."

"I want justice."

"In your justice, don't forget mercy."

William's gaze moved inexplicably to the kitchen, then back to Raven. He said nothing.

"If you're intending to hurt Professor Emerson, take this back." She picked up the gold bracelet from her nightstand and held it out to him. "I don't want it."

He scowled darkly. "It's for your protection."

"Which I no longer want."

"You wanted it badly enough a few minutes ago." William sounded bitter. "I see you return gifts from men with practiced ease."

"Men don't give me gifts."

"I have no interest in taking my revenge against a mother and child." His eyes sparked with anger. "My issue is with Emerson."

"Don't you understand, William?" Raven lowered her voice intentionally. "If you kill him, you destroy his family. I know what it's like to grow up without a father. Things happened to us after he died, terrible things. Please don't do that to Julia and Clare."

William started. "You know their names?"

"I met them, yes. And I liked them. Julia is kind and gentle and Clare is a beautiful baby. Would you condemn that beauty to a lifetime of sadness?"

William regarded her, his expression blank.

He glanced at the gold bracelet, but didn't take it.

His gray eyes moved to hers. "Good-bye, Jane. Be well."

"Wait." She struggled to her feet as he strode through the door.

Hurriedly, she grabbed her cane and made her way to the hall. "William, wait. I can't walk that fast."

By the time she reached the kitchen, he was gone. Mysteriously, the door was still locked from the inside.

Raven pulled out a kitchen chair and sat, on the verge of tears.

She hadn't expected his visit that evening, or the way her heart leapt when she saw him. She hadn't expected to feel so warm and desirable in his embrace, or to feel her spirits rise when he kissed her.

She hadn't expected him to say good-bye.

She looked at the bracelet, still in her hand, and felt loss.

William wasn't a friend and he wasn't a lover. He was something else—something for which there was no name.

He's Zephyr, hovering in the shadows. He took pity on Psyche and helped her and then he disappeared.

She felt unshed tears burn in her eyes.

You're selfish. Her conscience spoke. *You're crying over someone who isn't even a friend, while a whole family is at risk.*

Her conscience's reminder was enough to stop the tears. The Emersons were in danger.

She doubted he'd go after them tonight, when there were hunters in his city. He had more pressing concerns.

You need to warn them.

But how? She knew there was no point in writing a letter to Julia, pointing out that she and her husband had angered the vampyre prince of Florence. They'd think she was mad and probably persuade Dottor Vitali to dismiss her from the gallery and have her put in the hospital.

She had to do something.

If she couldn't warn the Emersons, her only alternative was to change William's mind. Based on his parting words, she doubted she'd be successful.

She wouldn't offer herself this time. She'd have to come up with some other way to persuade him.

Raven poured herself a large glass of wine and sipped it, trying to come up with a plan.

He wouldn't come to her again. He was through with her.

She would have to go to him.

Chapter Thirty-five

Two hours later, Ispettor Batelli stood on the other side of the piazza, watching the lights go out in Raven Wood's apartment.

He was not alone in his observations. At a nearby café, a man sat and smoked, keeping careful eye on both the apartment and the inspector.

Unbeknownst to both of them, a vampyre stood on the roof above, noting with interest the comings and goings of the apartment building opposite.

When the lights in Raven's apartment went out, the vampyre leapt across the rooftops in the direction of the Duomo, a group of hunters tracking him from the ground.

The vampyre saw movement below him and doubled back, moving in the opposite direction.

The hunters regrouped, some of them on motorcycles, speeding along behind him.

With one tremendous leap, the vampyre sprang into the air, his body hurtling over an alley toward the roof on the other side.

At that moment, a hunter who had been lying in wait aimed his crossbow toward the sky. When the vampyre came into view, the bow snapped and shot the arrow at its target.

There was the sound of something sharp piercing flesh and an agonized cry.

The vampyre was hit midair and fell like Icarus from the sky, crashing to the ground below.

Before he could rise, other hunters encircled him, quickly pouring a perimeter of salt around his body. Now he was trapped.

Black blood poured from the wound in his chest, the arrow piercing his heart. He lifted a hand to break the shaft, but one of the hunters threw holy water on him.

He screamed as the water ate into his flesh like acid.

Two hunters approached from behind, looping a closed garrote around his neck. They flipped a switch and stood back. A loud clicking sound echoed across the alley.

The vampyre lifted his hands to tear the metal cord from his neck, but it was too late. The garrote's mechanism clicked and tightened until, with one terrible, grotesque sound, the vampyre's head was severed from his body.

With lightning speed, the hunters moved the head some distance away, then set to work. In less than thirty minutes, the body was drained of blood and the corpse was left to decay.

A cursory observation of the vampyre's body, along with a quick test of his blood, indicated that he was no youngling.

The hunters cheered.

With one last triumphant cry, they retrieved the head and left the scene, bolstered by their success and eager to fell their next target.

Chapter Thirty-six

William was angry.

He left Raven's apartment after she'd ended things and immediately flew to Teatro.

He'd had her in his arms. She'd thanked him for coming to her rescue, again. This time, he felt the beginning of trust in her embrace.

They'd even talked about sex. Her ardor fanned the flames of his hope, cautious as it was.

Now she was willing to throw everything away, and for what? For a proud, arrogant thief.

He conceded the need to spare the lives of Emerson's wife and child. He'd already made that determination when he left their hotel room.

That was not enough for Raven. She wouldn't be satisfied until she'd saved the world.

He leapt into the air, landing lightly on the roof of the building next to Teatro.

The surrounding rooftops were empty. Vampyres young and old were either in the club or pursuing pleasure elsewhere.

He was glad of it. How could he explain to his brethren that he needed to feed at Teatro when he had a perfectly good pet at home? A pet with long, silken hair and soft, fragrant skin that smelled of roses.

A pet who guarded her body as if it were clad in a chastity belt.

He growled, rubbing his face.

Raven was not a pet and he wasn't angry simply because she'd tried to save Emerson. He was angry because she'd sent him away, as if their connection were tenuous and easily broken.

He'd allowed himself to hope, knowing that hope was vain. Just as quickly, his hope had been extinguished. And there would be no Raven to reignite it.

He leapt to the ground, standing in the alley outside Teatro's side entrance.

A burly security guard moved menacingly in his direction but stopped when he scented the Prince. The guard bowed.

"May I be of service, my lord?"

"Not at this time." William dismissed him.

A taxi drove up, stopping at the entrance to the alley.

As if on cue, the door to the club opened, and a young woman exited. She was slight of height and build, her eyes large and almost black, her hair dark. Her skin was a coppery brown and she spoke to the security guard in Spanish.

She was thinner than William preferred but he inhaled her scent eagerly; the spicy tang of her blood almost a taste on his tongue.

"Good evening." He addressed her in Italian.

She peered around the bodyguard with a frown. When she caught sight of William, she smiled.

"Good evening," she replied, in Spanish.

She turned as if to go to her taxi.

Suddenly William stood in front of her. "May I see you home?"

"I have a taxi."

"I'll walk you." He stared deeply into her eyes.

This was the test, of course. Would she look away or return his stare? She returned his stare and smiled.

William allowed the hunger in his belly to grow. He instructed the security guard to dismiss the taxi.

Offering the young woman his elbow, he escorted her from the alley to a side street.

"Your name?" he asked.

"Ana."

"Ana." He repeated her name, as if trying its feel in his mouth.

She didn't ask his name. Or perhaps she intended to but wasn't given the opportunity.

He quickly pulled her into another alley and pressed her back against the wall.

He didn't kiss her mouth, as he usually did in such moments. In fact, he closed his eyes and went for her neck, immediately.

She gasped as his tongue tasted her skin, her hands lifting to grip his biceps.

She rubbed herself against him, her breasts pert and high on her chest.

He placed his hand to her waist, leaning into her, before swiping his thumb across her nipple.

When she moaned and lifted her leg to place her thigh against his hip, he sank his teeth into her throat.

She cried out as he drank furiously, carefully counting the number of times he swallowed. Too much and she'd faint.

He drank quickly, but savored every mouthful. Her blood was light and sweet, like her body, with a delicate spice that hinted of recklessness.

When he reached the maximum volume he could drink from her, he carefully licked her wound. She gripped his arms tightly and orgasmed.

He waited until she stopped shaking, then carefully disentangled himself from her.

She murmured at him and tried to kiss him, but he kept her at arm's length, escorting her back to the security guard.

He'd given the young woman pleasure and fed from her, but he felt no joy. In fact, he felt even hungrier—hungry for blood, hungry for sex, hungry for hope.

He rubbed his eyes, trying to blot Raven's image out of his mind. His inability to take pleasure in the simple act of feeding did not bode well.

He instructed the guard to send the girl home in a taxi, then he melted into the shadows, feeling empty and conflicted.

Chapter Thirty-seven

Raven's head arched back, exposing her neck, as William's lips closed on her breast. His body, including his mouth, was cooler than hers. The feel of his tongue in intimate places was particularly arousing.

They were naked.

He was sitting up, his back against the wall at the head of her bed. She was straddling him, his arm encircling her waist as he thrust inside her.

At the sight of her neck, he growled, his mouth moving from her breast to her throat.

She moved up and down, riding him. She was close, a familiar tightening beginning below her stomach.

He kissed her throat, nipping and sucking the skin. His lips and tongue stroked across her flesh, her breasts brushing across his smooth chest.

"Cassita." He tugged her earlobe with his teeth. "I won't let such beauty die."

One more swivel of her hips and she climaxed, the words that tumbled from her lips incoherent.

With a snarl, he sank his teeth into her neck, piercing skin and artery until the blood flowed into his mouth. He sucked and sucked as her orgasm peaked, thrusting between her legs faster and faster.

With the blood flow to her brain diminished by half, she grew light-headed. But the sensation only compounded her climax, causing it to continue, like a wave that would not crash.

She was suspended in time, in the throes of absolute ecstasy as he drank, the blood flowing warm and liquid down his throat.

She grew more and more light-headed, the pleasure in her body still present, but she began to disconnect with it, as if she were losing the ability to feel.

She raised a weak hand to his shoulder, trying to push him away.

He shoved her arm aside.

Her eyes shot open and she began to cry out, begging him to stop, her limbs immobile.

Pain shot through her body, overtaking the pleasure. Her eyes rolled back into her head and she felt weightless, the pain as well as the pleasure gone.

When she collapsed in his arms, he laid her on the bed, lifting his bloodied mouth to kiss her.

"I'm sorry," he whispered. "I couldn't help myself."

Raven lacked the strength to respond. She felt the darkness close in around her as her heart stuttered and finally stopped.

Chapter Thirty-eight

To say that Raven was unsettled by the nightmare would be an understatement. She slept fitfully the rest of the night, finally giving up on sleep at around four o'clock in the morning.

She wrote short e-mails to Cara and to Father Kavanaugh, telling them she'd be glad to see them in the summer. She lied to her sister, saying that Bruno had canceled their date. She hoped Cara wouldn't pursue the matter further.

At six o'clock, it was still too early to get ready for work, so Raven spread her drawing paper and charcoals across the kitchen table and began sketching the lost Michelangelo painting that hung in William's villa.

It was difficult to draw from memory, even though Raven's memory (when not recovering from a life-threatening head injury) was very good. Still, it was worth a try, since it seemed unlikely she'd ever see it again.

An hour and a half later, she'd outlined the naked bodies of Adam and Eve. They were a fair approximation of the figures painted by Michelangelo.

Disturbingly, however, she'd drawn the faces of William and herself without realizing it.

Frustrated, she tossed the paper and charcoals into her knapsack and went to the bathroom to wash her hands. The drawing was ruined. And it certainly hadn't helped her put thoughts of William aside.

He was handsome, it was true. But he was dangerous.

He kissed like an angel. Or rather, what Raven thought an angel would kiss like if there were such things.

But he was cruel.

Her subconscious had placed interesting words into his mouth.

I won't let such beauty die.

But William would let beauty die. Moreover, he'd bring about its death directly, by killing Professor Emerson.

She chose a pair of black pants and a green blouse to wear to work, dressing listlessly. She pinned her hair into a bun at the nape of her neck and retrieved her glasses from the nightstand, where they sat next to William's bracelet.

He hadn't taken it.

As she looked at the gold, at the fleur-de-lis in the center, it occurred to her that returning it would give her an excuse to visit him. Then she could speak to him about the Emersons.

It was a flimsy excuse but all she had.

She placed the bracelet on her wrist, wrapped a scarf around her neck, and exited the apartment. After locking her door, she saw a woman on the landing, preparing to enter Lidia's apartment.

The woman bore a striking resemblance to Bruno, with the same dark hair and eyes.

"Good morning," she said. "I'm Raven."

The woman's face flashed with recognition.

"I'm Graziella, Bruno's mother."

"Um, I heard Bruno was in the hospital. Is he okay?"

Graziella appeared upset.

"He was attacked the other night. But he's doing much better. We think he will be able to come home tomorrow."

Raven exhaled her relief. "That's good news. How is Lidia?"

"Not so good. But a specialist from Rome is coming to examine her." She nodded toward the apartment. "She was refusing treatment until she heard her case had come to the attention of a distinguished oncologist. She decided she'd see him."

Raven found herself heartened by the news. "I'm glad to hear it. I didn't know she was sick. I'm so sorry I didn't try to help earlier."

"Would you like to come inside? Say hello?"

"Of course."

Raven glanced at her old Swatch discreetly. She had plenty of time to get to work.

When they entered the apartment, Dolcezza, the cat, darted toward the door.

Raven hung back, not knowing how the cat would react to her. It had hissed at her only a week previous.

But the cat seemed to have forgotten her previous bad temper and began threading itself through her legs.

Raven leaned over to pet the cat, hearing its throaty purr.

"Mamma, you have a visitor," Graziella announced.

Lidia was over seventy and small and rounded, with curly gray hair and dark, wise eyes. She was sitting on her couch in the living room, watching television. As soon as she saw Raven, she smiled.

"Hello, my dear." She waved her over and Raven crossed the room.

Lidia patted the couch next to her.

Raven sat down, placing her knapsack on the floor. "I'm so sorry to hear that you're sick."

"I'm fine, just old. How did your date with my grandson go?"

"Oh." Raven shifted awkwardly. "Well, something came up and he couldn't meet me."

"Really?" Lidia frowned. "That isn't like him. He told me he was looking forward to it. I'll have to speak to him. But you know he had an accident."

"Yes, I heard that. I'm so sorry."

"He's getting better. Now, what do you want for breakfast?" Lidia moved as if to stand, but Raven stopped her.

"I should be making you breakfast."

"I can still fix breakfast. I'm not dead."

Raven shot a worried look at Graziella, who rolled her eyes to the ceiling.

"I'm just on my way to work at the Uffizi. Maybe we could have breakfast another time."

"Anytime. Just knock on the door. But not tomorrow; tomorrow the doctor from Rome is coming."

Raven smiled and squeezed her neighbor's hand. "Good. I'll see you soon. If you need anything, please let me know. I'm just next door."

Raven hugged Lidia and took leave of Graziella, wishing with all her might that the specialist might find a way to help her neighbor.

❊ ❊

It was with great surprise that Raven saw Luka standing in the hallway of her building after she left Lidia's apartment. She'd thought that William would withdraw his protection after what had happened the night before.

She didn't bother asking him questions about William, for she knew Luka wouldn't answer. His lordship had trained his servants well and they always obeyed orders.

Luka was human. As far as Raven knew, all William's servants were human. Although at first she couldn't tell the difference between a human and a vampyre, now she found it easy. Vampyres were paler of skin, stronger, and more imposing physically than human beings.

An air of danger and threat clung to them, as well.

As she exited her building with Luka, she didn't see Ispettor Batelli watching her from across the piazza. Nor did she see him following the Mercedes from a distance.

She spent a quiet but constructive day in the restoration lab, working on the *Birth of Venus*. Patrick and Gina stopped by to invite her to lunch and the trio walked to a nearby osteria, on the other side of Piazza Signoria.

Luka drove Raven home after work, where she prepared a simple dinner, packing up half of it to deliver to Lidia. Lidia was grateful for the gift and prevailed on Raven to stay and enjoy a glass of wine.

Just as the sun was setting, Raven took leave of her neighbor and descended the staircase to the street. She put on her helmet, climbed on her Vespa, and drove to the Piazzale Michelangelo.

The Emersons' time was decidedly short. She didn't know how long the hunters were going to remain in the city. She didn't know when William would decide to go after the professor.

She was determined to see him and try once more to change his mind.

When she approached the gate to his villa, she heard a voice from the security speaker. She hadn't even announced her arrival.

"State your business."

"Um, it's Raven. Raven Wood. I'm here to see his lordship."

"His lordship is not at home."

Raven recognized Ambrogio's voice. She also recognized that he was being cool with her.

"Could I come inside and wait? I really need to see him."

There was a long pause.

When Ambrogio didn't reply, she decided to change tactics.

She lifted her wrist, displaying the gold bracelet to the security camera.

"His lordship ordered me to return this," she lied. "And his lordship's orders are always obeyed."

Raven bit her lip, trying to keep a straight face. It was too ridiculous.

"One moment."

Raven waited and the high iron gate opened, allowing her to pass through. She was shocked her strategy had worked.

She drove to the triple garage and parked in front of it, storing her helmet inside the Vespa's seat. She picked up her cane and walked through the garden to the door.

Ambrogio greeted her, directing her to Lucia, in the kitchen.

"Ah, Miss Wood. Sit down." Lucia gestured to the kitchen table, on which she'd already set a bottle of wine and a plate of fruit and cheese. She gestured to an empty glass. "Shall I?"

"Please." Raven tried not to drum her fingers on top of the table as she watched Lucia pour her a glass of red wine.

"His lordship is not here." Lucia corked the bottle and set it aside before placing the full glass in front of her guest. "In fact, he is not expected home this evening."

"Why not?"

"He has another residence that he sometimes uses. He stayed there last night and will probably stay there again tonight." Lucia's expression was carefully controlled.

Raven derived the impression that there was much, much more that Lucia was not telling her; none of it good.

"Can I wait for him?"

"I would not recommend that. As I said, he is not expected home." Lucia glanced significantly at Raven's wrist.

She removed the bracelet. "If you could return this to his lordship, I'd be very grateful."

"Of course." Lucia took the item.

"Can I still see his version of *Primavera*? He ordered me to give him my report for the restoration, but there's one part of the painting I need to see again."

Lucia smiled. "Please enjoy your wine, and when you are ready I will escort you upstairs. Will you need to have the painting removed from the wall?"

Raven shook her head.

Lucia gestured to a small bell that stood in front of Raven's plate. "Ring when you are ready."

With a nod, Lucia disappeared, leaving Raven to finish her wine alone.

While she sipped her wine and nibbled nervously on the fruit and cheese, Raven came to the conclusion that there was something wrong with Ambrogio, Lucia, and Luka.

They seemed to lack something, in addition to a sense of humor. And the way they mindlessly followed William's instructions . . .

William had mentioned something about mind control when he took her to meet his coven. Perhaps his household staff were under mind control, which was why they'd blindly let her in when she referred to his orders.

Having come to this momentous conclusion and having finished her remarkable glass of wine, Raven rang the bell. Lucia escorted her upstairs to the master bedroom.

As usual, the space was immaculate. The bed looked as if it hadn't been slept in.

Lucia instructed her to ring if she needed anything and closed the door behind her.

Raven examined the room carefully, searching for anything that would give her a clue as to William's whereabouts. But she found nothing.

It was possible, she reasoned, that he was at Palazzo Riccardi. Given what had happened the last time she went looking for him, Raven decided not to go there.

Surely he would have to return to the villa sometime. Unfortunately, Raven didn't have days to wait. She needed to be at the Uffizi early tomorrow morning for work.

What a mess.

In order to keep up the lie she'd told to Lucia, she decided to examine the painting.

She took a few photos of it with her phone, especially of the figures of Mercury, Chloris, and Zephyr. Then she sat, analyzing it.

Seeing William as Zephyr was jarring, especially since she now knew the story behind his depiction.

She examined the features of Chloris. It was difficult to make them out, since her head was turned. If what William had said was correct, the woman who'd fallen in love with him was the model for Chloris and for the second of the three Graces.

It was at this moment that Raven saw the painting in a new light.

Under the benevolent hand of Venus, Cupid pointed his arrow at the second Grace, who was already gazing with longing at Mercury. Mercury was busy stirring the clouds, his back to the Graces.

On the right side of the painting, Zephyr hovered in an orange grove, having captured Chloris. She was producing flowers from her mouth, marking the result of his fertile breath.

Without the figure of Flora, which appeared in the other version of *Primavera*, Botticelli's work was a dark morality tale.

Reading the painting from left to right and substituting the Renaissance persons for their classical counterparts, Botticelli told the story of Allegra, who fell in love with the handsome but indifferent William York. Subsequently, he was revealed as a monster. He captured her and had sex with her, but she fled from him.

Eventually, she killed herself.

Raven stared wide-eyed at the painting. It no longer seemed beautiful and serene to her. No, it was a portrait of horror and despair.

And he's had this painting for over five hundred years.

No doubt he'd stared at it daily, perhaps feeling guilt over the woman who'd loved him as one being, but killed herself when she realized what he truly was.

No wonder he'd never had a pet. Perhaps he feared the same outcome. If he was capable of feeling remorse.

Raven was fairly sure that William felt remorse and guilt, as evidenced by his reaction to her shaming him. Without guilt or remorse, shame was an empty emotion. Indeed, shame would not be shame.

Raven gazed with sadness at the second Grace.

What a tragic end.

She contemplated what William's overnight guests thought of the painting—if he'd ever told anyone its dark history.

Raven wrinkled her nose.

She tried not to guess the number of overnight guests he'd entertained over the centuries. The idea sickened her.

She threw back the curtains and opened the balcony doors, letting the night air into the room. She breathed deeply, staring up at the stars and the winking moon. With night blanketing the city, William and his coven would be free to walk the streets.

The hunters would come out in search of their prey.

She hoped William would be safe.

Raven returned to the painting and opened her knapsack, withdrawing some clean paper and her set of charcoals, which she spread across the hardwood floor.

Moving to lie on her stomach, because it was more comfortable than hunching over the paper, she began to sketch the second Grace.

Soon she was lost in the interplay of light and shadow, black and gray, her fingers ever moving over the page. She drew, she shaded, she blended with her fingers until her skin grew black. And finally, a few hours later, she had a large sketch she was proud of.

She signed her name at the bottom, as was her custom, and walked to the bathroom to wash her hands.

When she checked her watch, it was after midnight. William had not returned.

Maybe he'll return soon.

She could wait one more hour, especially to help the Emersons.

Raven sat on the bed, stretching her back and neck.

The bed was comfortable and her body was beginning to complain about having lain on the floor.

A few minutes later, she reclined, clutching a pillow. Then she fell asleep.

※ ※

Raven felt a breeze on her face.

She opened her eyes and was momentarily confused. She was in William's bed, his room swathed in darkness.

A light breeze wafted in through the balcony doors, causing the curtains on either side to lift and sway.

Raven turned on her side to face them and saw a figure standing in the doorway.

A light from somewhere in the gardens shone behind him. He was leaning against the doorpost, arms crossed over his chest, glaring at her.

"She awakes," he murmured.

Raven sat up. "I'm sorry. I didn't mean to fall asleep."

"What are you doing here, besides sketching my paintings?" His tone was abrupt.

"I came to see you. Where were you?"

He smiled, but it wasn't a happy smile.

"'I have gone round about the earth, and walked through it.'"

Raven rubbed her eyes. "I'll never understand how it is that a vampyre can quote scripture."

"Perhaps because he was taught scripture before he became a vampyre."

William pushed off the doorpost and approached the bed, his steps quick and purposeful.

"What are you doing in my bed? You made it quite clear whatever was starting between us ended."

"I was worried about the Emersons."

"Of course," he scoffed. "Raven is savior to the world. I believe someone else lays claim to that accomplishment.

"Go back to sleep. You can leave after breakfast."

He moved toward the door and Raven's heart sank.

"Aren't you tired?" she called.

He paused but didn't turn around. "We aren't capable of sleep."

"It must be exhausting not to have an escape from the worries of the day."

"It's necessary to rest the mind, if one doesn't want to go mad. We have various ways of doing that." He turned to face her, his tone somewhat ominous.

"And you?"

"I meditate."

Raven looked around the room. "Where do you do that?"

His chin jerked toward where she was lying. "There."

"Oh."

Raven pulled back the duvet and sheets to her right, where there was a pillow and an empty space. "Come here, then."

He eyed the bed with narrowed eyes. "Are you tempting me?"

"No, I'm apologizing for putting you out. We can share."

William walked to the empty side of the bed, his eyes fixed on hers. He placed a hand on the mattress, giving her a challenging look.

When she didn't retreat, he sat on the edge of the bed. He removed his shoes and reclined, lying on his back next to her.

She reached down to remove her shoes as well, before lying on her side facing him.

"Lucia presented me with your gift." He sounded unfriendly.

"William," she murmured. "Don't be angry."

"You're the most frustrating being—human or vampyre—that I've dealt with in centuries. And that's saying something, since I know Aoibhe."

Raven bristled at the female vampyre's name, but she tried to hide it.

"You said you felt shame when I offered myself in exchange for Bruno's life. Please don't be angry with me for trying to save a family and give a home to a little girl who needs one."

William sniffed but didn't respond.

She shifted closer to him on the bed.

"Did you capture the hunters?"

"No. They took down one of my brethren last night. The hunters have new weapons we weren't aware of."

"I'm sorry. Was the vampyre a friend of yours?"

"I don't have friends. It isn't in my nature."

"I'm sorry," she repeated. She reached out a hesitant hand across the mattress and placed it on his shoulder.

He didn't flinch but he didn't move into her touch, either.

"William, what happened to Angelo's body?"

"Angelo?" He turned his head toward her.

"The homeless man who died the night I was attacked."

William returned to looking at the canopy above the bed.

"His body was taken outside of the city and burned. That's what we do with corpses."

Raven's heart twisted. "Is there a grave? A place I could bring flowers?"

"You don't want to visit that place. It reeks of death."

"I suppose I could put flowers by the bridge, where he used to sit."

William exhaled loudly, as if her remark displeased him.

Raven touched his shoulder again. "Where did you find me? The night I was attacked?"

"There's an alley near the Ponte Santa Trinita. The animals dragged you into it. Why do you ask?"

"I still can't remember that evening. It's hazy."

"Be thankful for small mercies.

"Until the hunters are removed, I will do nothing about Emerson. But I make no promise for the future." He shifted to face her. "You have a day or so to manipulate one out of me."

"I'm not manipulating you. I'm appealing to your better nature."

"My better nature." He sounded bitter. "There is no better nature. Don't you understand?"

"You had compassion on me when those men would have raped and killed me. Who has the better nature between you and them?"

"You're comparing monster to monster—comparisons don't imply positives."

She shook her head. "Monsters aren't heroic."

William gave her a searching look, as if her remark truly surprised him. He soon recovered, however.

"Why are you so adamant about saving a man you don't even know? Emerson is arrogant and proud. I've seen him in public, parading his illustrations as if he were Dante himself, resurrected from the dead."

Raven frowned. "You don't like Dante?"

"The man was a mercurial egoist who panted after a married woman, neglecting his wife and family."

Raven's mouth dropped open. "Did you know him or is this merely your opinion?"

"I knew him. I knew Beatrice, too. She was lovely. And far too intelligent to leave her husband for such a fiend."

"I didn't think he was trying to persuade her to leave her husband. In *La Vita Nuova*, he talks about her as a kind of Muse."

"If she'd returned his attentions, he'd have committed adultery with her in the middle of the Ponte Santa Trinita. Don't fool yourself." He shifted on the bed so he could see her better. "My question remains. Why are you so intent on helping Emerson?"

Raven avoided his eyes. "I gave you the reason. It's unjust to kill him when he bought the illustrations in good faith not knowing they were stolen. And I'm worried about what will happen to his wife and child if you murder him."

William's gaze traveled the length of her body to where her legs rested under the covers.

"You said something happened to you after your father died. What was it?"

Raven rolled away from him, facing the balcony doors. "I don't want to talk about it."

William reflected on her answer and realized he truly wanted to know Raven's history.

(He didn't take time to ask himself why he was interested in her past. No doubt he would have been surprised by the answer.)

"That is my price. You tell me about your family, and I'll spare Emerson."

"I don't believe you."

"I give you my word. I'll spare the Emersons entirely if you answer my question."

"Just like that?" Raven was incredulous.

"Not just like that. A confrontation between Emerson and me is coming. I will have my satisfaction. But I won't kill him.

"I may predate psychology, but I can divine that whatever happened to you marked you. I'd like to understand why you're so hell-bent on protecting anyone and everyone."

"I'm not."

"Cassita." He approached her cautiously, moving his body to spoon behind hers. "You're a protector. The question I'm asking is, why?"

She didn't answer, but she didn't pull away, either. He placed his arm over hers across her stomach.

"Tell me what happened to your leg, then." His voice softened.

"It's the same story. And it's ugly." She tapped her fingers on top of the mattress. "If I tell you, I want your word you won't harm the Emersons, ever."

"I said I'll spare their lives, that's all I'll promise."

"William, I—"

"This is already a concession, Raven. I hate the man."

William's tone indicated his intractability.

"Fine." She sighed.

Raven closed her eyes, paused, and began her tale.

Chapter Thirty-nine

William was conscious of the tension in Raven's body, but she accepted his touch. He tried not to be distracted by the warmth and softness of her form, or the delight he had in wrapping himself around her.

He'd never held a woman this way before. He'd never asked a woman to tell him her secrets or share her hidden pain.

Raven was different.

He tried very hard to focus on her words and not be distracted by her scent, which had almost cleared of the vampyre blood he'd given her.

"I am not a victim." Her voice was low but steely. "I'm not telling you this story to inspire pity. I don't want that."

"Agreed." He spoke near her ear.

She mumbled a curse and he almost regretted demanding her history from her. Almost, but not quite.

"Everything began when my father died. I was eleven and we were living in Portsmouth, New Hampshire. My father was a construction worker. One day, he had an accident and fell off a roof."

Raven shuddered. "It was sudden, obviously. My mother went to pieces. We didn't have extended family so it was just my mother, me, and my sister, Carolyn. We called her Cara. She was four.

"My mother didn't function well without my father. He'd kept the house repaired and paid the bills and looked after the car. She didn't know how to do any of those things. Or if she did, she was too depressed to do them.

"We were going to lose our house. We didn't have money for food. So my mother got a job as a hostess in a local restaurant. That's where she met him." Raven shivered and William moved closer, wrapping himself around her like a shield.

"He was a real estate developer from Florida. He took a shine to my mother and asked her out. He didn't mind that she had kids. In fact, he told us he loved kids." Raven spat out the words.

"They started dating. Soon she was pregnant and they decided to get married and move us to Orlando, Florida, to live with him.

"Things were fine at the beginning. Mom was happy and pregnant. Cara was happy to have a new daddy."

"And you, Cassita"—William's voice was low—"were you happy?"

"I was relieved. When Dad died, I was left having to do things—buy food, try to cook, and remind my mother to pay the bills.

"After the first month or two in Orlando, I started noticing things about our stepfather. He barely spoke to me and when I tried to talk to him, he brushed me off.

"But he talked to Cara. And he stared at her, a lot. I didn't like the way he looked at her.

"One night I came out of my room to go to the bathroom and I saw him going into her room. I followed.

"He gave me some bullshit excuse of checking on her and tried to send me back to bed. I wouldn't go. I said I was scared of the dark and was going to sleep in her room.

"He argued with me but I wouldn't move. He was angry with me but eventually he left. That's when I realized something was very, very wrong.

"I tried to tell my mother, but she wouldn't listen. She was in a happy haze preparing for the baby and she didn't want to hear what I had to say. She didn't want to admit that something was wrong with her new husband.

"I started sleeping on Cara's floor every night. That made him furious."

"Did he try to hurt you?"

"Not directly. He'd ground me for no reason or try to convince my mother I was stealing from him. They tried to lock me in my room a couple of times but I figured out how to pick the lock with a bobby pin."

"What's a bobby pin?"

"A metal thing women use in their hair sometimes," Raven answered before forcing herself to continue. "I couldn't sleep at night because I was worried about my sister. I'd go to bed early, but set my alarm so I could wake up after my mom went to bed.

"I started having trouble in school because I was falling asleep. The teachers wanted to know what was going on at home but my stepfather just told them I was sneaking out at night with my friends.

"One night, I fell asleep and didn't hear my alarm. Or maybe he'd turned it off, I don't know. I ran to Cara's room and the door was locked from the inside. He'd switched the doorknob around.

"I went to my room and found a bobby pin and picked the lock. I opened the door and saw him sitting on her bed. He'd pulled Cara's night-gown up around her neck. She wasn't wearing any underwear.

"I started screaming. I picked up things and threw them at him. He pulled Cara's nightgown down and came at me, telling me to shut up or I'd wake my mother."

"Where was your mother?" William interrupted.

"In bed. Her door was closed but I know she heard me. She knew exactly what was going on but she was too fucking weak to stand up to him."

William felt Raven's arms tense as she balled her hands into fists.

"What happened next?"

"He hit me. I didn't even feel it, I was just trying to get to my sister. I started crawling on the ground toward her but he grabbed me.

"I was kicking and screaming and he was yelling at me to shut up.

"My mother chose that moment to open her door and come down the hall. I was struggling with my stepfather and shouting at my mother about what he'd done to Cara. I wouldn't shut up, so he pushed me down the stairs."

William's body went rigid.

She moved her head in his direction.

"Are you okay?"

"No." He tried to keep his voice calm, for her sake. "What happened next?"

"I don't remember. Actually, I don't remember him pushing me down the stairs. I just remember fighting with him and then I remember falling.

"When I woke up, I was in the hospital. The doctors said I broke my leg and ankle. A social worker came to see me, and after I told her what happened, my sister was put in temporary foster care."

William squeezed her lightly. "What's foster care?"

"Um, when children are in danger, sometimes the state steps in and takes them away from their family. Foster families look after the children until they can be placed somewhere safe."

"So they believed you."

"They believed the evidence—Cara was hysterical and she wouldn't talk about what happened. I was in the hospital and my stepfather was at the police station lying his ass off. He said he'd been drinking and it was a misunderstanding—that I tripped and fell.

"My mother knew. She *knew* and she did nothing," Raven whispered. "I told her something was happening with Cara. She said I was lying because I was jealous of my stepfather's attention; that I was trying to break up her marriage. To this day, she sides with him."

Raven inhaled deeply.

"Just once, I wanted someone to defend me. By the time we were placed in foster care, it was too late."

William's hand moved to her injured leg, ghosting over her scar.

"This happened because you were protecting your sister?"

Raven flinched. "I didn't protect her. He got to her while I was asleep. And I don't think that was the first time."

She stopped abruptly and William smelled the tang of salt. She was crying.

He buried his face in her hair, not knowing what to do.

"I failed her," she cried. "She was only five. She was just a baby. And it's my fault."

He grimaced. "How old were you?"

"Twelve."

William withdrew so he could look at her. "What twelve-year-old girl would have the courage to physically confront a man? Precious few."

Raven swiped at her eyes.

"I don't see how it is your fault that a pedophile went after your sister. You're the hero in this tale, Cassita."

"It's why I changed my name. I couldn't hear the word *Jane* without hearing his voice."

"So you chose *Raven*?"

"I wanted to prove to myself that I could be someone else. That I could be brave."

William brought his lips to her ear. "You are brave, Raven. You are very brave. A slip of a girl, fighting to protect her sister. That's heroic."

"Hardly."

"Joan of Arc had that kind of courage."

Raven shifted to look up at him. "Did you know her?"

"No. I came to Florence in the late thirteenth century. I've been here since then."

"You never leave?"

"Rarely. Vampyres in my position are expected to ask for permission before they travel across another prince's territory. I find the process tiresome."

He brushed a kiss against her hair. "What about your leg? Couldn't they repair it?"

Raven turned on her side once again. "They tried but it didn't heal properly. We were wards of the state at that point. I suppose if we'd had enough money for expensive surgeons and multiple surgeries they could have fixed it. But my stepfather was under a restraining order and he was the one with all the money. My mother was told she had to stay away from him."

"And did she?"

"Long enough to get us back. When I was released from the hospital, Cara and I were placed with a foster family for several months. My stepfather was brought up on charges but he plea-bargained and received a suspended sentence."

Raven exhaled loudly. "My mother lost the baby—probably because of the stress. I don't know. Eventually she was settled in an apartment and started working. We went to live with her.

"We were there only a week when my stepfather showed up. They said that we were moving to California. She said we were going to be a family again."

William growled, low, near her ear.

"That night, when we went to bed I grabbed my sister and we left. I stole my stepfather's wallet and used the money to try to get back to our old foster home. But I wasn't sure how to get there. We hopped a bus and ended up in a bad section of Orlando.

"We were at a bus stop trying to figure out how to get where we needed to go. My sister was crying and I was on crutches because my leg was still healing.

"A guy came up and started talking to us. He was creepy but we had nowhere else to go, we had to wait for the bus. He tried to persuade us to go with him, that he could help us. When I said no, he grabbed me. I fought him, hitting him with one of my crutches. He took my crutch and threw it away. I thought he was going to knock me out and kidnap us.

"Out of nowhere, a man and a woman appeared. They'd heard me yelling and came to see what was going on. The man who'd grabbed me ran off.

"The guy who came to our rescue was a priest. He asked me what had happened and I told him everything—about my stepfather, about my leg, about Cara . . ."

Raven cleared her throat. "He was the director of Covenant House, which is a shelter for teenagers. The woman was one of the shelter workers. They were making the rounds handing out food and trying to convince homeless kids to come to the shelter.

"They took us in and gave us a safe place to sleep. And they didn't call my mother."

William was puzzled. "Why would they?"

"Normally, you'd report missing children to their parents. But Father Kavanaugh kept us at Covenant House until he could figure out how to help us. In the morning, he called a friend of his who was a police officer and he came over.

"They called our social worker and we went back into foster care. It was over a year before we were returned to my mother. She gave up on my stepfather permanently and moved to St. Petersburg. Um, that's a different city in Florida."

"What happened to him?" William's hand curled into a fist.

"I don't know. He was in trouble with the police because he'd violated the terms of his sentence and the restraining order. He may have been sent to jail, I'm not sure. We didn't talk about him after that."

"And your mother?"

"I lived with her until I was old enough to go to college. I kept in touch with Father Kavanaugh. He paid for me to take art lessons when I was in high school. He helped me get a scholarship to Barry University. I left home and never went back."

"What about your sister?"

Raven squirmed in his arms. "She stayed with my mom. When she was a teenager, she got mixed up with the wrong crowd. She was promiscuous. I worried it was because of what had happened to her."

"And now?"

"She dropped out of high school for a while, but I persuaded her to go back. I was living in New York by then and going to graduate school. I think she realized that education was her ticket to a better kind of life.

"Father Kavanaugh helped her pay for college, and when she graduated she became a real estate agent. She's successful now and has a nice boyfriend. They're coming to visit me this summer."

"Is she all right?"

"She doesn't remember anything about that night and has basically accepted my mother's version of events." Raven shifted on the bed. "Maybe that's better than being tormented by the past."

"Are you tormented?"

"Every day."

William was quiet for a very long time.

"A priest came to save you, yet you don't believe in God?"

"What kind of God lets children be abused?" Raven's voice was low and very fierce.

"You don't need to tell me about the injustice of God. I agree. But his injustice doesn't entail his nonexistence."

"Maybe for you."

William stroked her hair softly.

"You cried for your sister but not for yourself."

Now he could smell the salt from fresh tears.

"She was a baby," Raven managed to say. "It was my job to protect her."

"It was your mother's responsibility to protect you both. And she didn't." William tightened his arm across Raven's middle. He sighed deeply, his tone tinged with regret. "I would not have asked you to talk about this if I'd known."

"A lot of kids had it worse than me. That's why I volunteer at the orphanage."

William swore, the muscles of his body tensing.

"I blame my father," she whispered. "I love him and I miss him, but if he'd been more careful, he wouldn't have died. None of this would have happened."

"Put the blame where it belongs, on your mother and stepfather."

"I blame her, William, believe me. We don't have a relationship because of this."

"I have considerable power, Cassita, and more than a considerable fortune. I will use both to have your leg repaired medically, if that's what you want. If you'd rather use alchemy, the best vintages of my cellar are yours."

She curled into herself. "William, I don't—I can't—"

"Take time to consider it," he interrupted. "You don't need to decide tonight. But more than that, I will give you justice."

"Justice?"

"You said no one defended you. I will." His tone grew frightening.

"It's too late."

He rolled her to her back and leaned over her.

"It's never too late for justice."

Raven looked away.

"I will deal with everyone who ever harmed you. All you need to do is name them."

"It won't change the past."

He placed his hand on her cheek. "It will stop the torment."

"Your justice involves death."

"I don't see why a death sentence for your mother and stepfather is problematic."

"I don't want you to kill my mother. Do you hear me?" She rolled away from him, exasperated. "Don't you get tired of death?"

His gazed burned into her back. "I get tired of evil triumphing over goodness. I get tired of the injustice inherent in the universe and beings, human and otherwise, standing aside and doing nothing."

Raven sighed.

"It must be sad to live forever," she said after a while. "Everyone you cared about is dead."

William shifted beside her. "I haven't loved anyone since I was human."

"Then I feel sorry for you. Love—even the love for family and friends—is a light that shines in the darkness. Without that light, I would have killed myself."

William frowned. "This is a morbid conversation."

Raven stifled a laugh. "Coming from a vampyre, that's funny."

She sobered and looked up at the canopy. "But it's true, William. I feel sorry for you. I wouldn't want to live forever—to carry this pain for eternity. I just want peace.

"No matter the justice you think you can get, I will always have this weight on my shoulders. I'm glad that someday I'll go to sleep and never wake up."

Raven curled her body into a ball, lying on her side, and tucked her hands under her pillow. Soon her breathing grew even and he knew she was asleep.

William was in desperate need of a few hours of meditation, simply to clear his mind and allow him to relax. But all he could think about was a twelve-year-old girl fighting a grown man to protect her sister and being thrown down a flight of stairs.

He could see her, the young girl with the black hair, lying at the foot of the staircase, her body battered and broken.

Cassita vulneratus.

Defensa.

He reached into his pocket and retrieved the gold bracelet that featured the symbol of Florence. He slipped it over her right wrist.

Everyone you cared about is dead.

"Not everyone," he whispered, pulling her against his chest.

Chapter Forty

Although William was unable to meditate while holding Raven in his arms, he was surprised to discover that the posture calmed and relaxed him. He closed his eyes and rested, allowing his mind to drift like a sailboat over the sea.

He felt a modicum of guilt for the way he'd treated her—first, allowing her to exchange her freedom for his assistance with her friends, and second, exacting her painful history in exchange for Emerson's life.

Don't you get tired of death? Her sweet voice echoed in his ears.

The truth was he did tire of it. When the Black Death scourged Florence and he had to scavenge for uninfected humans on which to feed, he tired of death. When the old prince allowed the brethren to kill without limit, including infants and children, he tired of death.

He overcame his fatigue by killing the Prince and taking over the principality. He accumulated wealth and power, he allowed his appetites to be fed, and he derived a measure of satisfaction from all his pursuits.

But he lacked hope. He lacked peace. The only way he could continue was to never, ever think of the future.

Of course, Raven couldn't know that vampyres didn't live forever. That the Curia had cursed them to a life of only a thousand years. Still, given his age, he had time and time enough to spare.

He'd outlive her.

The thought burned through him.

William released Raven as gently as he could, determined not to wake her. He retired to one of the guest bedrooms so he could shower and dress.

His considerable respect for her had increased a hundredfold. He was more determined than ever to make her his.

He simply needed to be patient, and patient he was.

❈❈

"Good morning." William looked down into Raven's wide green eyes.

"Good morning." Her tone was hesitant.

He leaned over and kissed her.

"Did you sleep well?" He spoke against her lips.

She nodded.

"What's the matter?" He sat next to her on the bed.

"I don't know," she confessed, avoiding eye contact.

"You came to see me; we had a meeting of the minds. Emerson is safe and you're wearing my protection." William gestured to her right wrist. "Is that an adequate summary of the evening's activities?"

She lifted her wrist to examine the bracelet, a small smile playing on her lips.

Her eyes moved to her protector's. "So you won't harm Professor Emerson?"

"If he commits an infraction within the city, there will be consequences. But I won't harm him because of the illustrations. I've decided to channel my energies in other directions." William's mouth extended into a provocative smile.

"What directions might that be?"

"Here."

He brought their lips together, this time seeking entrance to her mouth immediately.

Raven welcomed him inside, curving her hand around the back of his neck and pulling him closer.

William's lips pressed, devoured, tantalized.

His fingers spanned her waist. Then they ascended underneath her blouse to her breasts. He traced the opening before slipping his hand under the material to cup her bra, his hands cool.

She hummed appreciatively and he began circling his fingers, stroking and rolling.

Raven moved her hand to his hair, winding the strands. She tilted her head, languorously exploring his mouth, reveling in the feel and taste of him.

With a growl, William shifted, lightning fast. He pulled the covers from her lower body and brought his hips between her legs, arching over her.

His mouth descended to her neck, kissing and sucking at the flesh beneath her ear.

She moaned and he lowered his lips to her breasts, pushing her blouse aside and kissing across the skin that swelled above her bra.

"William," she whispered.

His arousal was pressing up against her, through their clothing. He slid his hand down her side, his touch scorching, and lifted her leg to wrap around his hip.

"William," she groaned.

He looked down at her, his eyes alight, his beautiful mouth parted.

"Let me pleasure you," he rasped, kissing her fiercely.

"I can't." Her voice was small, her expression conflicted. "What happened last night, what I told you—I'm a mess."

"Spend the night with me, here, in my bed."

"William, I—"

He lifted a hand to her face, his touch light and soothing.

"Come to me tonight."

"I'm not promising to sleep with you."

"Why not?" He kissed her again, this time gently.

"I'm worried about my heart."

He arched an eyebrow at the space between her breasts, his lips curving up into a half smile.

"Not that heart." Her eyes slid to the side. "When you laugh at me, it will hurt."

William's expression grew thunderous.

"Have I given you any indication that I find this funny?"

"No," she whispered.

"What I want most at this moment is to peel your clothes from your body and place my tongue between your legs."

Raven's eyes flew to his.

Naked desire shone in his eyes; electricity shot across his skin.

He traced her lower body with his finger. "Let me in."

"I know myself." Her eyes slid to the side again. "I know my failings and I know my fate. I'm supposed to be alone."

"I can't see how that's possible, since I believe you're supposed to be with me, in my arms, in my bed."

Her green eyes fixed on his. "I've had two lovers, William. Neither of them made me feel the way I feel when I'm in your arms. If we do this, I'll become attached to you."

He lifted her wrist, moving the bracelet aside.

"You are already attached to me." He began to kiss her wrist, drawing the flesh into his mouth and sucking.

"Vampyres may not have feelings, but humans do. You know this."

William paused.

"It isn't correct to say that vampyres are entirely without feeling. It depends on the vampyre."

"And you?"

"I lack empathy, like most vampyres. Except when it comes to you."

She lifted her hand and placed it over his heart.

She felt what she thought was his heartbeat, but it felt strange. It was stronger than a human heartbeat, but after it pulsed it would fall silent for several seconds.

"You have a heart."

"So I've been told."

"I didn't know vampyres had working hearts."

"We need our blood to circulate, to keep the body working. Life is in the blood."

"The other night, when you took me home after taking me to meet the others, you mentioned hope. What do you hope for, William?"

He frowned. "That I wouldn't be condemned to an eternity of empty darkness."

Raven cringed at his words. "Is that what you have?"

"Not exactly." His expression grew guarded. "Somehow the darkness recedes when you're near."

She withdrew her hand and he grasped it, kissing the back of it.

"Your skin smells of roses." He inhaled deeply. "It's exquisite."

He pressed his lips against the length of her arm, moving back and forth at a leisurely pace.

"This is my warning," she whispered. "My heart is part of my body."

He touched the space between her breasts. "I will treat you, all of you, with care."

Raven watched as the beautiful, flawless man above her kissed her wrist with absolute abandon and found words tumbling out of her mouth.

"I'll come to you tonight. But I don't promise to sleep with you."

William smiled slowly.

"I enjoy a challenge."

He kissed her once more, an embrace burning with promise, then he withdrew. He extended his hand to help her out of bed.

"I'll meet you downstairs."

Raven focused on his retreating back, part of her wondering why she had resisted him.

❊ ❊

After breakfast, William introduced her to another member of his security team, a tall, bald man with extremely broad shoulders.

"Raven, this is Marco."

"Polo," she blurted out.

William and Marco eyed her quizzically.

"I'm afraid you have him mistaken with someone who died many, many years ago," William said, his lips twitching.

"Sorry." She reddened. "It's good to meet you, Marco."

William gestured to his assistant. "Marco will follow you to the Uffizi this morning. After work, he will take you to your apartment so you can drop off your Vespa and pick up your things. Then he'll drive you here."

"I'm supposed to volunteer at the orphanage after work." Raven clutched her knapsack awkwardly. "And I'd like to see Bruno."

William appeared displeased. "He won't remember your time together. The head injury combined with the blood will have affected his memory."

"I realize that. I still want to see him." She sounded stubborn.

"Very well." William pressed his lips together as an indication of his displeasure. "Marco will escort you where you need to go.

"I have business to attend to in the early evening. I'll ask Lucia to prepare dinner for you."

"That won't be necessary. I'll eat with the children."

William examined her features. "Perhaps we could watch one of your films this evening."

She smiled. "I'd like that."

"Good. Call Ambrogio and let him know what you need in order to show the film."

William walked her outside to her Vespa and wrapped her in his arms. "You don't need to worry about the inspector. He won't bother you again."

"Thank you."

He gazed at her hungrily.

"I'm looking forward to tonight."

He kissed her firmly.

A few kisses, another embrace, and she was on her Vespa, speeding down the hill toward the Arno, with Marco following in the Mercedes. A few cars behind, Ispettor Batelli trailed them.

William returned to the house and summoned Luka to the library, handing him a folded piece of paper. "I need you to travel to Florida, in America, to the cities of Orlando and St. Petersburg. Find out everything you can about the persons I've named. Contact me for further instructions."

Luka unfolded the paper, read it, and placed it in his jacket pocket. With a bow, he exited the room.

William moved to the windows and looked out over his estate, lost in thought.

Chapter Forty-one

"I'm here to see Bruno Rostagno." Raven spoke to one of the nurses on Bruno's floor at the hospital.

"Friend or family?" The nurse didn't bother to look up from her computer.

"Friend." Raven shifted her weight, nervously glancing at Marco, who was standing a few feet away, looking intimidating.

The nurse was about to direct Raven to the correct room when a familiar-looking woman approached them.

"Raven, hello." Graziella greeted her warmly, kissing both cheeks.

"Graziella, hi." Raven smiled. "I'm just here to see Bruno."

"Good. I've just arrived also. Come with me." Graziella nodded at the nurse and took Raven's hand, leading her down the hall.

"How is he?" she asked, concerned.

"He will come home tomorrow, I think. He was supposed to be released today but the doctor wanted to wait."

They walked down the hall and made a left. Graziella stopped at the door to the third room.

"You say hello. I'll come in later."

"But you're here. I'm sure he wants to see you first," Raven protested, noticing that Marco had followed them.

Graziella just patted her arm and gestured to the door.

Raven's grip tightened on her cane as she entered the room with caution. She was worried about what she was going to find.

Bruno was lying in bed, looking remarkably well. In fact, there was no evidence of his previous injuries—no bruising, no bandages, no cords or tubes attached to his body.

He looked healthier than he had before, and perhaps even a little younger.

Raven wondered if anyone else had noticed the changes.

"Hello, Bruno." She greeted him with a cheerful wave.

He nodded at her. "Good afternoon."

Raven's smile faltered.

"It's me. It's Raven."

Bruno examined her face for a moment and then his gaze dropped to her cane. "Of course. You live next to my grandmother. How are you?"

"I'm well, thank you." She gestured at his hospital bed. "How are you?"

"Ready to go home." He grimaced. "They say I've made a miraculous recovery, but I'm still in a hurry to get out of here."

Raven swallowed thickly. "I heard about your accident. I'm so sorry."

"Thanks, it was nice of you to come by. Have you seen my grandmother lately?"

"I saw her yesterday. I've been trying to check in on her more frequently."

"Thank you."

Bruno fell silent, as if he were waiting for something.

It took a moment for Raven to realize he was waiting for her to say something.

She flushed. He didn't remember her. He didn't look at her with longing or ask her about herself or any of the other dozen special things he'd done during their one special evening. Sadness crept over her.

Raven forced herself to remain cheerful.

"Well, I'm glad you're feeling better. I saw your mother in the hall. Should I send her in?"

"Please. Thanks for visiting me." Bruno flashed her a muted smile, which she returned.

"No problem. Good-bye, Bruno."

Raven walked awkwardly from the room, leaning heavily on her cane. When she saw Graziella in the hall, she said, "He wants to see you."

"But you should stay longer. Come with me." Graziella moved to take her hand but Raven shook her head.

"I'm sorry. I have plans for dinner. But I'm glad he's all right and he's coming home."

"Thank you." Graziella kissed her cheeks again before waving good-bye.

Raven nodded at Marco and they walked to the elevator. But she didn't shed a tear until she was alone.

Chapter Forty-two

"As you can see by looking at the body, the hunters are using larger arrows, presumably shot from a crossbow." Stefan, the vampyre physician, pointed to the gaping wound that exposed the corpse's heart.

The Consilium members murmured in response, standing around the autopsy table.

"The cause of death?" The Prince addressed Stefan.

He held up the arrow and pointed to the barbed metal head.

"The arrow is armed with a capsule containing a powerful cardiac toxin. The capsule breaks on impact, releasing the toxin. The combination of trauma and toxin causes the heart to fail.

"Without the circulation of blood, the vampyre is weakened and potentially immobilized. I've identified the toxin but sent a sample to a lab in Switzerland for confirmation."

The Prince looked grim. "Other weapons?"

"Judging from the scene where the body was found, they used holy water and salt."

Aoibhe cursed loudly. "Have they no imagination?"

The Prince silenced Aoibhe with a look.

He turned his attention back to Stefan. "How do we combat the arrows?"

The physician appeared thoughtful for a moment.

"We could issue vests or breastplates. Armor would restrict movement, which would be detrimental in flight. There are newer materials used by various human militaries. We could test them to see how they might hold up."

The Prince pointed his gaze at Lorenzo. "Can you source those materials?"

He bowed. "Of course, my lord. But it will take time."

"We haven't got time. Get whatever you can immediately and coordinate testing with Niccolò." The Prince nodded in his direction. "If the tests prove successful, we'll outfit the entire principality, but each citizen must bear the cost."

"What about the toxin?" Pierre glanced anxiously from the corpse to the physician.

Stefan stroked his chin. "I've identified it as doxorubicin. It's a drug humans use to combat cancer."

"Is there an antidote?" the Prince asked.

"Humans would take digitalis drugs to thin the blood and bolster the heart. We've never tested them on our kind because we haven't had the need. We're impervious to human toxins."

"Or thought we were," muttered Aoibhe.

The Prince glared at Aoibhe before directing his attention back to the doctor. "What's your scientific opinion, then?"

Stefan shook his head. "An arrow isn't enough to fell one of us unless it ripped the heart to pieces. That isn't what happened to Matthias."

"The toxin isn't enough to fell one of us, either," Stefan observed. "It's the combination of the two that shocks the heart, causing temporary paralysis. Once on the ground, the hunters use water and salt to prevent the victim from removing the arrow and allowing the natural regenerative processes to begin. Then they take the head."

"The remedy?"

"Avoidance." The physician gestured to Matthias's body. "If digitalis or something like it were to work, it would have to be administered immediately. That isn't an option if one is surrounded by hunters."

"I want an antidote found," the Prince commanded. "Impress upon the lab our urgent need."

Stefan bowed. "Of course, but they are human scientists, ignorant of the true nature of their clients. I'd have to give them vampyre blood and a very imaginative explanation in order for them to produce an antidote."

"Then that's what you must do. Work through the human intelligence network, if necessary. Impress upon them the need to use mind control or physical coercion on the lab staff, as needed."

"Yes, my lord."

"Once an antidote is produced, we'll have to test it." The Prince looked over at Maximilian. "Perhaps you can convince a few of the recruits to donate their bodies to science."

The large man grinned. "With pleasure."

"Stefan, coordinate the testing of the toxin with Maximilian. I want reports as soon as possible.

"I'm sure I don't need to impress upon everyone the need for caution." The Prince laid stress on the word. "Matthias was felled from a rooftop in full view of witnesses. It's possible the hunters are here to do more than harvest blood."

He paused and two of the Consilium members exchanged a look.

"Such as?" Aoibhe pressed.

"Such as force us into an open confrontation that would attract the attention of the Curia."

At the mention of the name, the Consilium members looked troubled. Stefan fidgeted with his pocket watch, opening and closing it repeatedly.

"On my order as Prince of Florence, Teatro is now closed. I want the underworld evacuated and all communal gatherings canceled. Citizens are to remain in their primary residences and feed inside. This is for everyone's safety.

"Niccolò, now that the patrols are under your supervision, I expect that there will be no further breach. See to it.

"Pierre, the human intelligence network is to be charged with locating the hunters and discovering their supply lines. Someone knows where they're hiding. I want them found.

"Maximilian, until we have protective shields, no one is to escalate a confrontation."

"Yes, my lord." The Consilium members, augmented by Stefan, spoke in unison.

"You are dismissed." With a curt nod, the Prince strode out of the chamber, the weight of his principality heavy on his shoulders.

Chapter Forty-three

"You say this film is based on a novel? Was it written in Italian?" The Prince held aloft the DVD cover to *The Godfather*.

"No, English." Raven placed the DVD into the player and nodded at Ambrogio to turn on the projector. "That reminds me. You said *sard* was English. But in my dictionary, it isn't a profanity; it refers to a stone."

The Prince turned his attention to his servant. "Ambrogio, we'll ring if we need anything."

"Yes, my lord." He bowed and exited the room.

The vast sitting room on the second floor had been transformed into a theater. The curtains had been pulled over the windows and a large screen had been hung on the far wall. A projector sat on scaffolding behind a large antique sofa.

Lucia had even provided buttered popcorn and Coca-Cola.

"*Sard?* The stone?" Raven sat on the couch, tucking her uninjured leg under her.

William sat beside her. "*Sard* is Old English. I'm afraid my profanity is a product of my human life. I never quite caught on to the modern words."

She handed him the large bowl of popcorn, but he refused.

"You have to eat this when you watch a movie."

He looked at the contents of the bowl and wrinkled his nose. "What is it?"

"Corn that's been cooked. And buttered."

He pushed the bowl away. "We don't eat such things."

"Just try it." She handed him a single, buttered kernel.

He examined it closely.

He sniffed it.

He popped it into his mouth and began chewing. "Not bad."

"Good. I knew you'd like it." Raven grinned.

William picked up a paper napkin from the ottoman and discreetly removed the remains of the kernel from his mouth.

"What did you do that for?" She stared at him as if he'd grown another head.

"We can't digest human food." He balled the napkin up in his fist and put it aside.

"I guess I'll save the M&M's for myself. I think you'll like this film. It's about the Mafia."

He gave her a puzzled look. "Why do you think it would appeal to me?"

Raven pushed her hair behind her ear. "It's a great film with a great cast. The opening scene sets the tone for the entire movie—it's a meditation on justice."

She glanced up at him before focusing on her drink. "I think you'll find it interesting."

William observed her for a moment. Then he closed his eyes and inhaled.

He opened his eyes directly.

"You're anxious."

"No, I'm not." She reached into the popcorn, pulling out a healthy handful.

He took the bowl from her hand and placed it on the ottoman.

He moved closer. Too close.

"Tell me what's troubling you." He placed his hand on her knee and she tensed.

"Nothing." She moved away slightly and nibbled on her popcorn.

"You're lying. I can smell it."

She lifted her eyebrows. "How can you smell a lie?"

"Your body chemistry changes in accordance with your moods. You're anxious about something and every time you lie, your anxiety peaks." He moved closer and caught her chin, lifting it. "Whenever I touch you, I elicit the same reaction."

"William," she protested, looking away.

He pressed his lips to her temple.

"Are you anxious about going to bed with me?" His lips moved against her skin.

She closed her eyes at the sensation.

"I said I wasn't sleeping with you tonight."

"You're planning to engage in sex with me soon." He kissed her again, this time brushing his lips against her forehead. "Why not tonight? Why not now?"

She leaned into him but only for a second.

"You're going to spill my drink."

He took the glass from her hand, placing it on a tray next to the popcorn.

"Problem solved." He kissed the edge of her jaw, pulling her closer. "I am a vigorous lover. All vampyres are. Because you're human and because I—" He cleared his throat. "I'll be careful. You tell me what you want, how gentle, how hard . . ."

He brought her hand to his thigh. "I'll lead the dance, with you in mind. All you have to do is feel."

Raven felt her skin flushing and she mumbled a curse word.

He touched the apple of her cheek with his index finger. "It pleases me that I excite you. I'm looking forward to watching your face when you climax. Tell me, what do you enjoy? What do you crave? My tongue between your legs, in your mouth, on your breasts?

"Do you want my hands to roam your body or would you rather I lifted your arms above your head?

"Do you prefer to be above or below? Sideways? From behind?" He kissed her ear.

Raven shot off the couch so quickly, she almost fell.

"Stop." She pressed a hand to her face, trying to cool the heated skin. "Why?"

"I don't like bullshit and that sounds like bullshit. Stop talking to me like that."

William's expression changed in an instant. He stood, glaring. "What's the issue, Raven? I thought we'd come to an understanding."

She held up her hands. "I just want a quiet evening and a movie. Can't we forget about all that other stuff? And relax?"

William moved toward her but stopped, noting that she was extremely agitated.

She didn't appear afraid, but neither did she seem comfortable.

His seductive strategy was failing and that pricked his pride.

His features hardened. "We are going to bed together. You will welcome me inside your body. It's only a matter of time."

"I don't want to talk about it."

He gestured in frustration. "Why the hell not?"

"Do vampyres transmit sexual diseases?"

"Of course not!" His nostrils flared. "Do you think I would do that to you? That I'd knowingly give you a disease?"

"Humans have to discuss disease before they have sex."

"Vampyres are impervious to human diseases. We cannot contract them or transmit them. Next issue." He crossed his hands over his chest.

When she didn't respond, his eyes narrowed.

"This is all subterfuge. What's the true reason you won't go to bed with me?"

"I went to see Bruno," she blurted out.

"I know. And?"

"He didn't remember me."

"I warned you about that. Vampyre blood can cause memory loss."

Raven looked over at her cane, which was resting against the sofa.

"We went out. We had dinner and laughed. He kissed me. Today, he was completely indifferent. He barely looked at me." She gave William a tremulous look. "I'm tired of being invisible."

His expression softened. "Come here."

"No."

He extended his hand in her direction. "You aren't invisible to me. I think I've made that clear."

Raven turned to stare at the empty movie screen. "What happens when you really see me?"

"I don't understand."

"You wouldn't," she mumbled. "You're beautiful."

"You seem to be forgetting that I want you." He gestured to what stirred behind his trousers. "Badly."

She met his eyes and gave him a long look. "Tonight I don't need a lover. I need a friend. Can you give me that?"

"Vampyres don't have friends." William retreated a step.

He was about to deny her; she saw the resolve in his gaze.

Abruptly, his face changed.

"If that's what you desire," he said primly, gesturing to the couch.

She sat down, and this time he positioned himself a few feet away. He placed the popcorn bowl between them and handed her the drink.

"Thank you."

He didn't answer, his posture stiff, his face glowering.

She pressed play on the remote control.

❋ ❋

William was so engrossed in the film he didn't notice Raven set the popcorn bowl aside. Nor did he notice when she moved toward him.

During the scene when Michael comes to his first wife on their wedding night, she rested her head on William's upper arm. Without thinking, he shifted so that his arm went around her shoulders.

She burrowed against him.

"Is it dangerous?" she asked.

"Is what dangerous?" He looked down at her profile.

"Having sex with a vampyre."

His gaze returned to the screen. "It can be."

"For my body or my heart?"

He leaned over and pressed his lips to her forehead.

"I thought your heart was part of your body."

She met his eyes and the smile faded from his lips.

"I can't answer that, Cassita," he whispered.

Raven tried to focus on the film, pretending his words didn't trouble her.

❈❈

In the middle of the night, Raven awoke in William's arms. They were in his bed.

William was on his back, shirtless, stroking the skin of her shoulders, while she curled into his side.

The room was dark. The curtains had been drawn across the balcony doors. A small shaft of light shone from under the door that led to the hall.

She blinked up at him, trying to make out his features.

He smiled. "Hello, pretty girl."

The shadows made her bolder, as she forgot that he could see in the dark. She lifted her hand to his face and pressed against him. Her green eyes darkened with an unexpressed emotion.

Somehow, her feelings transferred themselves to her lips. She kissed him purposefully, nibbling his lower lip before taking it into her mouth.

William touched her neck, angling so he could deepen the kiss. As soon as their tongues touched, sparks flew.

Raven moved her leg over and between his, shifting so she was half on his chest. She rested her hands on his shoulders, enjoying the feel of the muscles under her fingers.

His tongue entered her mouth and retreated, enticing her to follow, while his palms brushed the length of her back to rest on the curves of her bottom. By all accounts, he liked what he felt, squeezing and kneading the flesh with his hands.

She licked at the seam of his lips before dipping inside. Back and forth and in and out.

William's pace was focused but unhurried, as if he were determined to enjoy every point of contact, every sensation.

He traced the hills and valleys of her spine before grabbing her old-fashioned nightgown and lifting it to her thighs.

"William," she murmured, pressing their lower bodies together.

He rolled her to her back and whispered fine kisses along her jaw and down to her neck.

She drew in a sharp breath.

"Please don't feed from me. Not our first time."

He lifted his head, conflict visible in his eyes.

He blinked slowly, like a cat.

"If that's what you desire."

He nuzzled her cleavage before slipping her nightgown from her shoulders, baring her expansive breasts.

"These are exquisite." He brought her breasts to his lips, eagerly licking and sucking.

His mouth, like his tongue, was cool. Raven enjoyed when he laved her nipples, before pressing them against the roof his mouth.

She wound her fingers in his hair, massaging his scalp.

"I could spend days right here. You truly are a work of art." He rested his chin below her breasts and gave her a wide, enchanting smile.

Once again, Raven forgot he could see clearly and believed only that he was referring to how she felt under his hands.

She tugged his head toward her and kissed him, allowing herself to explore the muscles of his back and lower down, where his hips met his backside.

William was lean and strong and, it seemed to her, controlled. But she could feel the power coiled beneath her fingers.

"You aren't attached to this nightgown, are you?" he whispered, fingering the fabric that pooled around her waist.

She shook her head. "It's yours."

"Mine?"

"It's what I woke up in the night after you took me home. You must have dressed me."

In a flash, the nightgown was torn down the middle and carelessly tossed to the floor.

"It must have belonged to one of Lucia's predecessors. I never should have put you in it." He rested his hand on her lower abdomen, gazing down at her appreciatively. "You're far more desirable naked."

He pressed a kiss to the top of her black lace underwear, coaxing her to spread her legs.

She bit her lip in anticipation, squinting against the darkness at the beautiful man who knelt before her.

"Very lovely," he murmured as his fingers traced a pattern over the lace.

Then, with a quick rip, her underwear was gone.

Raven held her breath, eyes wide.

"Cassita," he said gently.

He placed his hand over her heart. "Your heart rate is too fast. Breathe."

She struggled to breathe deeply, excitement and anxiety still overtaking her.

William's thumb stroked the skin beneath her right breast.

"You aren't a virgin. Why are you so anxious?"

"It's been a long time," she managed to say, feeling shy.

"Humans are fools," he muttered. "Your figure is perfect—lush and attractive."

He kissed down the center of her body, stopping just above her pubic bone.

He closed his eyes and inhaled.

"You smell incredible."

He reached up to whisper in her ear. "I'm going to lick you until you climax, then I'm going to enter you and you'll climax again. Don't forget to breathe."

He moved back and placed his hands on her upper thighs. "Open."

She did as she was bidden. Then his mouth was between her legs.

Raven's head sank back on the pillow and she closed her eyes, focusing entirely on the incredible sensation of his cool tongue on her most private places.

There was something exceptionally erotic about having a powerful being between her legs, eagerly giving her pleasure.

She clawed at the sheets, a series of moans escaping her throat.

William lifted his head, remarking her reaction with a wicked grin. Clearly he was enjoying himself. He teased and licked, nipped and sucked, before closing his mouth over her.

Raven's body tightened as she came, then she floated on a wave of pleasure before crashing down.

She tried to pull away, but he held her to his mouth, coaxing every last tremor out of her body until she finally collapsed against the bed.

Then he arced over her, hand against her hip, and pushed inside.

She was still sensitive and felt herself stretched beyond what she thought she could take.

William cursed and withdrew before filling her once again, very slowly.

He brought their noses to within inches of one another and brushed the hair from her eyes.

"Look at me," he ordered.

She glanced up at him, at eyes that burned into hers.

"Don't think. Give yourself over to pleasure." He moved inside her, withdrawing and plunging forward, again and again.

The strokes were deep, intense, but the pace was slow.

Raven placed her hands on his lower back and slid them to his backside, urging him to increase his speed. She felt his muscles flex and contract under her grasp.

He bent down to take her breast in his mouth and she closed her eyes, groaning in delight.

A few more strokes, a few more kisses and nips to her breast, and she was orgasming again.

William nuzzled her neck and licked at the flesh, biting her gently.

She ignored him, focused as she was on the feeling that spread from her insides throughout her entire body.

His pace increased slightly but he gave no sign of coming.

"Are you—?" she managed to say, still in the throes of an incredible climax.

"No." He grinned at her knowingly before kissing her neck once again. "I can go for hours."

Raven felt the last of her orgasm recede. She rested her hands on his lower back, stilling him.

"Did you say hours?" She panted, out of breath.

"Yes." He kissed her lightly. "Prepare yourself."

He began moving inside her once again.

Raven lifted up to kiss him.

"Nothing could have prepared me for this." She spoke against his mouth, her breathing uneven. "It feels incredible."

His expression darkened, but only for a moment. Then he rolled to his back, pulling her astride him.

She'd just come down from her third orgasm when he placed her beneath him once again, his rhythm increasing.

"Eyes," he commanded, his hand at her jaw.

She looked up and saw desperation and need.

His pace quickened, far faster than any human man could manage. She reached for his lower back, simply to hold on.

He strained and pushed above her, every muscle in his body tense. Then, with a roar, he stilled inside her and released. His mouth dropped to her neck and he sucked at her skin, a curious and extraordinary pleasure radiating from that spot throughout her entire body.

His release seemed to last much longer than normal, far outstripping the pulsing inside her.

When he finally opened his eyes and lifted his head, he regarded her curiously.

"Are you all right?" She touched his face, his brow, his chin.

He pressed his lips to hers.

"You've ensnared me, Cassita," he whispered. "I've never been less eager to escape."

Chapter Forty-four

D awn poured sunlight through the open balcony doors into the bedroom, spilling onto Raven's face.

She opened her eyes, peering with disappointment at the empty space
beside her.

William was magnificent. He was Cupid. A god.

He'd been attentive and passionate, truly an expert lover.

He hadn't showered her with pet names or paid her extravagant compliments. But he'd been tender and affectionate and when he orgasmed,
he looked as if he'd truly been overcome.

He was attracted to her and she believed she'd captured his interest, if
only until this morning. But he didn't care for her. Not really. From what
he'd confessed already, he never would.

She stretched her hand experimentally over the mattress, shifting her
legs. The space between her legs was tender, which wasn't surprising.
When William had confided that he had tremendous stamina, he spoke
the truth. She'd had three orgasms to his one, and that was only because
he was worried about hurting her. When she was used to him, he said,
he'd multiply that number.

The vampyre was insatiable.

She closed her eyes, chiding herself. She knew better than to become
attached, sexually or otherwise, to someone who didn't truly care for her.
And there was the small matter that William wasn't human.

In the harsh light of day, no doubt he'd seen her as she truly was and fled. It had happened before. This was why it was better to be alone and to accept one's solitude rationally and cheerfully.

"My lark awakes." A masculine voice broke into her musings.

Raven turned toward the balcony so quickly, she found herself entangled in the sheets.

"Good morning." William was standing in the open doorway, naked, his arm lifted above his head to rest on the doorpost.

In the sunlight, his pale skin burnished bronze, complementing his pale eyes and blond hair. His figure was a study in male perfection, every muscle defined and honed, especially his chest and abdomen.

"You're handsome." The words escaped her mouth before she could consider them, her eyes drinking him in.

He smiled and dropped his arm. "You're pretty. Especially now, with your dark hair mussed and your cheeks a little pink. You look as if you've been bedded and bedded well."

Raven smiled down at the sheets, unable to meet his gaze. "I was. Three times."

"I didn't mean to wake you."

"I noticed you were gone."

William nodded, noting the way she'd woven part of the sheet through her fingers. Her green eyes were fixed on it as if it had the answer to life itself.

"I held you for some time, but I grew restless."

She flexed her fingers.

He turned away from the door and she was treated to a frontal view of his body. Not even the greatest sculptures of the Renaissance could rival his symmetry of form.

"You don't need to wake up yet."

She smiled her thanks and tried not to stare.

"Why so quiet?" William's brow furrowed.

"Why me?"

"Why you?" he prompted.

Raven pulled the sheet up to her shoulders.

"There are lots of human women you could choose from. And there's the red-haired vampyre. She's gorgeous."

William wore a distasteful expression. "Aoibhe is an ally; nothing more."

Raven contemplated his answer, wondering why she felt suspicious.

"In comparison with the others, I'm practically celibate. I don't engage in intercourse everytime I feed and my assignations are carefully chosen." He watched her face to discern her reaction.

She gazed at him curiously. "You said once that you didn't know how sex as a vampyre compared with what it was when you were human."

William nodded, appearing uncomfortable.

"What did you mean?"

His jaw flexed. "I meant that as a human being I never engaged in sex."

Raven's mouth dropped open. "How old were you when you became a vampyre?"

William turned away to look out over the gardens. "The world was different then. I was different then. At the time of my transformation, I was a novice in the Dominican order."

"You were a priest?" Raven practically shrieked.

He pinned her to the bed with his dark glare. "I was in formation to become a priest. Novices take the same vows."

Raven murmured an oath.

"I haven't spent a great deal of time thinking about it, but it's clear the chains I wore in life still bind me. I enjoy sexual relations but intemperance repulses me."

"I don't see how a priest—I mean, a novice—could become a vampyre. Wouldn't you have crosses and relics on you at all times?"

"We are alike, you and I. We both hate God. You hated him into atheism and I hated him into a cursed supernatural transformation."

"I don't understand."

"If you continue to share my bed, it's possible I will tell you how it came about. But not this morning." William turned his back on her.

Raven realized she'd been dismissed.

Without a word, she swung her legs over the far side of the bed, facing the closet.

She wrapped the sheet around her naked body, fashioning it into a toga, and hobbled over to her overnight bag.

"What are you doing?"

She heard his voice but didn't look up. "I'm getting dressed and having breakfast."

"Why? It's early yet."

She withdrew underwear and a T-shirt from her bag. "You said 'if' I continue to share your bed. I know regret when I hear it."

He strode toward her. "What are you talking about?"

"I'm talking about being content with what I have and not deluding myself into reaching for something more."

"You aren't making sense."

"Actually, I've come to my senses." She glanced at him without making eye contact. "If you give me the room, I'll change and you won't have to watch."

William pulled the clothes from her hands. "Maybe I'd like to watch."

"So you can make fun?"

"Of what?"

She gestured to herself. "Are you really going to make me say it? Look at me."

His eyes bore into hers. "I am."

His look was heated, full of desire.

Raven turned her gaze to her feet. "Thin is beautiful."

He scoffed. "Thin is an indication of ill health and weakness."

Raven gave him a quizzical look.

He stroked his chin absently. "I'd forgotten about this aspect of human culture. For the most part, I ignore the workings of your world, unless there's something that particularly interests me. You, for example."

He placed a hand to her hip. "When I was human, slender women had a low survival rate. They were considered sickly, infirm, and definitely not beautiful."

"You don't mind my weight?"

He brought his hand to the top of the sheet, where she'd twisted it under her arms.

"Let me look at you."

"I'm naked."

"Precisely." His gaze darted to her breasts as he pulled the sheet from her body. He stood there, his eyes roaming her figure with undisguised appreciation. "You're an attractive woman, Raven."

She didn't meet his eyes. She felt conspicuous, embarrassed. She bent to pick up the sheet but he took her hand, leading her over to his painting of *Primavera*.

He stood behind her and placed his hands on her shoulders.

"I can see you may need a little convincing. Take a moment and examine the painting, focusing on the female forms."

"I know what they look like." She crossed her arms over her chest. "I'm an art restorer, remember?"

"You may have looked at them, but you haven't seen them. Look again."

Raven began at the left of the painting with the figure of Mercury and moved to look at the three Graces.

"They're certainly healthy."

"Look on the Graces before examining Venus. Remember, these are depictions of the ideal of feminine beauty."

"According to Botticelli."

William squeezed her shoulders. "Botticelli recognized beauty when he saw it. He admired Simonetta Vespucci, for example, and she was extremely attractive."

Raven turned her head to the side. "You aren't making me feel better."

"That's because you aren't paying attention. Look at the women's stomachs."

She did as she was told. "They're rounded."

"They're healthy." William brought his hands to her abdomen and placed them flat against her. "As are you." His lips found her ear. "And their breasts?"

Raven shuddered at his nearness.

"It's difficult to make out but they look full."

William brushed her hands aside and cupped her breasts, reveling in the weight. "You're far more voluptuous. Far more pleasing to my eyes, my hands, *my mouth*." He kissed her ear. "What about their bottoms?"

"They've got back."

"Back?"

"Um, they have substantial bottoms."

"Hmm." William slid his hands down the curves of her sides and her hips before gripping her backside. "You have an excellent, round bottom. It pleases me to hold it while I'm inside you."

He stepped in front of her, facing her. "In other words, Botticelli's ideal women look like women and not boys. They're soft and curvaceous. Healthy and rounded. Women of the size figured in this painting were considered beautiful for centuries, if not millennia. They were the aesthetic ideal during my lifetime and long after."

He brought his mouth to her neck before whispering, "My ideal hasn't changed."

Without a word, Raven wrapped her arms around his shoulders and kissed him as he carried her to bed.

Chapter Forty-five

"Someone is happy this morning." Patrick smirked as he saw Raven sitting at her desk with a dreamy smile on her face.

She was staring at an image of *Primavera* that she'd used as the wallpaper to her desktop computer.

"Earth to Raven?" He snapped his fingers, causing her to jump.

When she saw who'd surprised her, she shoved his arm. "Jeez, Patrick. What the hell?"

He laughed. "I called your name twice."

"I was concentrating." She turned back to her computer, logging out of the system.

"On what, your wallpaper?"

"Very funny."

"Why so happy this morning? Is it because Batelli got turfed?"

Raven glanced around the room at their colleagues. Fortunately, they weren't paying attention to their conversation.

"Ssshhh!" She gave Patrick a censorious look.

He lifted his hands in surrender. "Sorry."

"Summer is coming. That makes me happy." Raven grabbed her cane and walked to the wardrobe to retrieve her lab coat.

"Right." Patrick followed her. "Hey, if things with your wine collector are that good, why don't we go on a double date? Gina wanted to plan something for your birthday."

"It isn't until July."

"Well, she'll plan a party for then. But we should go out before that. Bring your friend to meet us."

"Um, I don't know." Raven tried not to look troubled.

"No big deal. I know how things are when it's new." He smiled again.

Raven returned his smile. "Things are pretty new with Gina. You guys have only been together a couple of weeks."

"Yeah, but it feels like longer because we were friends first. How's your collector?"

She directed her grin at her lab coat. "He's good. Thanks."

Patrick shook his head at her. "Now that we know everything is good, let me know when you're free. We can go out to dinner or meet for drinks after work. You decide."

He started for the door. "By the way, they're going to reopen the exhibition hall in a couple of weeks. The Prado in Madrid agreed to lend us a few pieces."

Raven gestured to him to come back. "Does that mean they've closed the investigation?"

"No. From what I hear, it's just moved off-site. There's no way Vitali is going to let the illustrations go without a massive investigation. By the way, be careful walking around the city at night. The newspapers are reporting that there's a motorcycle gang attacking people. They shot a guy with a crossbow Monday night."

"What?" Raven's jaw dropped open.

"I know. Ridiculous, right? The BBC is reporting that both British and American tourists are canceling their travel plans to Florence this summer. The theft at the gallery, plus those bodies they found near the river, and now the motorcycle gang have all hit the news."

"Is the gang attacking random people or are they targeting?"

Patrick gave her a quizzical look. "I have no idea. There were reports of attacks but when the police arrived, the victims had disappeared."

"Thanks, Patrick. Say hi to Gina. I'll let you know about dinner."

Her friend nodded and made his way to the archives.

Raven thought of one word as she walked toward the restoration lab. *Hunters.*

During her lunch break, Raven contemplated calling Ambrogio in order
to leave a message for William.

But she didn't.

He didn't communicate by telephone, text, or e-mail. If she asked him
to come to dinner with her friends, he'd decline, of course.

How could she introduce her . . . vampyre to her friends?

The answer was clear and concise.

She couldn't.

Raven didn't see William again until Saturday evening. He'd been busy
day and night trying to locate the hunters.

It was a plausible explanation.

But Raven couldn't help the doubt that crept into the back of her
mind. She wondered if he'd seen the red-haired vampyre while he was
hunting. She wondered who he was feeding from, since he wasn't feeding
from her.

She cursed herself for being jealous of his food sources.

On Saturday evening, at William's request, she put on a little black
dress that dipped very low in the back, exposing a great deal of skin. The
dress would have looked better with stilettos, but now that her leg was
back to its previous form, she couldn't wear high heels without excruciating pain.

She took time brushing and styling her long black hair, curling the
ends. And she made up her face with a light hand, accentuating the natural color of her lips and highlighting her green eyes.

William had said he was taking her out for the evening, but that she
was to be ready before sunset.

A knock sounded at the door and she looked through the peephole.

It was Marco.

She opened the door to let him in and retrieved her purse. "Where's
his lordship?"

"In the car." Marco moved past her, searching the apartment. When
he seemed satisfied with what he saw (or didn't see), he accompanied her

to the landing, keeping careful watch on the stairwell as she locked the door.

When she entered the Mercedes, she found William in the backseat.

"Good evening." He greeted her with a passionate kiss.

She kissed him back earnestly, for she'd missed him.

"I like this." His fingers descended to where the dress began at her backside.

"You requested it."

"I may have requested it, but only you could wear it." He grasped her wrist, moving her bracelet aside so his lips could meet her skin. "You're stunning."

Marco pulled away from the curb and they began driving.

"You won't need this tonight." William undid the scarf that covered her neck.

Slowly and sensuously, he slid the silk across her skin, allowing the end to trail across her breast.

Raven stopped breathing for a moment.

"Why not?"

"We won't be in public this evening." He touched her neck with a single finger. "But I need you to close your eyes."

"Why?" Raven looked out the window in alarm. "Are you taking me back underground?"

"No. Trust me."

Raven didn't trust him. Not completely.

But she swallowed her doubts and closed her eyes.

She could hear the sound of other cars and Vespas as they passed. She could feel the movement of the car, the acceleration and deceleration. There were several stops and several turns.

She had no idea where they were going.

All this time, William's thumb stroked the back of her hand.

Suddenly the car came to a stop.

"We're here."

Raven opened her eyes and saw they were in an alley. She didn't recognize the buildings on either side.

Marco opened her door and helped her out, reaching inside to pick up her cane.

"Thank you." She took it from him and walked around the back of the car to where William was waiting.

"That will be all, Marco. I'll ring you when it's time to return."

Marco nodded and returned to the driver's seat.

William stood in front of a rusty metal door. He pressed a stone in the wall to its left and a security panel emerged. He entered a long series of numbers and Raven heard a loud click.

William opened the door, allowing her to step inside.

"What's this?" she asked, her eyes peering into the dark space.

"This is Teatro."

Chapter Forty-six

"It doesn't look like a theater." Raven strained to make out the features of the room.

Behind her, William switched on the lights.

The lights were dim, but they illuminated a long bar that ran along one side, what looked like a stage that stood in front of a dance floor, and a series of couches and tables and chairs on the other two walls.

"It looks like a club." Raven gave William a curious look.

"It is."

"Where is everyone?"

"It's closed this evening for a private engagement."

He gestured to one of the velvet couches and Raven sat down.

William went to the corner, where the dj booth was located. Soon music filled the room.

Raven recognized it as Madeleine Peyroux.

"I thought you didn't listen to modern music," she called.

"I've been persuaded to expand my universe." He smiled as he approached her. "Can I offer you a drink?"

Raven looked toward the bar. "Do you have human drinks here?"

"This is a club for vampyres and humans."

Raven found herself disquieted by the revelation.

"I'd like red wine, please."

William bowed and withdrew to the bar.

Raven took the opportunity to examine the large space more closely.

There were flat-screen televisions on the wall, all of which were switched off. There were a few doors that led from the central room to places unknown.

It was, perhaps, a club like any other dance club. Except it catered to vampyres.

William approached with a bottle of wine and two glasses balanced on a tray. He poured a glass for her and one for himself.

"Going human tonight?" she asked as he handed her a glass.

"I enjoy red wine."

He settled next to her on the sofa and clinked their glasses together.

Raven tasted the wine. It was excellent.

"Do you spend a lot of time here?"

"Never." William sipped his wine pointedly.

"Why not?"

"Decadence bores me."

"Why? What happens here?"

William swirled the contents of his glass, his face studiously blank.

"Nothing of importance."

Raven's eyebrows knitted together. "It's a simple question; not a state secret."

His eyes flickered to hers.

"Secrecy is the currency that keeps me alive."

"Aren't you tired of keeping secrets?"

He placed his glass on the table in front of them, but didn't respond.

"I was under the impression that your secrecy would relax once we went to bed." Her green eyes held a warning.

William tried to hide his surprise at her rising anger but was unsuccessful.

"I'm not used to confiding in someone. I will concede that you should have answers to some of your questions, within reason." He relaxed in his seat, lifting his arm to rest across the back of the sofa. "I enjoy your company, Raven. I hope you enjoy mine."

"I do." She focused on her wineglass. "Very much."

"There are other human beings who enjoy the company of vampyres. They come here to offer themselves."

"In what way?"

"All ways."

She lifted her head. "And the vampyres?"

"They come here to feed, to have sex, to see and be seen."

Raven peered around the room.

"Do vampyres bring their pets here?"

"Sometimes. This is a place where one might find a pet, or borrow someone else's."

A sick feeling twisted in Raven's stomach and she, too, put her glass down.

"Cassita." He lifted her hand and pressed the back of it to his lips. "Look around you. Who's here?"

"Just us."

"Precisely. I wouldn't bring you here under normal circumstances."

"Why?"

"I think if you reflect for a moment, you'll discern the answer. Would you care to dance?" He gestured at the dance floor.

She lifted her cane so he could see it. "I can't."

"Are you in pain?" He leaned closer.

"No."

"Then you can dance."

She withdrew her hand.

"I'm unsteady."

"I'll hold you up."

"I can't really move that well."

"We'll stand in one spot."

She scowled. "You're one bossy vampyre, did you know that?"

He leaned forward to whisper in her ear. "*Yes.*"

Without ceremony, he lifted her into his arms as if she were as light as a feather and carried her to the center of the dance floor.

When she was on two feet, he pulled her into his arms.

The music continued; soft music that was conducive to slow movements. William held her close and they began to sway.

"I didn't know vampyres danced." She couldn't keep the amusement out of her voice.

"I wanted an excuse to touch you."

"You don't need an excuse."

"Don't I?" He pulled back to search her eyes.

She shook her head.

He lifted his hand and caressed her cheek.

"If you're uncomfortable, I can give you vampyre blood to help your leg."

Raven resisted the urge to pull away from him and instead focused her attention on the top button of his shirt, which was undone.

"I'm sorry it bothers you." Her tone hardened.

"Not in the slightest." He stopped. "I'm worried about you."

She shrugged. "The wine helps."

"As long as you're comfortable."

They resumed dancing, gently moving in concert to the music.

"You dance well," he observed.

"Not really." Raven blushed. "I took dance lessons when I was a little girl. Ballet."

"I detect it in your movements sometimes. Very elegant."

She stifled a laugh. No one had ever called her elegant since her accident. She regarded him skeptically. "Don't you want to fix me?"

William appeared puzzled.

"Why should I want to fix you? You aren't broken."

His answer pierced her.

Her eyes bore into his, searching for any sign of duplicity or mirth.

"Part of me wants to take the blood so I can run with you. I have a vision of the two of us, flying across the rooftops."

"Perhaps it isn't a vision. It could be a memory of the first time I brought you to the villa." He smiled. "When you decide you want to run, I have an entire cellar of excellent vintages at your disposal."

"I don't think so."

"I can run fast enough for both of us." He pressed his lips to her hair.

She toyed with one of the buttons on his shirt, staring at it as if it were the soul of fascination.

"Part of me feels like I would be betraying other disabled persons if I took the blood. That I'd be saying I'm not good enough. That my disability separates me from you."

William regarded her gravely—the set of her chin, her downcast eyes, the tension in her body.

He was quiet for a moment, struggling to find words that wouldn't add to her pain.

"I don't understand such things and I won't pretend to understand them. All I can say is that I think no one—human or otherwise—is perfect. If perfection is the standard for normalcy, we all fail."

"I like that." She lifted her chin. "I've always thought that human beings are all disabled in some way. It's just that my disability can be seen. It never occurred to me to think of other beings as disabled, too."

"One might think that vampyrism is a disability. It's certainly a curse." Raven saw the barest hint of despair in William's eyes.

She knew better than to try to soothe him with pretty lies.

"I'm sorry."

She reached up and kissed him, almost a brush of the lips.

He looked down at her gravely. "In many ways, we are the most perfect match. We see each other as we are, but neither of us views the other as broken."

William's words seemed to Raven to be more of a description of what he hoped was the case, rather than a statement of fact.

She squeezed his shoulders encouragingly.

"I think you're right, William. As long as I can lean on you, I don't need my cane."

"Then lean on me forever."

"Forever is a long time."

"Not long enough when you have hope dancing in your arms."

Raven saw desire and passion on William's face, his gaze startling in its intensity.

"Kiss me, William. Kiss me and pretend you mean it."

"I don't have to pretend."

His lips descended to hers.

Something had changed. Raven felt it the moment their mouths met.

He'd lowered his defenses and was kissing her with more than just his body. She felt his affection and want, his focus and attention.

Raven wrapped her arms around him. He took her weight, lifting her slightly.

When his kiss lessened, she pulled away and smiled. "Thank you."

"For what?"

"For that kiss. I felt it in my heart."

He brushed his lips against her forehead.

"Take me to bed," she whispered.

"Now?"

"Yes."

"Are you sure?" He ran the backs of his fingers down her cheek.

She nodded.

He swept her into his arms and strode quickly to one of the corridors that led from the large central room. They passed several closed doors until they came to the end of the hall.

William opened the last door and stepped inside.

The room was dark, but within minutes he'd lit candles and placed them around the space. Music could still be heard from down the hall but now it featured the rise of angelic voices singing without accompaniment.

"Who's singing?"

William approached one of the candles, staring into the flame. He reached out to toy with it, passing his hand through the fire. "They're called Stile Antico. They sing music that is more to my taste."

"It's beautiful. What are they singing?"

"A collection of Renaissance compositions on Song of Songs from the Old Testament."

Raven looked at her surroundings, at the large, central bed, which was dressed in black satin sheets. The walls were painted purple, the ceiling black. A mirror ran the length of one of the walls, reflecting the bed.

She turned her attention back to William.

"Song of Songs is the only book in the Bible devoted to sex," she observed.

"It isn't just about sex. 'The king hath brought me into his chambers: we will be glad and rejoice in thee, we will remember thy love more than wine.'"

"Beautiful." Raven smiled.

"It's about sex, seduction, and erotic attraction, but it's also about affection, tenderness, and play."

"So the book is about you." She gave him a saucy look.

"It's fortunate for me that you think so."

Raven's gaze traveled to the erotic photographs on the walls. They were all black-and-white: some featured a man; others featured a woman; but all paid special homage to the human's neck.

"What is this place?"

William focused on the flame once again. The set of his shoulders telegraphed his reticence.

"Some of the members of the club use these rooms for sex. Intercourse is not permitted in the public spaces."

Raven frowned. "Have you ever done that?"

"I've never had intercourse in the club before. I believe such assignations should be private." William stood at the foot of the bed, watching her. "We should go."

"Why?"

"This is not the place for you." He leaned over and blew out one of the candles.

"Wait." She caught his arm. "We're here alone. You're playing beautiful music. And I want you."

"That bed has its own memories." He jerked his chin. "So do the walls."

"Let's give them new ones. Good ones."

William stood before her, cupping her face in his hand. "I didn't bring you to Teatro for this. I simply wanted a place where we could enjoy one another."

"Then let me enjoy you."

She knelt on the bed, her fingers moving to the buttons of his shirt.

He stood, watching her eagerness with no little amusement.

"This is interesting."

"How so?" She removed his cuff links and peeled the black shirt from his body, throwing it to the floor.

"I'm used to being the seducer."

She brought her lips to his chest. She kissed across the smooth surface, enjoying his sharp intake of breath when she opened her mouth and tasted his skin.

His chest was hairless and well-defined, as were his abdominal muscles.

"You don't want me touching you?" She paused, tracing the space where his heart was.

He dropped his voice. "I didn't say that."

She felt his broad shoulders and smoothed over his biceps, fascinated by the lines and contours of his muscles, the muted strength.

She gently stroked his abdomen, pressing a kiss just above his navel.

He tangled a hand in her long black hair, letting it slip through his fingers.

Raven touched his belt, her eyes fixed on his.

He nodded.

She undid his trousers, pushing them over his hips. Then she sat back on her knees, taking a moment to admire the V that sloped from his hips.

William stood before her, proudly naked, his erection substantial and strong.

She looked up at him. "Do you ever wear underwear?"

"Never."

She wrapped her fingers around him, admiring his cool smoothness. Bending and kissing him softly, she brought him into her mouth.

He twined her hair around his wrist, a rumble escaping his chest.

He tasted different. That was the first thing she noticed.

His flesh felt human, but cooler, the skin no doubt tougher. But his flavor was . . . indescribable. Not delicious, certainly, but preferable to a human male, in her estimation.

She pleasured him with her mouth, hoping he was enjoying himself.

By all accounts—the fierce look in his eyes, the sounds from his lips, and the way he clutched her hair—she was successful.

But he was restrained.

He kept tension between his hand and her hair, but didn't tug or pull. Nor did he push her head down. In fact, he seemed quite content to remain still, allowing her to control the interaction.

"You delight me," he whispered. "You have an exquisite mouth. But now it's my turn."

She smiled up at him, more than a little proud of herself.

William deftly undid her dress, tossing it aside.

"Ah." He breathed out, staring at the black strapless bodysuit she was wearing.

She frowned. "Don't you like it?"

"I like it a great deal." His eyes moved up and down, taking in every inch of the satin fabric. "Black is my favorite color."

"I didn't know that." She winked.

He pressed a light hand to her chest, urging her to lie back. His lips moved to her breasts, through the bodysuit, as his fingers dipped between her legs.

"I like that," she murmured, squeezing his wrist.

"So do I." His hand moved to her bottom, where he traced the ascending strip that formed the thong.

He licked his lips.

He rolled her on her side, simply so he could admire her bottom, cupping and squeezing with both hands.

He slid a finger across the thong between her legs, tantalizing her.

Raven moved to her back once again and parted her legs. William's expression was triumphant as she moved in concert with his hand.

Without warning, his fingers withdrew and he was peeling her out of her bodysuit.

He took her hands in his and extended them to her sides before lowering himself to her body.

A few urgent kisses, a few tugs on her nipples with his mouth, and he pushed inside her.

She closed her eyes and exhaled. He stretched her almost to the point of pain, but she welcomed the fullness.

William moved slowly, his mouth joined to hers before it descended to lick her breasts.

She lifted her hips to meet him, enjoying every movement, every thrust.

"How do you feel?" He spoke against her collarbone, kissing a line from shoulder to shoulder.

"Beyond words." She flexed her hands in his, lifting her head to kiss his brow.

He released her hands and dropped his own to her backside, gripping her as he entered more deeply.

His eyes met hers and, for the first time, she saw uncertainty in them and not a little worry.

She pushed his hair back from his forehead. "Are you all right?"

"Of course." He stifled a groan.

"You make me feel pretty."

"For so you are. Noble and brave and pretty. Your body is soft and inviting." Now he groaned as if tortured. "You threaten my self-control."

"Then let go."

"I can't," he gritted out through clenched teeth.

"Feed from me."

He stilled, planting himself deeply inside her.

She felt his body tense and excitement radiate from his skin.

"Are you sure?" He traced the arch of her eyebrow, his eyes alert.

"I want to give this to you. To give myself."

His gray eyes grew eager but his expression was guarded.

"I can feed elsewhere and share what we have in this bed only with you."

"I'm offering myself to you because I—I care about you."

He saw it in her eyes, the depth of her feelings.

For a moment, he was tempted to deny her and himself.

But the moment passed.

"It will change things," he warned. "Once you give, you'll want to give yourself again and again. Once I taste you, I won't want anyone else."

"Please."

He gave her one last searching look before kissing her fiercely.

"Ignosce mihi," he murmured.

She felt his lips trail to her neck, cool and firm. Then she felt his tongue, licking and tasting.

Finally, she felt his teeth, nipping.

His hips pulled back and moved forward, pushing inside her quickly and deeply. A few more movements and she fell, her arms and legs clutching him as she climaxed.

Her orgasm was interrupted by a piercing pain in her neck. In an instant, the hurt was replaced by the pleasurable sensation of William's mouth, his lips and his tongue, sucking on her.

Her climax heightened, doubled, ascended out of her control.

He continued moving inside her, his pace quickening, his strokes lengthening.

She was still orgasming, the experience absolutely overwhelming.

Within five strokes, he released her neck, laving the wound with his cool tongue.

Their eyes met and Raven saw him lick his lips. His eyes seemed to glow in the candlelight as his strokes quickened, stretching her further.

With a growl, he pushed inside her and she felt a dull coolness fill her. A short time later he collapsed, burying his face in her throat.

Chapter Forty-seven

Raven floated on a cloud, accompanied by heavenly voices. She didn't know how long she lay, naked and wrapped in William's arms.

She felt dreamy and strange, as if she were drunk.

William stroked a finger up and down her spine, his face an expression of peace.

"I understand what you mean now." She nestled against his bare chest.

"About what?"

"About addiction. I want to have sex with you again and let you feed from me."

He chuckled and drew her closer. "Me, as well. But I can only take so much blood from you within a certain time. We'll have to wait and see how your body reacts."

"Is it safe?"

He kissed her forehead, stroking his thumb across her cheekbone.

"Raven, nothing about me is safe. But I can say that I will do all in my power to give you nothing but pleasure."

She burrowed into his chest, blissfully happy.

"In fact, when the city is free of hunters, I'd like to take you on my motorcycle for a ride into the countryside."

She laughed, a giddy sound.

"I'm not sure I can survive that. The last time you had me on your motorcycle, I was sick."

"This will be much more enjoyable, I assure you."

Another embrace, another caress, and he was helping her dress.

When her legs were too unsteady to carry her, he swept her into his arms, pausing to kiss her with every few steps.

They walked down the hall toward the dance floor, Raven gazing up at him in wonder.

She felt cherished. She felt happy.

She felt connected to him by a bond that was far more than just sex.

The experience had been nothing like she'd ever known. It seemed as if, with his mouth at her neck, she'd had a second, heightened orgasm, simultaneous with the first. Even now, she felt boundless satisfaction, the euphoria thrumming through her veins.

It had been a strange and wonderful experience. She couldn't wait to repeat it.

Just then, William stopped.

He rumbled and bared his teeth.

"Ah, so you've finally finished. I didn't want to interrupt, though I was sorely tempted." A woman's voice called from inside the main room.

Raven turned her head and saw the female vampyre, clad in a Renaissance-style gown of midnight blue velvet, sitting on one of the banquettes. Her fiery red hair cascaded down her shoulders, her face pale and perfect, her eyes sparkling.

She took a drink from a strange-looking glass.

"Aoibhe." William's tone was commanding. "Teatro is closed."

"I came to see what might prompt the Prince to break curfew." She nodded in Raven's direction. "I see I've found the answer. You smell of sex. Shall we share a drink?"

William's grip on Raven tightened.

"There are hunters about. Be vigilant when you leave."

Aoibhe put her glass on the table in front of her.

"If you've finished with your pet, send her home. We can enjoy the hours until sunrise. I think I left my chemise in your bedroom the other day. I'd like to retrieve it."

William muttered a curse.

Raven's mind moved slowly, but move it did. She'd heard Aoibhe's casual, offhand remark.

She remembered (albeit dimly) William dismissing Aoibhe as simply an ally. Everything about the female vampyre's tone and body language indicated her relationship with the Prince was far more intimate.

Raven put her hand over her eyes, as if she could blot out the sight.

"I see your pet understands English." Aoibhe noted Raven's reaction. "I must have said something that upset her. Her heart rate spiked."

Without a word, William crossed to the bar, gently placing Raven on a chair. He picked up a telephone, pressed a few buttons, and hung up.

All the while, Raven tried to make sense of what was happening, her mind struggling as if it were walking through mud.

"Did your pet leave this behind?" Aoibhe bent to pick up Raven's cane. "You surprise me, my lord, wasting yourself on a cripple. You could have anyone you wanted. And I do mean anyone."

"I am not a cripple." Raven's voice, defiant and steely, surprised even herself. She glared in Aoibhe's direction.

Swiftly, William moved to stand between the two females. He kept his eyes on the vampyre, but spoke over his shoulder.

"Marco is coming. We're leaving."

He'd barely pronounced the last word when Aoibhe threw the cane like a javelin, aiming for Raven's head.

William caught it.

Raven hadn't even seen him move. It was as if he'd plucked the cane out of the air like a magician pulls a rabbit from a hat.

"That was not a wise decision, Aoibhe." William's voice was deceptively quiet. "Leave before I lose my temper."

"Pardon, my lord. But your little one deserves punishment for speaking to me like that." Aoibhe stood, preening like a peacock.

"You insulted her and, by association, me. How is it that she deserves punishment?" William spoke sharply.

"Come now, my love. Let's not quarrel." Aoibhe flashed a smile. "Send your pet on her way and spend the night with me. Now that we've both fed we'll be more vigorous. Although lack of vigor has never been our problem."

Raven gave William a condemning look.

Aoibhe's eyebrows lifted. She was watching the interactions between Raven and William with more than a little curiosity.

"It appears your pet is the jealous type. Hasn't she learned her place?"

"That's enough," William snapped. He swung the cane through the air like a rapier, slashing in Aoibhe's direction. "Do you value your head?"

"Excuse the disrespect." She bowed very low. "I just find the situation . . . interesting."

"How did you know I was here?" William was abrupt.

"I called for you at Palazzo Riccardi, hoping to see you. They dismissed me, on your orders. I caught your scent in the alley outside." Aoibhe closed her eyes and inhaled deeply. A strange look flitted across her features.

William saw her reaction and moved toward her, his posture threatening.

"*Cave*, Aoibhe."

"It's her." Aoibhe opened her eyes. "It's the sweet-smelling one you found by the river. I didn't recognize her at the Consilium because her blood was muddled."

Raven felt her heart beat faster.

Aoibhe came a step closer. "I don't suppose you'd share?"

The Prince growled.

"I don't blame you. She's"—Aoibhe licked her lips—"exceptional. I thought you drained her after you found her. How did you manage to keep her? She was minutes from death."

Raven's mind began to clear and her stomach churned.

She lifted her eyes to William's as he walked toward her.

He handed her the cane, picked her up, and approached the door, careful to face away from the threat.

Aoibhe continued. "It wasn't your blood in her veins. You must have given her to someone else. Who?"

When William didn't respond, she cocked her head to the side.

"Why would the Prince of Florence save a delicious but crippled human? Is it because she fancies herself in love with you?"

Raven expelled a breath in shock, still in William's arms.

Aoibhe clucked her tongue. "Poor little pet. I'd keep her away from bell towers if I were you."

William lunged in Aoibhe's direction, growling and snapping his teeth.

Raven clung to his neck, terrified he was going to drop her.

Aoibhe backed away from the angry vampyre slowly, holding her hands up. "A thousand pardons, my prince. I'll take my leave."

She kept her back to the wall, inching toward the exit. As soon as her hand felt the door, she flung it open, disappearing into the alley.

William snarled at the closing door, his body trembling with anger. It took more than a moment for him to regain his composure.

When he stepped outside, Raven realized Marco and the car had not yet arrived.

And they were surrounded.

Chapter Forty-eight

Five men stood at one end of the alley, five men at the other. William, Raven, and Aoibhe were trapped.

The men were all large, muscular, and armed. One of the men on the left side held the leash of a massive German shepherd. The dog barked and reared, his master barely able to restrain him.

Aoibhe was huddled against the wall opposite Teatro. She lunged with bared teeth at the intruders, like a cornered animal.

The hunters, who'd been focusing their attention on her, immediately turned to William. A few murmurs lifted from the crowd as they realized the prize that stood a few feet away.

While the hunters were distracted, Aoibhe took that opportunity to begin climbing the wall to the roof.

The men reacted, shouting and moving forward. Two of them raised crossbows, releasing arrows. Sharp, whizzing sounds filled the air.

One of the archers missed his mark but the other was successful, his arrow slicing into the vampyre's back.

She screamed and began to fall, her red hair billowing like a cloud, her blue velvet dress like a sail.

"Aoibhe, no!" William cried.

He placed Raven on her feet and sprang into the air.

His body was a blur of black as he caught Aoibhe in his arms. The archers began to shoot at both of them, arrows flying from two directions.

William seemed to avoid the arrows easily, twisting and turning even as he landed, cradling Aoibhe to his chest. Her brown eyes were wide, her mouth open, and she was gasping, as if for oxygen.

"Stop," Raven croaked, leaning heavily on her cane.

The attention of the hunters turned momentarily to her.

She limped from where she'd been leaning against the door to the center of the alley.

"A feeder," one of the hunters pronounced. He sounded American. "Look at her neck."

Raven ignored the scorn in the hunter's voice. "Stop. She's hurt."

The hunter grinned. "That's the point, you stupid bitch."

A roar could be heard from the crowd, and scattered laughter, as if the situation were funny.

Raven found no amusement in the scene. She searched the eyes of their attackers, hoping to find some sign of humanity. But the only sign she could find was in William, who bent over Aoibhe's body, his face a mask of anguish.

While keeping careful watch on the hunters, who were still maintaining a cautious but aggressive distance, William sat Aoibhe up. He began digging into the wound in her back with his hand, black blood already staining her bright blue dress.

"They didn't attack you." Raven tried to reason with the men. "You don't need to kill them."

"She's crazy." A man armed with a crucifix and what looked like a small bottle of water pointed toward her.

"Of course she's crazy!" another exploded. "They go crazy when they fuck them. They probably had her together and fed from her."

"Shoot her."

The command came from Raven's left. A tall man, brandishing a garrote, jerked his chin at her. His eyes were hard, flat; his expression cool and detached. "We can't have witnesses."

"Raven, on the ground. Now!" William's voice came to her in Italian.

As if in slow motion, she saw him pull the arrow from Aoibhe's body and watched as her head lolled back, eyes wide and unfocused, body limp.

The archers took aim at Raven, just as William placed Aoibhe on the ground. He straightened from his crouch, holding the arrow in his right hand, Aoibhe's blood covering his fingers.

"I'm already a witness!" Raven shouted. "You're a death squad. You came here to kill beings who haven't done anything to you just so you can sell their blood."

"Shoot her," the leader repeated. "Before the neighbors hear."

Raven held her arms out, lifting her voice in Italian. "Look at me. I'm defenseless. You're going to kill a defenseless woman in cold blood."

"Raven, down!"

She ignored William's command, taking no thought for her safety, arms held wide.

She could think only about protecting William and the body of the vampyre who had just died in his arms.

"You're all murderers!" she shouted.

Something moved in her periphery.

William threw himself to her left, plucking an arrow out of the air, inches from her body. With a flick of his wrist and an overhand motion, he hurled the arrow back at the archer, where it caught him in the chest.

The archer fell to the ground, dead.

Spinning to the other side of Raven, William took the arrow he'd pulled from Aoibhe's body and flung it at one of the other archer's chests.

The crossbow fell from the archer's hand, clattering on the ground. He crashed down beside it.

William pushed Raven toward the door.

"Get down!"

She tumbled, scraping hands and knees as she landed on all fours.

At that moment, the dog broke free from his leash and began running toward them.

William whirled around.

The dog growled and snapped, lunging to bite William's leg.

He quickly grabbed the animal by its muzzle, slamming its mouth shut. Without effort, he lifted the dog and tossed it to the far end of the alley, where it crashed into a hunter, knocking him over.

The dog came to its feet, whimpering, and dragged its tail as it ran from the alley.

"Kill him," the leader ordered, pointing at William.

Three men ran forward, throwing what looked like water and holding out crosses.

William cursed as the liquid caught him in the face, stopping him in his tracks.

He shut his eyes, lifting a hand in the direction of the crosses, as if to shield himself from them.

Raven saw pain on his features. His face bloomed a bright red, as if it had been burned. She wondered if the hunters had thrown acid on his face.

"Stop!" she screamed. "Stop it!"

The hunters inched forward. The leader was among them, holding the garrote.

William's eyes were still closed as he groped with his hands blindly.

The leader threw the garrote at William's head.

The vampyre brushed the water from his face with his shirtsleeve, his eyes opening.

He batted the garrote aside and leapt forward, grabbing the leader by the shirt. He knocked the hunter's head against another. Both men dropped to the ground, eyes suddenly closed.

Raven couldn't tell if they were dead.

William sprang forward, avoiding the crosses and empty containers of water held toward him, repeating his attack on two other men.

At the sight of a vampyre who would not be deterred by holy water or relics, three of the hunters hopped on motorcycles and took off.

William walked toward the remaining one slowly.

The hunter took what looked like salt and threw it on the ground around his feet, making a small circle.

He stared in horror as William, undeterred by the salt, placed a hand on either side of the hunter's face and, with a sickening sound, broke his neck.

William tossed the body aside with contempt.

He surveyed the scene calmly, wiping his reddened face again with his shirtsleeve. Bodies were strewn across the alley, blood pooling on the ground.

His eyes moved to Aoibhe, who was lying motionless.

He cursed in Old English.

William's gaze flickered to where the motorcyclists had been, then back to Raven, who was cringing by the door.

"You tried to save me." His voice was filled with wonder. "You risked your life, tempting them to shoot you."

She felt her eyes welling up. "I couldn't watch them kill you."

His expression grew furious. "Never do that again. My death is the least of your worries. Do you understand?"

When she didn't answer, he strode toward her. He placed his hands on her shoulders, smearing Aoibhe's blood on her skin and dress.

"Do you understand?"

"Yes," she managed to say, fighting tears.

He released her as if he'd been burned.

"I have to go after them. They've seen what I can do and it's only a matter of time before they inform the Curia. I can't let that happen."

Before she could ask who the Curia were, he exited the alley on foot, running in the direction of the motorcycles.

Raven pressed a shaking hand to her mouth and tried very hard not to be sick.

Chapter Forty-nine

Raven paced the floor of William's bedroom until fatigue dictated she sit down. It had been an evening of revelations.

She'd discovered there were humans who voluntarily offered themselves to vampyres on a regular basis at a club. Whatever judgment she was tempted to pass on the pathology of others was tempered by her own willingness to offer herself to William.

He'd fed from her and she'd enjoyed it. Even now, as she stood in his bedroom, she fingered the wound in her neck, craving the experience. It had been so sensual, so ecstatic; she would let him feed from her again and again, possibly without limit.

Her desires disturbed her.

Over on the divan sat two of her sketches—the one she'd done of William from memory and the one she'd done of Allegra as the second Grace. William must have placed them there.

Put together in that way, Allegra and William made a handsome couple. But he hadn't loved her and she'd been so horrified to learn he was a vampyre, she'd committed suicide.

Raven thought of how high Giotto's bell tower was and cringed.

Aoibhe must have known the true story, for she'd mentioned Allegra, if only obliquely. Now Aoibhe herself was dead.

Raven didn't mourn her, but she felt something at having witnessed her death. To be hunted, cornered, killed, and left to rot in an alley . . .

If animals were accorded certain ethical treatment, why shouldn't a vampyre be accorded that same treatment? Vampyres were, like human beings, a kind of animal. They seemed to feel pain.

Raven lifted a blanket from the bed and wrapped it around herself like a shroud. There had been altogether too much death that evening. Bodies and blood and mindless killing.

William had massacred the hunters.

If she'd ever had a doubt as to his strength or abilities, she had none now. He was dangerous, he was lethal, and he had no compunction about killing. She shuddered when she thought about his quiet rage being unleashed on the Emersons.

Raven would have preferred that William knock the hunters unconscious, or evade them, rather than kill them. But she had to admit it was unlikely they would accept a warning to stay out of the city. They'd come to Florence to kill vampyres for their blood and they'd assembled themselves with fatal weapons, like an invading army.

William was defending himself, Raven, and his people. Surely that was just.

And he was still out there, possibly being hunted.

After William fled the alley, Marco had appeared. He was busy on his cell phone for a few minutes after he exited the Mercedes, his normally cool facade visibly disturbed.

Marco had helped Raven into the car and sped to the villa, where Ambrogio and Lucia had plied her with food and drink. They'd insisted she take what they said was an iron supplement.

She was still in shock. Although she should have refused the pill, she didn't, downing it with a glass of water.

It didn't have any discernible effect. Perhaps it truly was an iron supplement.

She'd taken the longest, hottest shower she'd ever taken, in an effort to clean herself of Aoibhe's blood. The shower regretfully removed William's scent and the evidence of his release from her body.

Raven moved the sketches from the divan and curled into a ball on top of it.

She couldn't lie on William's bed—on the bed he'd shared with Aoibhe. Perhaps the chemise she'd spoken of was hanging in the closet.

Raven didn't have the courage to look for it.

She tried closing her eyes, but all she could see was death. Death and the red-haired vampyre.

Aoibhe wasn't William's ally. She was his lover. She'd been in his bed only days before.

Raven had been betrayed.

Sickness and sadness wracked her body as she thought of the two supernatural beings together.

It had been a long time since she'd been betrayed by a lover. She hadn't had a boyfriend since. He'd been out of her league and eventually said so. He made her feel ugly, heavy, and crippled.

She resolved never to feel that way again.

Her first boyfriend, to whom she'd given her virginity, was nice. Nice in the way the color beige is nice—unremarkable and forgettable in almost every way. They'd parted company after a year.

William had brought color to her world, even if the colors were black and red. He'd liked her body—all of it. He hadn't wanted to fix her.

He'd awoken her body, her mind, her feelings. And he'd done the same with Aoibhe, presumably within hours of taking Raven to bed.

Which meant all his words and all his deeds were lies.

He'd said she was beautiful, but when the mood suited him, he'd taken a truly beautiful creature to his bed. Based on his expression of grief in the alley, he cared for her.

Raven was tempted to place her bracelet on his nightstand and slip out the back door. Fatigue and emotional upheaval prevented her from doing so.

It was only then, with her hand muffling her mouth, that she cried.

Chapter Fifty

William didn't return.

Raven woke up several times, both dreading and hoping to see him. He didn't appear.

It was Sunday. Lucia prepared an extensive breakfast, but Raven merely picked at the food. She accepted the coffee and orange juice, her mind fixed on what she would say to William when he came back.

Ambrogio reported that his lordship was well but engaged in business. He'd expressed his wish that Raven make herself at home.

Ambrogio gave no indication of when his lordship would return.

Raven spent the day with Lucia, examining some of the lesser pieces of his lordship's art collection, making notes on areas that would require restoration.

By the time the sun set, William still hadn't appeared.

At this point, Raven was agitated. She wanted to go home but Ambrogio suggested she was safer at the villa.

She knew his suggestion expressed his lordship's order. While she chafed at it, she didn't have an alternative. There were probably at least three hunters free in the city and they knew what she looked like. It was best to stay indoors.

Raven asked to be relocated to one of the guest rooms, but Lucia refused, stating that his lordship wanted her in his room.

Raven lacked the energy to argue with her and so, once again, she curled up on the divan.

Just before dawn Monday morning, she awoke to the sound of William entering the bedroom.

He stood by the closet, undressing with quiet, unhurried movements.

"I know you're awake. I heard your breathing change." He placed his clothes in a hamper and walked toward her, naked.

She allowed herself the luxury of admiring his form, even though it made her want to weep. "Where were you?"

William wiped his mouth with the back of his hand.

"Hunting hunters. I caught them, thankfully. I caught all of them, hopefully before they informed the Curia. For the moment, at least, the city is free of hunters. Why are you sleeping there?"

She sat up, pulling the blanket from around her and handing it to him. "We need to talk."

His jaw clenched. "Can it wait? I'm still weakened from the attack. I've been looking forward to having you in my arms."

"Just cover yourself, please."

William muttered a curse, but did as she asked.

Her expression softened as she examined his face. "Are you all right?"

The skin of his face was still reddened, as if he'd been sunburned.

He turned away from her. "It will heal."

"Since you're resistant to relics, I would have thought you'd be resistant to holy water."

He gestured to his face. "This is nothing. If they'd thrown it on Aoibhe, it would have eaten through her skin."

"Why is it different with you?"

His eyebrows knitted together and he looked irritated. "Can we just rest? It's been a difficult few days."

"You asked me why I wasn't sleeping in your bed. It's because of her."

"What the devil does she have to do with it?"

"She said she slept here—that she left you with her chemise."

William appeared confused.

Then a ray of recognition passed over his perfect features.

"She has never visited me here. This villa repels vampyres. She visited me at my other residence at Palazzo Riccardi."

Raven swore. "Is that supposed to make me feel better? You said Aoibhe was only an ally."

"She is."

"You lied."

"I did not. Aoibhe is power hungry and manipulative, but she's my ally and she's been one for a very, very long time. I don't trust her but she's the closest thing I have to a friend on the Consilium. I need her support when dealing with those vipers."

"Support," Rave scoffed. "You slept with her."

William lifted his chin. "I don't deny it."

"You've been sleeping with her while you've been sleeping with me, you arrogant bastard." Raven stood.

"No, I have not." William brought his hands to his hips.

"She said she left her clothes in your bed only days ago."

"Aoibhe's concept of time is somewhat . . . flexible."

"That's your defense?" Raven's voice lifted. "That time is flexible?"

"I haven't slept with her since we've been together. You have my word."

"Why should I trust you? You told me she was an ally; you didn't mention you were sleeping together. That's a lie of omission."

William's anger began to grow, his eyes snapping. "You are a self-fulfilling prophecy."

"What's that?"

"You say no man ever wanted you but when one does—and wants you badly enough to risk everything he's built for you—you tell yourself he's a liar."

Raven took a few steps on unsteady feet, her body clad in a long black nightgown.

"What are you risking? Tell me."

"I can't." His eyes grew shuttered.

"God, William. Just talk to me. Please," she begged.

He straightened his shoulders. "Some secrets I can't tell."

"Why not? Have I ever done anything to betray you? Or hurt you?"

William shook his head.

"Then why won't you talk to me?"

"Not now, Raven."

She threw her arms up in frustration. "You're like a walled city. I don't know how to get in. I don't even know what your real name is or when you were born."

"My name is William."

Raven lifted her arms in frustration. "You have secret lovers like Aoibhe. I know you feed from humans but you won't tell me about it. How do I know you aren't fucking around on me?"

He took a step toward her, his eyes flashing.

"What we share in bed, I'm not sharing with anyone else."

"Why should I believe you when you keep so many secrets?"

"My secrets are for my safety and for yours. If someone were to realize what I've told you already, you'd be in danger. They'd try to exploit you to get to me."

"I'm already in danger. Being with you puts me at risk."

"Undoubtedly. Which is why you need to let everyone think you're simply a pet. I'm convinced there's a group of traitors in my principality. I'm equally convinced Aoibhe is not one of them. That's why I need her help."

Raven's eyebrows drew together suspiciously. "*Need* her or *needed* her?"

William reached for her. "I need to explain. She—"

Raven retreated, avoiding his touch. "She's alive."

"The hunters shot her with a poisoned arrow but they missed her heart. I was able to remove the arrow and her body regenerated. I also fed her blood from my private cellar."

"I thought she was dead."

"If we hadn't been there, she would be. You saved her life as much as I, Raven, by distracting the hunters. You gave her time for her body to regenerate. And she knows this."

"Tell her to send a postcard," Raven sniped.

William adopted a conciliatory tone. "I don't think the hunters happened upon us. I think someone in my principality informed them of our location."

"Who?"

"I have yet to discover their identity."

"Then it could be Aoibhe."

"If she'd made a pact with the hunters, they'd have let her go."

"Not necessarily." Raven's eyes moved to William's. "Do you love her?"

William wore an expression of distaste.

"Of course not. The last time I saw her privately, we had an argument and I told her to leave the Palazzo Riccardi and never return. That was long before I brought you here on the motorcycle."

"But you rely on her."

"She is the least of a myriad of evils."

Raven looked stricken.

William watched her cautiously. He saw the hurt on her face. He could hear her heart and breathing, smell her anxiety. But he had no idea how to reassure her.

Truthfully, her reaction had taken him completely off guard. He didn't have the emotional awareness or experience that would enable him to defuse the situation.

He simply stood, staring.

Raven waited, hoping for a word or caress that didn't materialize.

She began to feel the icy fingers of despair encroaching on her heart.

"I know what I felt when they shot at you." Tears filled Raven's eyes. "I thought they were going to kill you."

"Cassita," he whispered, taking her in his arms.

Her tears rained on his chest as he held her, her shoulders shaking.

"You're the bravest person I've ever met." His voice broke on the words.

He held her more tightly, as if realizing all of a sudden what her sacrifice meant.

"I've been a vampyre since 1274 and no one, no human, has ever come to my aid before tonight. You've seen the monster and you haven't desired death to blot him out of your memory. You honor and astound me."

Gently, he stroked her hair, brushing kiss after kiss against the top of her head.

At length, she pushed him away.

He looked at her in confusion. "Cassita?"

"I honor you, but you won't trust me."

"I just trusted you with my age. I think the better question is, will you ever trust me?" He frowned.

"I'm standing here, William, begging for any truth you can give me. I want to know you."

He pressed his lips together, his eyes searching hers. But he said nothing.

She looked up at him with tremulous eyes. "Do you love me?"

He took a step toward her, but she held up her hand. "Answer me."

He spoke softly, patiently. "Vampyres aren't capable of love. Those feelings were taken with our humanity. As I said, I care for you. I have affection, passion, and respect for you."

She wiped her eyes and turned away. "I love you, William."

He froze, his body alert.

"I was drawn to you almost from the beginning. You made me feel things about myself and then I began feeling things about you. That's why I offered myself to you. I wanted to see how deep our connection could be. When I thought I was going to lose you, I realized that I love you."

He moved as if to take her in his arms again, but she resisted.

"For a long time, I thought love was not for me. Men who noticed me were few and far between. Almost all of them just became friends with me. You changed my mind. You changed my world. I started believing that maybe someone could love me and I could love him in return. I felt hope, William. You gave me that."

"Come here."

"I am not a cripple," she said fiercely. "I am not a pet."

"Of course not." William's voice was low, soothing. "You're my Raven."

"Don't you understand? If all you feel for me is affection, I am nothing more than a pet to you."

"That isn't true."

"Isn't it?" She swiped at her eyes. "You feel something for me, but it isn't love. You say you'll never love me. All I'm left with is the affection you feel for a friend, or maybe an animal you saw suffering and took pity on."

"Don't put words in my mouth." His eyes flashed. "I don't pity you."

"Perhaps not. But I will never be anything more than a pet in your world. A pet you can't even trust with your true name. I might not be as beautiful as Aoibhe, or have perfect legs like other women, but I deserve love."

William gazed at her, his face a mask of confusion and worry.

"I would stay with you, for as long as I lived," Raven said quietly. "But don't you see? I'd be miserable. Maybe you can't ever love anyone. Maybe you can't love me. I'll always wonder if today is the day you decide you want someone else and you throw me away."

"That won't happen," he protested.

"You can't say that. You don't know the future. But I know my own future, because I know myself. To stay with you, I'd have to give up my hope of having someone love me. I'd have to live with your secrets and my doubts until finally all hope was gone.

"If I stayed with you, William, you would kill my hope." Two tears trailed down her cheeks. "I won't let it die."

"Raven." His voice was hoarse. "If I were capable of loving anyone, it would be you."

Raven closed her eyes.

"You say you love me, yet you're the one leaving?" he huffed.

"I have to."

He paced the room, back and forth, his hands in fists.

"You're confused. You say you're leaving because of love, but really, you're leaving because of who I am. Because of what I am."

She opened her eyes. "That isn't true."

"This is the way the myth is always told. Psyche will not heed the warnings of Cupid and so she injures them both."

"Did you warn me not to fall in love with you?" Raven reproached him.

"I told you the story of Allegra. That should have been warning enough."

"I'm not going to fling myself off a bell tower, William. I'm just flinging my heart overboard, hoping you'll want it."

"I want it," he hissed. "I want you. I will elevate you to consort. You will be a princess among my people. I will shower you with gifts, whatever you desire."

Raven gave him an empty look.

"Your love would have been gift enough."

He didn't have a response for that. He looked around the room, desperate for something, anything that could persuade her.

"I care for you. Didn't our evening at Teatro demonstrate that?"

"Yes, you loved me with your body." She gazed at him sadly. "But not with your heart."

"My heart is part of my body," he whispered.

"Then love me."

William met her eyes, then turned away.

He strode to the closet, withdrawing an armful of clothes.

"If you want to go, go. But know this." He walked to the door. "You are the one who is ending what we shared. Not Aoibhe. Not another woman. And certainly not me."

He opened the door and entered the hall, slamming the door behind him. The paintings and light fixtures rattled on the walls.

Raven sank onto the divan, burying her face in her hands.

Less than thirty minutes later, Marco was driving her home. She left the sketches on the bed and the bracelet on William's nightstand.

Chapter Fifty-one

R aven grieved silently and privately.

    It would have been embarrassing to confess the explanation for her sadness—that she'd had her universe expanded in a short period of time, tasted passion and affection, and fallen in love only to discover her love would never be reciprocated.

She tried to take consolation in the fact that she'd progressed from thinking that love was not for her to hoping that, someday, it might be. Even if the dream was never realized, the prospect remained.

She tried listening to music.

The first time "White Blank Page" by Mumford and Sons played on her laptop, she switched it off. Then she listened to it several times.

It was while listening to this song that she came to the momentous conclusion that what William believed about the nature of feeding and addiction was wrong.

She craved the experience. She craved him. But her desires for him, sexual and otherwise, were not enough to overthrow her reason. They were not enough to impel her to cast aside hope and crawl back to him.

She took this as an indication that she was stronger than she thought.

She threw herself into her work, volunteering for any and all overtime offered by Professor Urbano. She went on a few day trips with Patrick and Gina, visiting Lucca, Siena, and Pisa.

There were evenings when she thought she saw a dark figure moving in the shadows across the street. Or when she was sure he'd been in her apartment, while she was sleeping.

"You're the shadow on my wall," she whispered to the darkness one evening. But the darkness was always silent.

There were no signs of hunters, no more bodies found in the street or down by the river. Whatever battle the principality had waged, it seemed to have won.

Raven found herself relieved the Prince was safe. But beyond that recognition, she did not allow her mind to go.

Instead, she focused on work, on her friends, and on bringing flowers to Angelo's favorite spot by the Ponte Santa Trinita, hoping that death had brought him peace.

Chapter Fifty-two

The Prince stood high atop the tower of the Palazzo Vecchio, staring down at the Uffizi Gallery. Tourists and locals congregated, sharing conversations and holding hands. Music could be heard in the distance. A few couples danced in the Piazza Signoria.

As his gaze flitted from figure to figure but failed to see the person he was looking for, his mood darkened. He tried to convince himself his longing was temporary—the result of sex and pleasure. But not even his coldest, harshest application of rationality could persuade him that he was unchanged by her.

"You're brooding." Aoibhe's voice sounded at his elbow.

He'd scented her a moment or two earlier. Despite her advanced age and skill, he'd heard her land on the tower's roof. He didn't turn around, confident as he was in his assessment of her loyalty and threat level, especially now that he had saved her life.

"I never brood." The Prince's voice was cool as he continued to search in vain.

"Then why are you up here, glaring? The night is ours. There's food and sport to be had, even for someone as dour as you," Aoibhe said, gently mocking him. "From what I hear, the police have given up their investigation. They have no evidence, no prospects, and a shrinking list of suspects. You must be very pleased."

"I don't know what you're talking about." He scanned the grounds one last time before turning to face her.

"Come now, my prince. While I've never seen your vast art collection for myself, I've heard rumors. I just don't understand why you chose to steal from the Uffizi now. Presumably, you already acquired the jewels of the Renaissance while you and Niccolò were enjoying the company of the Medici."

William sniffed. "I moved in their circle for some time. Niccolò had a fraught relationship with them."

"So I've heard. Could it be that he wrote *The Prince* for you?"

William offered her an indifferent look before gazing down at the gallery again. He saw a pair of lovers sitting on the steps of the loggia, kissing passionately.

"Where's the Prince's little pet this evening?"

"Out," he rumbled.

"I'm surprised you let her out of your sight, given the way you were with her at Teatro."

William opened his mouth to protest, but Aoibhe interrupted.

"Don't bother lying. One might almost say you're in love with her."

"Love?" he scoffed. "You know our kind too little."

"Ah, my prince. I know you only too well." She moved closer to touch his face.

He sidestepped her. "What do you know of love?"

"Precious little. I've tried to forget my time as a human. It made immortality much easier. But there was a boy . . ." She smiled, a faraway look in her eyes. "After the English lord raped me, the boy didn't want me anymore."

"This is your account of love?" William strode to the crenellations, placing his hands on one.

"Maybe the boy didn't love me. Maybe the ugliness of rape killed his love. I was young and unable to fathom such mysteries."

She tilted her head, regarding the Prince thoughtfully.

"One might say we have shared love, you and I. Our evenings together were certainly pleasurable. That's love enough for me."

"It isn't enough," he muttered, leaning forward on the battlements.

She stood next to him, following his gaze to the lovers who were kissing at the loggia. "The kind of love of which you speak is dangerous. It makes one vulnerable."

Satisfied that the woman entangled in the embrace below was not Raven, he tore his eyes from her.

"We are all vulnerable in some way."

"Then be vulnerable to me and make me your consort."

The Prince growled. "You have your answer, Aoibhe."

"Ah, but circumstances have changed. We both know there are those who are trying to overthrow you."

"Who are they?" He crowded her.

Fear streaked across her face and she stepped back.

"I would tell you if I knew. I swear it. I think you know I have a fondness for you, my lord. I owe you my life. I pay my debts, which means I'm your ally, at least until I've repaid you in kind."

"I am grateful for your allegiance." He nodded stiffly.

"I suspect the traitors live among us, that they are intelligent and crafty but not necessarily powerful. They've been manipulating others into doing what they could not do—colluding with Venice to have you assassinated, using the ferals to breach the borders. You executed Ibarra, which was probably part of their plan."

"Are you so sure Ibarra wasn't a traitor? He'd never failed his tasks before."

"Precisely. I took Ibarra to bed and questioned him in an intimate moment. He was loyal."

"Then why didn't you oppose his execution?"

"I'm fond of my head, my prince. I'd like to keep it."

William's body relaxed slightly. "I welcome whatever information you have to offer, Aoibhe, now and in future."

"I will make enquiries, discreetly, and report my findings to you. I think it's clear someone has been whispering to the hunters."

"See that you don't take anyone else into your confidence. We don't know how many of them there are."

"Of course. I suspect Max but he isn't intelligent enough to mastermind a plot. It's possible the Venetians approached him, but I doubt it." Aoibhe placed her hand on the Prince's sleeve. "Whatever vulnerabilities you have, they are small in number. I saw you fight the hunters. Their weapons had no effect on you."

He gave her a half smile. "I believe your perceptions at the time were somewhat altered."

"I was immobilized, not unconscious." She stared at him for a moment, challenging him with her eyes. "I pride myself in never underestimating others. I've known you a very long time and even I underestimated you."

His smile bloomed disarmingly. "I am an old one, Aoibhe. You know this."

She shook her head. "I've known old ones. I was the lover of one in Paris before I came here. He could not do what you do. No one can. Why would a vampyre with so much power content himself with the city of Florence when he could rule Europe, or the Americas, instead?"

He freed his arm from her grasp.

"Perhaps because I'm not as powerful as you think."

Aoibhe gazed on him with admiration. "An old Medicean trick—appear humble before the people, so as not to arouse their anger or jealousy."

He dismissed her remark with a wave of his hand. "Evil has its own logic."

"I've yet to meet an evildoer who's as concerned as you are with protecting the innocent."

"Pure pragmatism. We learned our lesson during the Black Death. If we feed on children, we'll destroy our food supply."

"Evil doesn't care about such things and we both know it." She shivered, glancing over her shoulder. "Besides, that wasn't the innocence I was referring to. Since you are without your pet for the evening, why don't you join me at my residence? You look weary and in need of diversion."

"I won't return to your bed," he rumbled.

"As you wish." She tossed her hair. "I'm sure you'll find me when you get lonely enough. While you're brooding, you should reflect on the story of Faustus, the Prince of Sardinia. He elevated his pet to consort and the principality rose up against him and destroyed her. They delivered him to the Curia."

"I have no intention of taking a consort, Aoibhe. You'd do well to recognize that."

"I'm not likely to forget it."

She bowed very low and leapt from the top of the building to the street behind the palazzo before disappearing into the shadows.

The Prince clenched and unclenched his fists before letting out a frustrated cry toward the heavens.

Chapter Fifty-three

Days turned into weeks, and soon it was July and Gina was making plans to throw a birthday party in Raven's honor.

"Who shall we invite?" Gina sat with Raven on the loggia near the Uffizi after work one evening. Her pen was poised above a pad of paper, waiting.

"You and Patrick, of course."

"What about friends from the restoration lab?"

Raven smiled. "Not Professor Urbano; I don't think he'd join us. But everyone else, I suppose."

"Even Anja?"

Raven sighed. "It wasn't her fault I was gone for a week and she was chosen to replace me. Sure, invite her."

"Anyone else? How about Bruno?"

"We aren't really friends. His grandmother said he's dating someone now."

Gina squeezed her arm sympathetically. "Is there no one else? No one special?"

Raven ignored the implication and put William out of her mind.

"My sister and her boyfriend were supposed to be coming for a visit but they've postponed it. I'd invite my neighbor, Bruno's grandmother, but she's getting chemotherapy and wouldn't feel up to it."

"I'd like to invite my cousin Roberto." Gina's tone was hesitant.

"That's cool." Raven glanced down at the guest list. It was very short.

"I think you and he would get along well. He's studying literature at the university. He's very handsome." Gina paused. "And he's blind."

Raven shifted her feet on the stone step, feeling very uncomfortable.

"Would it be all right if I introduced you to him?" Gina watched Raven's reaction.

She shrugged. "Sure. I don't want to be set up with anyone right now. But I'd like to meet him."

"I know he'd be happy to meet you." Gina changed the subject, asking Raven about the menu.

She gave polite but distant answers, her mind distracted by the subtext of Gina's suggestion about her cousin.

❀ ❀

Later, when Raven's lunch break was over and she was walking the corridors of the Uffizi, she had time to reflect on Gina's remark.

It was, perhaps, ungenerous to assume that Gina was trying to match her up with her cousin simply because he was blind and Raven walked with a cane.

But Raven couldn't help but feel that Gina, like many others, assumed that disabled persons should be matched with other disabled persons. As if one's disability defined one's entire existence. As if a person who didn't have a (visible) disability wouldn't be interested in someone who did.

The thought angered her.

While she mused, Raven found herself drawn to the second floor, fighting the tourists to enter the Botticelli room. Once again she stood in front of *Primavera*, staring at the figure of Mercury.

She admired him, as she always did. But this time her admiration was tinged with sadness.

Her gaze moved to Zephyr. Zephyr the monster, floating among the trees. He'd seen her disability. He hadn't insisted on fixing her. In fact, he'd said she wasn't broken.

In their last conversation, he'd made it sound as if she were leaving him because of his own disability—vampyrism.

She stood, eyes unfocused, as she recalled the conversation she'd had with him on that very topic, while they were dancing at Teatro.

Was it fair for him to compare vampyrism to a disability?

As a disabled person, Raven bristled at the suggestion.

But if her worldview was correct and there was no such thing as normal—if all beings, human and otherwise, had disabilities in some sense—then she had to admit that William was disabled as well. Certainly, existing without the ability to love was a disability.

Raven began to suspect she should have treated William with more compassion and more understanding—the way she, herself, desired to be treated.

But compassion and understanding didn't entail the denial of one's own basic needs. Raven needed love. She deserved love. All the compassion and understanding in the world would never substitute for it.

She sighed and took a step closer to the painting.

The difference between the *Primavera* in the Uffizi and the *Primavera* in William's villa was striking. Botticelli had added Flora to the Uffizi version, while William's painting featured only Zephyr grabbing a frightened Chloris.

William's version didn't portray a happy ending, perhaps because he hadn't experienced one. He'd captured Allegra, without love but perhaps with affection, and once she realized who'd captured her heart she'd killed herself.

Hundreds of years later, he'd captured Raven. She loved him but she hadn't stayed with him. She hadn't become his Flora.

William's happy ending still eluded him.

No doubt he'd find someone else in time—another Chloris—in the person of Aoibhe or a human being. And the cycle would repeat.

Forever.

What a miserable existence. To never love anyone.

Raven studied the painting.

She studied herself.

Her future looked a great deal like her past, filled with hard but rewarding work and a few good friends. There would be Brunos, perhaps, and Robertos. But there would never, ever be another William.

I could return to him.

The mere idea had her heart racing and the pain in her middle easing temporarily.

But the specter of despair haunted her whenever she thought of spending the rest of her life with someone who saw her only as a sexual partner with whom he shared a degree of affection, like a pet.

Maybe that's all love is—sex and affection.

Even as she thought the words she knew there was more. There was the absolute nakedness of being vulnerable with one's lover, trusting him or her to accept that vulnerability and not use it to destroy. There was the trust that came with sharing secrets, knowing that one would not be betrayed. There was the sacrifice of knowing one might be hurt, yet loving anyway.

All these things she hoped for, but he had not given them. Perhaps he would never give them. Perhaps he would one day find someone he could love.

In any case, she couldn't go back.

She whispered a farewell to the figure of Zephyr and slowly walked from the room.

Chapter Fifty-four

After her birthday party, July fifth, Raven returned to her apartment late at night.

She was wearing a vibrant green dress she'd bought herself. The neckline exposed her collarbone and a hint of cleavage; the skirt was full and flattering.

It had been a good evening. Gina and Patrick had hosted an excellent party, filled with food, music, and laughter.

She'd met Roberto and they'd struck up a conversation about their mutual interest in Italian literature and the rapier wit of Boccaccio. Afterward, she'd driven him home on her Vespa before making the trek to Santo Spirito.

She entered her apartment and closed and locked the door. She tossed her knapsack to the floor and hit the light switch.

She looked into the kitchen and screamed.

William was sitting on one of her chairs, waiting. As was his custom, he was clad all in black, his expression guarded.

She clutched a hand to her chest. "What are you doing here?"

"I was under the impression it was your birthday." He smiled cautiously, his gray eyes searching.

She leaned back against the door. Her body was tense, her hand gripping her cane tightly.

"What are you doing sitting in the dark?"

His smile faded. "I've always been more comfortable in the shadows."

He broke eye contact then, as if he were unsure of her reaction. He placed his hand in his pocket awkwardly.

Something about his lack of sureness pierced her.

"I'm sorry," she whispered.

Her words were sincere. She was sorry, very sorry, for a great many things, not least of which was his loneliness.

At the sound of her sincerity, he lifted his head. Cautious optimism flared in his eyes and it almost broke Raven's heart.

He approached her slowly, his eyes burning into hers. He moved as if to touch her face, but dropped his hand at the last second.

"That dress suits you. You look beautiful."

"Thank you."

"I have gifts."

She scowled and brushed past him, moving to the support of the kitchen counter.

It was as if he were an instrument that played only one tune. He'd tried to convince her to stay with him by promising riches. Now he was repeating the act.

She was insulted. And hurt.

"Your possessions don't interest me."

"Please." His tone was low, almost pleading.

Raven focused on his face, surprised. This was the first time he'd ever pronounced the word, she was sure of it.

She tried to soften her defensive posture, at least in appearance.

"It was nice of you to remember my birthday. But you're making this more difficult."

"I don't think anything could be more difficult than the past month." His expression was grave.

She arched an eyebrow at him.

"I mean it, Raven. I've known loss before, incalculable loss. It paled next to losing you."

She held out her hand, stopping him.

"William, please. I—"

"I want to show you something, then I have a gift I wish to give you. After that, you'll never see me again."

Pain lanced through Raven's body. Seeing him, hearing him, and being reminded that they were separated was almost more than she could bear.

He was gazing on her with what appeared to be hope. The hope was restrained, but still visible.

She could not kill that look.

"All right." She sighed in resignation. "But nothing has changed. I need you to understand that."

He moved toward her and gently took her hand in his, pressing it against his heart.

"Everything has changed," he whispered.

His eyes were focused and intense, as they'd always been. But there was something else in them. Something Raven hadn't seen before.

"What's changed, William? Tell me." Her voice hardened.

"I'd prefer to show you." He kissed the palm of her hand. "Leave the cane. Tonight you fly with me."

She leaned into his chest, internally cursing herself for reacting in such a way.

Then she snatched back her hand and placed the cane against the counter before following William to the bedroom window.

He held her with his left arm, clutching her close as he lifted her through the window and up to the roof. Then he ran with her, jumping from building to building, dropping to the ground only to cross the Ponte Santa Trinita.

Raven held on tightly, the speed both dizzying and exhilarating. The gentle midnight breeze blew her hair across her face. She fought with it, unwilling to have her vision obscured.

They scaled a building near the bridge and soon they were flying across the rooftops once again.

"Where are you taking me?" Her voice pierced the silence between them.

William stopped on one of the buildings opposite Giotto's bell tower.

"I want to show you my city."

She gazed out over Florence, at the red-tiled roofs and open spaces, at the tourists and citizens walking below.

"Incredible," she said breathily.

"A better view can be had from Brunelleschi's dome." William gestured to the great structure that loomed above them.

She gazed at him skeptically. "It's holy ground."

His eyes met hers.

"Holy ground bothers me the way the sun bothers me. It's a discomfort I can manage."

"Relics don't affect you."

"That isn't quite true."

"You gave me a relic. You touched it with your hands."

He hesitated. "I have a few items in my collection from a single source that have no effect on me whatsoever. Other objects, including holy water, cause physical pain. But their effect on me is nothing like their effect on my brethren."

"Is that why you looked in distress when the hunters waved their crosses at you? Because it caused you pain?"

"Yes." He shifted his weight. "I didn't realize you'd noticed that."

"Of course I noticed it, William." Her tone reproved him. "You mean something to me."

"Do I?"

She turned away. The tone of his voice, earnest and almost optimistic, was excruciating.

"You'll always mean something to me. But I asked you to share your secrets and you wouldn't. It's too late."

He touched a lock of her hair, winding its end around his finger.

"You were right. The secrets function like a wall. They serve their purpose with everyone else, but not with you. Never with you."

He didn't give her the opportunity to respond. Instead, he pulled her close and leapt with her to the ground. No sooner had they landed than he ran with her at top speed to the side of the church.

With practiced ease, William scaled the wall with one hand, his figure a ghost in the darkness, a patch of green visible under his other arm.

Raven closed her eyes as they climbed, unwilling to watch the safeness of the earth as it fell farther and farther away.

Finally they stood at the top, under the shade of the gold globe and cross.

William stood behind her, his arms wrapped around her waist for safety. She fancied she felt him nuzzle her hair with his nose.

"It's so beautiful," she mused, not knowing where to look first.

From their vantage point, she could see the stars winking above them, the antlike creatures below, and the great vista of the magical city that spread around them in all directions.

She could look across the river to the Piazzale Michelangelo and see the lighted copy of *David*. Beyond that, she could see the small hill on which William's villa was situated.

"We're up so high."

"The best view of the city is from here. This is where I spend every sunset. But I've never shared it with anyone."

She glanced down at the ground and quickly lifted her head, closing her eyes.

William noticed her reaction—the speeding of her heart and quickening of her breathing, the way anxiety began to roll off her body. He drew her against him more closely, her back to his chest.

His lips found her ear. "What's happened? What's wrong?"

"My father fell from a roof."

William's body tensed.

"I'd forgotten about that. This wasn't the best idea." He sounded apologetic, but also disappointed.

"Wait." Raven wanted to take one more moment to absorb the view, knowing she would never see it again.

William paused, his gaze alighting on Giotto's bell tower. His grip on Raven tightened. He could sustain a great many things, but not the loss of her.

The realization continued to haunt him.

"We should go."

Raven turned her head toward him. "What happens if one of the others sees you up here?"

He shifted his weight. "They'd realize holy ground isn't a deterrent. The more powerful I appear to my people, the more likely they are to want to kill me."

"Then why risk it?"

He was quiet for a moment, as if he were choosing his words carefully.

"You brought beauty to my world. I wanted to do the same for you, if only for one night."

An anguished sound escaped Raven's lips. Their distance from the ground was the only reason she didn't struggle to free herself from him.

"Don't torture me."

"It's the truth. For years, I thought my days and nights were filled with beauty. Beautiful things, a beautiful city, and beautiful women from time to time. Then you appeared and I realized I'd been deceived."

Raven closed her eyes. "We need to go. It's painful for me to be here and I don't want you to be in danger."

"I'm sorry for causing you pain. We'll go at once." His hand brushed against hers. "But don't spare a thought for my danger. What can they do to me? I've already lost the only thing I value."

"What's that?"

"You."

She shook her head. "I gave you my heart and you handed it back to me as if it were nothing."

"It isn't nothing." He spoke in her ear. "I value it and I value you. I think you know this."

"It doesn't matter. I won't relegate myself to a life of misery, loving someone who doesn't love me."

"You're the only one I want."

Now Raven struggled against his arms, albeit carefully. "Take me home."

"Just a moment, that's all I ask. Please." He appeared to force a smile. "I've learned a verse for you. Do you know it?"

> "'*Cupid being now healed of his wound and Maladie,*
> *not able to endure the absence of Psyches, got him*
> *secretly out at a window of the chamber where hee*
> *was enclosed, and (receiving his wings), tooke his flight.*'"

"Apuleius."

"Yes."

"You speak in riddles."

"Only because language fails me."

"Are you saying you're healed of your malady?" she asked, fearing his answer.

"There's no cure for vampyrism except death. But for coldheartedness, I think there is a cure." He turned her in his arms and looked at her gravely. "The warmth of a pure heart, for example. And the stunning pain of loss."

He stopped, his arms wrapped around her waist.

"My human memories are indistinct for the most part. We all have the same complaint. Memories are stored in the brain. When our biology changed, our brains changed as well. It affected our ability to access those memories."

"Why are you telling me this?"

"I'm trying to share a secret."

Raven stilled. She felt his worry, his uncertainty.

She placed her hand over his.

Tentatively, he laced his fingers with her own.

"Everyone, including Aoibhe, thinks I'm English, but that isn't true. I'm not Anglo-Saxon; I'm Norman. My name is William Malet. I was named after an ancestor of mine who was one of William the Conqueror's companions in the Battle of Hastings. My family lived in York in the thirteenth century and that's where I was born. My first language was Anglo-Norman French. I was the oldest son of a noble family and destined for a certain life, but I fell in love with a merchant's daughter. Alicia."

He gazed out over the city, a haunted look in his eyes.

Raven squeezed their connection, prompting him.

He looked down at their fingers.

"Because of the difference in our stations, and the fact that she was Anglo-Saxon, my family opposed the match. But we were young and in love. We thought the differences between us were meaningless.

"We decided to flout my father and elope. Alicia was supposed to meet me in York one night so we could run away together. She never appeared. I went looking for her, and after searching for hours I found her, lying by the wall." He cursed. "She was alive, but barely. A group of men had happened upon her while she was on her way to meet me. They took their pleasure and broke her body. She died in my arms."

"I'm so sorry." She held his hand firmly.

William's expression was tortured.

"She'd been a virgin, secretly betrothed to me. The way she suffered and died . . ." William's voice trailed off into a curse. "I should have met her at her father's house and not compelled her to wander the streets alone. Or I should have let her go and she could have married someone else."

"You loved her," Raven said quietly. "And, from what you've said, she loved you, too. You couldn't have known what would happen."

"She died nonetheless." William struggled to continue. "I tried to avenge her death but couldn't discover who had done it. In the interim, my father arranged to have me marry a girl from another Norman family. It was a political and economic alliance, as most marriages were in those days.

"I had no wish to marry anyone, let alone a spoiled aristocrat I'd never met. Angry and in despair, I fled my father and went to Oxford. I was there only a short time when the Dominicans took me in. I began my studies at Oxford and later went to Paris."

"Was she beautiful?"

William squeezed Raven's hand. "Very. She had red-gold hair. I've never quite seen its likeness. And she was kind and very sweet. I fell in love with her the moment I saw her."

He cleared his throat. "When Alicia died, I knew my ability to love died with her. I became a novice with the Dominicans, taking a vow of chastity. My intention was to become a priest."

His eyes lifted to Raven's, a strange fire in them.

"When I saw you that night, pressed against a wall, those animals beating you, you reminded me of her—this beautiful, gentle girl. You were going to die because you'd been walking a dark street alone. I couldn't let that happen.

"Aoibhe and some of the others found us. Your blood smells sweet and they wanted it. By then, I knew I wasn't going to feed from you. I told them you were mine and took you away."

"William," she whispered, "thank you for having mercy on me."

He stiffened. "I don't think *mercy* is in my vocabulary."

"But you acted mercifully. You honored her memory by saving my life."

"I may have saved your life, Cassita, but I lost you just the same."

The despair in his voice both wounded and irritated her.

She disentangled her hand from his. "You only lost me because you don't love me."

"You are mistaken." He pulled her against him, his expression earnest. "This past month I've been waiting, thinking what I felt for you would recede. If my ability to love died with Alicia, or if it ended when I became a vampyre, I should have been able to forget you.

"I couldn't. Every morning and every evening, my thoughts fixed on you—on your face, your smile, your very being. I found myself wondering what you were doing, if you were safe, if you were jumping between someone and his attacker."

He took her hand and kissed it, running his thumb across her life line.

"Your name suits you, you know. Raven—the beautiful, fearless black bird. I've been in mourning for centuries but nothing has distressed me as much as losing you."

"You aren't the only one who was hurt." She tried to swallow back the rising emotion.

"Forgive me." He cupped her cheek. "I came to you tonight because I couldn't allow the light of my life to be extinguished without seeing you one last time."

"Then tell me," she whispered.

His expression faltered. "I lack the words, in any language."

"Just say it." She reached up on tiptoe and placed her hand against his face. "Say what you feel, William. Be brave."

His fingers closed over her wrist, holding her hand to him.

"When I spoke to you about hope the night I took you to the Consilium, my hope was that you could see beyond the callous contract I was foolishly trying to make. That you would stay with me and be mine because you wanted me as desperately as I wanted you."

She gazed up at him sadly. "We're from two different worlds."

"Maybe we can create a new one."

"Only at great risk to you and your city."

He inhaled deeply, his eyes fixed on hers.

"What are a thousand cities to me if I am without you?"

Raven searched his eyes, which were dark and desperate. She felt his fingers nervously tighten around her wrist.

"Are you certain?" she asked, returning his stare.

"If I lose you, I lose everything. You are the only goodness in my world."

"You've been alone a long time. You suffered a great loss. I'm sorry for that," she said softly. "I can understand your reticence to tell secrets. But love isn't secretive or one-sided."

"It isn't," he said fiercely.

"Then tell me."

He kissed her forehead. "*Je t'aim.*"

Raven savored the moment, letting the old words burn into her consciousness.

She took in his expression, his eyes, his posture. He was clearly earnest and unsure how he would be received.

She answered him by bringing their lips together.

He kissed her intently but reverently, his mouth desperately seeking their connection.

At length they parted, and he brought their foreheads together.

"I didn't know what darkness was until I lost you."

"You found me again. I love you, too."

He kissed her, this time more passionately, his hands moving to press against her backside. Then, with a devilish smile, he tucked her under his arm.

"Hold tight," he ordered.

She clung to him, arms wrapped around his neck. "Where are we going?"

"To celebrate by loving one another with our bodies." He squeezed her waist.

She peered down at their perch. "Not here."

He laughed. "Certainly not. Not even I am bold enough to join with you on holy ground." He moved to whisper in her ear. "There is another venue I think will please you."

He tightened his hold on her and they leapt from the dome, to a lower half dome, before descending the great stone structure.

Chapter Fifty-five

From the terrace atop the Loggia dei Lanzi, one can see the Palazzo Vecchio, the Uffizi, and the beautiful and spacious Piazza Signoria. One can also see Brunelleschi's dome rising in the distance.

Not that Raven and William were looking.

They were in one another's arms, passionately kissing against a wall.

"I can't believe you're in my arms," he murmured, stroking her neck.

She hummed at his words, returning his embrace with eagerness.

William's tongue teased her mouth, slipping inside before retreating. He enjoyed reciprocity, the way she responded to his touch.

Her back was to the wall, his body flush with hers. His hand paid homage to her collarbone, smoothing across her skin and tracing the neckline of her dress.

She shivered in anticipation and need, her mind and heart full of everything that was William—the one who truly loved her, all of her, as herself.

She tried to pour her love and affection into her eager touches, exploring his broad shoulders and the muscles that rippled from underneath his shirt before dropping down to appreciate the planes of his chest.

Growling, William brought their hips together.

She scratched his scalp, smiling against his lips at his guttural reaction.

He nipped her lower lip and kissed along her jawline, pressing himself more tightly against her.

"Are you cold?" He moved so he could see her face.

"It's July." She grinned.

He placed his palm to the wall beside her hip. "I don't sense temperatures as well as a human. The stone must be cool against your back."

"All I feel is you."

With a tilt of her head, she exposed her neck. He brushed her black hair aside and pulled some of her flesh into his mouth, sucking gently.

"Feed from me," she whispered.

His lips descended her throat, kissing a path to her shoulder. "No."

"Why not?"

William lifted his head. Even in the semidarkness Raven could see he was conflicted.

"You're exquisite. I want you. But what we share tonight is a different kind of sustenance." He toyed with her hair, watching as the long strands spilled over his fingers.

"But I love you. I want to give you this."

He kissed a lock of her hair before releasing it. His arm wrapped around her waist and he lifted her, winding her legs around his hips.

"Let me love you, Raven, with my heart."

She blinked hard, if only to keep the rising emotion at bay. Now was not the time for tears, not when he was gifting her with everything she had ever wanted.

She kissed him deeply as his hand slid from her breast to her ribs and down to her backside. Raven held her breath as he lifted her skirt and placed his palm against the outside of her thigh.

He made a circle against her skin before squeezing her hip. A single finger traced the top of her panties before descending between her legs.

She moaned her appreciation as he touched her over the silk. In an instant, her underwear was gone and he was stroking her, testing her.

Her mouth found his ear. "Please."

His hand moved between them, removing the barriers. Then, with eyes fixed on hers and an animalistic sound, he plunged inside. Raven clutched at his shoulders, focusing on the pleasurable sensation.

His movement wasn't slow. He thrust deep, his hands underneath her backside, lifting and squeezing her. Raven flexed her hips, trying to bring him farther inside her.

She clung to him, their chests rubbing against one another.

He was rumbling in her ear. Her pants and cries spurred him on.

Deeper and faster, he moved at a feverish pace.

She couldn't keep her eyes open, focusing only on the feelings he elicited from her, the way every stroke, every movement, sent her ascending higher and higher to bliss.

Her heels dug into his ass as she gripped him with her thighs, well beyond words.

Suddenly she was gasping and crying out.

Her body stiffened in his arms and still he continued, thrusting and swirling inside her. When she grew limp and buried her face in his neck, only then did he allow himself to climax.

Her name was the first word on his lips.

Raven was breathing heavily, her heartbeat racing.

William listened to the foreign and rhythmic sounds of his lover's body, knowing with pride that he'd caused those reactions.

They stood for what seemed like an age, the young woman and the centuries-old vampyre, holding one another desperately on a rooftop that overlooked the Uffizi.

They were the most improbable of lovers. Yet it was manifest to both they were indeed a perfect match.

Raven's heart was full, her mind relaxed, her body sated.

"Now that you've given me your gift, I must give you mine." He stroked her cheek, his eyes alight.

Raven placed her hand flat against his chest, over his heart. She felt the strange rhythm under her palm, and the almost frightening silence.

"This is the only gift I want."

"You have it." He lifted her fingers and kissed them, one by one. "But you'll want the other gift I'm going to give you."

He extricated himself from her body, placing her on unsteady feet.

He righted his trousers and withdrew a handkerchief from the pocket. Supporting her with an arm around her waist, he lifted her skirt to press the linen between her legs.

Raven leaned into him and sighed. "This is my gift," she said quietly. "The way you touch me, I can tell that you love me. But I'm still happy to have the words."

"I love you," he whispered. *"Defensa."*

She smiled against his shoulder. "That's a new name. I'm no longer wounded; I'm a protector."

"You've always been a protector." He kissed her forehead before tracing the faded scar that marred it. "You told me once that no one ever defended you. Tonight, I will."

"What?" She pulled back, confused.

William tossed the handkerchief aside.

"I promised to give you justice. I keep my promises."

A wave of anxiety passed over her. "William, what have you done?"

He smiled at her slowly. "It's what I am going to do. Come."

He pulled her tightly against him and they climbed to the roof, their bodies disappearing into the night like a wisp of smoke.

Glossary of Terms and Proper Names

(NB: This list contains spoilers)

ALLEGRA—Fifteenth-century woman and lover of the Prince.

AMBROGIO—William York's servant.

ANGELO—Homeless man and friend of Raven Wood.

AOIBHE—*Pronounced "A-vuh."* An Irish member of the Consilium.

ISPETTOR BATELLI—Police inspector in Florence.

THE CONSILIUM—The ruling council of the principality of Florence. It consists of six members: Lorenzo, Niccolò, Aoibhe, Ibarra, Maximilian, and Pierre. The Prince is an ex officio member.

THE CURIA—Enemy of the supernatural beings.

GABRIEL EMERSON—The professor is a Dante specialist who teaches at Boston University. He is the owner of a famed set of Botticelli illustrations of Dante's *Divine Comedy*, which he lent to the Uffizi Gallery in 2011. His story is told in the Gabriel's Inferno trilogy: *Gabriel's Inferno*, *Gabriel's Rapture*, and *Gabriel's Redemption*.

JULIA EMERSON—Doctoral student at Harvard University. She is married to Gabriel and the co-owner of the Botticelli illustrations.

FEEDERS—Derogatory term for human beings who offer themselves up as a food source to supernatural beings.

FERALS—Supernatural beings who live and hunt alone. They display brutal, animalistic behavior.

GREGOR—Personal assistant to the Prince.

HUMAN INTELLIGENCE NETWORK—Human beings who are contracted to provide information to the supernatural beings. They also provide security and perform specific tasks.

THE HUNTERS—Humans who hunt and kill supernatural beings for commercial purposes.

IBARRA—A Basque member of the Consilium and head of security for the principality of Florence.

FATHER KAVANAUGH—Former director of Covenant House in Orlando, Florida, and friend of Raven Wood.

LORENZO—A member of the Medici family and second in command in the principality of Florence. Also a member of the Consilium.

LUCIA—Ambrogio's wife and servant to William York.

LUKA—Servant to William York.

MARCO—Servant to William York.

MARCUS—Also known as the Prince of Venice. Former ruler of the underworld principality of Venice, now deceased.

MARIA—A young girl with special needs who lives at the Franciscan orphanage in Florence. She is introduced in *Gabriel's Redemption*.

MAXIMILIAN—A Prussian member of the Consilium.

THE MEDICI—Famous ruling family of Florence during the Renaissance.

GINA MOLINARI—Friend of Raven Wood, employed in the archives of the Uffizi Gallery.

NICCOLÒ—Famous Florentine and member of the Consilium. Head of intelligence for the principality of Florence.

OLD ONES—A special class of supernatural beings who, by virtue of having attained seven hundred years in their supernatural state, enjoy tremendous power and special abilities.

GIUSEPPE PACCIANI—A professor of Dante at the University of Florence. His backstory is given in the Gabriel's Inferno series.

KATHERINE PICTON—Retired Dante specialist and former professor at the University of Toronto. Her backstory is described in the Gabriel's Inferno series. Friend of the Emersons.

PIERRE—A French member of the Consilium. Oversees security and liaises with the human intelligence network as well as the police services.

THE PRINCE—Ruler of the principality of Florence, the underworld society of supernatural beings.

RECRUITS—New supernatural beings, formerly human.

THE ROMAN—Ruler of the principality of Rome and also the head of the kingdom of Italy, which includes all the Italian principalities.

AGENT SAVOLA—Interpol agent assigned to Florence.

SIMONETTA—The Princess of Umbria.

Stefan—A supernatural physician of French-Canadian origin.

Professor Urbano—Director of the restoration project working on the *Birth of Venus*. Raven Wood's supervisor.

The Venetians—Supernatural beings living in the principality of Venice.

Dottor Vitali—Director of the Uffizi Gallery. He appears in the Gabriel's Inferno trilogy.

Patrick Wong—Canadian citizen and friend of Raven Wood. Works in the archives at the Uffizi Gallery.

Carolyn (Cara) Wood—Raven's younger sister. Carolyn is a real estate agent in Miami, Florida.

Raven Wood—American citizen and postdoctoral restoration worker at the Uffizi Gallery.

William York—A wealthy Florentine and patron of the Uffizi Gallery. He appears briefly in *Gabriel's Redemption*.

Younglings—Supernatural beings who have yet to attain one hundred years in their supernatural state.

Acknowledgments

I am indebted to Sandro Botticelli and the incomparable space that is the Uffizi Gallery. I'm also indebted to the citizens of Florence, who gifted me with hospitality and inspiration.

I've used poetic license in locating Raven's restoration lab at the Uffizi, since it would have been undertaken at one of the labs operated by the Opificio instead.

Quotations from Lucius Apuleius's "The Golden Ass" are from William Adlington's translation, as presented in Project Gutenberg.

I am grateful to Kris, who read an early draft and offered invaluable constructive criticism. I am also thankful to Jennifer and to Nina for their feedback and support.

I've been very pleased to work with Cindy Hwang, my editor. Thanks are also due to Tom Guida for his wisdom and energy. And thanks to the copyediting, art, and design teams who worked on the book and its cover at various stages.

My publicist, Nina Bocci, works tirelessly to promote my writing and to help me with social media, which enables me to stay in touch with readers. I'm honored to be part of her team.

Elizabeth de Vos, Bee W., Elena, Becca, Ellie, Heidi, Tiffany, and Chris all contributed in their areas of expertise. Thank you.

I would also like to thank those who have offered support, especially the Muses, Erika, Argyle Empire, and the readers from around the world who operate the SRFans social media accounts.

Finally, I would like to thank my readers and my family. Your continued support is inestimable, especially as we return to Florence for a new adventure.

—SR
ASCENSION 2014

Keep reading for an excerpt from
the sequel to *The Raven,* the second
book in the Florentine series.

Coming soon from Berkley Books

William leaned over, bringing his lips to Raven's ear. "Happy birthday."

Raven stood, staring at the man in the cell, a feeling of horror paralyzing her.

William noticed her pale face, her pounding heart, and the obvious scent of fear that lifted from her skin.

"That is not the reaction I was hoping for," he said dryly.

She lifted a shaking finger, pointing toward the cell.

"What's he doing here?"

William frowned. "I should have thought that would be obvious."

Raven's eyes met his. She blinked. "What?"

"I swore I'd give you justice." He extended his hand in the direction of the prisoner. "This is justice."

"How?" she asked, her breath hitching.

"I brought him here so you can kill him."

"Stelle Su Firenze"

An Outtake from *Gabriel's Redemption*

"I think if we sat here long enough, the whole world would walk by."
Julia's voice was wistful as she rested her head on Gabriel's shoulder.

It was their last night in Florence. They'd spent the evening dining at a romantic restaurant overlooking the Arno River. Then they'd wandered the narrow streets before arriving at the Loggia dei Lanzi. From this vantage point, they could watch the Piazza della Signoria come to life after dark.

Tourists and locals milled about the Piazza or enjoyed a drink at one of the cafés. Nearby, a string quartet played Verdi, filling the square with a beautiful melancholy.

Julia watched in fascination as street vendors launched glowing cylinders into the air, the toys sparkling like firecrackers against the ink-black sky. But always, the objects would fall to the ground, their brief foray into the heavens ended by gravity.

A strange sadness crept over her. "We try to touch the stars, but we always fall back to earth."

Gabriel drew her closer, wrapping his arm around her waist. "That's true, but it isn't like you to despair."

"I'm not in despair. I just don't want to go back. Not after . . ." Her voice trailed off.

"I don't want to go back either, but summer has to end eventually."

He brushed a light kiss against her dark hair before pulling her to her feet. As the music continued, he walked her to the center of the piazza. Then he took her in his arms and began to sway to the music.

She closed her eyes, floating over the stone beneath their feet as he expertly moved them.

He tightened his grip on her waist. "I'm sorry we've been fighting."

Julia opened her eyes. "Me too."

"I promise I'll make it up to you."

"You brought me here."

"I'm the reason you're constantly falling back to earth." Gabriel's blue eyes were earnest and searching. "I drag you from the stars—from where you belong."

She gave him a sad smile. "It's the human condition. We're bound to fall."

He stopped dancing, his eyes boring into hers. "You should never have to fall, Julianne."

He kissed her gently and they continued dancing, stopping only when the last strains of Verdi no longer echoed through the night.

They returned to the loggia, sitting side by side on the stone bench. His fingers traced the folds of her silk dress in what he hoped would be a comforting manner.

"I wish I could sit in this piazza forever." She gazed at the elaborate fountain nearby, and the elderly couple who were standing next to it, holding hands. "We could grow old here."

Gabriel followed her gaze, the edges of his lips turning up.

"If you remained in this piazza, you'd be cold when winter comes."

"Not if I had you to warm me."

A smile pulled at his mouth. "I'm glad you find me useful, if only as a warming device."

"You're also an excellent tour guide."

"Another way in which I'm useful."

"And since your Italian is better than mine, you're an effective translator."

He brought his mouth to within inches of hers. "Shall I translate my favorite words? *Labbra? Lingua? Seno?*"

She traced the fullness of his lower lip with her middle finger. "*Lips. Tongue. Breast.* You're very provocative this evening."

"You've forgotten the most important way in which I'm useful."

"And that is?"

His gaze grew heated and he lowered his voice. "As your lover."

He nipped at her finger slightly, before drawing it into his mouth. He toyed with her for a moment, laving her skin with his tongue, before releasing her.

"I'm afraid that if you persist in staying in this piazza, my capacity as a lover will be sorely diminished."

She lifted her eyebrows. "Diminished?"

"For example, I couldn't possibly do this in a piazza." He brought their lips together.

Julia hummed her appreciation and Gabriel deepened their connection, his tongue stroking hers.

His hands moved to her face as Julia's slid to his shoulders, pressing him closer.

"And I couldn't possibly do this." Gabriel spoke against her mouth as his thumb glided down the side of her breast.

She shivered.

"Or this." His hand slid over the curve of her waist and around to her lower back. He ran a single finger just above the waistband of her panties, almost as if he were contemplating their removal.

"Or this." His eyes suddenly alight, he covered her bare knee with his palm before coaxing her legs to part.

Julia's skin grew warm at his touch.

"Move your hand any higher and we're going to get arrested," she whispered.

His eyes appeared to darken. "It will be worth it."

She placed her hand over his, stopping the slow, teasing ascent.

"I think we've been the subject of enough scandals, Professor."

"Then you're going to have to leave this piazza before I slip my hand under your dress and show you what comes next."

"Where would we go?"

"I know a much quieter piazza nearby."

She stifled a laugh. "Is that the best you can do?"

"There's always the hotel. I have a view."

She cocked her head to one side. "A view?"

He lifted her hand and pressed a kiss to her palm.

"The only sight worth seeing in this city is you. But the view from my hotel room isn't entirely unfortunate."

She lowered her eyes and blushed.

He squeezed her hand. "Florence has exceptional architecture and art. But Brunelleschi's dome lacks your compassion. And no painting in the Uffizi could ever capture the beauty and warmth of your love."

She lifted her gaze to meet his.

"Are you flirting with me, Professor?"

Gabriel brought his mouth to her ear. "This isn't flirtation, Julianne. This is seduction. And I won't rest until I enjoy the wonder that is your body, lying underneath me again."

He kissed the shell of her ear, before moving down to the side of her neck. He pressed unhurried kisses against her skin, brushing against her collarbone.

"This is just the beginning," he whispered, his hand caressing her side. "Think of the delights that await you."

She hummed softly. "I'd like to hear more about that."

He stood, holding out his hand.

"I'll do more than tell you. But I'm afraid you'll have to leave this piazza."

Julia glanced over his shoulder at the fountain. She sighed.

"It's hard for me to leave, knowing what awaits us at home."

"But we'll be together." He tugged her into his arms. "Tonight I'll help you touch the stars. And when you fall back to earth, I promise to catch you."

She looked up him, at his tender, intense expression, and lightly cupped his angular jaw.

"What about you, Gabriel? Don't you want to touch the stars?"

He smiled his slow, sweet smile.

"You're the only star in my sky."

She kissed him fiercely, before taking his hand and walking hurriedly toward their hotel.

Fin.

"An Umbrian Swim"

An Outtake from *Gabriel's Redemption*

July 2011
At a house in Umbria . . .

"Julianne."

Gabriel's voice startled her and she sat bolt upright at her desk.
He was standing in front of her, watching her hungrily. He was clad only in a pair of black swimming trunks, a towel slung over his shoulder.

"Oh, I didn't hear you come in." She admired his bare chest over her laptop, her fingers poised over the keyboard.

"It's time for a swim." His voice was a throaty whisper.

She gave him a guilty look. "I have so much work to do."

"Ah, yes. I do recall having to work now and then when I was a graduate student." His lips twitched, as if he were resisting a smile. "And what is Signora working on this evening?"

"I'm brushing up on my French."

His blue eyes fixed on hers. *"Pourquoi?"*

"Because it's one of the languages I need for my research."

Gabriel nodded and walked toward her. "This is very good news."

"It is?" She looked up at him, for he was tall.

"Yes. Not only do I speak French, but I'm proficient in their kissing style as well." He lifted his hand to sweep her dark hair behind her shoulders, running the backs of his fingers down the column of her throat.

"I seem to remember that. I think I needed to ask you for a translation."

"No translation necessary. I know you speak the language of love." He brushed their lips together.

Their mouths met, innocently at first. Then the moment Julianne parted her lips, his tongue teased hers, retreating backward until she followed.

"Come on." He spoke against her mouth.

"I'm working, Gabriel. I can't."

"You can't kiss me like that and go back to work." He frowned. "Have mercy on me."

"I don't mean to tease you." Julia glanced down at her French dictionary. "But there's so much to do."

"Just a few minutes. A midnight swim will clear your head of all the regular and irregular verbs and you'll *parles français* in no time." He kissed the palm of her hand, his eyes darkening slightly.

When she didn't move, he continued. "Paris wasn't built in a day."

Gabriel leaned forward, bending at the waist. His eyes focused on hers. "And I want my Julianne back for a few minutes."

They exchanged a long look.

Julia nodded.

He kissed her hand once again and led her to the master bedroom. She changed into a purple bikini while he retrieved another beach towel. Then they walked hand in hand to the outdoor pool.

Julia watched as Gabriel eschewed the outdoor lights and instead lit a series of candles, placing them around the perimeter of the pool. Soon the area was dappled in a warm, flickering glow.

"Bathing suits are optional." Gabriel smirked, placing their towels over a chair.

"I don't think so." Julia lowered herself into the warm water.

"Our nearest neighbor is over a mile away. I think your modesty is safe."

Julia tilted her head to one side, regarding him in the semidarkness. "My modesty is never safe when you're around."

Gabriel joined her, swimming to her side in three short strokes. "Oh really? I'd like to hear more about that."

"You—do things to me."

"Let's explore that. What kinds of things?"

He pulled her into his arms and kissed her deeply, delicately exploring her mouth.

Julia wrapped her arms around his neck just as he pulled away.

"You amaze me." A look of admiration softened his features.

"By my ability to stand in the shallow end and kiss you? I don't think I'd qualify for the Olympics."

He chuckled and kissed the end of her nose. "I was referring to the way you are—the way you kiss with abandon, and laugh easily. The way you accept me." His expression grew grave.

Julia pushed a lock of his hair back from his forehead. "I love you, Gabriel. Of course I accept you."

"Not everyone would be as forgiving as you. Not after what I did." He grimaced, lowering his gaze.

She pressed her hand against his stubbled jaw, forcing him to look at her. "Love is hearing the truth and still choosing to love. You chose to love me despite what I did."

"I can't imagine my life without you."

"Good." She smiled.

She stretched out in his arms, lying on her back on top of the water. She looked up at the stars as they winked at her from an ink-black sky. The moon was a sliver, its light pale and remote. She moved her hands lightly over the surface of the water.

"I love this time of night—when everyone is asleep and the world is quiet."

His hands moved to her hips, cradling her.

"I like it, too. It reminds me of my birthday." His thumbs stroked her hips, just under the band of her bikini bottom.

"What about?"

"Our hotel in Rome. The balcony." He brought his mouth to the side of her neck.

Julia closed her eyes and hummed. "I remember the balcony. There wasn't a moon that evening."

"A good thing, too. We were lucky we weren't arrested."

Julia's eyes popped open. "Arrested? You told me no one could see us."

Gabriel's eyes glinted and his attractive mouth widened into a self-satisfied smile.

"No one could see us, Julianne, but they could damn well hear us. You're . . . loud."

Julia abruptly moved to stand, the water swirling about her. "Do you think someone heard us?"

"I think the Vatican heard us. And they were miles away."

"Gabriel!" She reached out to catch his bicep. "That's embarrassing."

"Why?" He trailed a finger over her collarbone, back and forth. "You're a healthy young woman who obviously enjoys sex. I should think the moans would be inspiring. Probably the best sex sounds Rome has heard in a millennium." He winked, pulling her closer.

She covered her eyes with her hands. "I can't believe you didn't say anything."

"What should I have said?"

"I don't know—*stop*?"

"Never." He moved to whisper in her ear. "It was hot."

She was quiet for a moment, and he began to regret telling her. Then her shoulders started shaking.

"Julianne? Don't cry." Gabriel's voice sounded slightly panicked.

She removed her hands so that he could see she was laughing.

A wave of relief washed over him.

"We put on a sex show." She spoke through her laughter, trying to catch her breath.

"Yes."

"I can't believe I did that."

"You seem to have gotten over your embarrassment rather quickly." He gave her a puzzled look.

"I wouldn't say that." She closed her eyes, tipping her face to the sky above them. She shook her head slowly.

"I'm sorry, Julianne. I should have said something. But I was enjoying myself too much. I love hearing you—knowing that I'm the one pleasing you and causing you to cry out."

"Don't be sorry." She brought her lips to his ear and lowered her voice to a whisper. "It was hot."

He kissed her firmly and she wrapped her arms around his neck. When he pulled away, he spoke against her mouth.

"I know something that would be hotter."

She pressed herself more firmly against him. "And what would that be?"

"Skinny-dipping. With me." He began tugging at the tie around her neck.

"Gabriel!" She protested halfheartedly, resting her hands on his shoulders.

"Our nearest neighbor is far away. I'm going to have to do an extraordinary job of pleasing you this evening, Julianne, otherwise no one will hear you but me." His lips turned up into a half smile. "Now drop the bikini."

"Aoibhe and the Virgin"

An Outtake from *The Raven*

May 2013
Florence, Italy

"I brought you a gift."

The Prince regarded Aoibhe with cold detachment as they stood in one of the corridors near the Council Chamber. "That isn't necessary, Aoibhe."

She smiled, her beautiful face alight. "We had a falling-out, my prince. It's customary to try to make amends, especially with an ally."

She winked. "And you'll like this gift, I assure you. I seem to have a talent for locating the only virgins left in Florence."

Before the Prince could protest, Aoibhe approached him and touched his sleeve.

"I will be taking my own refreshment nearby. You should join me when you're finished."

She kissed him on the cheek once and disappeared into the room across the hall.

The Prince stood for a moment, inhaling the human's scent. Virgins had a noticeable fragrance and one that was highly prized among his kind. But for reasons having to do with a human memory he had not been able to forget, the Prince tended to avoid virgins.

Still, he found himself hungry and Aoibhe had delivered food.

He opened the wooden door and closed it behind him.

"Who's there?" a young woman called into the darkness, speaking Italian.

When he didn't answer, she stood.

"I know someone is there."

The Prince could see in the dark and so he had an excellent view. She was standing next to a low, armless couch, her arms wrapped around her waist. Her hair was long and fair, and her eyes were wide and very blue.

She looked, he thought, a great deal like Simonetta Vespucci.

"Please answer me," she whispered.

"How old are you?" he asked, watching her.

At the sound of his voice, her face moved in his direction. She took a step backward and almost toppled onto the couch.

He was beside her in a flash, grasping her elbow to steady her.

Slowly, as if she were worried about his reaction, she pulled away.

"I'm eighteen."

He could hear her heart beating and smell her scent, which was heavy with innocence.

"Why are you here?"

"I don't know." She twisted her hands. "One minute I was in a club with my friends, the next minute I was here."

He stepped closer and lifted her chin with a single finger. "Never board a ship unless you know its destination."

She whimpered, her blue eyes lifting sightlessly to his.

"What are you going to do to me?"

He paused, indulging himself by tracing the edge of her jaw.

"I'm going to kiss you."

At her sharp intake of breath, his finger dropped to her neck, stroking at the speed of a snail.

He sifted his hand through her hair until he was cupping the back of her head. Then he brought their lips together.

Her heart rate increased immediately and he could feel the heat steal over her skin.

"Who are you?" she whispered, her lips moving against his smile.

His smile disappeared.

"I am darkness made visible."

The woman let out a shaky breath.

"Are you going to hurt me?"

He studied her breathing, the flow of adrenaline through her body, the tension in her muscles.

"On the contrary, I came to give you a gift."

"What is it?"

"Pleasure."

He kissed her again, wrapping his arms around her.

She began to relax a little as he held her, tentatively lifting her hands to his shoulders.

Her mouth was sweet. Almost as sweet as the scent of blood that lifted from beneath her skin.

In the old days, when he'd been young, he would have fed from her by now, most likely killing her in the process. But those days were long past.

He was an old one. He fed when necessary but rarely did he feel the overwhelming hunger and desire of his youth.

The young one in his arms aroused his appetite and his senses but she did not threaten his control.

He explored her mouth languorously, his tongue playing with hers.

She responded in kind, but clumsily.

He kissed her until she pressed her breasts against his chest, molding their bodies together. He slid his hands to her bottom, gripping and kneading the firm flesh.

Her lips parted and she breathed heavily against his neck.

"Lie down," he commanded.

"What about the lights?"

"Don't you know the myth of Cupid and Psyche? Some lovers prefer the dark."

He backed her into the couch and brought his body atop hers when she reclined.

She opened her mouth to protest but he silenced her with his own, kissing her again at an unhurried speed.

He cupped her breast through her blouse and squeezed, before lightly running his fingers back and forth.

She murmured her pleasure, wrapping her arms more tightly around his shoulders.

He slid his hand down her side and lifted her thigh, angling it against his hip.

"What are you doing?" she whispered.

"I'm going to touch you."

He drew up her skirt while he kissed her intently, exposing her skin. He teased her inner thigh, dropping his lips to her throat.

He tasted her skin, nipping and kissing at an increased pace. And all the while his fingers ascended her thigh to between her legs.

He pressed a single finger against her, perhaps expecting her to pull away.

But she didn't. She tugged his head toward her neck and moaned in his ear.

His fingers pushed her underwear aside, exposing her to his touch.

She lifted her hips to meet him, panting in his ear as he circled and pressed.

She began to tense beneath his fingers and he took that opportunity to sink his teeth into her neck.

She climaxed beneath him with a low cry as her blood flowed, warm and sweet, into his mouth.

He dipped his tongue in the nectar, savoring the taste, while she shuddered in his arms, her orgasm continuing.

Pain and pleasure mixed together in her body as he drew the life from her artery, drinking slowly.

When her climax had ended and she grew still beneath him, he released her neck.

His tongue moved to lick her wound, ensuring not one drop of her blood was wasted.

With a satisfied smile, he spoke in her ear.

"Sleep, young one. Rest well, remembering nothing of our time together. Don't return to Teatro again."

The young woman in his arms closed her eyes and began to breathe deeply.

In a moment, she was asleep.

He lifted himself from atop her slight form and stared down at her, taking one last moment to inhale her tantalizing scent.

For reasons known only to himself, he left her unplucked to pursue more carnal pleasures in the room across the hall.

※ ※

"Was she delicious?" Aoibhe greeted him, dabbing her lips discreetly with a piece of red silk.

"Very." The Prince glanced at her mouth. "And yours?"

"Tasty enough as a starter." She patted the bed on which she was sitting, naked. "I prefer the main course."

"Where is she?" The Prince sniffed the air, noting that the human scent lingered but not strongly.

"Taking a nap." Aoibhe indicated a door that led to an inner chamber.

"Did you pluck her?"

"Absolutely."

"If I'd known what you were doing, I'd have arrived sooner." The Prince's eyes moved to the inner door.

Aoibhe rose to her knees and bowed atop the black silk sheets. "Don't tease me, my Lord. It's been some time since you've allowed yourself to watch."

He chuckled to himself, as if remembering a secret.

"I watch when sufficiently motivated."

She sat back on her calves, gazing up at him, her long, fiery red hair streaming across her shoulders and covering her chest.

"Come here," he commanded, his expression shifting.

She moved toward him.

He raised his hand and pushed her hair behind her back, exposing her breasts.

Aoibhe closed her eyes, pressing herself against him. "I can smell her innocence on you. I assume that innocence is ended."

The Prince pressed his hand over her breast, feeling the weight of it in his palm, before swiping his thumb across her nipple.

"Enough speech," he growled, dropping his mouth to her shoulder.

She encircled her arms around his neck, before kissing him deeply.

Then with a low laugh, she led him toward the bed.

For those readers who missed the introduction
of the Prince of Florence in

GABRIEL'S REDEMPTION,

here is his scene from that book.

As Julia scanned the crowd, one face stood out. A young-looking, fair-haired man with strange gray eyes stared unblinkingly in her direction, his expression one of intense curiosity. His reaction was so different from the other guests, Julia couldn't help but return his stare, until Gabriel nudged her, drawing her attention back to their host.

Dottore Vitali painstakingly traced the provenance of the illustrations from the Emersons back to the nineteenth century, where they seemed to have appeared out of nowhere.

The Uffizi was proud to display images that had not been viewed in public since, perhaps, their creation.

The audience murmured appreciatively and broke out into enthusiastic applause as Vitali thanked the Emersons for their generosity.

Gabriel moved his arm in order to take Julia's hand, squeezing it. They nodded and smiled their acknowledgments. Then he walked to the podium and offered a few words of thanks in Italian to Vitali and the Uffizi.

He turned his body sideways, his eyes fixed on Julia's.

"I would be remiss if I didn't mention my wife, Julianne. The lovely lady you see before you is the reason why this evening came about. Without her, I would have kept the illustrations to myself. Through her words and her deeds, she has shown me what it is to be charitable and good."

Julia blushed, but she could not look away. His magnetic gaze was focused entirely on her.

"This evening is only one small example of her philanthropic work.

Yesterday, we spent the day at the Franciscan orphanage, spending time with the children. Earlier today, my wife was on a mission of mercy with the poor and homeless, in the city center. My challenge to you this evening is to enjoy the beauty of the illustrations of Dante's *Divine Comedy*, and then to find it in your hearts to celebrate beauty, charity, and compassion in the city Dante loved, Firenze. Thank you."

The crowd applauded, with one exception. No one seemed to notice the fair-haired man's cynical reaction to Gabriel's call to virtuous living, or the contempt he expressed when Dante was mentioned.

Gabriel returned to Julia and kissed her cheek chastely before facing the applauding crowd. They posed for photographs and cut the ribbon that was strung across the doors that led into the exhibition. The exhibit was declared open, to the sound of much applause.

"Please." Vitali gestured to the room, indicating that the Emersons should be the first to view the collection.

Gabriel and Julianne entered the room and were immediately awe-struck. The space had been renovated, its normally pale walls painted a bright blue to better display the pen-and-ink illustrations, only some of which were in color.

The illustrations were arranged in order, beginning with Botticelli's famous *Chart of Hell*. In viewing the collection, one was able to witness the journey of a man's soul from sin to redemption. And of course, there was the inevitable reunion of Dante with his beloved Beatrice.

"What do you think?" Gabriel held Julia's hand as they stood in front of one of their favorite images, Dante and Beatrice in the sphere of Mercury. Beatrice was wearing flowing robes and pointing upward while Dante followed her gesture with his gaze.

"It's beautiful." She linked their pinky fingers together. "Do you remember the first time you showed it to me? When I came to dinner at your apartment?"

Gabriel lifted her hand to his lips, pressing a kiss to her palm. "How could I forget? You know, I showed them to you on impulse. I hadn't even told Rachel about them. Somehow, I knew I could trust you."

"You *can* trust me." Her dark eyes grew serious.

"I know." He appeared conflicted and for a moment Julia thought he was going to confess his secrets, but they were interrupted.

The attractive, fair-haired man approached, angling to view the illustration.

As if in a dream, Julia watched the stranger move. His body almost appeared to float across the floor, his footsteps light and fluid. He appeared tall but was actually an inch or two shorter than Gabriel. Julia perceived that although the man was trim, his elegant black suit hid muscles that rippled beneath the fine material.

The Emersons politely retreated, but not before Gabriel locked eyes with the other guest. Wordlessly, Gabriel placed his body between the stranger and Julianne, blocking her from his view.

"Good evening." The stranger addressed them with a British accent, bowing formally.

To Gabriel's trained ear, the accent sounded Oxonian.

"Evening," Gabriel clipped, his palm sliding down Julia's wrist in order to grasp her hand.

The guest's eyes followed the path of Gabriel's hand, and he smiled to himself.

"A remarkable evening," he commented, gesturing at the room.

"Quite," said Gabriel, gripping Julia's hand a little too tightly.

She squeezed back, indicating that he should release the pressure a little.

"It's generous of you to share *your* illustrations." The guest's tone was ironic. "How fortunate for you that you acquired them in secret and not on the open market."

The stranger's eyes traveled from Gabriel's to Julia's, pausing briefly. His nostrils flared and then his eyes appeared to soften before he turned to the drawing nearby.

"Yes, I count myself lucky. Enjoy your evening." With a stiff nod, Gabriel moved away, still gripping Julia's hand.

She was puzzled by Gabriel's behavior but elected not to ask him about it until they reached the opposite end of the gallery.

"Who was that?"

"I have no idea, but stay away from him." Gabriel was visibly agitated, and he passed a hand over his mouth.

"Why? What's going on?" Julia stopped, facing him.

"I don't know." Gabriel's eyes were sincere. "But there's something about him. Promise me you'll stay away."

Julia laughed, the sound echoing across the gallery. "He's a bit odd, but he seemed nice."

"Pit bulls are nice until you put your hand in their cage. If he moves in your direction, turn around and walk away. Promise me." Gabriel dropped his voice to a whisper.

"Of course. But what's the matter? Have you met him before?"

"I don't think so, but I'm not sure. I didn't like how he was looking at you. His eyes could have burned holes in your dress."

"It's a good thing I have Superman to protect me." Julia kissed her husband firmly. "I promise to avoid him and all the other handsome men here."

"You think he's handsome?" Gabriel glared at her.

"Handsome the way a work of art is handsome, not the way you are. And if you kiss me now, I'll forget him entirely."

Gabriel leaned forward and caressed her cheek with the backs of his fingers before pressing their lips together.

Also available from
New York Times bestselling author
SYLVAIN REYNARD

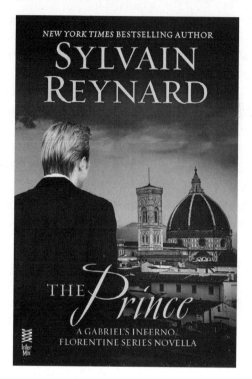

Praise for the Gabriel Trilogy:
"The Professor is sexy and sophisticated...
I can't get enough of him!"
—*USA Today* bestselling author Kristen Proby

"An unforgettable and riveting love story."
—Nina's Literary Escape

sylvainreynard.com
facebook.com/AuthorSylvainReynard
penguin.com

T432-1114